M000085203

THE GOLDEN CORD

BOOK ONE OF THE IRON DRAGON
SERIES

THE GOLDEN CORD

PAUL GENESSE

FIVE STAR
A part of Gale, Cengage Learning

GALE
CENGAGE Learning

Detroit • New York • San Francisco • New Haven, Conn • Waterville, Maine • London

GALE
CENGAGE Learning

Set in 11 pt. Plantin
Printed on permanent paper.

LIBRARY OF CONGRESS CATALOGING-IN-PUBLICATION DATA

Genesse, Paul.
 The golden cord / Paul Genesse. — 1st ed.
  p. cm. — (Iron dragon series ; Bk. 1)
  ISBN-13: 978-1-59414-659-6 (alk. paper)
  ISBN-10: 1-59414-659-4 (alk. paper)
  I. Title.
PS3607.E537G65 2008
813'.6—dc22   2007044408

First Edition. First Printing: April 2008.

Published in 2008 in conjunction with Tekno Books and Ed Gorman.

Printed in the United States of America
1 2 3 4 5 6 7 12 11 10 09 08

This novel is for my wife, Tam—the love of my life.

ACKNOWLEDGMENTS

Writing this book has been a journey into a dream. I resisted that journey for many years, telling myself that I did not want my work to join the ranks of books on the shelves. I turned away from the call, telling myself there were other journeys I should take instead, but the need to write would not go away.

Now, years later this book is in your hands. I could have never written it without the support of so many people who helped me find the courage and kept me motivated. The most important person in this whole process has been my wife, Tammy, who has been there every step of the way. I am very fortunate to have her in my life. She has been patient and kind, never discouraging me from my goals. Tam has always given me the love and support I needed.

My best friend and college roommate, Patrick Tracy has helped me immeasurably, suffering through multiple drafts and endless discussions about plot or character. His words grace this manuscript in many places. Pat is such a good friend and a very talented writer. Also, Brad Beaulieu's expert critiques and suggestions have made this a much stronger book. He has taught me a lot about writing and I am very thankful for his keen insight and help. I consider myself his biggest fan.

The early manuscript readers who were the first to read rough drafts of this book and the whole *Iron Dragon Series* gave me invaluable support and suggestions over the years. I am very thankful to MarLeice Hyde, Deborah Blankman, Aundra Bello,

Acknowledgments

Bryan Stowe, Julie Reynolds, Jeanene Senten, Lu Schmelter, Jeanette Staker, Jode Allen, Kim Parsons, Karrie Taggart, Jan Cook, Marilyn Tracy, Kathy Larsen, Michael Larsen, Jan Condie, Holly Davies, Thomas Stratton, the SLAG Writers Group, Louise Marley, Kerrie Hughes, Jordan Stephens, Natalie Wilson and Jason Wilson. They all made me believe I could do it. Also, Stephenie McKinnon, who helped get the project moving. Without her encouragement I may have never started writing. Then there are the real heroes who inspired the fictional ones: Adam Davies, K.C. Anderson, Chuck Hill and Craig Lloyd. Their contributions are truly legendary.

I am also grateful to my high school English teacher, Richard Stephens, who gave me the foundation needed to become a writer. He helped open my mind to the world and showed me what dedication to your craft can accomplish. My other excellent writing teachers, Kij Johnson, Janet Deaver-Pack, Jean Rabe and Michael Stackpole, taught me what being a fantasy writer was really like and graciously shared their vast knowledge and wisdom.

There are so many others who have helped me on this journey, especially my friends at the hospital where I work as a nurse. They are my second family and keep me going, helping me more than they know. My parents have also been there, encouraging my love of books and supporting my aspirations of becoming a published writer. In so many ways, this book is because of them.

The person I would most like to thank is my editor, John Helfers, who believed in me and this novel. A writer could not ask for a better mentor and friend. He has helped bring this book to life and his ideas have been so important. I am forever grateful to him and to you for coming with me on this journey into a dream.

Paul Genesse
May 2007

THE GOLDEN CORD

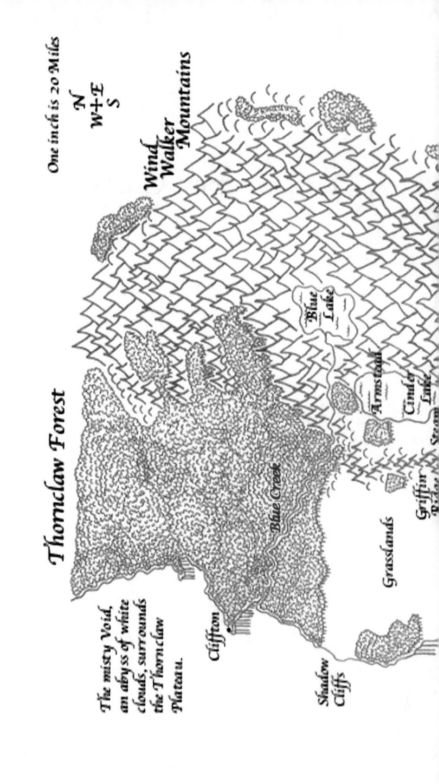

One inch is 20 Miles

N
W+E
S

Wind
Walker
Mountains

Thornclaw Forest

The misty Void,
an abyss of white
clouds, surrounds
the Thornclaw
Plateau.

Blue
Lake

Armstail

Cinder
Lake

Blue Creek

Griffin
River

Grasslands

Clifftop

Shadow
Cliffs

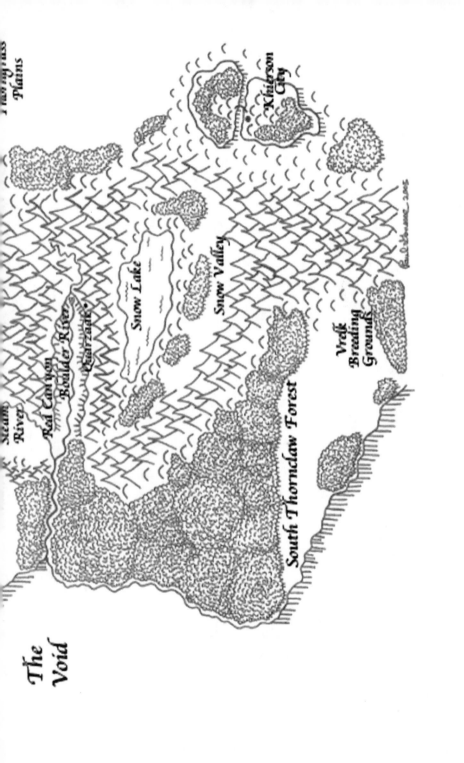

PROLOGUE

Don't look back.

Drake fought the urge to leave the trail and hide in the tangled undergrowth of the Thornclaw Forest. He knew the predator was behind him, thanks to the shrill warning call of the ferretlike surikat.

Don't let them see your fear.

The young man marched a step closer to his father and the party of eight veteran hunters bound for the mountains. He clung to the faint hope that the early morning darkness would hide them from the griffin following close on their heels. Even though one of the eagle-headed demons could tear him apart in an instant, he kept telling himself it didn't matter that he was last in line. As the youngest—only fifteen winters old—his people's customs placed him in the back, where his courage would be tested.

Acting naturally, so as not to alert the prowling griffin, Drake tapped his father casually on the elbow, then made the hand sign for griffin—a fist with three fingers hooked like talons.

His father brushed his hand away dismissively, infuriating the young man.

The surikat's ululating call faded and Drake held his breath as an unnatural silence spread across the forest. All he heard were the hunters' vrelkskin boots on the moss-covered path. The griffin had to be much closer now, ready to strike.

Another piercing cry erupted behind them.

13

Drake and his father whirled and stood motionless. The bushy tail of a surikat vanished into the tangled canopy of thorny branches and serrated leaves. Drake scanned the ironbark trees, but saw nothing. He turned to look into his father's dark-brown eyes, so much like his own, and made a questioning hand sign. Tyler Bloodstone's eyebrows scrunched together and his expression showed that he'd known all along—something was following them. The confirmation made the hair on Drake's neck needle into his skin.

Tyler whistled a short and sharp signal. The hunters turned stern faces toward him as he relayed the information with rapid hand signals. His cousin Rigg, Uncle Sandon, and the other men took Tyler's cue and walked faster. Their hurried steps on the curdle-moss-covered trail released a caustic odor that burned Drake's nostrils and filled his mouth with the taste of sour milk. His undesirable position at the end of the line guaranteed he would endure the strongest vapors.

Switching his empty crossbow from hand to hand, Drake fought the urge to bend back the thick cord with his iron crank-lever and nock a broadhead bolt. It took all his willpower not to break tradition and cock his weapon. He wanted to ask his father for permission, but Drake shook his head. Such a foolish question wouldn't be tolerated. He'd be told what to do and when to do it. For reassurance, Drake gripped the handle of his forward-curved Kierka knife sheathed on his hip. He glanced backwards, his mind racing as he thought about what kind of creature could have landed to hunt them. Few wingless beasts would pursue ten men. It had to be an aevian; probably a griffin or wyvern. *Please not a dragon.*

Swallowing the sour taste of fear mixed with curdle-moss, Drake knew if he fell behind the monster would strike. He matched the older men stride for stride, almost bumping into his father when the hunters slowed their fast-march at a wide cleft in the trees. Drake focused on the predawn sky above. It was large enough to prove fatal if an aevian was circling, waiting in ambush. Perhaps they were being herded to the forest window where a flight of cunning griffins waited to pounce.

None of the hunters spoke as they crossed the open space. Ten pairs of eyes searched for the slightest sign of danger. Drake held the butt of his crossbow against his shoulder, aiming his unloaded weapon upwards and wishing it held a sleek broadhead or a stout, steel-tipped war bolt. Empty, it was an ineffective wooden club.

Drake's father ducked under a branch crossing the trail without turning his eyes from above. The young man tried to imitate his father's expert movements, but grabbed a tree limb to steady himself. Before he realized his mistake, a long thorn pierced his left palm. Muffling a curse, he pulled away as the pain spread across his hand. It would have been unforgivable for Drake to cry out under the opening, but having a bleeding hand was worse. Griffins loved human flesh and could smell blood on the wind. He might as well have lit a torch and screamed. He sucked on his bleeding palm, tasting the bitter poison, which would burn for at least an hour and leave another tiny scar. Thornclaws always left their mark, and the namesake plant of the dark forest was fond of his flesh.

The trilling song of a staerling as it flew off made his father glance back. Drake concealed his discomfort and hoped his father couldn't see the blood oozing from his hand. It was only a tiny wound and the curdle-moss would mask his scent from the griffin. He hoped.

Drake stifled a gasp. *The griffin will smell my blood on the thornclaw vine!* The aevian demon would do anything to eat his flesh once it picked up his trail. It would never stop hunting him. His heart sank into the rising acid pool in his stomach.

Even if he lived through the day, Drake feared this would be the first and last mountain hunt his father would ever take him on. He'd be stuck in Cliffton, trapped in the village. He'd never climb the slopes of the Wind Walker Mountains, visit his cousin Rigg's home in Armstead, or explore the famed Red Canyon his grandfather had spoken about so often.

A hard glance from his father chilled Drake's blood. He had opened his mouth to admit his mistake and whisper a warning about the blood on the vine, but his father's frown struck him silent. Tyler squinted his left eye and tightened his jaw. He'd seen that look a lot, ever since Roan Graywood had been killed by a griffin three months ago. Since that day the Bloodstone household had been a very troubled place.

Drake's skin bristled with a pulse of warning he couldn't shake off as he considered his father's familiar expression. He couldn't escape the feeling of something creeping up behind him in the darkness—something he desperately didn't want to face.

The trill from another staerling caused Tyler to stop and spin around. His father's eyes became tiny black orbs as he locked his gaze on his son. "Get rid of him."

Drake shuddered. He knew what followed them. It was worse than a griffin. His father's tone and expression made perfect sense. Drake hesitated, his lips forming words of protest.

His father cut him off. "I want you to take care of it. Alone."

Drake's sour mouth turned dry as sand. He tried to think of a way to get out of the distasteful task, but he was dumbfounded.

"I'll go with him." Cousin Rigg stepped toward the rear of the line.

"No." Tyler barred seventeen-year-old Rigg from moving closer to Drake.

The young men's eyes met. More than anything Drake wished that Rigg were his brother, not just his favorite cousin from a distant village. "But, Father. . . ."

"Alone." Tyler Bloodstone fixed his stern gaze on his son. "You carry a thorn bolt. You're a hunter now."

Nothing came out of Drake's mouth, but his mind screamed, *Don't make me do this alone!*

"Catch up when it's done." His father turned and strode away with Rigg and the others, leaving his oldest child to face the challenge on his own. A hundred words Drake should have said echoed in his mind. He should've stood up to his father.

Turning, Drake clutched his crossbow. The drying blood from his pierced palm coated the stock, making it sticky in his trembling hands. He held the weapon close, searching for courage in the fine grain of the wood, then moved off the trail to set up an ambush and wait for his quarry.

Drake braided himself into the fabric of the forest, disappearing into the prickly brush and waiting with unblinking eyes. The excitement he had first felt about the adventure in the mountains had disappeared long ago. Dread clung to him like a clump of foul mud. He knew what he had to do, but his mind sped in a hundred different directions, *There has to be another way.*

Something moved on the trail. Out of the dimly lit forest a small figure on gaunt legs limped toward him. A slight tremor twitched the muscles of one of the young man's thighs, making his gait labored and unsteady. A small backpack rested awkwardly over skeletal shoulders and a child's crossbow with a slack string dangled in wizened arms. The ailing youth tried to maintain the quick pace of the hunting party he pursued, but his rapid breathing showed the strain on his weak lungs.

Drake wished a griffin would have appeared, instead of Ethan. His father would help him with an aevian, but not with his best friend.

At this moment, Drake hated his father even more than any aevian.

A nauseating thought almost made him retch with despair: A bolt through the heart might be the kindest thing anyone could do for Ethan. He could almost hear one of the older hunters—or maybe his father—saying the words.

Rejecting the hideous notion, Drake watched Ethan trudge along with his usual determined stare. Drake had always admired Ethan's willpower, and for a moment he considered letting the other boy trundle past without ever revealing his position. But Drake knew he couldn't.

He had to stop him.

Ethan would not survive the trek to the mountains, or the dangerous vrelk hunts once they arrived. Drake slipped out of the brush and stepped onto the trail. He stood rigid, a different grim determination etched on his face.

Ethan took one more laborious step before coming to a wavering halt. "Drake, I'm coming with you. We'll see the vrelk herds and the mountain meadows . . . and Red Canyon. . . ." The smaller boy's words trailed off as he read Drake's dour expression.

Drake couldn't find the words he had to say to his adopted brother. He didn't want to do it. How could he? Ethan's only crime had been being born physically weaker than everyone else. For that he'd been labeled the outcast, the misfit. Ethan could never be more than half a man in the eyes of almost everyone in the village—except Drake.

"You knew I was following?"

Drake nodded.

"How far away are the others?"

"Not far."

"We better get going or they'll get too far ahead."

"Ethan. . . ."

"What?" The young man's intense eyes belied his frail body, but not his sharp mind.

"You know my father said you can't come."

"So what. My father would've let me go. He'd let me try anything. He never held me back."

Drake couldn't say it, but he thought: *Your father's dead, Ethan. Roan Graywood is dead. The whole village thinks he'd be alive if he hadn't taken you on a hunt. He was worrying about you and he should've seen the griffin before it killed him.*

"You're not stopping me." Ethan stepped forward with his head held high.

Drake took a wide stance. "I don't want to, but—"

"Why're you in my way?"

"My father wants me to send you back."

Ethan shook his head. "I don't care. He's my Watch Father, not my real one."

"He just doesn't understand you."

"I'll make him. Keeping me in Cliffton is wrong. It doesn't matter what your father says. I'm going to see all the places beyond this damned forest. I'm not hiding in Cliffton forever."

"But you have to do what my father says." Drake's tone pleaded for his friend to be reasonable. "I'm sorry. He doesn't know what you're capable of."

"Just because I live in the Bloodstone house doesn't mean your father owns me like some Nexan slave."

"He took you all in. He loves you. He just wants to protect you and your family. What would your mother or sisters say if they knew you were here?"

Ethan sighed, but didn't answer.

"They don't know you're gone, do they? And what about Jaena?" Drake didn't want to bring her into it, but he had to use everything—and everyone—he could think of. "You're supposed to watch out for her while I'm gone. Remember?"

"Shut up, Drake. Your father just doesn't want me around. I'm just a burden to him. He wanted to get away from me. So did you. Admit it. My mother'll be glad I'm gone for a while too. She blames me for my father's—"

"That's not true. Don't say that. It wasn't your fault." Drake wanted to believe what he was saying, but he couldn't.

Pain and guilt spread across Ethan's face as he hung his head in shame. He never talked about his father's death. Drake figured it was still too painful for him. "My father just wants to keep you safe, and so do I."

The terrible palsy affecting Ethan's body made his right hand shake uncontrollably. Drake wanted to pick his friend up and rush off to see the village healer. Priestess Liana Whitestar and her golden-haired daughter, Jaena, could stop the grotesque tremors, but they would always come back with a vengeance. Ethan was cursed.

"I can take care of myself, Drake. Now let's get going." Ethan hid his hand.

"Wait. You've got chores back in the village. You're the path warden for the next two weeks. And you promised to feed my new pups. You're supposed to watch over both of them and all the other dogs. You've always done your share. Don't stop now."

"Feeding guard dogs and pruning cover tree paths isn't the goal of my life, Drake."

"Keep your voice down." Drake scowled and glanced at the canopy, hoping they hadn't attracted any predators.

"I'm tired of getting the worst jobs in the village. Anyone else can do them better than me. It's not fair. They won't even let me go into the forest to hunt and I want to see the mountains for once. This is my chance. Mountain hunts don't come very often. You told me yourself."

Ethan was right. The sojourns to the mountains were rare. He didn't know what to say. When Ethan made up his mind nothing would stop him. Seeing his father killed hadn't broken Ethan's spirit—at least Drake didn't think it had.

"Let's go. We're falling behind."

Drake realized his only option was to block the trail himself. He didn't know what else to say or do. He needed time to think.

"Do I have to push you out of my way?" Ethan glared at him, his thin eyebrows raised. After laying his crossbow on the side of the path, Drake folded his arms across his chest. He hated resorting to brute strength to stop his best friend. Trying to intimidate Ethan made Drake feel like one of Cliffton's bullies.

"Move out of the way," Ethan's high-pitched voice cracked with emotion. "You promised."

Remorse washed over Drake. He wished he could take back what he'd said after Ethan's father's memorial ceremony. It had been a mistake to promise that they would go to the mountains together.

"Move." Ethan stepped forward. He was much shorter, but he put his frail chest against Drake's strong one and tried to push past. Drake shifted to keep the smaller boy from slipping by and nudged his friend backwards. Ethan lost his balance and fell hard to his knees, sprawling on the ground. Drake reached down to help, but Ethan slapped away his hands and bared his teeth. "Don't touch me!" He struggled to stand as Drake knelt on the mossy trail, extending his open palms.

Ethan locked his bony fingers onto Drake's hands, grappling for dominance.

"Stop it." The words hissed through Drake's teeth. He held firm in spite of his friend's powerful aura of courage and the stabbing pain from the thorn wound now being squeezed. They stared at each other, neither giving up. The realization that Ethan wasn't going to quit gave Drake a desperate idea. He didn't dare bring up Roan's passing and slur the memory of a fallen hunter, but there was something else he could say.

21

"You don't carry a thorn bolt. You're not a true hunter. You're just a boy. You can't go on the mountain hunts until you have one." Hating every word that fell from his lips, Drake spoke like all the bullies who had ever picked on Ethan. "That's Cliffton's law. You're bound to it. Your body's not strong enough. Face it and go home."

Ethan's lips quivered, but words erupted as if he didn't care if every griffin in the forest heard him. "The Council won't even let me try to get a damned thorn bolt. You know that, you dung eating woodskull!"

Drake felt like he had just shot his best friend in the back with a poisoned bolt. Every hunter in the village had gone to Thorn Bolt Rock; but when Ethan had reached his fifteenth birthday he had been forbidden to go. It was too dangerous. Everyone knew it, but the leash intended to protect Ethan had become a noose. Shame clawed at Drake as he towered over his friend. "That's because you can't get one. There're some things you just can't do. This hunt is one of them." Releasing his grip on Drake's hands, Ethan's shoulders sagged with despair. Drake heard the words he had just spoken, but they were said with Tyler Bloodstone's voice. He had repeated what his father had told Ethan the night before.

Now Drake hated himself even more than he despised his father.

Ethan shrank a bit at Drake's betrayal, looking like a ravaged sapling dying from a bark-beetle infestation—but his obstinate expression remained.

"Doesn't matter. I don't need a thorn bolt to be a hunter." Ethan's voice was just a whisper as he fought back tears.

Drake knew he had to press his argument further to land the telling blow. He blurted out the words before he could think. "Go back before you summon a griffin down on our heads and get us killed like. . . ."

"Like my father?" Humiliation turned to rage. Ethan's face became bright red and he clenched his fists. Drake thought his friend was going to punch him in the face.

"I hate you. You're not my friend."

Drake wished Ethan would have hit him instead.

The afflicted young man staggered to his feet and stumbled down the path toward Cliffton. Tears welled in Drake's eyes. He wondered if shooting Ethan would have been easier.

When there was no sign of his friend, Drake mustered enough willpower to catch up to his father and the others. The sun appeared above the treetops as he hustled along, turning the Thornclaw Forest from shades of gray to many variations of dark green. Drake had been looking forward to the light, but now it brought more attention to the barbs and stinging nettles of the lush undergrowth.

A strong hand reached out of the brush and grabbed Drake's shoulder. The young man drew his knife even as his father said, "You're lucky I wasn't a skulking aevian gone to ground."

You're lucky I didn't cut off your damn hand! Drake thought, pushing his Kierka blade back into its sheath and glaring at his stone-faced father.

"You sent Ethan back?" Tyler stepped onto the path facing his son.

Drake wished he'd stood up to his father before ambushing Ethan and sundering their friendship.

"Well?"

"I sent him back."

Tyler nodded. "The village needs all of us to come back alive. With him along—"

"I would've looked after him."

"You can't protect him all the time. Roan was a veteran of the Thornclaw and he's dead. What makes you think you

23

could've done better than his own father? Do you want to end up in an aevian's belly? This isn't a children's game out here."

"It's just not right." Drake said what Ethan would have. Things were always right or wrong with Ethan.

"I know it wasn't easy." Drake heard the pride he longed for in his father's voice. "But you did what you had to do." He didn't hate his father so much at that moment. Tyler put a hand on Drake's shoulder. "He's lucky he lives in Cliffton. Our village is a good place for little Ethan, even though he'll never be a hunter."

Drake touched the ceremonial thorn bolt in his leg-sheath and wondered if Ethan would ever forgive him. A cold chill crept up Drake's spine, rooting him in place.

"What?" Tyler scanned the canopy and surrounding bushes preparing to loose a killing bolt at whatever had spooked his son. "I don't see anything."

Spirals of fear pulsed through Drake's chest. His eyes opened wide. He knew what Ethan was going to do.

"What's wrong?"

Drake flung his pack and crossbow to the ground, then sprinted back down the path.

"Where're you going?!" Tyler called as he scooped up the discarded gear and chased after his defenseless son.

"To stop him!"

Drake ran as fast as he could down the trail, dodging the low-hanging branches and poisonous vines. He outran his pursuing father, moving faster than he ever had through the dangerous forest. He almost didn't care about the chance of ambush by an aevian demon. His friend's life was at stake and he was willing to risk his own for his adopted brother.

Drake's face and hands were soon cut and bleeding after a few minutes of rushing through the Thornclaw. He ignored the pain, accepting it as fair punishment for what he had done to his best friend.

The village was close and the trail became less wild as it approached Cliffton. He spotted the open ground between the forest and the village's long palisade wall. The wide firebreak was barren except for countless tree stumps and small ground-hugging plants. He glanced at the open ground, then up at the thick domes of the cover tree grove before dashing away from the village gates.

Drake ran back into the untamed forest, veering toward the edge of the great plateau, near where Cliffton had been built. He took the path to the Lily Pad Rocks and the edge of the Void. He could almost sense the yawning abyss of the Underworld as if it called his name, tempting him to come closer.

Any moment now, the ground would fall away and the sea of clouds would begin. Drake nearly tripped over Ethan's pack and crossbow, and the sinking feeling in his stomach intensified. He hoped he wasn't too late as he approached the terminus of the plateau. *Please Goddess, let me be in time. I'm sorry for what I did.*

The brightness at the end of the forest tunnel made him blink. Blinded for an instant, he respected the danger of falling into the Void and slowed his mad sprint. His eyes adjusted to the glare and he saw the lip of the stony cliff.

Beyond the sheer precipice, an ocean of clouds stretched to the horizon. The deep green of the forest contrasted with the sea of pure white mist reflecting the morning sunlight. Drake swerved left at the edge of the unfathomable gulf. The surface of the wavy mist began five hundred feet below the cliff. He had no idea how deep the fog extended before the Underworld began. Not wanting to find out, he ran alongside the chasm taking careful strides—a stumble would mean death.

At last, Drake spied his destination. The six Lily Pad Rocks poked up from the Underworld like long demonic fingers of grayish stone. The summits of the flat-topped towers were the same height as the plateau where the Thornclaw Forest had sunk its roots. Five of the spires were barren except for a few patches of crusty lichen.

Drake spotted Ethan staring at the sixth and furthest rocky island. His friend's back was to him. The frail youth stood wavering in the strong breeze and appeared unaware of Drake's arrival.

Despite his fear, Drake was impressed Ethan had made it so far out. Leaping across all but one of Lily Pad Rocks was quite an accomplishment for a person with his strength, but Drake knew he wouldn't stop until the end.

There was one more jump to make, the longest of them all. Drake glanced at the rare and ancient sikatha tree clinging to the sixth rock where it had watched over the Void for hundreds of years. The squat and thorny sentinel grew on the most remote island—Thorn Bolt Rock. Thick barbs projected like quills from its fat trunk.

To become a fully recognized hunter Ethan needed one of the thorns, but Drake had to stop him before his friend fell to his death. Drake prepared himself for his jump over the Underworld. If he missed a step he would plummet into the abyss, where his soul would be forever doomed to wander as a ghost.

Drake launched himself toward the nearest Lily Pad, easily making the short hop onto the first of the six pillar-shaped rock islands. He had made the long step several times before. For him the mental challenge had always been greater than the physical one. There would be no hunters covering them, and a person never knew if demons were watching and waiting to fly up and attack.

Ethan stood motionless, ready to attempt his final jump at any moment. Drake knew Ethan didn't lack the heart, only the body for the last challenge.

"Ethan, stop!" Drake screamed, knowing that all the heart in the world wasn't enough sometimes. Ethan heard the plea and turned his grief-stricken face to Drake, who recognized the mournful expression he had seen since Roan Graywood had been killed. His face showed defeat. The final leap was impossible. The Void had finally crushed his friend's unrealistic hopes of becoming a hunter.

Drake vaulted over the fourth gap and bounded across the rocky spire. He'd be at his friend's side after one more easy jump.

Ethan shook his head at Drake.

He's not turning back. Drake could see it in his friend's eyes. As Drake neared the fifth crevasse, Ethan lurched toward Thorn Bolt Rock. Drake nearly miscalculated his own leap when Ethan shambled toward the depths separating him from the far island and the prize growing on the venerable sikatha tree.

Ethan picked up speed, but it wasn't enough. His friend flung himself forward, arcing over the chasm.

Drake sucked in his breath. Ethan wasn't going to make it. There was nothing Drake could do. He blamed himself for the nightmare unfolding in front of him. He had pushed his friend to this ultimate moment of insanity. Drake's arrival had spurred Ethan to try a desperate attempt to become a hunter. Now his best friend was going to die.

Ethan's bony hands and palsied arms barely caught the lip of the rocky island. His lower body slammed into the stone tower. Drake gasped when he thought he heard the sound of his friend's bones breaking.

But there was a chance. Ethan hung on.

Drake's legs had felt like tree trunks at times during his desperate run through the forest, but he reached deep into his soul and sprinted the last few paces.

Ethan dangled above the gaping mouth of the Void as Drake reached the final gap and leaped with all his remaining strength. He sailed over Ethan's head and landed hard on the weathered ground. Momentum pushed him forward, but Drake whirled around and lunged for Ethan's hands.

Their eyes met.

Ethan fell.

"Ethan!" Drake shrieked and reached out to his friend, almost hurling himself over the edge. Ethan screamed as the opaque fog of the Underworld enveloped his withered body, devouring him.

Ethan was gone.

Drake lay paralyzed on the cold rock and stared into the misty chasm. His wide, unblinking eyes searched in vain for his lost friend. Drake's body shook as the wind whipped at his face. A whisper escaped his trembling lips, "Ethan, I'm so sorry. Please come back."

Only the empty, mocking Void stared back at him.

★ ★ ★ ★ ★

PART ONE
THE CLIFFTONER

★ ★ ★ ★ ★

I

After years of searching, The Dragon is finally within my reach.

—Final entry in the Lost Journal

Bölak Blackhammer screamed as the dragon fire melted his flesh. The huge tunnel blazed with light and for an instant he spotted the dragon's head at the eye of the firestorm. The dwarven warrior flung away his white-hot metal shield. The round disk had blocked most of the wyrm's fiery breath, but it had become like a branding iron, searing through his clothing and roasting his skin.

Fighting through his pain and the thick cloud of smoke, Bölak saw the monster's long black horns jutting forward like a bull's as it prepared to charge. The dragon's gigantic mouth filled with flames and its eyes shone red as it locked its gaze on him.

Choking on a sulfurous cloud, the band of dwarven warriors struggled to breathe as the sudden inferno consumed the air itself. Bölak fell to his knees with the others, taking shelter behind a pockmarked boulder. For a fleeting moment a fading crimson glow surrounded the dwarf's body. He realized that the powerful Earth magic shielding him and the other dwarves from fire had been shattered by a vile Draconic spell an instant before the conflagration.

Peering over the rock, the dwarven warrior saw the charred bodies of Gillur and Tharak on the cavern floor. The flames had been hot enough to melt their armor and the half-molten

31

puddles of metal and flesh barely resembled the two dwarves slain by the wyrm. "Fall back!" he yelled, as those with unburned eyes saw death approaching.

"To the small tunnels! Run! We'll make a stand there!" Bölak shouted, wincing in pain from the smoking burns on his arm. As they fled, he blinked away tears, as much from the pain and caustic air as from the deaths of his friends.

Blood sprayed across Bölak's neck. He glanced back to see a giant claw tearing through the chain mail of Doran, whose burning boots had hindered his retreat; but the brave dwarf's sacrifice didn't stop the raging creature.

Stones rumbled as the beast closed in. Their rear guard, Karek, loosed a steel-tipped crossbow bolt, which darted through the smoke-filled tunnel. Enchanted with powerful Earth magic, the missile flared with silver light as it pierced the scaly hide of the dragon's neck, sending jolts of silvery-white energy surging across the dragon's iron-gray scales. Roaring in pain and rage, the colossal beast checked its charge and threw back its horned head.

Knowing the Priests needed time to reinvoke the magic that would protect them from the devastating flames, Bölak stopped running. He yelled to his followers, "Go! I'll hold here!"

Bölak's best friend paused. Nalak's neck swiveled and his always-stony expression fractured like a rock hit by a sledgehammer. Sadness poured from the old dwarf's eyes as Bölak realized Nalak would rather die than leave his side.

A pain much sharper than his burned shield-arm filled Bölak's chest when he stared at his most loyal friend; but taking advantage of Nalak's delay, he flung the smoking pouch holding his rune-inscribed journal to his second in command.

"Go! Live!" Bölak screamed as his friend of so many years clutched the journal to his chest. Nalak gave him one sharp nod and gritted his teeth before fleeing down the tunnel with the other warriors. In the span it took Bölak to whirl around and face the approaching dragon he prayed to Lorak. "Let them return and finish our Sacred Duty."

Bölak shouted the war cry of his clan, "Blackhammer!" His deep voice reverberated off the cavern walls as he brandished his ancient warhammer.

The iron-gray dragon stopped and stared down. Fury and loathing beamed from the dragon's eyes. Scalding spittle dripped to the rocky floor as the beast opened his cavernous mouth and lunged at the lone dwarf blocking his path.

As the massive head descended, Bölak had only a heartbeat to take aim before throwing his magical blacksteel hammer at the dragon's forehead.

The sword-length fangs approached at incredible speed as the hammer flew to its mark.

In the next instant, the battle was over.

Bellor Fardelver bolted up from his mossy bed under an ironwood tree. The old dwarven War Priest snatched up his axe even as he opened his weary, golden-brown eyes. As the verdant trees came into focus Bellor lowered his guard. He thought, *What did I see? A terrible fight between my kin and Draglûne? Was it a vision of the past, or the future?* Bellor noticed Thor Hargrim, his much younger dwarven companion, standing watch over their primitive camp in the depths of the Thornclaw Forest. "Dreaming of battle again?"

Bellor nodded. *Perhaps it was just a dream.* He couldn't be certain and tugged nervously on his graying beard, which had a few streaks of loamy brown running through it.

Thor rubbed the green stains and debris of the forest off his round shield emblazoned with a black warhammer. When Bellor noticed the Blackhammer clan symbol his mind filled with images of melted dwarven bodies, a dragon's mouth spewing fire, then glaring at him with hate-filled eyes.

Bölak stood alone in the path of Draglûne. I saw the wyrm through Bölak's eyes. "It was so real," he whispered to himself. Bellor decided to record the frightening images in his journal for later study. He took out his small, leather-bound book. Rather than writing down the horrific dream, however, he found himself praying that he and Thor would find the village where they would attempt to hire a guide. *Perhaps the humans will know the fate of our lost kin? I can only hope that they do and this trek into the wildwoods will not end in our deaths. We must find Bölak and the others.*

Praying silently, Bellor rocked back and forth. Thor stopped his fastidious polishing. The young dwarf's lips parted behind his dark-brown beard, but he didn't ask another question. Grateful for Thor's uncommon silence, Bellor prayed for guidance and considered what he had seen. In his mind he saw the dragon fire killing his kin again . . . and again.

Bellor's eyes shot open. *The vision was a warning! We cannot fail!* The old War Priest struggled to his feet, locking his wild gaze on his friend. "We've rested too long. We've got to move."

A sudden gust rustled the leaves. "What's wrong?" Thor raised his shield and scanned the looming trees.

"That's not wind." Bellor lifted his axe. "It's an aevian's wings. It's landed behind those trees."

II

The Void is the source of all evil.

—Priestess Liana Whitestar, litany from the Goddess
Scrolls

Drake stared into the Void from high atop Cliffton's wooden watch tower. The ocean of white clouds below brushed against the sheer walls of the plateau as the wind blew them south. Leaning forward, he searched for any break in the mist stretching to the horizon. Wispy vapors floated in the air like restless ghosts. He had seen it a thousand times before.

Mist and fog. Nothing solid, only ephemeral vapors rising from somewhere in the Underworld. In the five years since Ethan had been taken, the veil over the unfathomable abyss had never parted, but Drake kept looking into the depths where his best friend had fallen. For some reason, he felt like today of all days, he needed to be watching the Void and treetops.

A sudden breeze tousled his dark-brown hair. A vortex of mist caught his eye and he wondered if some creature churned the clouds from below. The superstitions about the Void were many, and the old villagers often said that a misty vortex was an omen of danger, perhaps the sign of a demon coming up from the Underworld.

Drake snatched his crossbow, slipped his foot into the stirrup on the front of the stock and began bending back the cord with his split-tipped iron crank-lever, or dog's foot, as his grandfather called it. His muscles bulged as he fought against over a hundred pounds of draw weight until the cord latched into place. Without ever turning away from the Void, he slipped a feathered bolt from the quiver on his hip and loaded it into the track. He almost hoped for something to break the monotony of the never-ending clouds and moved his finger to the smooth wooden trigger carved by his grandfather's expert hands.

Drake waited long enough to see that no creature, demonic or otherwise, was rising up into the sunlit world. *Nothing. Just the Void tormenting me.* His lips curled into a grimace as the vortex subsided. *I must stop listening to the superstitious ravings of the rest of the village,* he thought, dry releasing his crossbow. He took a deep breath of the early spring air to clear his mind. He always expected the breeze from the Void to be smoky and foul, but it smelled fresh and moist. How could the Priestess be correct about the ever-smoking fires down there? It didn't seem right, and the more Drake had thought about it recently, it never had.

But who was he to question the Goddess Scrolls of Amaryllis? "Face it, Drake," old man Laetham had once said, "Ethan's soul is damned. Stop questioning the wisdom of the Scrolls or your spirit will be punished for unbelief."

Unbeliever. Good.

Even though he liked the sound of that, Drake hoped the rest of the villagers didn't think of him so poorly. He worked hard to gain their respect—though at times he didn't think he'd been very successful. What did it matter if he didn't believe exactly how they did? *I do my duty and serve the village. That's what should matter the most.*

The faint, high-pitched laughter of a small child floated to Drake's ears. The boy was close to the watch tower, playing in the cover tree pathways.

"Neven, help Mommy find the herbs."

Drake recognized the voice. *Mae Boughcutter. Jaena's friend.*

The boy's laughter faded away, swallowed by the trees of the large unpopulated garden-grove where the small fields had been planted. Drake was pleased that he had finished pruning the cover paths so Mae could navigate the trails without getting stabbed by thorns while keeping an eye on her four-year-old son. Clearing all the paths in the garden-grove had taken several hours, and his right arm ached from swinging his Kierka blade. But the pain didn't matter. There was still much work to be done.

The loose hinge on the east gate had to be tightened before his father and the others returned from their hunt. They'd be back from where Blue Creek plunged into the Void in a few hours. Carrying the butchered meat was the hardest part of their trip, and always put his father in an awful mood. Tyler Bloodstone would berate him in front of all the hunters if the gate wasn't fixed before they returned.

I do the work of two men and Father still isn't satisfied, Drake shook his head. *Path warden and village guardian. No one else does both jobs, but still I'm ridiculed. They ambush a vrelk after sitting under a tree for a few hours and they're real men?*

"*Nev-en!* Where are you?" The fear in Mae's voice slapped Drake in the face. He realized that while he was feeling sorry for himself the little boy had run off into the grove. His hunter's intuition whispered ill tidings and the young mother's urgency compelled Drake to slide rather than climb down the ladder. *The gate can wait. Damn my father.*

As he hit the ground, Drake had the terrible feeling that leaving the watch tower and the alarm horn was a mistake, since no one was watching over the village. He couldn't shake the feeling as he concealed himself within the shadows of interlocking cover trees and listened for Mae's voice. He heard the sound of his two bullmastiff dogs panting and suspected the boy had passed nearby.

Jep and Temus whined and wagged their tails as Drake hurried toward them in the bushes. Their black frowning faces with pendulous jowls stared up at him as the dogs rolled on their backs, showing him their bellies.

"We've got to find Neven. Get up, boys." Drake patted their bellies and dust rose from their fawn-colored coats. "Find him. Come on." Temus didn't understand and licked Drake's boots with his pink tongue, but Jep jumped up and sniffed the ground where a path led into the grove.

"Jep, do you smell Neven?" Drake knelt down touching Jep's back as Temus arrived to help. "He came by here, didn't he?" Drake pointed at the ground and the dogs' noses snuffled over the trail. Drake bit his lower lip waiting for them to find the scent.

"Nev! Where are you, baby? Come to Mommy." Mae's distant, panicked voice sent slivers of ice into Drake's guts.

A loud *woof* announced that Jep and Temus had found the boy's trail.

"Find him."

The dogs trotted down the path, following their noses. Curdle-moss would have made tracking by smell impossible, and Drake was thankful the shade-clover blanketing the trail didn't obscure Neven's scent. The dogs led him toward one of Cliffton's many hidden cover tree paths. He slipped through a tight thorn-door after the dogs, turning his broad shoulders sideways and ducking to allow his nearly six-foot frame to fit through the space between the iron-strong branches. He had pruned the barbs, but kept the thorn-door narrow to keep out big aevians.

As he passed through the doorway the strong, peppery scent emitted by the broad leaves repelled the hook flies buzzing around Drake and the dogs. *At least Neven will be free from them,* Drake thought, but he worried about the child stumbling into a nest of the nearly impossible-to-eradicate fever ants. One step on a hidden mound and the boy would be stung to death.

Being under the most sacred kind of tree in the village usually made Drake relax, but his shoulders tightened as he passed the cover tree's thick central trunk. He scanned the ground where the lowest layer of the tall branches arched down and into the dirt to form a wide circle around the base of the trunk. The lower boughs drooped to the ground and took root, caging the area and forming a dome. The wooden bars grew close together where they had melded with the ground, and only small animals like surikats or thorn vipers could pass between them. Larger creatures would be held back after feeling the poison sting of the thorns.

Drake hoped Neven hadn't slipped through a small break where he couldn't follow. Even if he had an axe, it would take at least half an hour to hack through the branches. His arm was already sore from pruning the thorns from the cover trees doorways, but wherever Neven went he would follow.

The dogs led Drake from one giant cover tree to the next, tracing the boy's scent down the camouflaged pathways. *Neven's probably lost and afraid.* Anyone unfamiliar with the grove would have difficulty navigating the thorn-doors and the hard-to-see trails. Any footprints on the lush shade-clover would have already disappeared as the soft ground cover sprang back to its original shape, but Drake searched for any sign of the boy or his mother. Mae's voice had grown distant—then silent. He realized she was too far away for him to hear. Mae must have gone the wrong way.

The vortex of mist Drake had seen in the Void swirled in his mind. Right after he saw it was when Neven had run away from his mother. *Don't be a fool.* He chastised himself for the superstitious thought, but he couldn't shake an uneasy feeling that made the old scars on his forearms itch as if fever ants were crawling all over him. His nervous touch broke open a fresh scab from his morning work.

Drake didn't pause to staunch the oozing blood and instead glanced through the branches of an adjacent cover tree, searching the shadows. Another path ran parallel to the one he and the dogs were following.

Laying face down in shade-clover was Neven's tiny body.

"Neven!" Drake rushed toward the boy, but a cover tree barred his way. He reached through a gap in the ground-rooted branches, ignoring the thorns scraping against his shoulder. Stretching as far as he could, he grabbed the boy's slender arm.

Neven lifted his face from the soft shade-clover with a playful smile. "How you see me?"

Drake sagged backwards. *Just a game. Thank the Goddess* "Neven, stay there. I'm coming to get you." He glanced at the adjacent path where Neven had been hiding. He'd have to backtrack past a long screen of cover trees separating him and the four-year-old.

"No. Dwake. I play hiding."

"*Neven.* Stay there."

The boy's cherubic face beamed a smile before he darted away. "Jep, Temus. Find him." Drake pointed down the trail and the dogs took off while Drake ran the other way to trap the boy between them. He sped down a path beside a vegetable garden, always keeping an eye on the patches of open sky. A flight of small birds, thorn shrikes, sat in a line on a branch where they had impaled a tree frog on a thorn. They picked at the frog's flesh with their sharp bills and watched Drake with their little black eyes. He stomped past the shrikes, which took flight and disappeared. Superstitious thoughts flitted through his mind. *The little demons might report my position to one of their larger cousins. I'll have to be ready.*

Drake arrived at the spot where Neven had been laying. The boy had scampered away, but Jep and Temus loped down a nearby path after him. Drake took a different route to cut Neven off and saw rows of vegetables growing in the open ground.

Scanning the crop area, Drake made certain Neven hadn't taken a shortcut. The children of Cliffton were taught to stay under cover, but Neven was so young he might forget. A griffin or some other aevian could swoop in and snatch him before anyone would know what had happened—especially with no one in the watch tower.

Passing the garden where old Tearl, Jep and Temus' sire, had been killed defending Tallia, Drake's sister, made his heart skip a beat. She had twisted her ankle running for a cover tree, but Tearl had held off the rogue griffin long enough for her to crawl to safety. The aevian flew off with the valiant bullmastiff clutched in its talons instead. Drake wished he had been there with Tallia, instead of being on a vrelk hunt. *What a waste of time. Even at thirteen winters, I was needed here. One well-placed bolt and Tearl would still be alive. My first dog was taken while I was away. Never again.*

A second griffin skull would be on the basement wall in the Bloodstone family home, matching the one his grandfather had killed years before. The young men wouldn't tease him for volunteering to be guardian all the time if he slew a griffin. He was tired of them urging him to shirk his duties at home and join them on the boring hunts. *Why don't they understand?*

A chorus of high-pitched squeaks and short trilling barks erupted from a troop of surikats in a nearby melon patch when he appeared. The ferretlike animals foraged across the entire village-grove killing and eating fever-ants, beetles, and thorn-snakes. They were always on guard during the day keeping such a sharp vigil that most of the Clifftoners called them watchkats.

One or more of the kats was usually in a tree keeping watch over the thick canopy and keeping in contact with the troop on the ground with chirps and barks. He listened to their calls, recognizing the meaning: "The sky is clear." But after a lifetime listening to them he also heard another message revealed in the urgent tone. Fear.

Drake spotted a mob of the foot-tall watchkats standing on their hind legs in the garden. The surikats' short brown and grayish fur with black stripes stood erect from head to tail. Their black eyes darted back and forth and Drake's hunter's intuition told him to load his crossbow. *Now.*

The watchkats' shrill ululating call for "Big aevian!" echoed through the grove.

Neven screamed from somewhere close. Drake sprinted forward. The high-pitched child's wail sliced through Drake's spirit. The boy's shriek ended abruptly and there was no time to cock a crossbow. Jep and Temus sniffed at a thorn-door leading into a garden. The dogs growled and bared their teeth at something in the open ground.

Unsheathing his Kierka blade, Drake stood with his dogs, ready to repel any aevian demon. He stared into the garden, looking at the sky above the tall treetops. There was no sign of a griffin or worse demon. His eyes were drawn to a child's footprints across the soft ground. A few paces from the thorn-door a little shoe lay in the dirt.

"Neven!" Drake shouted as he scanned for any other signs of the four-year-old boy. *This can't be happening.*

Despair sapped the failed village guardian's strength, and his numb body sagged against sharp branches. *My fault. I can't take this again. Not again. Not a little child.* He stared at Neven's shoe in the garden. There was nothing else.

Something moved inside the grove behind him. He heard small gasping breaths coming from behind a tree trunk. Springing toward the sound, Drake ran around to the other side of the tree where he found little Neven huddled against the trunk. He swept the boy up in his arms as waves of relief and joy swept aside his anguish. Jep and Temus stopped growling after a moment; but the dogs stayed on guard at the thorn-door.

Looking into the boy's eyes Drake asked, "Nev, what did you see?"

Neven's entire body shook with fright as his eyes filled with large tears. Drake could feel the tiny boy's heart pound as he hugged him close. "It's all right. You're safe. I'll protect you."

The watchkats' alarm calls had stopped, but they echoed in Drake's mind, sending jolts of worry through his body. *What was it?* He glanced at the dogs, wishing they could tell him what they sensed. Both remained rigid, ears up. Drake wondered if the aevian—or whatever had been out there—was gone. He wanted to ask the boy more, but decided he'd been through enough for one day. Hugging Neven, Drake asked, "Did you run for cover when you heard the watchkats?"

Neven nodded.

"Good boy. Always listen to them and don't go out in the open."

Tears fell from Neven's big brown eyes as he nodded. Drake remembered a time when he was a little boy, perhaps six years old. He and his mother were in the garden planting seeds when she had grabbed him and ran under the nearest cover tree. An instant later a flight of griffins passed overhead. After the danger had gone his mother had knelt in front of him, putting her face in front of his so he would pay attention. Her eyes were so big and shiny. He could still hear her urgent words and recalled her trembling hands clutching his small shoulders.

"Remember that sound. Hear it now? Listen carefully . . . that's the danger call for big aevians. Promise me, if you ever hear that sound, run for cover as fast as you can. Promise?"

"I promise, Mommy."

She had cried and hugged him tight. Drake remembered being very afraid, just like Neven.

"Neven!" Mae Boughcutter ran down the path and took her son into her arms.

"He's all right." Drake made his voice as calm as he could manage.

"I heard the watchkats and your shout and I thought that. . . ."

"Everything's all right. He ran for cover. You taught him well." Drake showed her a confident smile, but in the back of his mind he knew that whatever Neven had seen was still out there.

III

The forest is endless and filled with all manner of barbs and briars. I wish to feel the smooth stone halls of home under my feet again.

—Bellor Fardelver, from the Thornclaw Journal

"Lorak's blood!" Thor untangled his brown beard from a spiky plant. The unyielding foliage of the Thornclaw Forest appeared to have a single duty—shed dwarven blood.

"Thor. Please refrain from using Lorak's name so . . . irreverently. Have I taught you nothing?" Bellor made a disgusted sound in the back of his throat and thought, *Thor will never change his ways, and two weeks of floundering in this green prison hasn't helped.*

"Humans," Thor fumed as he ripped away from the bush snagging him. "Only a species as short-lived and as shortsighted as them would inhabit a forest like this."

"Please, calm down and pay attention to where you're going."

"Where I'm going? I don't have any idea where I'm—"

"I'm certain the human village is close by." Bellor rubbed his square jaw and broad nose. "We must find a guide."

Thor pulled his much sharper facial features into a scowl. "There probably isn't a village, and they won't help us anyway."

"Of course there's a village. Now please be silent."

"This forest is driving me mad."

"I think it's driven you mad already and not eating for two days hasn't helped." Bellor felt guilty when he saw Thor's exasperated expression.

"Hrrmmff." Thor frowned.

"I'm sorry. The humans fled to this frontier to keep us away, so please don't prove their fears correct when we find them."

"But why can't there be a trail? Is that too much to ask? I know they can make trails. It's one of their few skills. I just don't know why any sane human would—"

"Be silent, will you? If the aevian is around it'll certainly hear you ranting."

Following behind Thor in the relative quiet for a moment, Bellor wished the impassable brambles were their only enemy. He was more concerned about the aevian beast pursuing them. He seldom saw its shadow as it flew over the canopy, but knew the monster was waiting for a chance to strike. Bellor thought it ironic that the sharp leaves and poisonous thorns were keeping them alive—or perhaps just killing them much slower than the aevian would.

Mumbling vulgar Drobin and Nexan oaths, Thor plowed through the forest like an irritable bulldog. Amused, Bellor watched as Thor took out his frustrations on the plants blocking their way. After an hour of listening to Thor's gruff swearing, Bellor called for a much-needed rest and they drank water collected from the leaves. Thor sat gnawing on a twig and swatting at hook flies.

The War Priest napped against a tree until Thor woke him. "Hear that?"

"What?" Bellor roused himself, then focused on the sounds. Something large crunched through the brush, then stopped.

"A vrelk?" Thor lifted his crossbow as the sounds started again. "We need food."

"Too big, and it's coming closer." Bellor pulled his battleaxe from the leather baldric suspended across his back.

Bellor led Thor backward, looking for a place to run or hide. Nettle shrubs formed a thick hedge hemming them in. *Why didn't I pick a better place to rest?* Bellor rebuked himself when he saw they were trapped.

A thunderous crack resounded through the canopy as a dead tree snapped and fell just beyond the bushes in front of them. The dwarves ducked behind a large ironwood tree as the beast closed in. The thrashing sounds stopped on the other side of their hiding place.

The monster's breath sawed in and out of its lungs as Bellor's eyes darted around, searching for a way to escape. The impenetrable hedge of nettle plants stretched into a vast thicket as far as he could see. He dropped to his knees, dug his fingers into the soil and noticed a small opening leading through the hedge. Bellor motioned for Thor to follow him as he crawled into the tunnel-like passage.

As Thor wriggled after Bellor, the creature crushed the entrance to the thicket an arm-length behind Thor's legs. It tore up the plants as both dwarves crawled away as fast as they could. Bellor thanked Lorak for the ground-hugging animal trail that had prolonged—if not saved—their lives.

The aevian's frantic thrashing faded as Bellor and Thor crawled further into the maze of nettle shrubs. They lost themselves in the impenetrable thicket and Bellor wondered if they would ever find their way out.

"Is it still there?" Thor slipped his shoulders between two biting nettle plants, using his shield to keep the stinging leaves away from his face.

"We must always assume it's there." Bellor searched the tenebrous ceiling for evidence of the beast. Blinking his dark eyes at a bright patch of sunlight ahead of them, he smelled a fresh breeze almost unfiltered by the musty trees and decaying leaves.

Hoping they had eluded the creature, Bellor stood up at the edge of the thicket and scanned the trees. Thor followed his lead and both dwarves stretched their cramped bodies. Hours of crawling under the sharp plants had left them sore and covered with small scrapes from the nettle plants that stung like cold fire and left their fingers numb and painful.

"Thor, angle to the right, there's a clearing ahead we must avoid. We don't want to get caught in open ground."

Thor grunted in disgust to protest Bellor's order as he moved ahead through the endless thorny shrubs.

"The aevian could land there." Bellor dodged a nettle plant. "We can't risk it."

"I only need to stretch my legs for a moment away from this thicket. You act as if it's a spawn of Draglûne."

"Shhh." Bellor sunk to the moist ground and scanned the treetops. His intuition whispered another warning. The two dwarves hunkered back to back and searched for whatever had spooked Bellor.

The screeching of nearby thorn shrikes drew their full attention. The birds' high-pitched cries echoed across the forest, then died out.

Where are you, aevian? Bellor felt something hidden watching him. Waiting.

After a few moments of vigilance, Bellor pointed in the direction he thought they should go, making a drastic course change.

"I hate this," Thor complained as he broke the trail, step by laborious step. "Let's set a trap for it. We should be doing the hunting."

"No. Too dangerous."

Thor rolled his eyes and Bellor remembered all the young dwarves he had seen killed because of Thor's impatient attitude. The War Priest wondered how much longer he could keep his

48

friend from doing something foolish that would end in his death. He had resigned himself to keep Thor alive, foolish or not. He was the only one left alive that Bellor could trust to accompany him. Grinning to himself, Bellor pondered the subtle difference between foolishness and bravery.

"Is this the right way?" Thor pushed past a tangle of sharp stalks trying to pierce his light chain-mail hauberk.

"Of course it is." Bellor spoke in the same encouraging voice he had used hundreds of times in the past weeks to reassure his precocious comrade. Bellor thought about what Thor would say next: *But how do you know for certain?*

"But how do you know for certain?" Thor asked for the tenth time that day.

Bellor knew the routine better than his friend. And in spite of all his protests, Bellor enjoyed the game. It got their minds off their pursuer, and Thor required much more religious instruction if he was to ever take on the mantle of a full War Priest.

"Is your faith wavering again, my Earth Brother?" Bellor smiled. "Because if it is, take heart in knowing that Lorak, Our Maker, has given me the gift of finding the way. Trust in Lorak and—"

"I was just asking a simple question! I'd hate to break a trail for you in the wrong direction, *Master Bellor.*"

The beams of sunlight invading the forest in front of them were interrupted as something passed overhead. The shadow cast a pall over the two dwarves, silencing their conversation. Both dwarves crouched under a low tree branch as they checked the tiny patches of sky all around them.

"It's here," Thor whispered, his right hand resting on the warhammer hanging from his belt. "Should we span our crossbows?"

Bellor nodded, keeping his fear hidden behind his thick beard as they bent back the braided strings on their weapons with small steel crank-levers, then loaded scale-piercing quarrels.

"Curse this forest." Thor spit on a thorn bush covered with dozens of spider webs. "I wish we could see it."

"It's the same creature that's been following us. I recognize its shadow. It has a very wide wingspan."

"How wide?" Thor eyed the canopy.

"We'll be safe as long as we stay in the thick forest."

"It'll find a way to get to us eventually." Thor wrinkled his nose.

"Lorak will help us."

"Have you forgotten that you also taught me 'by committing to action Lorak will help us'? I say we find it first."

"I also taught you to be patient and trust Him."

"I'll trust my steel. I have great faith in it." Thor grabbed his blacksteel hammer in one big meaty fist and held his crossbow in the other. "I'm too hungry and too tired to sit here and wait for it any longer."

"Then let's get going." Bellor pointed south. "The village is that way. We'll have to fight soon enough."

Thor hesitated for a moment, grumbled to himself, then plowed through the undergrowth. They entered an area of sapling burnwood trees and saw light streaming down from the sparse canopy. The soft-wooded trees were perfect for cutting and burned well once they were dried—but they didn't provide much protection when they were young.

Bellor realized the short trees were replacing old growth, which must have died or rotted away years before. Remnants of old logs and a few stumps poked out of the ground. Bellor saw the telltale signs of axe cuts on the wood. "We're close to the human village." Any celebratory thoughts soon faded to despair. The short trees had allowed malicious thornclaw shrubs to grow to tremendous sizes, making the dwarves' advance much more difficult. Each step involved eluding the snaring branches that hooked their clothing.

Bellor couldn't get out fast enough. He encouraged his companion to move quicker. Sweat poured off Thor as he cut the trail through the clawing bushes that fastened onto him like the talons of tiny demons. Thor and Bellor were soon dragging disembodied thornclaws from the exposed links of their chain-mail coats.

Leading with his shield, Thor pushed through a tangled mass of scratchy thorns until he reached the far side. His lead foot didn't find the ground.

Thor started to fall, momentum carrying him forward.

Lunging, Bellor caught the back of Thor's belt just in time and latched onto a thick bush with his other hand. Both dwarves teetered on the edge of the cliff. Far below, the tops of white clouds lapped against the sheer face of the plateau like waves. Bellor stared over Thor's shoulder at the clouds separating the living world of Ae'leron from the churning cauldron of the Underworld.

"Pull me up! Pull me up!" Thor's arms flailed for a handhold and were cut by the thorns.

Bellor dragged Thor back to solid ground and they collapsed into a pile of beards and short limbs.

"That's no way for a warrior to die." Bellor patted Thor's shoulder.

"I'm indebted to you again, Master Bellor."

Bellor nudged him off. "I shouldn't have pushed the pace so much. I'm sorry." The War Priest looked out of the hole Thor had made in the brush and realized they were on a small southern facing peninsula jutting out of the plateau. They ducked back into the shrubs and scanned the light canopy above them. "We're going to have to backtrack and then follow the edge if we want to go south."

"The Void lured us off course again?" Thor raised a bushy

eyebrow. "That's never happened before."

Bellor ignored the jabs and gazed out into the infinite abyss. "We'd better turn back. I wish we had a guide. I'm sorry, but I've led us into a dead end." Bellor immediately regretted his choice of words as the shadow of the aevian passed overhead again. He wondered which would finish them off first, the aevian, the forest, or the Void.

IV

The treasures of the forest are not only the trees, but the folk who tend them.

—Priestess Liana Whitestar, litany from the Goddess
Scrolls

Drake and his dogs watched over Neven and Mae, escorting them through the dense garden-grove. They made their way toward the heart of the village, and Drake's eyes searched the shadows for threats.

"Walking with Nev and I is most kind." Mae hugged her son close to her chest. "If you hadn't found him. . . ."

Drake reached back and brushed his hand through Neven's fine hair. He forced a smile at Mae, and suppressed his guilt about not reaching the boy sooner. *He could have been taken.*

"Mommy, kats told Neven hide."

Mae and Drake grinned at each other upon hearing the boy's first words since his sighting of the aevian. Mae kissed Nev's soft cheek. "Thank the Goddess for sending the watchkats to us. And bless Priestess Liana and Jaena for keeping the trees healthy and strong."

Mae's prayer played through Drake's mind. Every day he was more amazed at Liana's skill as an arborist. No tree under her care had ever died and the path they followed was well shielded, but the aevian was still out there. He wouldn't relax until the young mother and her child were safe. Then he would check on his own family and Jaena. He suspected a griffin or one of its cousins, perhaps a manticore, might be circling the village. He scanned the canopy for signs of the aevian and looked at the trail behind them. Mae was about to speak, but she looked away. "Mae, what is it?"

"Nothing. I was just wondering if you knew Jaena and Liana visited my house this week."

He tried not to become distracted from his task of guarding them, but he did recall a lot of visitors going to her house in past days and he turned around. "Didn't my grandfather deliver some paint?"

"He did, for our arboreum." Mae's beaming smile said it all. "Priestess Liana says the baby will come in five months!"

"Mae, I'm so happy for you!"

"I knew I was with child, and Liana told me when I would give birth. It was so wonderful. I even think I felt the baby move inside me when Liana touched our tree and used the magic of the Goddess. She says my baby will be healthy. I'm so happy."

A wave of protectiveness flooded over Drake. Something deep in his soul demanded that he get her home. "Come on, Mae." He took Neven in his arms, the dogs guarded their flanks, and he marched down the trail.

A moment later they approached Mae and Neven's home, which nestled under the arches of a five-hundred-year-old cover tree. The two-story log house abutted one side of the middle-aged trunk, leaving plenty of room for the growth of the tree, which would be accelerated by Tree magic during healings and ceremonies. The small ceremonial structure was connected to the main house and touched the tree, giving easy access to the trunk.

Neven's great-grandmother opened the door and the four-year-old squirmed out of Drake's arms and ran to her. He waved from inside and smiled at Drake. Mae stepped toward the doorway, then turned back. Her eyes misted over with tears and she couldn't speak. "Sorry." She wiped her eyes, looked away. "Thank you for being there for us."

He didn't know what to say, but when he met her gaze Drake decided to paint her arboreum himself. Tomorrow. Two coats.

Mae wiped away her tears. "You'll make Jaena a good husband"—she touched his arm—"and you'll be a good father someday. My mother told Liana she thinks you'll bring Jaena a marriage branch soon. Will you?"

Lame excuses came to his mind. He had so much to do and Jaena needed to finish her priestess training. He didn't want to distract her from her studies any more than he already had. She hadn't been able to use the Tree magic successfully yet, and Drake wondered if her slow progress was because of him. He nodded at Mae, trying to hide his embarrassment at living three winters past seventeen and not being married yet.

"I never thought your sister would be married before you. Remember when we were little and your mother watched Jaena, you and me? I knew that you two would marry."

It's always the same. He hid his discomfort with an awkward smile. Father had told him at least twice in the past month, "By the time I was your age, I'd been married for almost four years. I'm tired of your daydreaming and skulking around the village by yourself while the rest of us hunt. Wake up. When are you going to marry Jaena?"

Drake forced his father's words out of his mind and looked at Mae. "Sorry, I've got to go."

Jep and Temus followed on his heels as they jogged past the house where Ethan's mother and her second husband lived. He passed a few other dwellings, stopping at the front thorn-door of the Bloodstone family home. His place of birth was much like Mae's. A tiny ribbon of smoke wafted from the stone chimney poking out of the domed tree. He enjoyed the mixed fragrances of the peppery cover tree leaves, the rich burnwood smoke, and especially the wild onions and thyme. Grandmother was cooking a vrelk roast.

Drake breathed a sigh of relief when he saw his sister Tallia sitting on the front porch with Mother. Tainting the mouthwatering scent of cooking meat were fumes from a pot of Grandfather's vrelk-hoof glue. He wrinkled his nose as Tallia dipped the tip of a crossbow bolt shaft into the pot, then affixed one of the new iron points, which Father had bartered for in Nexus City. Temus sneezed, shaking his jowls as the mingling odors drifted through the air.

The mob of watchkats playing next to the porch called out with chirruping barks to greet Jep, who bounded forward to play while Temus lay down. *Damn! I wasn't going to stop. I've got things to do.*

Tallia glanced up from her work, but his mother's eyes focused on sewing white cloth flowers onto Tallia's wedding dress. His seventeen-year-old sister's face lit up when Mother lifted the almost-completed dress for inspection.

Learning about Mae's pregnancy sparked him to remember what Tallia had told Mother a few weeks before. "The Priestess said I won't have any trouble conceiving healthy children. She has foreseen it."

"Good, Tally. Just wait for after the wedding to—"

"Mother!" Tallia's cheeks turned pink. "Of course Vance and I will wait."

With her wedding only two weeks away, Drake suspected he'd be an uncle in less than a year. For Vance's sake—and his sister's honor—he hoped it would be at least nine months.

Jep *woofed* and rolled on the ground with the watchkats. Drake stepped toward the porch, muttering to himself. *I'll only stay a moment.*

Tallia gave her brother the contemptuous smile she reserved just for him. "Get tired of daydreaming in that old watch tower, Drakie? Can't you find something else to do?"

He rolled his eyes, then realized from her playful mood that there hadn't been any sign of the aevian over the village itself.

Mother glanced up. "You can't be done with the trails already."

He held up his hands showing the fresh scabs from eight hours of pruning. "They're done."

"Oh." Mother's eyebrows raised a little. "Have you fixed the hinge on the gate?" She stitched another cloth flower onto the linen dress.

"I will."

"You'd better before Father comes home." His sister pointed a shaft at him.

Jep ambled over and sniffed at the pot of glue beside Tallia's feet. The big dog sneezed, nearly blowing over a watchkat.

"Get this mutt out of here before he drools on my dress." Tallia pushed Jep away with her bare feet.

Drake grabbed Jep's collar and pulled him away.

"Keep those dogs away from my dress." Tallia glared at Jep.

"All this wedding work is making you surlier than usual, Tally." Drake held Jep, but let him lick Tallia's feet, prompting her to squeal and scrunch up her face.

"Hush," Mother scolded, "you're both distracting me, and I want this trim to be perfect."

Tallia smirked. "Get out of here and take those dogs with you before I find a crossbow and shoot one of these up your—"

"*Tallia!*" Mother flashed her a disgusted look.

"With your aim, I'm not worried." He grinned at his feisty little sister.

Tallia dipped an unfinished bolt in the glue and threw it at Drake.

Jep jumped in the air and caught the shaft. Tallia frowned when her sticky dart missed the mark. Jep displayed his catch, wagging his tail. Laughing, Drake tugged and groaned for added effect as he tried to pry the bolt out of Jep's jaws. Tallia giggled as Jep battled Drake like his doggy-life depended on keeping the bolt. Even Mother chuckled a little while the big dog held on, no matter how hard Drake pulled. Temus watched from the thorn-door, leaving his more playful sibling to have fun for both of them. The watchkats observed the tug-of-war and their little black eyes lingered on the growling dog with fascination.

"Drop it!" Drake commanded, causing Jep to open his mouth. "Here, Tally." He tossed his sister the slobber-covered shaft, which had dirt and leaves stuck to the tip.

Tallia deflected it away with her hand. "Achhh!" She wiped the drool off and stuck out her tongue at her brother.

"Off with you!" Mother shook her head. *"Children."*

Satisfied he had won that particular exchange, Drake smiled and strutted away. "Good dog." He scratched Jep on the head and patted Temus, who yawned. "Come on, boys. We've spent too much time here already. Let's check on Jaena."

The dogs trotted down the path toward the Shrine of Amaryllis. Jaena and Liana would be teaching the children, unless they were out tending ill villagers. Visiting home had calmed him, but the sense of urgency he'd felt while escorting Neven and Mae returned.

Nothing must happen to Jaena or her mother. Without them the entire village could be wiped out by sicknesses that only the Tree magic could cure. Mae's baby could die at birth, and his grandfather might already be dead from old age without Liana's healing hands. He swallowed the lump of fear that collected in his throat. *Everything is fine. The village is safe. But what's out there?*

Despite the dangers of aevians and the harsh forest, he

thanked the Goddess for her blessings. At least the Clifftoners were free, unlike most of the Nexans who lived under the steel fist of the Drobin Empire, where Amaryllian Priestesses were persecuted and often killed. Dwarven Priests held sway over most humans, and the Temple of Lorak branded Amaryllians as heretics and rebels; but the arms of the stunted folk didn't reach this deep into the Thornclaw Forest.

Drake reaffirmed a vow made long ago. *Nothing will ever happen to anyone I love, especially Liana or Jaena, while I'm the village guardian.* He would do anything to protect his people from aevians or dwarves. His life would be an easy trade and he knew the rest of the men of the village felt the same way. All enemies of Cliffton would be slain without mercy. He would make certain of it.

V

An unexpected chasm, real or imagined, always seems to get in our way.

—Bölak Blackhammer, from the Lost Journal

Thor and Bellor ran along the narrow peninsula of rock, trying not to give the aevian time to cut them off. The immense Void lay in wait just beyond their vision. "Careful, Thor," Bellor said, trying hard not to make an ill-advised step of his own.

The young dwarf grunted and moved as fast as the clawing bushes would allow. Bellor knew they had to backtrack into the older, more protective forest. If they were cornered at the edge of the Void in the lightwoods, their Sacred Duty would come to an abrupt and unpleasant end.

The thunderous cracking of tree branches behind them sent icy needles of fear shooting into Bellor's stomach. "It's landed, run!" The two dwarves struggled forward, but the dense undergrowth coupled with their short legs didn't allow for much speed.

Something large smashed through the bushes a few paces behind them. Bellor heard the creature's scales scraping over the thornclaw thicket. The large predator closed the distance with a leap. The ground shook when it landed.

Bellor felt the aevian's hot breath on his neck. He thrust his head forward as the creature's jaws snapped together and ripped out a chunk of his gray hair. He barely noticed his ringing ears or felt the pain from his bleeding scalp as he dove after Thor, who had scurried under an arch made by a fallen log.

The beast's head smashed into the rotting wood behind him, sending an explosion of bark blasting over Bellor. The War Priest scrambled forward on his hands and knees, then rolled down an embankment after Thor. They both crawled under the exposed roots of an ancient tree and ducked into the thicker woods.

The monster fell back and Bellor realized they were in the older forest. The smaller trees gave way to an extensive and thick canopy filled with layers of thorny branches.

The loud thrashing sounds faded, then stopped.

Bellor realized the monster couldn't follow them inside the tangled foliage. The dwarves' four-and-a-half-foot-tall stature helped them outdistance the larger aevian as they continued.

"A trail, look." Thor jumped onto the narrow path leading south.

"Follow. . . ." Air wheezed out of Bellor's lungs. "Go."

Thor jogged down an animal trail snaking through the forest. Bellor's old legs weren't as energetic as his younger comrade's, and first he fell behind, then dropped to the ground, utterly exhausted. The old dwarf hid within the raised roots at the base of a tree trunk. Thor slumped down next to him to catch his breath. On guard, Bellor prayed they would be safe. The shadow of the large creature circling overhead crushed his hopes.

"We've got to keep moving!" Thor grabbed Bellor's arm and hauled the exhausted Priest down the trail.

"No." Bellor gasped for breath and shook off Thor's grip. "I can't . . . run any . . . more." He scanned the interlocking branches of the canopy above them, looking for any sign of the beast.

"Let's stand and fight!" Thor raised his hammer. "Before we're too weak to give a good accounting of ourselves."

The loud flap of the aevian's wings made Bellor gasp and

look upward. The layered ceiling of the forest blocked his view as the monster's claws raked across the canopy. Snapping branches exploded above them as the creature landed on the ironbark sentinel where they had taken shelter. Broken tree limbs and leaves rained down, and they guarded their eyes as the plant material pelted their bodies. Bellor cringed as the canopy sagged under the weight of the aevian.

Hundreds of leaves fell to the ground and Bellor stared upwards through the storm of vegetation. Huge wings blocked out the sunlight, creating jagged shadows on the forest floor. The beast's distorted silhouette loomed over Bellor as thick boughs bent and creaked.

The dwarves froze, waiting in silence with weapons drawn. Thor brushed away a leaf that landed on his face and Bellor scanned their surroundings for a way out. His heart sunk as he realized the trail and all their avenues of retreat passed under breaches and thin areas in the canopy.

Bellor thought, *If we run, it will pounce. Cornered at last.*

Thor looked at his mentor and asked with a hand sign, *What now?*

The War Priest's eyes measured the outline of the demon perched above them before reexamining possible escape routes. "Thor Hargrim." Bellor used his commanding battle voice. Thor's body tensed as if he were ready to leap into the tree, climb the towering ironbark's trunk and attack. "Before we draw its blood," Bellor spoke with all the determination he could muster, "we're going to build a great fire. Gather green wood and tinder."

Thor squinted at Bellor, but gathered dry leaves and several armloads of branches sent down from above. The aevian shifted its weight several times as they waited beneath the tree—caught in its trap at last.

Sharp cracks punctuated the groans of the splintering

branches as the aevian's bulk sunk deeper into the collapsing roof of the forest. Thor glanced upward with every loud sound. Bellor didn't flinch as he cleared a small area, dug a fire pit, and built a mound of earth beside the hole.

Thor pushed several armloads of dead leaves into the pit and Bellor quickly arranged the fuel so it would give off as much smoke as possible. Then he reached into his belt-pouch and withdrew a rectangular red stone as large as his thumb. Bellor placed the smooth rock under the tinder and made certain the archaic Drobin rune painted on its surface faced the sky.

"*Feör.*" Bellor spoke the command in Old Drobin and a flame erupted from the black symbol. The leaves caught fire and the green wood began to smoke. Bellor added several handfuls of leaves and blew into the flames, which grew stronger; but didn't ignite the wood still moist with tree sap.

"*Löshun,*" Bellor whispered and the fire from the rune stone extinguished itself. The leaves kept burning as acrid wisps of smoke drifted into the forest.

Using a stick, Bellor plucked the warm rock from the fire and put it back into his leather belt-pouch. He withdrew a similar-sized rune stone of white marble, this one painted with an intricate silver pattern across its surface. Bellor saw the question in Thor's eyes.

"It's a Chanting Stone." The old dwarf traced his finger over silvery symbols. "Given to me by my mentor over a hundred years ago. I have no others, but this can be saved no longer." The War Priest put the rune stone on the mound of earth in front of the smoking fire. He knelt to pray and touched the ground with the palms of his hands. He felt the dampness of the soil as he channeled the Earth magic. Bellor began to chant Lorak's Song of Fire and his deep voice carried into the woods. "Sûng-**gen** feör um-**Lor**-ak."

A faint glow shone from the rune as he chanted the ancient

words of power and silvery light mixed with gray smoke.

"Sûng-**gen** feör um-**Lor**-ak!" Bellor's voice became louder and Thor joined in, singing at an even lower pitch. Their voices filtered through the forest and soon a third and fourth voice echoed their own. On Bellor's cue the two dwarves stopped singing, but the magic of the Chanting Stone continued their prayer-song even louder.

Thor pointed up, then punched toward the aevian, *Climb the tree? Attack?*

Shaking his head, Bellor pointed south toward an avenue of escape concealed under a choking cloud of smoke from their green-wood fire.

Thor scowled, then signed with terse, slashing gestures, *We kill it now!*

The War Priest's right hand moved patiently, *No. We Drobin kill aevians on the ground. Not in trees.*

The loud chanting continued as the dwarves slipped away into the smoky forest. The sound of their voices faded as they got farther away, but Bellor knew the singing continued. Sadness at leaving such a precious rune stone behind prevented a triumphant grin, but relief stopped a frown.

Thor halted on the path they had been following and pointed to another trail burrowing through the trees like an underground tunnel. Foul-smelling curdle-moss covered the new path, and Bellor gestured for Thor to take it and head southwest—back toward the Void. The sour stench irritated his nostrils, but the aevian wouldn't catch their smell if they stayed near the moss.

Following close behind his companion, the War Priest held the weariness sweeping over him at bay. The Earth magic had taken its toll, and he concentrated on putting one foot in front of the other. He didn't ponder long before a glowing beacon of sunlight appeared at the end of the forest tunnel.

Approaching with caution, Bellor's eyes adjusted to the light as they looked across exposed ground dotted with short tree stumps. Forty paces away stood the log walls and sturdy gate tower of a human settlement.

Thor grinned. "I knew this trail would lead to their village."

Bellor rolled his eyes and shook his head at Thor while they stared at the dozens of dome-shaped trees that sealed off the village from the sky above. Bellor wondered if they would be safer in the village with the humans, who undoubtedly hated them, or outside the walls with the horrors of the Thornclaw Forest.

VI

If one is lost, follow the roots of Amaryllis back to the source, where they will find the love of the Goddess.

—Priestess Liana Whitestar, litany from the Goddess
Scrolls

Drake marched toward the center of Cliffton, hoping to find Jaena there. He performed the ritual of honor to the Goddess by tilting his head back and admiring the uppermost branches of the gigantic central cover tree. He headed for the steps of the most sacred place in the village, the shrine of Amaryllis, silently thanking the Goddess for Neven's life.

A cluster of watchkats spotted him and his dogs as they entered the enormous arbor dome. The little animals called out with a shrill ululating cry, "Groundwalkers." A few scurried into their burrows under the stone foundation of the Hunters' Meeting Hall, where two old men sat on the porch of the long wooden structure. Their harsh eyes followed his every step.

"He stayed home again." Hallan Greenbow, the old pugnacious hunter, didn't bother to whisper.

Mae's grandfather, Craik Boughcutter, sighed. "Not right for a Bloodstone to miss so many hunts."

Greenbow scowled. "I wouldn't stay home if I could still hunt."

"Maybe his eyes are as bad as yours, Hal."

The men sniggered and Drake bristled, but he kept his chin

high and didn't look at them. The oldsters' ridicule quickened his pace as he entered the patchwork of shadows and sunlight surrounding the shrine. Varnished log walls formed a large rectangle around the base of the holy tree. As he approached the front entry, inspecting the red tile shingles and the narrow stairs going to the small moon-prayer platforms in the upper branches. He peered into one of the rainbow-hued, stained-glass windows transported with great effort from Nexus City—where they traded for all of their glass and metal goods. His shoulders relaxed when he saw the familiar silhouettes of Jaena and her mother. *She's safe. Thank the Goddess.*

Pausing, Drake watched a small gathering of children and one elderly man at the base of the steps. Old man Laetham, Cliffton's self-proclaimed historian and Elder Councilman, sat in the shadows facing the youngsters. *Of course he would be in my way.*

A dozen children sat in a half-circle listening to one of the tales Elder Laetham had learned when he was a soldier in the Drobin king's army. The old man's raspy voice became deep and quiet. Drake recognized the final lines of the "Tale of the Two Gods" as Laetham leaned into a patch of sunlight and spread his battle-scarred arms wide. "Mount Nexus erupted in fire and smoke that rose all the way to the moooon! But the Goddess brought rain to the volcano, putting out the great fire. This angered the Mountain God, Lorak, who had raised the plateaus above the Underworld. Foolish Lorak wanted to raise the peaks higher than the moon and block it out from the sky forever!"

The smallest children gasped, their horror at losing the silver moon imprinted on their faces.

"Prideful Lorak had made Mount Nexus explode with fire a hundred times already, and He wanted it to explode a hundred times more until it grew tall into the sky. But before the

67

mountain could erupt again the Goddess sent a great storm of clouds, more clouds than all the mist in the Void. Lorak and Amaryllis argued for hundreds of years as Her rain fell and the wind blew, cooling off the burning mountain—and with it, Lorak's anger.

"In the end the Goddess stood beside the Mountain God and the sky was clear. The Two Gods decided to work together to make the folk of Ae'leron and began under the light of a full moon. They used Mount Nexus as a giant cauldron and combined the Earth and Tree magic."

Shaking his head, Drake thought about how the dwarves told a much different tale to their own offspring and the human vassals bound to serve the rulers of the Drobin Empire. According to Grandfather, the Lorakian Priests said the humans had been created to be the loyal servants of all Drobin, who watched over them as wise, all-knowing fathers—fathers who should be obeyed at all times. *Vrelkshit.*

Laetham continued, "Amaryllis and Lorak created the people of Ae'leron within the cauldron of Mount Nexus. From the tall trees once growing on the mountain she created our Nexan ancestors. And from the short stone boulders and the fire the first dwarf king and his Priests were born."

"What's a dwarf?" a little girl asked. It was Edeline, the second child of Ethan's older sister.

"Later, child," Laetham snapped, "that's another story." He took a deep breath. "The folk were born from the mountains and trees and have lived on the great plateaus ever since, with the blessing of the Two Gods. Remember always, children, the Mountain God raised the plateaus to separate us from the demons that dwell in the Void mist.

"The plateaus are high above the Underworld, but without the trees of Amaryllis we would never be safe. So, all of you mind the teachings of the Priestess and stay under cover. Don't spend your days looking into the Void or playing by it, or you'll call up a demon who'll carry you away."

Drake swooped in and picked up the curious little Edeline, who screamed and then laughed as he snarled like a dog.

"What're you doing here?" Laetham glared at him. "Don't you have work to do?"

Drake hugged Edeline. "It'll get done."

Laetham's mouth wrinkled. "Don't be like him, children, and spend your days staring into the Void. Listen, wee ones, the men of Cliffton should spend their time hunting, not hiding."

Drake shook his head.

"Do you hear me, Drake Bloodstone?" Laetham asked, "You know you should be out with your father and the other hunters, not lazing around here."

The muscles in Drake's jaw tensed and he put Edeline down. He met Laetham's gaze. Harsh words sizzled on the tip of his tongue, but he turned to walk away.

Edeline hugged Drake's leg. "Don't listen to him," Edeline looked up at him with soft brown eyes that reminded him of Ethan's. "You're the best guardian in the village. Don't ever go away." She squeezed his leg as the other children nodded, their young faces echoing Edeline's sentiments.

Laetham snorted. "Don't worry children, we'll always find someone to watch over Cliffton."

"How about me?" A smooth and playful feminine voice asked from the top of the stairs. "Inside, children, time for the afternoon lesson. You mustn't keep Priestess Whitestar waiting." Jaena smiled as the children scampered up the steps and Edeline waved at Drake before going inside.

Jaena stood supervising the kids as they entered the shrine. She gently touched each of them as they passed. Drake gazed at her long, curly blond hair, which caught the few rays of light and shone like dew on golden-yellow roses. Her white, long-flowing dress with green and blue threads woven into the fabric intensified Jaena's sapphire eyes.

Drake shifted uncomfortably in his dirt-brown vrelkskin tunic, patched pants, and scuffed knee-high boots. He knew Jaena didn't care about his hunter's clothes. His spirit of determination and service was just one of the things she loved about him. Jaena always understood Drake's need to protect their people, and he understood her calling to provide everyone with health and support. They had different ways of accomplishing their goals, but they were both guardians of Cliffton.

Love for Jaena filled him, and he realized he'd been gawking like an awestruck little boy ever since she appeared. His eyes glanced away and he rubbed his chin, reassuring himself that he was clean-shaven, just the way she liked him. He remembered their tender kisses before he had left for the watch tower and hoped his cheeks would still be smooth enough for her liking later in the day. She probably wouldn't have time, but he could always hope.

The memory of her soft skin and the smell of her hair when he held her close made him slowly let out his breath. His yearning for her during the last several months had been difficult, especially since Jaena had been talking more about having children someday. He watched the last little child go inside and wondered if someday they would have beautiful, blond babies who looked like Jaena.

Drake's mouth went dry as twenty-year-old wood and he felt his pulse pounding in his ears. *No. I wish I could marry her, but I can't be a father. What if I can't protect our children? What if they die? I can't do it.* Shame washed over him and he knew he was weak. *I wish I was more like Rigg. He could face anything.*

"Too bad you like this unbeliever, Jaena." Laetham picked himself up off the ground and dusted off his tattered pants. "There are other men who deserve your attention."

Laetham's words spurred Drake and the challenge gave him a burst of confidence. *I will ask her to be my wife. I must. Soon.*

"Elder Laetham," Jaena's smile spread across her face until tiny dimples formed in her cheeks, "it would be difficult to find someone as devout as you." Her soft tone and disarming expression made Laetham pause. He chuckled to himself before hobbling toward his friends at the Hunters' Meeting Hall.

Another victory for Jaena's smile. Someday I'll resist it, but not today. Drake stood mesmerized as Jaena glided down the steps to embrace him. She didn't go down the last one and stayed just high enough to remain at an equal height with him. He held his unloaded crossbow in front of him in mock protest. "I'm village guardian and path warden today. I don't think I have time for—"

"I think you'd better put something long and sharp in that weapon if you're really a guardian." She pushed the crossbow away and wrapped her arms around him. The little wooden star charm he had carved for her hung from her bracelet and tickled his neck. Jaena's rosy lips beckoned and Drake lost himself in the warmth of her body as they kissed.

VII

Premonitions are so common among us, but why don't we Amaryllians always heed Her warnings?

—Priestess Liana Whitestar, from her personal journal

Jaena hugged Drake tight after their lingering kiss. She couldn't resist, though her mother would not approve of kissing him on the steps of the shrine. Besides, she had heard Laetham insulting him, and Drake needed cheering up. She whispered in his ear, "I'm glad you're here."

He forced a smile, and they pulled away from each other to a more discreet distance. Jaena stared into his handsome face. *I've got to tell him about my dream, or whatever it was.*

Jaena made her expression serious, and his smile disappeared. He glanced up at the branches. "What's wrong, Drake?"

"Nothing." His eyes lingered on the tall branches for a moment. "Tallia's wedding and. . . ."

She caressed his tense, muscular forearm, trying to relax him with her soft touch.

"Everyone, especially Father, has been pressuring me to. . . ." Drake bit his lip. "You know . . . ask you to . . . to be my. . . ."

Jaena couldn't think of what to say. He didn't need to hear that from her too, though she wanted him to ask her to marry him more than anything.

"I'm sorry, Jaena. I just. . . ."

Jaena read the lines on his face like they were words on the

Goddess Scrolls. *Guilt. Fear. Shame. Why can't he see what he's doing to himself?*

Jaena struggled to find the words to lift his spirits. "You don't have to prove yourself to me or anyone—especially Elder Laetham or your father. I know you're one of the best hunters in the village." She eyed the new scabs and scratches on his hands. "And you do more work than anyone."

"It doesn't matter. Father always wants me to leave the village and go with him on the hunts."

Jaena lifted his chin with her delicate fingers. "You're one of the best crossbowmen in the whole village. How many thistle deer and vrelk have you shot when you were on the wall or in the gate tower, scores of them? I've seen you shoot them when they're the entire length of the open ground away. Not many can do that."

"Father can. And no one thinks that me shooting stupid animals who've wandered into the firebreak makes me a hunter."

"But you are." Jaena sighed and thought about all the hours she had spent watching Drake and his family practice their fast, intuitive way of shooting. No other family in Cliffton could duplicate the Bloodstone Way.

"Look at me. Don't think of anything else." Jaena fixed her startling blue eyes on his dark brown ones and everything became irrelevant as they connected with each other. Jaena and Drake became the only two people in the village. "I love you. No matter what anyone else thinks. I know who you are, and I love you."

A true smile spread across his face and his shoulders straightened as some of his stress lifted.

"Jaena, I love you more than anything." His smile broadened. "And my sister isn't the only Bloodstone getting married before the next full moon."

Jaena kissed Drake hard on the lips and didn't care if anyone saw.

Holding hands, they sat on the wooden steps of the shrine, and Jaena couldn't stop smiling. Jep and Temus lay panting at their feet while the children's high voices inside the building repeated Priestess Liana's well-enunciated words. Jaena listened to her mother teach the children about the outside world and remembered when she had sat with Drake and Ethan learning the same things, repeating the same lines.

"I can't stay long." Drake shifted his weight. "I've got to work on the east gate before Father gets back. And won't your mother be upset since you're not helping her in there?"

"She will, but for a few minutes she'll be fine." Jaena hesitated, struggling to find a way to explain her dream to him. It was hard to put the images into words. She couldn't focus as she thought about getting married and her strange dream. She needed to get back inside, and the sound of the children echoing her mother's lesson further distracted her: "Cliffton, Armstead, Nexus City, Drobin City. . . ."

"Jaena, remember when we were kids and your mother taught us exactly what she's teaching them right now?"

"My mother made you, me, and Ethan sit in the front." Jaena winced and looked at Drake. *Why did I say that?* She wished she had spoken of her dream, or their wedding, anything but their dead friend. "He would've liked today's lesson because it's about the world outside Cliffton." Drake leaned backward, resting his elbows on the steps.

"He always wanted to leave, didn't he?" Jaena sighed, resigned that she had spoiled a time when they could have had a happy conversation about their wedding.

"Wouldn't you want to leave if you were him?" Drake asked.

"*No.* Remember when he said it was a curse that I was going to be a Priestess bound to Cliffton?"

He nodded.

Jaena tapped her fingers. "I can't remember what he wanted us to do in Nexus City."

"He said he could be a fletcher or a scribe, you'd be an herbalist, and I could make crossbows or hunt dangerous aevians for bounty. Just children's dreams."

Jaena shook her head. "I never wanted to be an herbalist in Nexus."

"Why not? You'd be a good one. Hundreds of people would come to you."

"No, I want to be a Priestess and use the Tree magic of the Goddess. I couldn't practice magic in Nexus City. If the dwarves found out, they'd either kill me or exile me into the forest to die."

"I'd never let them hurt you." Drake sat up straight.

Jaena knew he could never protect her from the power of the Lorakian Priests. They both sat for a moment, and she realized she had to finish their conversation about Ethan before they could talk about anything else. "Going to Nexus City was a fine dream for twelve-year-olds, but this is our place. We belong here, not out there with all the Nexan thralls."

"You sound just like your mother."

Jaena poked his shoulder. *"Do you want to prune the cover tree paths with your bare hands?"* They both grinned because she used Priestess Liana's favorite warning.

"But Jaena, don't you ever want to see for yourself if all the things we've been taught are true? No one our age has ever been to Nexus City."

"Thank the Goddess for that, and shall I remind you that living in Cliffton has its advantages?" Hoping to lighten his mood, she flashed a mischievous smile, and pulled away so he could see her feminine curves. He stared for a moment, then turned away with the familiar look in his eyes: Drake was always questioning what they'd been taught. "Come on, my mother would never lie."

"I know, Jaena, but don't you ever wonder if Ethan was right?"

She felt a chill in the air and Drake pulled away. Jaena couldn't explain it, but she sensed a presence hovering around him—as if Ethan was still there. She caught a glimpse of some vague shape out of the corner of her eye, then saw nothing when she looked. She had felt and seen similar things many times since the Void had taken Ethan. Jaena shivered as Drake rubbed his forehead.

What is he not telling me? She moved closer and put a hand on his leg. "We're doing what the Goddess intends us to do. Both of us are doing Her will. This is how it is supposed to be. I'll follow in my mother's footsteps, and in time you'll be my husband."

"Being your husband isn't what I want to change."

"I know." She rested her head on his shoulder and wished things had been easier for him. He made his choices, no matter what others said or did, and suffered the consequences. Jaena wished she could be more like him, but her role in life had been decided before she was born. It was all meant to be. As she had many times before, Jaena accepted her duty. "Things can't be different. Our path in life is predestined by fate. I will be the next Priestess of Cliffton. I can never leave my duty."

"I know. Neither can I." He scanned the branches above him with a guardian's searching gaze.

Worry poured from his eyes and beneath his over-protectiveness of the village she sensed a restless spirit hiding in the back of his mind. Before Ethan's death all Drake wanted to do was hunt in the mountains, but that changed because of the Void's treachery. For five years he had avoided the long hunts, only going on short patrols near Cliffton where he could be summoned by the alarm horn.

Jaena put her cheek on his shoulder and an arm around his waist. Her mind cleared and she remembered what she needed to tell him. *My dream.* Jaena also thought about going into the shrine and helping her mother with the children. *No, I can't keep something so unusual from him. It's too important. I need to tell him.*

She was confused about what she had seen. *Was it a vision of the future?* Jaena stood up, paying homage to the colossal cover tree above them by gazing into the branches. She searched for the protected platform in the upper boughs where she and her mother had meditated the night before. Under the light of the moon she had seen the vision. *Please, Goddess. What did it mean?*

"Do you see something?" Drake stood up and scanned the upper branches with her, as if she had seen an aevian flying overhead.

"Drake, I had a strange vision last night when Mother and I were performing the Moon Ritual. Instead of seeing the moon in the sky I saw. . . ." She touched the middle of her forehead, activating her invisible third eye of prophecy.

"What did you see, a griffin?"

"No. I saw you. You were standing—"

The loud barking of several bullmastiffs in the distance stopped her in mid-sentence. Jaena could tell they weren't bellowing at some harmless forest animal that had strayed into the open ground outside Cliffton to graze.

Jep and Temus sprang to their feet. "The watchdogs at the east gate." Drake grabbed his crossbow. "I've got to go!" He sprinted along with Jep and Temus toward the guard dogs in their pen under the gate tower.

Jaena's third eye sensed the danger and throbbed painfully in her forehead. She knew without question, something terrible had come to Cliffton.

VIII

I survived because of my vigilance. The Giergun War taught me to never let down my guard.

—Gavin Bloodstone, from the *Bloodstone Chronicles*

Drake sprinted to the east gate tower. He tore down the cover tree paths, darting through the thorn-doors until he reached the palisade wall at the edge of Cliffton's grove. Half a dozen bull-mastiffs barked and howled inside the gate tunnel, which ran straight through the wooden guard tower. He could tell the outer gate, made from ancient ironbark trees, was closed tight. The heavy wooden crossbeam, thick as a man's chest and lifted by a counterweight, lay securely in place as he ran toward the closed doors on either end of the tunnel. A ladder went into the fortified watch tower where he could see the entire open field, but he decided to check on the dogs first. They saw or smelled something they didn't recognize. Something dangerous.

Five more bullmastiffs running at full speed appeared on a path. Drake grinned as the pack of guard dogs that freely roamed Cliffton arrived to back him up. As they appeared he opened the inner gate, which was half again as tall as he was. Drake cursed the loose hinge and shut it behind him so the male dogs couldn't mix with the females in the kennel-tunnel. He grimaced when the gate wouldn't shut tight because of the slack hinge, but forced it into place.

Ignoring the strong smell of dog, Drake faced the agitated

bullmastiffs in the tunnel. "What is it, girls? What do you smell?"

Some of the dogs stopped barking and whined. A few of the younger ones sniffed his hands for food. When they smelled nothing to eat, they returned to their loud barking. The gruff barks thundered in the confined space and hurt Drake's ears. He fought through the mass of dogs and tried to see what was causing the commotion.

Peering out a shooting window in the outer gate, he saw the expanse of green grass dotted with hundreds of old tree stumps. He was confident that the treeless firebreak would act as a killing place for anything uninvited approaching Cliffton. Nothing moved on the gravel-lined path.

The dogs apparently barked at something in the dense woods forty paces away; but he couldn't see a threat. Drake's hand brushed against a rope hanging down through one of the shooting holes in the ceiling of the tunnel. A hunter—probably his father—had threaded it into the grooves of the gate after tying it to the counterweight lever in the tower. The end of the rope had been buried under the front gate, where someone on the outside could grab it and pull.

The hunters away at Blue Creek could easily open the gate in case they were in a hurry and couldn't wait for him to heed the summons of their horn call. Drake hated it when his father left a pull-rope without telling him. He snatched the rope away from the ground so no one but him could open the gate and began searching the edge of the trees for any sign of what the dogs were watching.

Something moved. Two small figures stepped onto the path. "Quiet!" he commanded the dogs, who stopped barking as he took a better look. *No. It can't be. Two dwarves? What're they doing out here? Impossible!* Wondering how many more of them were in the forest, Drake knew he needed to sound the alarm horn hanging beside him. He had to try to warn the hunters from Blue Creek and gather the men from the village, but if he blew the horn he couldn't surprise them. Drake chose not to use it. Not yet. He also decided that the Drobin must be scouts for a larger war party. If he killed them both, they wouldn't be able to tell their war party about the village. In the span of a single breath he made his decision.

I've got to kill them.

He bent back the cord of his crossbow then loaded an iron-tipped war bolt. Keeping an eye on his quarry, he saw the pair of stunted folk scanning the sky from their covered location. They didn't carry a truce branch and didn't use the hailing horn hanging on a tree next to them. Everyone knew the custom and by not blowing it to announce their presence they named themselves hostile. *Definitely scouts.*

The two dwarves sneaked out of the woods and kept low to the ground. They tried to hide behind tree stumps, but were still easy targets. They were foolish to give him an open shot at such close range.

Comparing them to the tree stumps, Drake estimated the pair were at least four and a half feet tall, though he had imagined dwarves would be much shorter. The Drobin were very wide at the shoulders and wore thick beards drooping over their upper chests. He thought about climbing into the guard tower where he could get into the armory and have a second crossbow spanned and loaded for a follow-up shot. They'd be easier targets from up there, but he might not have time to get into position. He'd have to shoot two bolts through the tiny window in the gate.

The dwarves kept coming. Drake wondered if they were worried about getting killed by a hiding sharpshooter. Tremors of fear streaked through his body. He couldn't look away from the enemies he was about to kill. He wanted to leave the tunnel, climb the ladder, do anything but stand and wait for them.

Soon he would have to look them in the eyes and shoot.

The dwarves marched past the numerous tree stumps, which looked so much like the headstones in Cliffton's cemetery. *I'll bury the dwarves in the field beside a stump. What names will I use? It doesn't matter.* He would kill the first one when the pair reached the gate. The other would run away and have to cross the full forty paces to retreat. *I might not have time to reload after the first one falls, but I can't let the second one make it back to the trees. He won't get far. I'll hunt him down.*

The dwarves hastened forward and Drake got a clear look at them. Both were armored in lightweight chain-mail coats, but the interlocking rings appeared quite durable. Even with a war bolt, he decided he should shoot them in their necks or legs to avoid the chain-mail links. The first dwarf had a well-groomed brown beard and carried a circular metal shield with a black hammer emblazoned across the surface.

The lead warrior would be killed first before he could lift his dented metal disc. The dwarf also carried a warhammer on his belt and a small crossbow hung across his backpack. Drake reasoned that from his fine traveling boots and expensive clay-colored cloak, the dwarf must be from a clan of noble warriors. *Odd choice for a scout.*

The other dwarf was much older and wore an earth-colored cloak similar to his companion's. His beard was also well-kept, consisting of intermingling streaks of brown and gray hair. The second Drobin turned to look back at the forest, and Drake saw a long-handled battleaxe in a baldric slung across his back. The vicious curved blade was made for cutting flesh—not trees. The intricate pattern on the axe blade glinted in the sunlight and Drake caught his breath when he realized its tremendous value. The amazing craftsmanship was similar to Grandfather's long-sword, *Bloodguardian*.

The older dwarf also had a crossbow strapped to his back

and carried a small pack. Drake's sharp eyes noticed the axe-carrying dwarf was quite different than the shield-bearing warrior. The gray-bearded fellow walked with an air of caution. He had more observant eyes than the younger warrior, who looked straight ahead, while the older warrior glanced in many directions—but especially at the gate tower where Drake waited.

I'll shoot the elder one first.

He wondered why the dwarven fighters had come all the way to Cliffton. Perhaps he shouldn't kill them? *No. Both must die.* He took aim through the shooting window at the older dwarf's throat. His finger touched the smooth trigger.

The winged form of a wyvern appeared over the forest. Drake suddenly knew why the dwarves were risking their lives by approaching the gate. The two-legged dragon creature glided over the treetops on its batlike wings stretching over forty feet from tip to tip. Black and dark-orange scales absorbed the sunlight as two talons thrust forward like an eagle anticipating snatching up one of the dwarves and carrying him off. The swooping wyvern opened its long mouth filled with dagger-like teeth while whipping its barbed tail forward. Poison dripped from the curved stinger aimed at the dwarves' backs.

Drake chose his target and pulled the trigger. The quarrel flew toward the dwarves, but the missile shot past the surprised Drobin and struck the wyvern, piercing its chest. The shaft buried itself until only the feathers protruded from the fatal wound. The wyvern's claws snatched only air as it sailed over the heads of the Drobin before crashing to the ground, banging into several tree stumps and sending a cloud of dust rising into the air.

The two dwarves were upon the wounded serpent-dragon before it realized its death was at hand. "Blackhammer!" The younger one's war cry echoed above the crunching sound of breaking bone as his hammer split the creature's skull.

The old dwarf swung his axe with two hands and chopped into the neck of the snakelike dragon, causing a gush of blood to spurt onto the ground. A death spasm caused the wyvern's long tail to lash out. The wicked scorpionlike stinger hit the shield of the hammer-carrying dwarf and knocked him backwards. Dark poison squirted out as the aevian shuddered and fell limp as its soul returned to the Void.

Drake blew the alarm horn to alert the village, then cocked his crossbow while keeping watch over the two Drobin. As he put a new shaft into the bolt channel he thought about what had just happened. His shot had not been aimed with his eyes, but with his instincts. The Bloodstone Way had taken over. By pure reflex he had released a killing strike. Some hunters would say it was a lucky hit, bringing the wyvern down with a single shaft, but Drake knew better. The dwarven fighters had finished off the dying serpent before it could attack them, but it was already dead from the bolt piercing its heart. It just hadn't known it yet.

Drake realized he had almost shot the gray-bearded dwarf and had planned to let the wyvern finish the other. He didn't remember deciding to shoot the demon. His heart had made the choice for him, his hatred for aevians outweighing his loathing of the Drobin.

Clifftoners climbed into the gate tower. The click of crossbow strings being latched into place made him feel even more confident. He pulled the rope to the counterweight lever and the bar lifted. He kicked open the gate and stood tall, eying the monster's corpse while scanning the sky for danger. In addition to the men assembling in the tower, six huge dogs in the gate tunnel were ready to attack. Low growls rumbled from the back of their throats. They would kill on his command. Lifting his chin higher, Drake thought, *I won't kneel to them like a Nexan thrall. Never.*

The older dwarf stepped forward after cleaning off his axe on the grass. He slid the long handle into the baldric on his back and showed his open hands to the sky. It was the ancient peace gesture his grandfather had taught him, but Drake didn't trust them.

The gray-bearded dwarf called out in perfect Nexan, his refined accent and dialect more proper than the Clifftoners. "Friend, we thank you for your assistance and excellent shooting. May the blessings of the Mountain God go to you and your village."

Drake suspected that the dwarf spoke the servant language so perfectly because he often dealt with Nexan thralls.

"I am called Bellor Fardelver and am a humble War Priest of Lorak. We come as friends."

The Clifftoners in the tower grumbled. Grandfather Bloodstone had said Drobin War Priests were very powerful and had potent Earth magic. They were not to be trifled with, and Drake heard the nervous chatter of the men in the tower confirming this.

"My companion and I seek shelter." Bellor took a step forward. "We wish to purchase food and information from your village. Is there an Aethling we may speak with?"

"There's no Aethling here. Nobles have no place in our village." Drake pulled the wooden crossbow stock against his shoulder, targeting Bellor's throat. "I speak for the village."

The hammer-wielding dwarf stepped in front of the older one and angled his shield to turn aside any missile. Drake studied his foe and the hammer he carried. The flat smashing side and single claw on the back of the head were small, but he'd already seen the savage impact of a blow on the wyvern's skull. It couldn't be thrown very easily across the fifteen paces that stood between them. Up close it would be more devastating.

Thoughts of a duel with the seasoned Drobin warrior weren't comforting. An image of the expertly wielded hammer smashing the skull of the wyvern flashed through his mind. He imagined his own skull being split open. Gripping his crossbow tighter, Drake changed his aim to the hammer-wielding dwarf's throat, deciding to kill him long before he reached the gate.

"I am Thor Hargrim, crossbowman. You made a good shot, if it was meant for the wyvern." The dwarf pointed his hammer at the dead monster. "But if it was meant for us, you've a lot to learn."

The older dwarf sidestepped his companion and bowed his head. "Forgive our manners. We've had a long journey through the forest. Thank you for aiding us, crossbowman. The wyvern would've left its mark had it not been for your expert shooting. If I may ask, what are you called? It is our custom to record the names of men to whom we're indebted."

"I am a guardian of Cliffton, Drake Bloodstone."

The two dwarves glanced at each other for an instant and Drake suspected they had some trick planned. He wanted to let them think he was a foolish backwoodsman and lowered his weapon to give them a false sense of security. He held the crossbow with one hand and rested his other on the bloodstone gem affixed to his iron belt buckle. The polished green stone, streaked with red flecks that looked like drops of blood, would help him detect the lies of his enemies—if family lore was correct. "Have you traveled all this way alone, or are there more of you in the forest?"

The older dwarf's jaw tightened. "We're alone, and at your mercy, Guardian Bloodstone. We seek shelter, and upon our sacred honor vow our friendship to you and your village."

The younger dwarf balked after the War Priest's words. He started to raise his shield, assuming a fighting stance. The older dwarf's hand on his shoulder stopped him.

In the gate tower, old man Laetham whispered, "We can kill them now, Drake. Don't be a fool. Never trust the Drobin."

"We'll release our bolts after you shoot." Hallan Greenbow appeared in a window and Drake guessed Mae's grandfather, Craik Boughcutter, and a few others were also there.

The Hunter's Law. I saw them first. I have the first shot. No one shoots unless I miss or defer my right. Drake suppressed a grimace. They had given the peace gesture, asked for shelter, promised friendship on their honor—as if Drobin had honor. And there were only two of them. They didn't look like scouts and it would be a simple thing to pull the trigger. He had to protect the village. Sacrifices had to be made for the safety of his people.

What would Grandfather do? Shoot them. No. Drake removed the bolt from his crossbow and rested the weapon against his abdomen. "Under the protection of the Hunter's Law." He glared in the direction of the old hunters in the tower before turning to the dwarves. "You may enter the safety of my village."

"Woodskull!" Laetham shouted as Greenbow and some others in the tower reacted with other vulgar words and hateful remarks. Drake showed a hand to the sky. "You Drobin will find that we Amaryllians also have honor."

"We're twice indebted to you, Guardian Bloodstone. Thank you very much." The older dwarf bowed his head low—the gesture of a Nexan servant. Mouth hanging open in shock, Drake never imagined he would see a dwarf bow to him. Humans bowed to dwarves, never the opposite.

Some of the men in the tower stormed down the ladders as the two Drobin approached. Drake wondered if he'd regret letting the dwarves live as Elder Laetham stomped toward him. Laetham stepped past Drake so close he could almost feel the anger seething from the wiry old man. He planted a booted foot on the ground in front of the younger man's right shin and looked Drake in the eyes with a cruel gaze. Before he knew what was happening, Laetham shoved Drake from behind, tripping him hard to the ground. The front of Drake's crossbow hit the ground first and the butt poked into his gut, the wooden stock driving the air from his lungs. Gasping on the ground, he couldn't believe what had just happened. Rolling on his back he found himself staring up at Laetham, who aimed a cocked crossbow at Drake's face.

"You traitorous pile of vrelkshit." Laetham's whole body shook with rage. "You disgrace your family offering Drobin safety here." Two of Laetham's fingers touched his crossbow's trigger and he leaned forward, the tip of the bolt pointing at Drake's chest.

The pain in Drake's abdomen turned to cold fire. His face flushed with shame and anger. He wanted to leap up and see how many yellow teeth he could knock from Laetham's mouth. He glared into Laetham's eyes as he got to his knees, his hand touching the handle of his Kierka knife.

Laetham fingered the trigger, his body tensing. "I've put you down once today, boy. I'll do it again."

Drake stood up slowly, his chest thrust forward, daring the old man to shoot. Anger surged through him, and he slid his knife halfway out of the sheath.

"*Laeth.*" Mae's grandfather, Craik Boughcutter, put a hand on Laetham's shoulder. His eyes moved toward the Drobin and he gestured with his own crossbow—aimed at the dwarves. "Laeth and I will cover the Drobin. Now pick up your crossbow, Drake," Craik ordered, "this is still your watch."

Before leaning over to pick up his weapon, Drake shook his head at Elder Laetham and turned away trying to keep his anger from erupting. His face flushed and his pride stung at being bested by the old man. His gaze fell hard on the Drobin and Drake knew the day was only going to get worse.

IX

Wyrms must be respected, studied, then killed without mercy.

—Bölak Blackhammer, from the Lost Journal

The scaly wyvern lay in a tangled heap of broken wings and twisted claws. The aevian reminded Drake of a gigantic winged snake with the hind legs of a lizard and no forefeet—only leathery wings with dark branching veins. Even keeping upwind, it reeked worse than the fumes from a stink-beetle nest.

Estimating its fully extended body would be over twelve paces, Drake couldn't take his gaze away from the wyvern's corpse. He suspected it was the creature Neven and the watch-kats had seen over the garden-grove. Drake shuddered when he thought of the monster snatching little Neven in its talons and flying away with him. *Not on my watch.*

Villagers gawked from the gate tower at its ugliness. A few shouted congratulations to Drake on an impressive kill, while others whispered, probably about his confrontation with Elder Laetham. Many of the people's faces were filled with disdain for the dwarves and scorn at him sparing them. He wished Jaena was at his side, but she was with her mother at the urgent meeting of the Council of Elders. All the Elders had gathered, except his grandfather. Gavin Bloodstone had wanted a look at the wyvern and the dwarves before he met with the Council. He had told Drake he would be the deciding vote if the others were evenly split on what to do. Drake already knew what Elder La-etham would say. *Kill them, and Drake with them.*

Waiting while the Council discussed the fate of the two Drobin made acid bubble in Drake's stomach. He would have rather been out with the groups of hunters who were searching the forest for more dwarves. They had to verify if the two were alone.

Time passed slowly while they all waited for the Elder Council to finish their discussions in the Hunters' Hall. The setting sun painted the western sky pale red. The once-yellow orb seemed to cloak itself in scarlet mist as if the Void was rising up to drag the globe of light below the horizon.

Night was coming much sooner than Drake expected. He berated himself for giving in to the old Nexan superstition—but he still thought it was an ominous sign. There had been many bad omens today, starting with the vortex of mist before Neven disappeared in the grove. Perhaps the Council would vote to kill the dwarves, even after his invocation of the Hunter's Law and his promise of safety to them. *I'll find out soon enough. Priestess Whitestar can't let the sun set before the aevian is taken care of. Traditions must be followed.*

As the sun dipped farther into the Void's scarlet mist, Drake stood waiting near Cliffton's palisade wall with thirty armed hunters who watched over the dwarves with him. They had returned from Blue Creek and all were armed with loaded crossbows. If the dwarves tried to leave or a demon appeared, either would be riddled with bolts from sharpshooters in the gate tower and by the men on the ground.

The Drobin stood away from the hunters, under guard, whether they knew it or not. They said very little and none of the Clifftoners approached them. Drake couldn't tell if the strangers minded that he received all the credit for slaying the serpent-monster. He couldn't read the guarded expression of the Drobin, though he guessed the one called Thor trusted him very little. The older one, Bellor, had much better manners. He was the one to watch.

Grandfather Gavin and Drake's father strode toward the aevian. For the third time they inspected the black-and-dark-orange hide of the wyvern. Tired of standing and waiting, Drake followed them.

Grandfather knelt down and wrinkled his brow. "I've never seen a wyvern colored like this one before. It doesn't look like the ones from the Wind Walker Mountains or from the Northern Thornclaw Forest. Where did it come from?"

Father shook his head.

Bellor ambled closer to the wyvern after Grandfather's words. Thor stepped behind him and seven of the hunters came closer, keeping their sharp eyes on the dwarves.

"Those have to be scars on its neck just below the axe cut." Grandfather examined the two large s-shaped lines running from side to side on the scaly throat. He ran his fingers across raised marks mirroring each other. The lines stood above the creature's hide like giant skewed letters.

"They're claw marks." Bellor stepped closer. "From an encounter with another wyvern . . . or some other dangerous creature. They mark this wyvern as very powerful himself, since he survived the clash with whatever nearly slit his throat many years ago. Those scars are old."

Some of the gathered hunters nodded their heads, grudgingly agreeing with the dwarf's words. It surprised Drake to see his folk concur with Bellor.

"It was a killing shot. I taught my grandson well." Grandfather slapped Drake's father on the shoulder. The patriarch of the Bloodstone family pointed to the bolt piercing the wyvern's scales. It poked out at the heart level below the two s-shaped scars. "This one will make a fine companion to the griffin skull in our basement, don't you think?"

A guarded smile showed on Drake's face as he stood among the gathered hunters. Some of the men glared at him, then back at the wyvern. He pretended not to notice. His injured pride healed slightly at knowing he had slain the beast before it had attacked the village—despite Laetham getting the better of him.

One of the hunters whispered to another after the dwarves backed away from the men. "Too bad the aevian didn't kill the dwarves before Drake slew it."

"We could finish them now."

"We can't."

"Why?"

"Drake offered them safe passage."

"Foolish."

"The Council will order them slain."

Drake's ears burned as he listened to their mutterings. He couldn't take it anymore. Drake turned so only the men could hear him and said through slightly clenched teeth, "What about our honor? They didn't attack us."

The men bristled.

Grandfather Bloodstone cleared his throat, shook his head, then pointed at the wyvern. "I wonder what our wives are going to say when they see this?" He frowned a little. "They've never minded the vrelk antlers, but anything aevian. . . ."

Tyler sighed. "We better keep the skull out of sight or they'll have Tallia throw it in the Void."

Drake didn't blame the women of the house. Grandmother, Mother, and Tallia were all more religious than the Bloodstone men and took Priestess Liana's admonitions against aevians very seriously. All three women abhorred the griffin skull perching in the basement and made sure it was displayed in the darkest corner.

Grandfather's, Father's, and Drake's non-aevian trophies got more visible locations upstairs. The wyvern was sure to suffer the same fate as the griffin. It would end up hidden in a shadowy corner or a worse place. But when Drake stared at the monster he realized he would rather never see it again. He imagined that without flesh its skull would be even more hideous.

"Are you finished admiring the demon spawn?" Priestess Liana Whitestar asked as she and Jaena arrived next to the carcass with the Council of Elders.

The hunters parted as the Priestess and her apprentice arrived wearing ceremonial blue and white robes. The attire of the blond women provided a startling contrast to the drab vrelkskin hunting clothes of the men.

Drake searched for any sign of the fate given to the dwarves. Anger simmered in Laetham and Liana kept a stern countenance. Jaena kept her eyes on the ground.

"I asked, *Drake Bloodstone,* if you were *finished* glorifying the aevian?"

"Yes, Priestess." He almost stammered with embarrassment when he realized she had been talking to him.

"It's time to cleanse this land and return the demon to the place of its birth." Liana pointed to the Void.

"We will claim the trophy of the hunter." Grandfather Bloodstone put a foot on the creature's head. "It's our right."

Liana scowled at him. "If you must, Elder, but do it quickly. The Void is taking the light of day. We must finish this task before the sunlight is gone or risk a curse worse than we've already suffered. I expected you men would've been moving the creature by now."

She glanced at Drake with contempt.

"Sorry, Priestess." Humiliation turned Drake's face red again and he hoped Jaena wasn't looking at him.

Father and Grandfather freed the wyvern's head from its body after a score of chops from their Kierka knives. Thick blood oozed onto the ground, staining the grass reddish-black.

The dwarves watched the lengthy beheading and spoke in Drobin a short distance away from the large group. Bellor inspected a small copper vial that had already been filled with the wyvern's blackish blood. The dwarf corked the small vessel, tucked it away, and inspected a shiny black scale he had collected from the beast.

Twenty men dragged the wyvern's headless and bleeding body toward the edge of the Void seventy paces away. They tried to avoid the stumps, but the wings became snagged several times as they approached the cliff. The dwarves watched, but didn't help with the ancient Nexan custom.

During the backbreaking process a dozen others kept watch on the dwarves and the dusky sky with their crossbows ready. Drake pulled as well, silently cursing the old tradition of throwing dead aevians off the plateau's edge. But if the superstition was right, the aevian's spirit would be condemned to the Underworld for eternity—if they threw it in before the light of day was gone. A dim glow bled over the horizon, but it would be dark in a few moments.

"We must hurry." Priestess Whitestar's voice conveyed her urgency as she directed the final progress. Some of the Clifftoners were stained with dark blood as they reached the edge of the cliff with the heavy carcass.

Drake stared into the abyss. Gray swirling clouds writhed and flowed like a great river hundreds of feet below the plateau. Liana began her prayer to Amaryllis in a somber tone as the men heaved with one final push. "Goddess, we ask you to banish this demon from our land and condemn it to the Void for all time. We pray for this place to be cleansed of its evil."

"May the sky be clear." The Clifftoners offered their most common prayer.

Drake and the men pushed with all their remaining strength.

The wyvern fell toward the churning mist—just after the horizon faded to darkness. *We're too late,* he thought, still hoping they had succeeded in beating the sunset and condemning the spirit of the aevian to the Void.

Unable to watch the corpse fall, Drake turned away and shivered. He tried to suppress the memory of Ethan's face as his best friend had plummeted into the mist at Thorn Bolt Rock. Since that day he couldn't watch anything fall into the Void. He turned his gaze to Jaena and made eye contact. Using subtle gestures he pointed to the dwarves with a flick of his chin, then pushed his thumb to his heart as if scratching an itch: *Are the dwarves to be killed?*

Jaena mouthed a reply. He read her lips: *Not yet.*

Breathing a sigh of relief, Drake's shoulders relaxed, but his imagination needled him with the vision of the dwarves' dead bodies being cast into the Void.

Priestess Whitestar led the hunters back to the gate tower, while Thor lingered on the edge of the cliff. The dwarf spit into the Void and balled a fist while making some forceful statement in Drobin.

The action sparked a vague memory in Drake. His grandfather had told him something, but he couldn't quite recall the story. He guessed Thor made some kind of oath or curse to the dead wyvern, though no translation was needed to understand the bitterness and anger in Thor's voice. Turning to his grandfather he asked, "Did you see the dwarf spit into the Void?"

Grandfather nodded.

"Why did he?"

"Disciples of Lorak make offerings to the Void. They believe it's the most powerful way to make a pledge or an oath. They think blood given to the Void is powerful magic."

"Is it?"

"I've seen it work before." Grandfather fixed his dark eyes on his grandson.

Nodding, Drake recalled Liana teaching him, "Never cast anything but dead aevians into the Void. You'll risk the wrath of the demons below." *Vrelkshit. Just another stupid superstition to scare the children.* Still, he wished they had beaten the sunset.

X

Alliances tempered with hatred and doubt shatter like brittle blades in the heat of battle. I must forge a friendship with the humans tempered with respect and honor.
        —Bellor Fardelver, from the Thornclaw Journal

The scent of rancid dog urine filled Bellor's nostrils as he stepped into the gate tunnel. The pack of dogs snarled from the rear of the passage, their growls rumbling off the log walls. For the first time Bellor saw the animals that had been barking at him and Thor. He recognized the wide jaws and large heads of Drobin bulldogs, though they had the frame of tall Nexan mastiffs. *Clever breeding,* Bellor thought. *These are not simple folk.*

The young village guardian, Drake Bloodstone, held the dogs at bay with an outstretched arm and a terse word that instantly silenced their barks. Bellor knew the obedient animals would lunge forward and attack with a simple command. Still, he worried more about the men above them, especially the one called Laetham who had pushed Drake to the ground. Bellor's old dwarven eyes pierced the darkness at the ceiling of the gate tunnel. Men with armor-piercing bolts loaded into their crossbows aimed at him and Thor. The humans watched them through murder holes and rested their fingers on the triggers of cocked weapons. *Please Lorak, let this have been the right decision.* Bellor clung to the hope that by hiring a guide he and Thor would stay alive long enough to find their lost kin.

Drake opened the inner gate. The young man winced as it sagged on a loose hinge. The War Priest pretended not to notice the gate and kept away from the dogs as he and Thor entered the massive arbor dome of a venerable cover tree that grew into the guard tower and wall. The group of hunters and the two Amaryllian Priestesses ahead of them disappeared around the wide trunk of the tree, their footfalls silenced by soft ground cover.

"Follow me." The Clifftoner strode past Bellor with two large male dogs at his heels. The pair of bulldog-mastiffs sniffed at Thor before loping after their master.

"These trees smell. . . ." Thor's loud sneeze made the dogs whirl around and stare at him with their curious brown eyes. "Smell . . . terrible."

Bellor shook his head, relishing the peppery fragrance, which cleansed the putrid urine smell from his nose and kept away the flying insects. The War Priest fell in line behind Thor, the dogs, and Drake. They circled the broad trunk and Bellor searched for a trail leading out from the cage of ground-rooted branches. There appeared to be no way out, but Drake stepped toward the thorny wooden bars and slipped through a slender portal hidden by leaves. With no sign of the large party of humans preceding them, Bellor wondered if the villagers had taken another way. He heard low angry voices as several grizzled hunters followed as Drake led Bellor and Thor deeper into the grove. They passed under domes of various sizes, taking a twisting, circuitous route through the camouflaged portals.

After only a moment in the maze of random hidden paths, Thor whispered in Drobin, "Which way back to the gate?"

Shrugging, Bellor realized he had no idea. *Clever folk indeed.*

Thor's sigh became a groan, attracting the raised ears of the dogs. "They never should have built their village so close to Void. This is madness. We can't trust these Nexans. Leading us in circles." Thor glared at their guide and the armed men behind them.

"They're far from being servants, and the young guardian saved our lives." Bellor's golden-brown eyes rested on Drake. "And he has the earth name, Bloodstone, like the man from Nexus City."

"I know. I'm not stupid"—Thor emphasized the harshness of his Drobin words—"and he wears the same belt with the bloodstone gem, just like the man in the city did."

"Same clan." Bellor slipped through a thorn-door. "Say nothing about it. I'll tell what we know of his kin when the time is right."

"Where have I heard his hearth-name before?" Thor hid his mouth with his shield. "Isn't *draek* a Drobin word?"

"It's of the Old Father Tongue, yes." Bellor touched his beard. "It's in the sagas about our ancient allies, the *draeks*. But who named the young man in the first place? Only a Lorakian Priest could access those histories."

Thor frowned. "He may have a Drobin name, but he's man-blood."

"He did help us, Thor. We may have found an ally."

"More likely a servant." Thor squinted at the Clifftoner, who flashed them a suspicious glance.

"He wonders what we're saying." Thor spoke his Drobin words louder. "Perhaps I should tell him what I'll do if these forest-crawlers betray—"

"Keep your tongue behind your beard. I speak for us here."

Grimacing, Thor lowered his voice. "We're not staying long, are we?"

Bellor shook his head. "We might join the wyvern at the bottom of the Void if we do, especially if I let you handle the negotiations."

Thor snorted.

"But above all"—Bellor glanced at Thor—"we can't linger here. I'll not have us bringing ruin to their village. The Void is so close, and the wyvern—"

"You think I'd ruin their village?" Thor smirked.

Bellor's mouth wrinkled. "I know it's hard for you to imagine, Thor, but there are things more dangerous than you. There could be another wyvern, or a worse thing hunting for us now. Have you forgotten how close we are to the Void?"

Thor shook his head.

Bellor sighed. "I won't have the blood of these folk spilled because we delay here like fools. I've seen enough death to last me ten lifetimes."

Thor shrugged and fixed his gaze on Drake. "Spilling man-blood doesn't bother me."

"I know." Bellor rolled his eyes. "That's what worries me."

XI

Good allies bring many blessings, but finding those we can trust is most difficult.

—Bölak Blackhammer, from the Lost Journal

Sitting at the head of the longest table in the Hunters' Meeting Hall, Drake watched more than fifty villagers milling about or huddling together and whispering. People glanced furtively about the smoky room, reminding him of funeral suppers, rather than the first feast where he had been named the Honored Hunter. Few congratulated him for slaying the wyvern. They stayed away and sipped bitter ale, further puckering their already tight lips.

Hallan Greenbow and Mae's grandfather, Craik, discussed how Drake had "invited" the Drobin into the village and Hallan didn't even lower his voice. People glanced at Drake with nervous or condemning eyes, and the young man sunk into his chair with crossed arms and a clenched jaw.

More villagers arrived and Drake wondered if the people were looking at him at all, but rather the door behind him where the whole Council of Elders and the dwarves were meeting. He heard raised voices from the Council chamber and with each angry outburst he wished even more strongly that the Drobin had never come to Cliffton. He sighed, then sat up straighter to listen to his family, who were making plans for Tallia's wedding feast. Father, Mother, Grandmother, Tallia and her soon-to-be-husband, Vance, sat to either side of him on long benches. They saved a place for Grandfather, who would join them once the Elder Council meeting ended, but the cooks weren't waiting.

Mother presented him with an excellent cut of tender vrelk steak, and Drake decided the smell of roasting meat was the only pleasant thing about the Hall. As the first one served, the people's eyes fixed on him. He chose not to eat, waiting for the plates of sizzling vrelk, roasted vegetables, warm biscuits, and pitchers of ale to be placed on the tables. Tallia filled her brother's tankard with Cliffton's dark brew.

"You're pouring me ale?" Drake's eyes widened.

"Just today. Don't get used to it," Tallia said in her mocking voice, then flashed a smile. Blinking in shock, Drake noticed a few of the people were now grinning at him as they raised their mugs. Mae and little Neven waved, while her husband, Rett nodded his head in apparent thanks for Drake's help of his family earlier in the day.

"Eat, eat." Mother patted Drake's shoulders and smiled. "What's wrong? This feast is for you. Eat!"

Shrugging and staring at his food, Drake couldn't decide if the villagers were proud or upset because of what he had done.

"Can't you just enjoy your dinner?" Tallia raised an eyebrow and laughed. "I'm the only one here who really despises you."

Drake put a piece of juicy steak in his mouth and tried to savor the taste of the moment.

The Hall became louder as the villagers consumed the meat and ale. Drake wondered if they had forgotten about the Council meeting and the Drobin. After drinking his mug he did too, but when he finished his food Grandfather's seat still remained empty.

Glancing at the door to the Council chamber, Drake decided that Grandfather, Jaena, Liana, Laetham and the other Elders would be there all night. He stared at his plate and overheard some of the old men grumbling. The most vocal ones appeared to be former sharpshooters in the Drobin king's army. Hallan Greenbow said, "We could have killed them and dropped them into the Void with the wyvern."

"Want some more?" Mother asked, oblivious to the oldsters. Drake shook his head.

"No sulking. Eat." Mother put a piece of redberry pie in front of him. "Everyone has come to honor you tonight."

"Some honor." Drake rolled his eyes. His mother groaned and sat down.

"They're here to see our *guests,* if they ever come out of there." Father grimaced before sipping his ale.

Matching his mood, the redberries tasted extra sour to Drake. He swallowed a few bites, then stopped eating when the last hunters searching the forest arrived. He could tell by their faces that no signs of other dwarves had been found. The pair was alone.

"Clifftoners!" Tyler Bloodstone shouted as he stood up and lifted his tankard. "We can't wait any longer for the Elders to join us. Before the ale is gone, a salute to my son, and the best shot he's ever made. May he always have such good aim."

"Drake!" Some of the Clifftoners shouted as they raised their mugs and banged on the table. The intensity of the Clifftoners' response made Drake sit back in his chair in shock.

"Say something, son." Father slapped his only son on the shoulder and motioned for him to stand.

Drake froze. He didn't know what to say, but he stood up at his father's prodding. His throat tightened as if a mass of constrictor vines had lashed themselves around his neck. He tried to take a swig of ale to wet his throat, but the mug was empty.

"Uhh . . . thank you all . . . very much. I was just on watch, and . . . uhh. . . ." He stood dumbfounded as over half the village stared back at him.

"To Drake!" His father raised his mug for another toast, saving the Bloodstone family any further embarrassment. The young man sat down and breathed a sigh of relief as Father clapped him on the shoulder. "Son, you shoot better than you talk. Leave Jaena to make the speeches, if you ever get up enough nerve to bring her a marriage branch."

Before Drake could tell his father about his plan to ask Jaena to marry him, the main door to the Hall burst open. An out-of-breath thirteen-year-old girl named Lyndra dashed inside, and scanned the room with wild eyes. Drake reached for his Kierka knife, wondering if the men on guard were about to blow the alarm horn.

"Where's the Priestess?" Lyndra questioned the folk near the door.

Releasing the handle of his knife, Drake remembered that Lyndra's mother was due to have her fourth child. A woman pointed the girl toward the Council's meeting room and Lyndra rushed past Drake's table and pounded on the door. "Priestess! Priestess Liana!"

Jaena opened the door and Drake glimpsed the dim chamber inside. The dwarves sat on one side of a broad table and the four Elders plus Liana sat on the other. Grandfather wore a grim visage, as did most of the others. Elder Laetham scowled and Thor shot an angry look back at him, while Liana wore a calm expression and fixed her eyes on the frantic girl.

"Mother's baby is coming!" Lyndra shouted.

Jaena grabbed the girl's shoulders, steadying her. "Has the birth water come yet?"

"Yes, and she's having the pains."

Jaena glanced back at her mother.

"Go in my place, Jaena," the Priestess ordered, "make the preparations and make sure Lyndra's mother is in her arboreum.

I'll come as soon as I can. You know what to do."

Jaena nodded and took Lyndra's hand. "It'll be all right. You and I will go to your mother now. The Priestess will be along soon." The young girl gave an anxious smile.

Jaena's blue eyes suddenly met Drake's. He saw a message hidden behind her long lashes. She didn't speak, but Drake tried to interpret her gaze as she glanced back at the meeting room and then at him. *What's she saying? Is she warning me? Are the Elders talking about me?* Nervousness coursed through him as the dwarves and the Elders stared at him.

Jaena shut the door and led Lyndra away. She looked back at Drake when she reached the outside door. He saw fear in her eyes.

Jaena slipped into the night with Lyndra on her arm. Drake locked his gaze onto the closed Council chamber and wished Jaena hadn't gone. His foot tapped the floor as he waited for news, wondering what she had tried to tell him. Was it a warning? Was he to be punished for allowing the Drobin into Cliffton?

Soon after Jaena had departed, the Elders filed out of the room. Grandfather Bloodstone sat on Drake's left with an impassive expression. The dwarves came next, with Liana walking behind. Conversations stopped as all eyes fixed onto the Priestess and the dwarves.

Liana raised her chin and took a deep breath. "Clifftoners, the blessings of the Goddess are with us. A dangerous aevian has been slain by one of our bravest and most dutiful sons." She nodded to Drake. "Travelers have come to our village and are under our protection now. They'll stay as guests in the Bloodstone home tonight."

Murmurs of discontent rose up from the people. "They'll soon depart, as their journey continues deeper into the forest.

To those of you who haven't met them yet, let me present our guests."

Thor climbed atop a bench at Liana's direction and spoke in slightly accented Nexan, "I am Thor Hargrim, twelfth son of Karrick and Daerna Hargrim. I hail from the halls of my kin in Drobin City."

The hunters muttered to each other. Drake heard disparaging remarks about the Drobin Empire's largest enclave. Humans weren't allowed into the subterranean halls of the Drobin city, where their king reigned from his Granite Throne.

Thor rested his hand on the head of his warhammer. "I served in the army during the last Giergun War and attained the rank of Champion before I left my regiment to dedicate my life to Lorak, and study with Master Bellor Fardelver." He bowed his head to the older dwarf and sat down.

Grandfather Bloodstone whispered to Drake, "Only the most skilled warriors are given the rank of Champion." The patriarch tapped his hands loudly on the table as a sign of respect for Thor. Only a few of Cliffton's veterans followed Grandfather's lead.

Bellor stepped onto the bench, then bowed his head. Drake thought he saw an aura of faint light surrounding the older dwarf's body. *Are my eyes deceiving me?* Drake wondered if anyone else could see the white glow, but no one appeared to have noticed the faint nimbus.

Bellor spoke in perfect Nexan, "I am Bellor Fardelver, twentieth son of Thera and Goren Fardelver."

Drake whispered to Grandfather, "Twentieth son? I thought you exaggerated how many children they have."

Grandfather grinned. "I told you their women are fertile for eighty years, though their pregnancies are longer that our women's."

Mouth agape, Drake couldn't believe it. Maybe the Drobin

really did live to be three hundred years old?

"I am a War Priest and a humble servant of Lorak." Bellor bowed his head. "We thank you esteemed Clifftoners for your protection and hospitality, and especially thank and honor you veterans of the last Giergun War. Though I have not met any of you before, the deeds of the sharp-eyed crossbowmen of your Hunter Regiment are known to me. All the Drobin and Nexan folk are in your debt. I salute you, and thank you again for your victories. It is most kind for you to allow us inside your village."

The Clifftoners tapped on their tables as Bellor bowed once again to them. "As some of you know, Thor and I have traveled for several weeks across the frontier of the Thornclaw Forest. We came to find your village and seek the assistance of your people. Please be assured, we come alone, and as friends."

Hallan Greenbow yelled, "You better not have come to recruit our sons! We've given the Drobin army enough of our blood already."

"Have no worry. Neither the army nor the Elders of Lorak's temple have sent us. We come of our own volition, with no ill intentions toward any of you. As I've already explained to your wise Council, no other Drobin know we are here. Thor and I have pledged in front of your Elders to keep our knowledge of your village secret. Your men, who fought so bravely, deserve to find some peace after serving so stalwartly in the last Giergun War. Thor and I honor your wishes."

Laetham rolled his eyes and many of the other Clifftoners re-acted with the same skepticism, flashing suspicious glances at Bellor.

"Please let me explain why we're here. Thor and I have come to find our Drobin kin who passed near here forty years ago. They didn't come to Cliffton, but traveled through the village of Armstead, which we have learned is hidden somewhere in a high valley a few days' march away.

"We come seeking to learn the whereabouts of the small group of Drobin who were known to have established a mine and made it their home in the mountains south of Armstead. We must discover news of our lost kin and find where they settled."

Liana stepped forward. "Elder Laetham has confirmed that a group of Drobin passed through Armstead four decades ago. Please tell us again, Elder Laetham."

"Indeed, I remember." Laetham glowered at Liana, then Drake. "I was in Armstead after my wife's passing"—his voice dropped—"when a group of heavily armed dwarven raiders arrived outside the walls. But when they realized they couldn't breach the defenses, they decided to barter for supplies instead. They said they were going on an expedition into the Wind Walker Mountains. It must've been the kin of these two, as they're the only Drobin ever known to come this far into the Thornclaw."

"Thank the Goddess," Hallan Greenbow raised his voice. "We don't need them here."

"It was a long time ago when they came," Laetham spoke over the others. "Nothing has been heard of the Drobin in many years. They disappeared in the mountains."

Hallan spoke to Laetham, "The Armsteaders probably killed them. We should do the same." Several men near Laetham gripped their Kierka knives as Thor sized up the hunters. The dwarf bared a toothy smile, as if challenging them to face him.

Before other men could voice their harsh opinions or draw blades, Liana cut them off. "Master Bellor and his companion, Thor, are our guests. They wish to travel to Armstead, regardless of some Council members' opinions."

Laetham squinted and turned away.

Bellor cleared his throat, and Drake admired the old dwarf's calm demeanor in spite of the volatile atmosphere. "It's true."

Bellor smoothed his beard. "We haven't heard from our kin for many years, but that's why we are here. We must find out what has happened. Thor and I have made it our Sacred Duty to find them, whether they're alive or dead. Thank you again for your assistance and hospitality. We are most grateful." Bellor bowed his head once more before stepping down from the bench and taking his seat. The white cloud of light disappeared and Drake guessed he must have imagined it.

"The Council has voted," Liana said, "however, we are deadlocked on what to do. I will not vote in this matter, though I have made my opinion known to our four elders."

"Which is?" Hallan asked while crossing his arms.

"We must help our guests," Liana said with confidence.

Grandfather Bloodstone suppressed a grin as Laetham shook his head.

"The Goddess teaches us to help those in need," the Priestess continued. "Her Scrolls implore us not to merely tell the way to travelers, but to show the way. We must honor the Goddess. I believe that it falls upon us to guide them to our sister village. We cannot abandon Master Bellor or his companion in the vastness of this deadly forest."

"Let them die in the Thornclaw," Hallan Greenbow grumbled, "our blood-debts are paid to the stunted folk tenfold. We owe them nothing."

Liana shouted above the clamor of harsh words. "No! We owe them honorable treatment regardless if we help them further, though I believe one of us must guide them."

"See!" Hallan shouted. "They came for one of our sons!"

"Listen!" The Priestess raised her arms. "We will provide them with a guide only if someone is willing to go."

"They want our blood for nothing!" Hallan reached for his knife.

Liana turned away from the angry old hunter. "Master Bellor

has offered to compensate our village for the absence of one of our men, and reward us for defending them from the wyvern. Twenty silver aer'bors will be paid to the hunter's family who goes with them, and twenty to the village coffers for slaying the wyvern."

Murmurs spread across the Hall as the people whispered about the small fortune.

"Blood silver, bah!" Hallan spat on the floor. "They should have paid for a Nexan up north. Clifftoners can't be bought."

Liana glared at Hallan with cold eyes. "Helping them has nothing to do with payment. We must honor the Goddess by doing our duty as Amaryllians."

Hallan Greenbow had stared down a griffin in his youth. Drake remembered the story well, but now he flinched under Liana's withering gaze.

Why is helping them so important to her? Is it truly about duty and honor? Drake wondered, *What is Liana not telling us?* He found nothing on Grandfather's face that gave him a clue.

The precious aer'bors would mean a lot to the village when the barter season arrived and a trading party trekked north for the things Cliffton could not produce. Still, the Council wouldn't have been influenced by any amount of silver.

Liana raised her arms once again to quell the muttering in the Hall, waiting for the dissenting voices to die down. "Please, Clifftoners. The Elder Council has failed to reach a decision, and now the choice rests with you." She lowered her arms and took a deep breath. "Will one of our hunters lead our guests to Armstead, and help them find the lost mine of their kin?"

Silence. No one spoke and some of the veterans glared at Liana with disgust. The Priestess swept her gaze over the entire room, searching for a volunteer. Turning from Liana, Drake surveyed the men, women and children in the Hunters' Hall. No one accepted the burden of guiding the enemies of Cliffton.

Men sat unmoving while their children fussed and asked their fathers not to leave them.

Fear leaked from the eyes of young mothers. He realized, *I'm the only man who has reached twenty winters and isn't married.* Almost every other man had a wife and children, or, like Rett and Mae, had a baby coming soon. The men couldn't leave, nor should they. Their families depended upon them for food and protection. He imagined Rett being killed by a griffin while guiding the dwarves to Armstead. How would Mae and Neven and the baby deal with such a terrible loss? Twenty aer'bors was nothing compared to one dead Clifftoner and his fatherless family.

Damn Liana for putting our people in such a dangerous position. Shuddering, Drake remembered when Roan Graywood had been slain by the griffin. Ethan, his mother, and three sisters had been taken into Drake's home and put under the protection of Tyler Bloodstone, who had asked the Council to be their Watch Father. Ethan's death made it even worse. Two years passed before Nola had chosen a new husband and moved out.

Drake surveyed the faces of his people. Tallia and Vance held hands next to him, and Mother and Grandmother nervously glanced at him. He couldn't live with the possibility of any of Cliffton's families being torn apart like Ethan's had been. No one else but him should accompany the dwarves. He had let them into Cliffton and he should guide them to Armstead. Once they arrived, his cousin Rigg could help locate the Drobin mine. It was his duty to sacrifice for the village. *I won't fail my people like I failed Ethan.*

Doubt suddenly exploded in Drake's mind as he thought about Jaena. *I can't leave her. Not now. I should stay and ask her to be my wife.* But with one last search of the room, he realized no one else would volunteer to guide them.

Father whispered to Grandfather Bloodstone, "I haven't seen

Sandon in a while. And Liana wills this. I'll take them. I know the way to my brother's village better than most." The older Bloodstone didn't reply, but instead glanced at his grandson.

Mind racing like a speeding bolt, Drake looked at his mother and knew he couldn't let Father take the risk. His chair scraped across the wooden floor as Drake stood up to face Liana and the entire Hall. He tried not to think about Jaena as words came out. "I'll guide them. I know the way."

Villagers shouted their disapproval, and Tyler Bloodstone tried to stand and protest, but Grandfather kept his son from rising. "No," the Elder said, just loud enough for Drake to hear over the clamor. "This is his calling. Not yours."

Liana approached Drake and took one of his calloused hands into hers. "May the Goddess bless you for your courage. When Cliffton has needed a service, you've always answered the summons. I thank you for all of us."

The Clifftoners hesitated, some muttering curses at the dwarves, but after Grandfather Bloodstone began, they joined the old veteran in tapping out a slow rhythm on the tables. Drake turned to see the faces of his people. More looked relieved than angry. He guessed many were upset that he would choose to help the Drobin and abandon them.

For a moment he thought of staying and asking Jaena to be his wife; but as if her mother had read his thoughts, Liana hugged him and whispered in his ear, "Jaena would want you to know that she loves you and would support you, even if it means going away."

The Priestess pulled back and stared into Drake's eyes. He thought she could see his deepest and most closely guarded secrets. "My daughter and I know what you must do, and it must be done away from Cliffton." She gripped his hands firmly. "Sever the ties to the spirit of the past. You know he holds you back."

The lips of the Priestess stopped moving, but Drake heard her voice inside his mind: *He has bound you for too long. Cut the dark cord. Let him go.*

The Hunters' Hall disappeared and a heaviness pulled Drake toward the edge of the Void. Paralyzed, he sat teetering on a cliff, staring into the abyss like he had for the past five years. The terrified face of his best friend falling to his doom surged from his memories. A great weight tried to drag him down.

Ethan! Drake heard himself scream as the chill wind of the Underworld whipped at his cheeks. Opening his eyes, Drake saw Liana, his family, and all the people.

Liana hugged him again, banishing the chill of the Void away from his soul. The Priestess whispered, "Go with my blessing, and when you're ready, come back and marry my daughter."

XII

There is a whispering of doom in my ears. I cannot listen.
If I do the voices of all the restless Drobin warriors who've
died under my command will return and drive me mad.
—Bellor Fardelver, from the Thornclaw Journal

Bellor knew something was out there, waiting for him to fall
asleep. Eyes wide open, he stared through the darkness, listening to the scraping and tapping of the cover tree against the
roof of the Bloodstone family home. He focused on the sounds
in the physical realm, refusing to hear the murmuring from
beyond the grave—the whispers he refused to hear.

The night wore on and the tree's tapping became more
insistent, as if it were translating a desperate message from the
spirit realm. Not even his prayers to Lorak could calm his
troubled mind. The hostile mood of the villagers made him
wonder if some of them would come for him and Thor, planning to tie them up, then throw them into the Void. They
wouldn't go without a fight, unless the humans caught them
asleep. . . .

Thor lay on the wooden floor beside him, snoring quietly,
unaffected by the sense of dread inside Bellor's heart. A sudden
chill made him pull the musty-smelling blanket higher on his
chest. He guessed it was long after midnight, and the cold from
the Void must be creeping into the village. The humans had
foolishly built their homes much too close to the edge.

The chill grew stronger and Bellor's eyelids drifted shut as the falling temperature sapped his resolve to stay awake. His arms wouldn't move as he tried to pull the blanket higher. Needles of cold prickled his feet, then moved up his legs.

In his mind's eye, the shadowy face of an emaciated young man materialized from the blackness.

"It's coming, wake up!" A human voice screamed in Bellor's mind as phantom hands on his shoulders tried to shake him. The spirit could not move him physically and only transferred some of its icy fear. The young man glanced over his shoulder, and when the pale face turned back, terror filled his already haunted eyes. *"You have to wake up! No one else can!"*

A draconic face with glowing red eyes loomed over Bellor and the young man. The old dwarf recognized the now-ghostly visage of the wyvern slain outside Cliffton. Its wings, larger than they were in life, wrapped around the entire house, enveloping it in a frigid embrace, suffocating the life out of the people inside as the very breath in their lungs began to freeze, sending white plumes into the night as the heat fled their bodies.

"Please! Wake up!" The young man pleaded as the chill of the wraith penetrated Bellor's chest. The paralyzing numbness affected the dwarf's entire being, as if he was being held down by blocks of ice on his limbs. A jolt of fear made him realize the others in the house had no chance of surviving the attack unless he could awaken. He knew what he had to do and felt the power of the Mountain God within him. *Great Lorak*, Bellor spoke the prayer in his mind, *I summon Your Sacred Fire. Burn within me. Protect me from the spirits of the Void. Give me the strength of the mountain.*

Red and orange flames banished the darkness that had invaded Bellor's mind. The wyvern-wraith recoiled, as did the mysterious young man—both pushed away by the prayer to battle spirits of the Void. Bellor forced open his eyelids and sucked in the frigid air of the room. The bitter cold threatened to cause a spasm in his lungs. He endured the white-hot pain in his chest and sat up.

Thor lay asleep, clouds of cold air rising from his mouth as he exhaled. Bellor needed help and nudged his friend's side. His companion could not break the power of the wraith and did not awaken. Bellor began the prayer himself, speaking aloud. "Sacred Fire. Burn within me. Protect me from the spirits of the Void." He closed his eyes and saw the wyvern's barbed tail coming toward him in the ethereal realm. Unless blocked, the stinger would stab into his soul, injecting ghostly white drops of barb-shaped venom that oozed from its tail.

Arm raised, Bellor summoned a glowing shield of fire in the spirit realm and deflected the wyvern's stinger. The venom ghosts exploded in puffs of glowing ectoplasm as they struck the barrier. Twice more the wyvern struck, Bellor's fiery shield turning the stinger away each time. The drops of venom shrieked as they burned in Lorak's Fire, as if each one were a condemned spirit facing final judgment.

The hate-filled, red eyes of the wyvern bored into Bellor. He heard the creature's voice in his mind. *"I will not stop until you are dead. You will wander the Void, filled with my venom so you can never find rest."*

"You've already been slain, wyrm. Go back to the Underworld where your spirit belongs." Bellor's shield flared with holy power and the wyvern covered its eyes from the radiance of Lorak's Sacred Fire.

"My task is undone, dwarf, and I shall fulfill my master's wishes even in death. Draglûne will prevail! All of your puny kind, alive or dead, will be his slaves!"

"Not while I stand." Bellor's aura expanded into a globe of pulsing white light, pushing the wyvern's evil spirit back even further.

"You stand alone. Cursed to watch all of those around you die. After all the others in this house are dead, I shall take your soul to Draglûne. None will be left to oppose him when you are gone. His time will come, and you will see the end of your folk."

The wyvern's tail darted at Thor, who shivered in his sleep, still unable to break the paralyzing power of the wraith. Bellor lunged to block the stinger. The barbed-shaped droplets squirted out of the wyvern's tail and scattered like a swarm of wasps speeding toward Thor's spirit. Bellor burned some of them away with his fiery screen, but others stabbed into his aura, piercing his soul, injecting themselves into his core.

Before the poison could take full effect, Bellor summoned the Sacred Fire and bathed Thor's body in its cleansing power, banishing the venom ghosts trying to poison his friend. Bellor hoped Thor would be all right as he turned back to face the wyvern, only to find it had disappeared—though the cold emanation remained.

"You cannot save them all," the wyvern's voice whispered in Bellor's mind. *"I will have my vengeance."*

Bellor threw open the door to the main room of the Blood-stone family home, cursing himself for not warding the house. The embers in the hearth glowed faintly, but Bellor closed his eyes and saw the serpent-like head of the wyvern-wraith floating over the kitchen table. It leered at the small, shadowy spirit of the same young man who had awoken Bellor. The young man now blocked a doorway, somehow keeping the wraith at bay with force of will alone.

"You are worth nothing to me," the wyvern said to the spirit. *"I will enslave you if I must."*

Bellor strode into the room, shouting into the ethereal realm. *"You will take no one from this house!"*

The wyvern-wraith's smoldering eyes flashed at Bellor. *"I will have the human who shot me!"*

116

Bellor raised his arm, the fiery shield pulsing in the spirit realm. The ghost of the wyvern recoiled as Bellor took up a position where the young man had just been. Something moved in front of the hearth as a longsword was being taken off the mantle. Drake's Grandfather, Gavin Bloodstone, held the sword with two hands and faced the direction of the wraith, trying to see the invisible apparition attacking his home.

The wyvern held its place near the front door as Gavin squinted in the darkness, his breath coming out in puffs of cold air. Frost coated the blade of the sword, now raised adeptly in the high-guard position. "What's happening, Master Bellor?"

"The wyvern has returned from the Void as a wraith. It's come for vengeance." Bellor blinked with amazement that the old human could have fought off the power of the creature and awoken when Thor could not. "Pray with me. We shall send the wyvern back to the Void and protect everyone in this house from its power." Bellor took in a cold breath and stood beside Drake's Grandfather. "Sacred Fire. Burn within me. Protect us from the spirits of the Void. Give us the strength of the mountain."

The wyvern hissed and bared its teeth, the venom ghosts dripping from it tail. The holy power emanating from Bellor and bolstered by Grandfather Bloodstone, who also spoke the words, pushed back the wraith. Gavin repeated the words with Bellor, not letting down his guard as he knelt with the Drobin Priest. They prayed, saying the words again and again as Bellor peered into the spirit realm. A dark cord of energy connected the wyvern to himself, Thor, and then trailed off into the room where Drake slept.

Gavin placed the tip of the sword onto the wooden floor. As the blade neared the dark cord connecting Drake to the wyvern, the cord weakened and tried to slither aside, avoiding the sword and the ancient Drobin magic Bellor realized was contained within.

The force of the prayers drove back the creature as it snarled and spat. Its eyes met Bellor's in the plane of ghosts. Hatred twisting its loathsome face, the wyvern fled the house at last, forced out by Lorak's Sacred Fire. Its ghostly wings, which had been wrapped around the entire home, pulled away as the wraith flew back down into the nearby Void.

Bellor shivered for a long moment, trying to shake off the lingering chill.

"What happened?"

"It's gone now." The War Priest rubbed his hands together to warm them.

Gavin looked at the area where the wraith had been, then at Bellor. "It was after my grandson, wasn't it?"

"It wanted revenge on him, as well as Thor and I. It's marked us for vengeance and we're too close to the Void here in your village."

Gavin sighed, then glanced at the dying embers in the hearth. "I'll build a fire."

"That would help fight off this chill."

Gavin set some logs onto the embers and created new flames with his exhaled breath. After it was going, he asked, "Will it be back?"

Bellor wanted to say no, to explain why the wyvern was so intent on killing them, to apologize for endangering his family, but the veteran hunter spoke first.

"Get my grandson away from here. Away from the Void." Gavin stared into Bellor's eyes. "Look after him. Please."

Another stone added itself to the heavy weight of Bellor's responsibility. "I'll take him as far as I can, because until he gets away from the Void, the wraith will keep coming back until your grandson is a restless spirit, damned to never find peace."

"Don't let that happen, Master Bellor, please," Gavin poked at the fire, "there are already too many ghosts in this house."

XIII

The Giergun War taught me what is most important in life.

—Gavin Bloodstone, from the *Bloodstone Chronicles*

The sounds of the swaying cover tree failed to lull Drake to sleep. Every creak and rustle added more troubled thoughts to his already racing mind. *I've got to finish packing my gear, carry enough food. But what's enough?* He didn't even know how long he would be gone. Uncle Sandon and Rigg would replenish their supplies once they got to Armstead. Then where were they going? The dwarves weren't very forthcoming with information. After they had given him the fifty silver aer'bors in the Hunters' Hall they had walked off with his grandfather before he could ask more questions.

Not knowing made it even worse when he had come home. Handing Mother the pouch of silver aer'bors should have been a proud moment until she refused to take them. "I'd rather you stay here than accept any amount, especially from Drobin."

"I have to go." Drake put the bag in her arms.

"No. You don't." Mother's trembling hands made the coins jingle.

"I'm coming back."

"When?" Mother's eyes moistened and Tallia glared at him.

Drake turned away from them both, shrugged.

"You're going to miss my wedding!" Tallia screamed before

running to her room and slamming the door.

Tears rolled down Mother's cheeks. "What about Jaena? You haven't even told her you're leaving. We'll give back . . . the aer'bors." Mother began sobbing. "Stay here, marry Jaena . . . settle down before you go off and into . . . I just don't . . . I mean, I don't understand. You're leaving . . . with those . . . *dwarves.*"

For a long time, Drake had hugged his mother before Father finally took her away. He couldn't hear Mother's sobs anymore, just the swaying tree. He wondered if Jaena was sleeping and what to say to her. He rehearsed different speeches as his thoughts flowed in many directions at once. Clear thinking seemed impossible as fleeting images flashed through his mind's eye: Jaena's sad face in the Hall, the dwarves walking toward Cliffton in the open ground, the wyvern falling into the Void, Ethan screaming.

As he lay on his bed, the visions swirled inside his mind as the sharp snap of his crossbow releasing a shaft played in the background. The bolt *thunked* into the wyvern over and over again. At the edge of unconsciousness, Drake didn't realize he listened to the branches of the cover tree creaking and tapping on the roof.

The streaking bolt missed the wyvern. Drake cringed as the serpent-dragon carried Bellor into the air, crushing the old dwarf's bones and slicing open his flesh with sharp claws. The War Priest screamed as the aevian stabbed him in the back again and again with its curved stinger. The monster flew toward the Void, dropped Bellor's bleeding body into the abyss. The dwarf's limbs flailed as he fell headfirst toward the Underworld where his soul would be damned forever.

Drake found himself standing on the edge of the cliff as mist boiled over the rim. A bitterly cold wind blew the ground-hugging fog onward making it impossible to tell where the plateau ended. He staggered back as the icy fog swallowed his feet and legs. His entire body became numb as the mist flowed over his thighs, draining his warmth, leaving him shivering and weak.

In the distance, the wyvern turned in midair. Drake raised his crossbow, realized it wasn't cocked or loaded. He struggled to pull back the cord, his fading strength barely able to span the weapon. His bolt quiver was missing from his leg, so he slipped out the only shaft he carried—his thorn bolt—from the special pocket on his leg. Numb fingers tried to put the shaft in the track. He fumbled with the bolt, dropped it into the mist. His heart stopped when he didn't hear the shaft clatter against the ground.

The wyvern's vengeful eyes fixed on him. It dove toward him with its stinger and claws poised to strike. He reached into the freezing mist. Icy needles stabbed into his hand and arm. On his knees, the mist touched his chin, chilling him to the core as he desperately searched the frigid rock. His hand only found the emptiness beyond the edge of the cliff.

The wyvern's wings blocked out the fading light of the sun. Black talons reached for him. He couldn't move. The cold mist froze him to the ground. Something inside the fog pushed him sideways. The hooked talons scratched against the stone where Drake had been as the beast flew by. The monster climbed into the darkening sky as he sat up wondering what had saved him and what was happening.

The force of the wyvern's wings parted the fog. Drake's chest tightened. He sat on a slender spire of rock surrounded on all sides by the Void. The mist flowed back around him, a sheet of thick cloud hid the open air. Trapped on the tower he forced himself to stand his ground and not give in to the overwhelming fear or biting cold. He couldn't hold onto his crossbow and let it clatter to the rock.

A wisp of cloud rose up and a face formed in the vapors, took on the shape of a young man. Drake recognized the spirit's sad eyes. *"Ethan."*

The ghost's ethereal hands raised Drake's lost thorn bolt. Ethan's eyes stared at the shaft, the symbol of manhood he could never gain in life.

"I'm sorry, Ethan." Drake grasped the bolt, his cold hand almost unable to feel the wood.

Ethan's eyes filled with sorrow, then determination. The ghost turned to face the diving wyvern, his incorporeal body gathering mist around him and becoming a shield in front of Drake.

"Ethan? What're you doing?" He could barely speak, his body numb and almost paralyzed by the cold, but Drake couldn't shake the feeling that Ethan was offering himself as some kind of sacrifice.

I won't let it take you, Ethan's voice sounded in Drake's mind. The wyvern dove toward them, eyes burning with hatred.

A flash of light, as if a fiery sun had suddenly burst out from behind the clouds, blinded Drake. When his vision returned, there was no sign of Ethan or the wyvern. Afraid his friend had given up his soul to save him, Drake searched the endless gray expanse with his blurred vision. The freezing wind gnawed at his bones, sapping the last of his strength. He gave up his futile search in despair. Trapped on the tower of rock, Drake slumped to the stone and the Void mist covered him. He closed his eyes, giving into the cold and letting the sleep of death claim him.

A strange tapping intruded into his senses and Drake forced himself awake. He stared at the shadowy ceiling of his small room in the Bloodstone family home. The cover tree drummed on the roof and he jerked up in bed. A lingering cold assaulted his skin as the nightmare came back to him. Thinking of poor

Ethan made him realize what he had to do before he left with the two Drobin.

Battling grogginess and the cold, Drake quickly pulled on his favorite hunting clothes, a pair of patched brown pants and a matching long-sleeved tunic made of tanned vrelkskin. The thick material, soft on the inside and tough on the outside, would repel all but the sharpest barbs in the Thornclaw, but his clothes felt like ice against his legs. He hoped the material would warm up soon, and thought it bizarre that this time of year the night had been so cold.

Around his waist he strapped his belt with the Kierka knife and its small quiver already attached. Touching the empty quiver made him shiver as he remembered the nightmare. He slipped his thorn bolt into a pocket on the opposite side in a long leather pocket. Grandfather said thorn bolts never missed. Though a hunter vowed to shoot the ceremonial bolt only if his life was in jeopardy. He tightened his belt, trying to avoid touching the cold bloodstone gem on the buckle.

After rolling his forest-green cloak, he stuffed it into his hunting pack, which already held a few supplies. The cape would warm him at night and keep him dry during the almost nightly rains. He loaded a large quiver with twenty good bolts, making certain the fletchings were straight and undamaged. He pulled on his supple vrelkskin boots that reached all the way up to his knees. Mother had made them well and he slid a long, slender dagger into the sheath she had stitched into his right boot. Glancing up, he almost took the parchment map down from the wall by his bed, but he knew every detail, plus dozens more about the Thornclaw and the Wind Walker Mountains.

As he walked into the hearth-room, the blazing fire drew his attention. He packed some dried goods from the pantry, then warmed himself beside the flames. His eyes were drawn to the weapon above the mantle. Grandfather's longsword rested slightly askew on the rack of vrelk antlers. He ran his fingers over the beautiful wooden scabbard, then shifted the weapon to its normal position. Some forgotten craftsman—possibly a dwarf—had carved the sword's name into the wood, *Bloodguardian*. Drake picked it up and unsheathed the blade, examining the archaic Nexan script decorating steel above the pommel: *STRENGTH* on one side, *COMPASSION* on the other. The words reminded him to carry on the time-honored tradition of the Bloodstone Way.

"You don't need a sword." Grandfather sat in his rocking chair beside the hearth. At seventy-five years old, Grandfather still possessed the stealth necessary to sneak up on his distracted grandson.

The long blade made a slight metallic sound as Drake slid back into the scabbard. He placed it carefully on the antlers. "Such a beautiful blade."

Grandfather stopped rocking. "Swords are for killing, for protection. That's no decoration. Never forget what's in our *Chronicles*."

Wishing he hadn't opened his mouth, Drake glanced at the leather-bound book on the mantle that had helped him learn to read. He read the old-style lettering, *THE BLOODSTONE CHRONICLES*. His family's lineage had been penned by many different hands going back almost twenty generations. The bits of history found on the brittle paper proved Grandfather's words were correct: the sword had taken the lives of many Giergun, several men, and probably a few Drobin—judging by the names of the slain.

How many Giergun has Grandfather alone killed with this blade? Drake rested his hand on the sword, turned to the old patriarch, formed the question in his mind.

"You don't need such a weapon to guide Drobin through the forest." Grandfather stared at his grandson, who pulled his hand back. "You're a crossbowman. Not a swordsman. Don't forget it."

"I won't." He wondered why he had even thought to ask and touched the Kierka knife on his belt.

"Listen to me." Grandfather leaned forward. "I want to be the last Bloodstone to ever use a sword." He started rocking again. "The *Chronicles* say that no one in our family who has carried *Bloodguardian* into battle has ever been slain. There's only one way to make absolutely certain that will remain true. Do you understand?"

Drake nodded.

The old man rubbed his eyes. "We're hunters now, not soldiers."

A heavy clarity came to the young man and he knew he had done nothing compared to his grandfather, the man who had taught him everything, who had always been his teacher and friend.

Struggling to find words, Drake blinked back tears. "Thank you, Grandfather . . . for everything." He wanted to say more; tell him how much he loved him and how he would miss him. The old soldier and master hunter had named him when he was born, giving him so much attention over the years. Drake wanted to blurt it all out, but he stood in numb silence.

Gavin Bloodstone wiped his eyes. "Be careful out there. These dwarves attract trouble, and there are things they aren't telling us. Those odd scars on the wyvern's throat aren't from a fight. They were carved there, very precisely."

"By what?" Drake furrowed his brow.

"I don't know, but that wyvern didn't come from the Thornclaw." Grandfather's eyebrows bunched together. "There might be another." Grandfather shifted in his chair, shivered despite the fire. Drake wondered what manner of demon from the Void could have sent the aevian after the dwarves. Was that even possible?

"You aren't planning to leave without saying good-bye to the others, are you?"

"No, I. . . ." Drake looked at his feet. "I've got something to do first."

"Will you be back for breakfast?"

"No."

"Off with you then, the sun is about to rise." Grandfather gestured toward the door. "We'll meet you at the south gate two hours after daybreak."

The old man sniffled as Drake strode out of the hearth-room. He had never seen his grandfather cry before. He would miss him more than anyone else in his family. Suppressing his sadness, Drake concentrated on shouldering his pack and carrying the crossbow his grandfather had made for him. Once outside he stopped at the front thorn-door of his family's yard. He inhaled the peppery fragrance of his home cover tree as Jep and Temus ran up and mobbed him for attention, pressing their cold noses against his hands. Petting his dogs while turning around to stare at his home, he tried to forget about the bad times and remember the good ones.

Pangs of guilt at leaving his family made him hang his head. He couldn't leave them defenseless. The dogs couldn't come with him. With an unsteady voice he told them, "Stay. Guard the house." They sat down panting with pink tongues hanging out of their mouths. Their sad eyes and droopy faces made him wince with regret. Jep whined, begging to accompany him, but both dogs obeyed.

"Good dogs." His voice cracked. Jep and Temus stayed inside the borders of his family's cover tree while he headed toward the south gate. Drake tightened the straps on his pack and slung his crossbow over his shoulder. The dogs whined louder, the sound tearing at his heart. He fought back tears and girded himself for what he was about to do. There was one person he couldn't leave behind.

XIV

Ghosts of the past haunt me in my dreams. Why do they
linger at my side?

> —Bölak Blackhammer, from the Lost Journal

The village's bullmastiffs pawed and nuzzled Drake as he passed
under the south gate tower. The pack clamored for attention as
he stepped outside the gate, letting the heavy bar fall into place.
He clutched his loaded crossbow and scanned the dawn sky for
aevians.

Empty.

The dim glow of the rising sun appeared in the distance, as if
signaling its blessing for the Clifftoner to proceed. He crossed
the forty paces of the clearing and ducked into the tangled
woods, glad he had left his bulky pack in the village.

The sharp-scented curdle-moss tingled in his nostrils as he
inhaled the familiar scents of the forest. Insects buzzed in the
shadows and thorn shrikes sang shrill songs in the dense canopy.
He dodged low, hanging vines and spiky foliage as he followed
the trail. A trickle of blood ran down his neck, alerting him to
an attack by a hook fly that had made off with a bit of his flesh.
The initially painless bite stung now, and he chastised himself
for failing to notice its initial landing.

Drake ducked under a spiny branch that would have gouged
out an eye and slapped another hook fly on his arm. His feet
moved with the rhythm of an experienced forest walker. He

danced with the Thornclaw, sometimes using the stirrup or lathe of his crossbow to move brush aside, cutting vines with his Kierka only as a last resort.

Instinctively avoiding the bloodletting plants, Drake's mind strayed to another time when he had rushed down this same track five years ago. The Lily Pad Rocks had been his destination and Drake remembered the sense of urgency he had felt then—but this time he didn't run.

After several minutes of wending his way down the prickly path, the trees lost their dominance at the edge of the plateau where the Void began. Near the cliff, he spied the six pillar-shaped rock islands jutting up from the mist. The barren flat-topped Lily Pads were the last bit of solid ground before the white clouds of the Void stretched to the horizon.

The squat sikatha tree grew on the farthest rock island, a lone sentinel of thorny branches sprouting from a fat trunk. With one long stride he easily crossed the first gap. He jumped over the next crevasse and then the next, making his way toward the sikatha tree, crossing the short gaps until he faced the final leap.

This is where Ethan died. As Drake stared over the edge, he remembered his friend falling. The terrified shriek haunted him again like it had in his nightmares. Seeing Ethan in his dream had forced him to act. He took a deep breath and shouted, "Ethan! I'm going away . . . and you're coming with me." *My friend, my little brother, I'm sorry I failed you. I'll get away from this evil Void for both of us.* "We'll both be free of it!"

After backing away from the edge, Drake put down his crossbow, then ran at full speed toward the chasm. His legs drove him toward the yawning gap between him and the sikatha tree. He heard Ethan scream from beyond the grave, suppressed the memory and sprinted ahead, leaping as far as he could. The clouds roiled beneath as he sailed over the abyss. He landed on the stone, stumbled forward, falling in front of the short tree covered with long sharp thorns. The thick spines were the same size as his crossbow bolts.

Drake unsheathed his Kierka blade. He searched the tree inspecting every branch and not caring about the risk of lingering in the open. He stood there longer than any hunter ever had until he found a perfectly straight thorn as long as his forearm. He felt a rush of sadness that became grim resignation, then he chopped off the thorn. His hand closed around it and Drake knew he had to do something else. With the wooden barb clutched in his palm he strode to the edge of the rock island. He gazed into the depths of the swirling mist where Ethan had fallen, then stabbed his finger with the sharp thorn. Blood dripped into the Void.

"Ethan, I've got your thorn bolt! You're a hunter now! Do you hear me! I'll see the world with your spirit at my side." Drake fell to his knees. "By my own blood, I pledge this. You are a hunter."

A voice from the Underworld shouted, "Ethan, I've got your thorn bolt!"

Drake's eyes opened wide with fear, before he realized he heard the echo of his own words. The Void mocked his pledge, minimizing and distorting the words and carrying them on the wind for the demons to hear. A gust of chill wind swirled up, and the cold air stung his skin.

Guilt filled Drake's heart as he searched the endless clouds. A wisp of mist rose from the Void, drifted on the wind. Ethan did not appear like he had in the nightmare, but Drake sensed something, a presence filled with shame, wanting to be free.

I have to leave. Drake understood that now, both for himself and for Ethan's lost spirit, who he felt in the wind clinging to his side.

XV

The demons of the Void come in many guises. Never underestimate their power or forget their many names. Guilt. Shame. Anger. Greed. Fear. Hatred.

—Priestess Liana Whitestar, passage from the Goddess Scrolls

Jaena watched as Drake leaped across the Void, a spine from the sikatha tree clutched in his hand. The echoes of his pledge resonated in her mind. She knew the shaft would become Ethan's thorn bolt. Jaena cursed it, a physical symbol to further anchor Ethan's spirit to this plane.

How could he offer his blood to the Void and make such a vow? Is he being tempted by demons? Jaena's suspicion deepened as Drake's eyes glazed over. Appearing half-asleep, he picked up his crossbow from the rock island. As if in a trance he jumped over the next four gaps of the Lily Pad Rocks while Jaena hoped a griffin would not come.

When her beloved approached the final gap, Jaena stood tall. Her long, flowing white dress with green and blue embroidered threads made her stand out like a jewel on the edge of the plateau. Lost in his daze, Drake failed to see her until he was in mid-air of his jump. Her golden hair streamed across her face as Jaena's eyes met his—just before he landed. She heard a loud *pop*. His right ankle twisted awkwardly as he fell hard to the ground.

What have I done?! Jaena ran to Drake, who sat grimacing near the edge of the cliff. She knelt beside him and they both stared at his hurt ankle, his boot hiding the full extent of his injury. "I shouldn't have come out like that. It's my fault that you—"

"I'm fine, just help me up." He gritted his teeth and put his hand out for her. She stood up, holding firm as Drake pulled himself to a standing position. He balanced on one leg, unable to put much pressure on his twisted ankle.

"Let's get under cover so I can see how bad it is." Jaena put his arm over her shoulder, then helped him hobble toward the forest. Judging by his pained expression, she wondered if he'd broken any bones. Suddenly she realized that regardless of the damage, Drake would not be leaving the village with the Drobin. Someone else would have to guide the dwarves.

"How could you possibly know I was here?" he asked, cringing with every short step.

"I knew." She spoke with the confident priestess voice she had learned from her mother and didn't tell him she had just missed him at his house and followed when he left Cliffton.

"How long have you been here?" Drake glanced at the sky.

"I heard your pledge." *Reckless and blasphemous,* she thought. As if he'd been shamed by her thoughts, Drake turned his face away from her.

They ducked under the edge of the trees, and Jaena found herself in the unprecedented position of leading the way for him. She held back a branch so he could pass and they headed for a solitary, young cover tree a few paces from the edge of the Void. Balancing on one leg and keeping a hand on Jaena's shoulder, Drake hacked off dangerous barbs from the poorly maintained thorn-door.

They slipped inside and Jaena helped ease Drake down. They sat on the soft bed of sweet smelling shade-clover, both avoiding a thick root of the cover tree that snaked across the ground. She knelt in front of him then focused on his dark-brown eyes. "I've got to take your boot off."

"No. Leave it."

"I can't leave it. And it's going to hurt."

He nodded and took a deep breath.

Jaena pulled off the knee-high boot as gently as she could. Drake gasped in pain, collapsing on his back when it finally slipped off. She stared at his ankle, the flesh already swelling, and knew it was badly injured. Her fingers gently probed the enlarged area, and she guessed he'd torn muscles and tendons, possibly broken bones. For an instant, Jaena wished she could heal him, but invoking the Healing magic was beyond her. For the first time, she was grateful not to be a full Priestess. Now Drake would have to stay. Guilt nagged at her.

He sat up on his elbows and stared at his puffy ankle. The normal bump on the inside had swollen to twice its normal size. "Why did this happen today?" He shook his head.

"I'm so sorry. It's my fault."

"No, it's mine." Shadows cast by the tree made his face look even more grim. "This never would have happened if I hadn't. . . ."

Jaena sensed great shame as he hung his head.

"I had to come here and get this." He held up Ethan's thorn bolt.

Jaena touched the freshly cut sikatha thorn. *Ethan's spirit bolt. It should be destroyed to free him, even though it was never really his.* "What will you do with that?"

Drake shrugged.

"Custom should be followed." Jaena stared at the thorn.

"I'm not burning it." He pulled away and slid the thorn into his leg quiver.

"Thorn bolts tie a hunter's spirit to this world. They must be burned if the owner is dead."

"I'm taking it with me."

Jaena frowned. *The bolt or Ethan's spirit?* The words she wanted to say didn't come. Others spewed out much harsher than she had planned, "You're not going anywhere. You're staying in Cliffton."

Shoulders sagging, he lay back down. "When my father finds out what happened, he'll think I'm a bungling fool. Everyone will."

"No they won't and. . . ." Jaena hesitated.

"It doesn't matter. My father will take this injury as a sign that he should guide the Drobin. He'll say he's meant to go in my place, ordained by the Goddess. Not even your mother will argue with that."

He was right.

"I can't go to the gates," Drake said. "You'll have to say farewell to everyone and tell the Drobin I'll meet them in the forest. Say I'm waiting for them."

"What? You can't even walk. You'll never make it to Armstead like this."

"I'm not going to show my father and the whole village what a fool I am and hobble through the gates like a . . . cripple."

The color drained from Drake's face. Jaena moved closer and put her arm over his chest while tucking her head into his shoulder. They embraced for several moments and Drake said, "Ethan was a good friend to me. But sometimes I wish. . . ."

She hugged him a little closer.

"I wish"—guilt scrunched up his face—"that Rigg had lived in Cliffton. Then he would have been my best friend. Or maybe together we could have stopped Ethan."

"No one could have." Jaena squeezed him. "It was his fate to be taken by the Void."

"But he's not gone. Whenever I'm at the Lily Pads . . . I feel

Ethan with me."

Jaena considered her next words with care. "Perhaps he's always with you." She paused, still unsure if she should tell him of her suspicions, but decided not to keep it from him any longer. "Sometimes I sense a presence with you."

Drake's eyes met hers, and she knew he felt it too. Jaena knew she must speak with utter kindness and care. "Maybe you're right. Maybe his soul wasn't condemned to the Underworld."

"I've never thought he was, no matter what your mother taught me."

"I know." Jaena rolled away and picked at the soft shadeclover.

"He's not damned." The sourness of Drake's words puckered his lips.

"Why did you speak to the Void?" Jaena moved back to him. "You tempt the demons of the Underworld."

"I talked to Ethan, not the Void. My vow will help both of us find peace."

"My mother says it's not good to carry the spirits of the dead with us. You should let him go to Amaryllis." *If it's still possible.* "My mother told me what you must do, cut the dark cord between Ethan's spirit and yours."

Drake shook his head and pulled up a big handful of shadeclover. Anger radiated from his body and she brushed a hand down his cheek, trying to calm him.

"You believe what your mother said, don't you?"

She nodded.

He turned away, then muttered, "Your mother doesn't know everything and I don't care if the people think I'm a fool believing what I do."

Jaena rubbed his shoulder. "The people don't think that. They love and respect you for what you do for the village."

Drake shook his head.

He never wants to believe the truth. "Everyone knows you put too much pressure on yourself. Your father and the hunters think you just need a break from being a guardian once in a while. You can't let it consume you."

Drake rubbed his forehead.

"I want to help you see what you're doing to yourself," Jaena soothed, "but I don't know how anymore. *Stop punishing yourself for the selfish decision of another.*" Five long years of failing to mend Drake's tortured spirit made her eyes fill with tears. In that moment she decided she would always be a terrible healer, not because of failing to heal others, but because she was unable to comfort the man closest to her. His pain would become a reminder of her greatest failure.

At least he would be alive and with her in Cliffton. Jaena's vision from the night before made her suspect with every fiber of her being that if he left with the Drobin he would not come back. She suspected that when he saw her—and then hurt his ankle—she had saved his life. But if that were true, why did it feel so wrong?

Jaena sat up and wiped her eyes. She stared at his ankle, noticing it was even more swollen than before. The injury would keep him in Cliffton, exactly what she wanted. Doubt and remorse gnawed at her. He had to leave if he was ever going to cut the dark cord between him and Ethan.

Lifting her head toward the upper branches of the cover tree, Jaena prayed silently to Amaryllis, pleading for guidance. She shook her leg and a sandal fell off. Jaena's bare foot touched one of the tree's surface roots. The wood pressed against her toes and she had her answer.

After crawling to a spot in front of Drake's feet, Jaena placed her hands upon either side of his ankle. Her fingers touched the swollen joint and her intuition told her it was broken. She slipped off her other sandal and all her toes found the root. Jaena pressed against the wood, beseeching the Goddess to allow her to channel the Healing magic and repair his ankle. "Please, Amaryllis, bless him with Your Light."

For several minutes she prayed, wanting him to be healed more than anything. Nothing happened. The outcome she desired eluded her once again, just like all the other times she had tried to use the Healing magic in the past months.

Drake looked into her disappointed eyes. He said, "It's all right. We'll go back together and face the village. My father will be their guide."

Jaena suddenly realized why she had failed. She wanted it too much and her desire for him to be healed had gotten in the way of the magic. Praying again, Jaena asked Amaryllis to do what the Goddess wanted, not what the novice Priestess Jaena Whitestar wanted. After a moment of intense prayer she felt her spirit separating from her body, her awareness of the physical world slipping away as she became a being of pure light. Her ego, fears, and petty desires were left behind. Jaena became free of judgment as she floated invisibly above Drake. Her physical body held his broken ankle and manifested the magic that would make him whole again. The moment she accepted her power to heal, Jaena's spirit rejoined her physical body as the magic coursed through her.

A soft, golden-green glow emanated from Jaena's palms, encapsulating Drake's ankle. She gasped as the Healing magic flowed from within the tree, through her feet, and out through her palms. She knew that the warm surges would overwhelm her—sap away her life—if she broke contact with the root. Time became irrelevant and the forest disappeared. Jaena's skin tingled as tumultuous magic swirled around Drake's lower extremity, bringing his injured ankle back to the perfect state of health.

The light faded and Jaena opened her eyes before carefully withdrawing her hands. Wide-eyed with amazement, she whispered the proper words, "Thank you, Great Tree. May we be worthy of your sacrifice."

"You've done it." Drake grinned. "You're a full Priestess now."

Jaena's smile disappeared. Now he would go. Probably never come back. She realized that her action to mend his ankle may have cost him his life. Shoulders sagging, she crawled over him. Drake pulled her down and wrapped his strong arms around her.

As he rubbed her back Jaena whispered, "You're going to take a part of my spirit with you wherever you go too." Tears streamed from her sapphire eyes and she snuggled against him, praying she had made the right decision.

"What does your mother say about taking the spirit of a living person with you?"

Jaena sobbed in his embrace. "What if you never come back?"

Drake caressed away her tears with the tips of his fingers and she savored the tenderness of his touch. Jaena calmed down and stared into his soft brown eyes. She could almost see his aura and the golden light of love connecting them.

After holding him for several long minutes, Jaena found her words at last. "Our souls will always be connected. Once spirits meet, they are joined for all time. No matter where we go in this life or the next, there will be a bond between us."

He ran his fingers through her soft curls. "Jaena, I'm so sorry for being the way I've been. I've wanted to, but I just couldn't ask you to be my wife . . . then yesterday I decided I would . . . and now this happens. It's not fair." He hugged her. "I'm sorry for having to leave today. I'm so sorry for everything. I've made so many mistakes. I've failed so many people."

Jaena put a hand on his face. "Leaving is your chance to heal your heart. It wasn't your fault Ethan died."

Drake's face wrinkled with grief. She knew he was haunted by that terrible day when his best friend "fell." He had remembered the event many times in the past years. She had heard him talk about it with his family, though Drake spoke of the final moments of Ethan's life only to her.

After listening to all of Drake's recollections—and omissions—Jaena suspected one thing: Ethan had killed himself. Suicide. Jaena knew Ethan couldn't make the final jump. Everyone knew it, especially Ethan, who was too smart to miscalculate his own abilities.

The Void had lured Ethan into making a selfish choice, a choice that the entire community of Cliffton paid for during the past five years. It had pulled the boy into the Underworld with its evil malevolence. Liana agreed. Her mother had seen Ethan's fall in a vision the morning he died. Only the Goddess could have altered the afflicted boy's destiny and prevented the ripples caused by his passing.

No one could have stopped him, though Jaena knew Drake had come very close to saving his friend from "falling." She wondered if he would ever say if Ethan really fell . . . or let go of the cliff. "Drake, you can't let his death hold you back anymore. You have to face it once and for all, and forgive yourself."

His face took on a stony resolve. "His dying made the fire in me stronger. That's all."

Jaena could tell Drake believed the lie he had told himself so often. "I think that I was able to heal you because I know if you stay here now, things may never change. I've held you back, and maybe you've held me back from accepting my own destiny as a Priestess."

"I'm sorry. I didn't mean to."

"I know. We've both been fighting our futures. Now is the

time for us to accept our fate, even though it's painful. My mother believes you must leave for a time. She says it's important for you to get away from here." Jaena's shoulders quivered and she struggled to speak. "I'll"—her voice cracked— "miss you . . . so much."

"I love you, Jaena." He pulled her close to his chest again.

She let herself enjoy his embrace and tears fell from her eyes, dampening his tunic. A few moments later Jaena took control of her grief. "Drake, I was going to tell you at the shrine yesterday, but the Drobin came."

"Tell me what?"

"About my vision." Jaena leaned away from him and stared off into the forest through the arching branches of the cover tree. "I saw you looking into a beautiful valley surrounded by tall, snowcapped mountains. Gnarlpine trees were all around, and you were looking for something in the valley. Two eagles flew over your head and screeched a warning."

"What was I looking for? The Drobin mine?"

"I don't know," Jaena hesitated. "But I don't think so. It was something else. I don't know why I know this, but I do. Amaryllis spoke to me." Jaena's voice trembled. "If you go into the valley . . . your life, and the lives of everyone in Cliffton will be put in danger. Drake, if you go into that valley, you'll be gone for a very long time. You may never return."

Drake rocked backwards in stunned silence.

"Amaryllis gave me this vision and knowledge of your future, perhaps to warn you and protect the village, but the only thing I truly know is that I love you so dearly that the thought of losing you. . . ." Jaena used all her self-control to prevent herself from crying.

"I'm coming back, Jaena." He hugged her and they sunk into the deep green shade-clover. Their lips touched, devotion translating into a burning kiss Jaena promised herself she would never forget.

Their bodies pressed into the ground leaving the outline of their passionate embrace molded in the shade-clover. Drake whispered his love into her ear and she felt his warm breath on her skin as he breathed in her fragrance.

"I can't wait for you to return." Jaena pressed her cheek to his chest. "I can't bear to be apart from you for too long."

"You won't have to . . . but if something happens . . . and I don't come back . . . I would understand if you married—"

"Don't say that!" Jaena burst into tears. They held each other and lost themselves in a desperate embrace. Jaena didn't want to let him go, but she knew his inescapable fate would soon take him away, perhaps forever.

The sun rose higher above the thick branches of the cover tree arbor. Threads of light shone upon Drake and Jaena's bed of shade-clover. He released her and rose to his knees. She couldn't look away from him as he put on his boot and secured his traveling gear. *He's really leaving.* Jaena grasped his hands desperately, her tight grip willing him to stay for a few more minutes—or forever.

She pulled herself up and they hugged one last time, fighting the urge to beg him to stay, while knowing he had to go. A single tear fell from his eye and landed on her cheek. She touched it with her fingertip and pressed the salty drop to her lips. He brushed away one of her tears and brought the moist finger to his own mouth in a silent kiss.

"I love you so much, Jaena," he held her close, "but I must go now."

She nodded, choking back her sorrow. He pulled away slowly and held eye contact as he backed out through the thorn-door. On her knees, she prayed as she watched him go.

Though his ankle wasn't hurt, each of Drake's steps away

from her appeared harder than the last. She wondered if he wanted to run back, hold her in his arms and tell her to come with him. He didn't. He kept going, toward his destiny—away from Cliffton—away from her.

Jaena lost sight of him in the forest. She offered a prayer for her one true love, "May the sky always be clear for you, and may the forest protect you." Collapsing on the ground, she wept, watching his outline in the shade-clover slowly disappear.

XVI

We have all left behind the ones we love. Some in graves, others in homes we wonder if we will ever see again. Lorak only knows if we're ever going home.

—Bölak Blackhammer, from the Lost Journal

Drake pushed through the dog-filled tunnel under the south gate tower as he entered Cliffton. He found the cover tree arbor beyond the gate brimming with people and heard Bellor thanking the villagers. He had expected his family and maybe a few others, but almost the entire village had come to say farewell. Over a hundred and fifty men, women, and children had packed themselves under the large dome, sitting on the lowest branches and filling all three levels of the gate tower. He'd never seen anything like it, not even when a big hunting party returned home. Enveloped by the shouting crowd, Drake stood with his mouth agape.

"I told you he didn't run off!"

"Thank the Goddess."

"Drake, we'll miss you!"

"Watch out for aevians!"

"Maybe if you hurry you'll be back for Tallia's wedding. You've got two weeks."

"May the sky be clear for you."

Mae stepped forward and hugged Drake. "The children were always safe when you were on watch. Thank you for watching

144

over Neven and all the others."

"Dwake." Neven latched onto his leg. "I wuv you."

Many of the hunters and their wives clamored for handshakes and hugs. He tried to comprehend what the heartfelt farewell meant to him. He could almost hear Jaena saying, "I told you. Don't you see?" He wished he could tell her she was right. Overwhelmed, he couldn't think of what to say to the people, and thought this sendoff too much, since he might only be gone for a few days. Then he remembered Jaena's vision.

Out from the crowd Ethan's mother stepped forward and embraced Drake. He wrapped his arms around her thin body, putting his cheek against her wispy gray hair, once a lustrous jet-black. He felt her body shaking and her voice trembled. "Come home safe."

She couldn't lose anyone else. It would kill her. Drake wanted to tell her about his vow, show her Ethan's thorn bolt. The specter of his shame clouded his mind. "I'm so sorry. I tried to save him."

Ethan's mother looked up with her dark-brown eyes, the same as her dead child's. "It's time to let go of that day. It's not your fault Ethan's gone. You're my only son now, and I've always been proud of you."

A shuddering gasp caught in Drake's throat. *No. I will not cry.*

Little Edeline pushed past her grandmother as sobs shook her body. She hugged Drake and he patted her head, resigning himself to be strong for his people. Ethan's mother kissed Drake's hand and led her weeping granddaughter away.

Liana's eyes fixed on him as she stood at the edge of the crowd with the two dwarves. He stared back at Jaena's mother, trying to decipher her gaze. *She knows something.*

Drake's family circled around him, while Liana and the two dwarves joined them near the gate. Mother and Tallia hugged him.

Tallia squeezed him hard and rubbed his back. "I wish you could stay for my wedding."

"Maybe I'll make it back in time."

His sister wiped her eyes, tried to smile.

Mother and Grandmother cried as they hugged him. Both said, "Find good cover."

"I will."

Father shook Drake's hand. "Say hello to your uncle Sandon and his family for me. It's been a while since I've seen them. Janek and Ellie must be a lot bigger now, and Rigg is probably married."

The dwarves exchanged a strange, knowing glance. Drake wondered what it meant, then suddenly remembered a task he hadn't finished. "Father, I didn't fix the east gate, and I was going to help paint Mae's arboreum, and the watch tower's roof needs—"

Tyler held up a hand to silence his son. "I'll take care of it all. You've done more work in the last few days than another man could do in a week."

Swallowing hard, he couldn't ever remember hearing praise from Father about what he had done for the village.

"What about Jep and Temus?" Father asked as the two bull-mastiffs nuzzled Drake's legs with their wet noses.

Drake rubbed the big heads of his dogs, then hugged them both. "Father, please watch them for me. I don't want to take them away from the village." While petting them, he realized Jep and Temus had no idea he was about to leave them behind. They'd be heartbroken. He felt like he was leaving little children without explaining why. Saying farewell to Jaena, his family, the dogs, and all the villagers hit him like a falling tree.

"Take the dogs with you, son. They've always made good trail companions and I brought their packs." Father touched Jep and Temus on their necks. "You need them. You'll be alone without

Jep and Temus."

Drake considered it, inspecting the loaded saddle-packs strapped onto the dogs. "No. If I'm not going to be here, I want them to guard the family."

Father embraced his only son. "You are the family." Tears came to Drake's eyes, but he forced them back.

Lastly, he hugged Grandfather. "You're the only forest walker on this trek, so be extra cautious. Get as far away from the Void as you can tonight. Don't go near it."

Drake nodded, heard the warning, wondered why he was so insistent.

Liana Whitestar called everyone to look upwards for a prayer. "May the sky always be clear for Drake and his companions. May they find their way free from the brambles and make haste toward their destination. In the name of the Great Goddess, I bless you three travelers. May the smile of Amaryllis be upon you all. Go with Her Grace and pass through this land in harmony and peace. May the canopy be strong, and may the sky be clear."

"May the sky be clear." The villagers repeated her words, concern in their voices.

Desperate to keep in his tears, he waved farewell and moved ahead of the dwarves and into the darkness of the strangely cold gate tunnel.

Old man Laetham emerged from the shadows near the outer gate. Even in the dim tunnel Drake could see his bloodshot eyes and the raised white scars on his arms. Laetham's voice struck as a sharp whisper, "Blue Creek trail is the fastest route to Armstead, but the hunters who were there last week said it's still a dangerous path, especially for outsiders." Laetham sneered at the dwarves, who said farewell to Liana. "They might not make it through a rough place like that."

"You want me to let them be killed?" Drake clenched his

teeth as a chill ran down his back. He blinked and saw the hideous face and the arched tail of the dead wyvern hovering above Laetham, as if it rode on the old man's back. Ghostly white drops of poison leaked from the wyvern's barbed stinger. Drake opened his eyes and the image had disappeared.

Malice shot from Laetham's eyes. "If you're smart, you'll be back for Tallia's wedding. Maybe even one of your own to Jaena. If you're not back soon, I'll make certain Jaena marries someone else."

A sliver of icy pain stabbed into Drake's chest. Hatred filled his soul, then the sliver pulled out, making him stumble forward. Rage filled the young man and one of his hands clutched Laetham's throat. The old man grabbed Drake's tunic with surprising strength and drew him closer, then choked out the words. "No one will miss the Drobin, but we need you here, boy. Can't you see it? The village needs you, not them. That's why half the Council voted against helping them. There's another way. You'll know what to do when the time comes. Get rid of them at Blue Creek, then come back home."

Bellor and Thor pushed past the curious bullmastiffs in the tunnel. Bellor's face was filled with concern as Drake wrenched away from Laetham. The young man seethed with anger, swallowing his rage when he faced the two Drobin. He yanked on the rope to the counterweight lever and opened the outer gate. Drake's proximity to the demon called Laetham forced him outside.

Bellor and Thor also stepped into the open ground filled with withered tree stumps and long grass. Several of Cliffton's crossbowmen covered them from the gate tower and gave him the "all clear" hand sign. Drake checked the sky anyway, then spanned his crossbow and loaded a broadhead into the track. He fought the urge to whirl around and shoot the shaft into Laetham's chest.

148

Forget yourself. Focus on the moment. Permit no distractions. The Bloodstone Way whispered in his ears, but all he wanted to do was see how many chops it would take to sever Laetham's head.

"Which way?" Belior asked, his voice tense as he scanned the thick woods, a worried frown on his face.

The chill and the pain lingered in Drake's chest. He didn't feel like himself and shivered despite the heat of the day. He motioned with his crossbow, then marched ahead, leading them south and east into the depths of the Thornclaw Forest. One thought dominated all the others in his mind. *I'm going to lead them down the trail to Blue Creek.*

★ ★ ★ ★ ★

PART TWO
ARMSTEAD

★ ★ ★ ★ ★

XVII

We must travel with those who know the way. We have no other choice.

—Bölak Blackhammer, from the Lost Journal

A razor-sharp leaf scraped against Drake's neck, accumulating his blood along its serrated edge. Unflinching as the acid sting pulsed on his skin, he strode down the trail. The pain was nothing compared to his anger at Laetham. The old man's bitter words replayed in his mind: *Get rid of them at Blue Creek, then come back home. If you're not back soon, I'll make certain Jaena marries someone else.* The vile notion and the disgusting threat turned his stomach, as did the memory of seeing the ghostly wyvern above Laetham.

The two dwarves spoke quietly in Drobin as he glanced back. *They don't trust me.* Frowning, Drake decided he shouldn't trust them either. He picked up his pace, wanting to put more distance between his exposed back and the pair of Drobin. They endeavored to match his speed and managed to stay close behind him, though sweat poured off their brows. He heard their loud breathing as they trotted along.

After an hour of traveling through the muggy air saturated with the scent of rotting leaves, the two Drobin still maintained the grueling pace without a word of protest. Drake was forced to admit they had great stamina and courage to have made it so far into the wild. He would help them find their kin at the lost mine and aid them in laying the dead to rest if need be, but nothing else. A shiver ran across his arms as he thought about unquiet dead.

Glancing back repeatedly, Drake noticed the gray-bearded War Priest watching the canopy and shadows all around them with suspicious eyes. He stopped to scan the interwoven branches above them. "Priest Fardelver?"

"Please, call me Bellor."

Drake glanced back again. "Is there something else that might be following you?"

Thor's eyes flashed at Bellor. Drake suspected they were keeping much from him—just as Grandfather warned. He expected a lie to come from Bellor's lips and he touched the bloodstone gem on his belt, hoping it would help him see through the Priest's upcoming attempt at deception.

"It was alone." Bellor rubbed his brow. "Though it had been shadowing us for over a week."

He holds something back. If the wyvern had been following them for "over a week," it would have passed through several areas of forest claimed by other wyverns—and the territorial creatures almost never entered the hunting grounds of another, except to mate. It didn't make sense for the creature to have followed them for so long. The wyvern's tan markings were also different from the green-bellied ones native to the Thornclaw. *Where did it really come from? Why won't they tell me the truth?*

Drake locked his dark eyes on Bellor and faced the Drobin. "I can't guide you if I don't know what waits for us . . . or what could be coming."

Bellor pressed his lips together and shook his head. "Lorak only knows what is in our path."

Just like Jaena's mother when she's keeping secrets. Drake wore a scowl learned from his father. A few strides later he turned off the path—in case something trailed them, or waited in ambush.

The fronds of a fern brushed against his chest as he motioned for the dwarves to follow.

"We're leaving the trail?" Thor's mouth hung open.

"For a while." The Clifftoner surveyed the thick forest to the southeast.

"Does this route lead us away from the Void?" Bellor asked.

"It does." Drake remembered his grandfather's warning about staying away from the Void and wondered what the connection was to Bellor's question.

Thor moaned before mumbling, "Can't we use a trail for longer than two minutes, just once?"

Unsheathing his Kierka, Drake pushed through the bushes as far as he could before using the machete-like weapon to slash apart a tangle of vines blocking the way. "Don't worry. I'll cut us a path."

Bellor and Thor winced as he sheared through the plants. He wondered why they were so afraid of leaving the trail.

Thor asked, "Why do all you men of Cliffton carry the weapon of the *Kierkaan* tribe?"

"*Kierkaan* tribe?" He turned around and wrinkled his face, realizing they had reacted to the sight of his curved Kierka blade—not leaving the trail.

Bellor shook his head. "No, his blade's not Giergun forged, Nexans forged them."

"*Zûrbrecken briettle schteel.*" Thor turned up his nose at the knife.

Drake's eyes narrowed at Thor. "I'd rather you spoke my language."

"Forgive us," Bellor said. "Drobin is normal for us after fifty years together, not to mention Thor's stubbornness about speaking Nexan."

"Fifty years?" Drake remembered hearing how long dwarves lived, but he doubted the stories were true. "How long have you spoken my language?"

155

Bellor tugged on his beard. "Ever since my sixth year. All Drobin children learn Nexan, as well as basic Giergun, and of course Drobin. The three languages are actually quite similar. It took me quite a few decades, but I've learned to be proficient in them all. Though I've rarely spoken Giergun since the Twelfth War ended."

Drake focused on the elder dwarf. "That was nearly fifty years ago. How old are you?"

"I'm two hundred and forty-three years old, and I believe Thor's only a hundred and fifty-six. As I'm certain you can tell, he's still a young one among our people."

"He's over twice as old as my grandfather." A fern slipped out of Drake's hand, smacking him on the cheek and sending the spores attached to the underside of the frond drifting into the air.

Bellor chuckled. "Five-hundred-year-old dwarves are not uncommon, though I doubt I'll reach that lofty age, especially considering my affinity for journeys like this one."

Staring back at the dwarves, Drake realized the unbelievable stories had to be true. "I had no idea you were so . . . old."

"I apologize for Thor and I speaking in the Father tongue. It's so natural for us. We were actually talking about your . . . knife. Thor and I have confronted that type of blade before. We're quite surprised to have seen them on the belt of nearly everyone in your village. Where did you get them?"

"We have them made. A weaponsmith in Nexus City forges them for us." Drake showed the blade to Thor, who scowled with distaste. "There's nothing wrong with my knife." To prove his point he hacked through a mass of vines.

"Master Bellor and I have seen those on the battlefield." Thor rubbed a thin scar on his neck, which was mostly hidden under his beard. Hair didn't grow on the white line and Drake imagined a Kierka knife opening the wound.

"Curse the metal of the Giergun." Thor spit on the ground. "They forge those blades and carry them into battle against our kin with poison staining their steel. What you carry is the symbol of the Giergun clan who call themselves the *Kierkaan*. Other Giergun use the knives as well, and blades just like yours have killed seven of my brothers. Why is it that you Clifftoners carry them? Don't you realize how dishonorable it is for you to use—"

"Thor." Bellor's voice silenced his friend. "Not everyone follows Lorakian customs. Sorry." Bellor frowned. "We didn't expect to find the weapon of our enemy in Cliffton. It brings back . . . painful memories of the Giergun Wars."

Grandfather had told Drake of the war. He scanned the bushes, imagining the warlike Giergun, rumored to be like men in every way except for their monstrous faces, gray-green skin and tendency to have yellow eyes. Thankfully, they had not come across the Void on their skinwing mounts. The Giergun weren't foolish enough to invade the Thornclaw Forest—not even the Drobin were that stupid.

Drake wondered if the fighting over the home plateau of the Drobin, where both folk had built their greatest cities, would ever come to an end. How many more conscripted human soldiers would march and die under the banner of the dwarf king?

"This way." Drake ducked under a branch, thinking about how every Giergun War had raged inside the caverns and on the slopes of the Dark Spire Mountains. All twelve known wars had ended the same way, with a virtual stalemate after too many lives—mostly Nexan—had been taken.

"You must understand," Bellor raised his square jaw, "seeing your people carry the weapon of our enemies . . . makes us wonder—"

"I don't wonder," Thor interrupted, "I know the Nexan and Giergun are connected by blood. Man-blood and Giergun-

157

blood are the same. I know."

Keeping his anger hidden, Drake suspected that Thor had killed both men and Giergun. He thought, *But I'm not Giergunkin, and my people will never ally with them, no matter what you damn Drobin and your paranoid Lorakian Priests say.*

"If you don't mind telling us. . . ." Bellor tried to make eye contact with Drake. "How did your people come to use the chosen weapon of the *Kierkaan?*"

"The Hunter Regiment asked for short swords during the war. Their Drobin commanders didn't give them what they were promised." Drake snorted. "So my grandfather and the others seized knives they called Kierkas, from the Giergun they killed."

"Scavenged steel." Thor spat and wrinkled his sharp nose. "Dishonorable."

Shooting a sideward glance at Thor, Drake felt a chill as he pondered Laetham's suggestion of leaving the dwarves at Blue Creek. At that moment he found the idea much more palatable. He took a deep breath, held in his anger and fixed his eyes on his knife. He slowly wiped the accumulated plant sap onto his sleeve, imagining it was dwarf blood.

"Knives like this one kept my grandfather alive." Drake's eyes didn't stray from the edge of his blade. "But getting one meant killing a Giergun. Now we Clifftoners follow the same tradition as the Giergun. We give up our Kierkas only when we're dead."

Drake slashed and chopped away his anger, beating a constant rhythm during their trek through the Thornclaw Forest. For half a day, they slipped through the grasp of the fierce undergrowth. He led them on a secret route through a grove of young cover trees, then navigated a maze created by a snarl of nettle plants oozing with poisonous ichor.

"Even without a trail we're traveling much faster than Thor

and I did on our way to Cliffton," Bellor told Drake.

Thor grimaced. "We would have covered more ground if we'd stayed on that trail."

We might have been dead if something was following us. Drake flashed Thor a sideways glance while slicing through a knotted vine that bristled with hair-like fibers. Careful to avoid the tiny spines, he raised his arm and cut another, then a dozen more. He paused when faced with a hedge of nettle bushes, and touched his ear as he listened to the sounds of the Thornclaw. The dwarves listened along with him. He guessed they had no idea he had stopped to rest his arm, not listen to the forest.

"I don't hear anything." Thor shrugged.

Drake's arm felt better after a moment, and he found a way past the nettles, picking a course where he didn't have to use his Kierka very much.

An hour later, the camouflaged entrance to a stand of towering cover trees beckoned. "There, a good place to rest." Drake sighed with relief at the sight of the refuge inside cage-like trees whose sharp, peppery fragrance filled the air.

Thor wrinkled his nose. "At least this stink keeps the bugs away."

After cutting back newly grown barbs, Drake gestured to the once-hidden thorn-door and led the dwarves into the shelter where wooden benches had been constructed. He checked for thorn-snakes and fever-ants, finding only the remains of a dead snake, with telltale bite marks from wild watchkats that had feasted on the serpent.

"You come here often?" Bellor asked.

"My father camps here a lot. There's good hunting nearby." Drake tried to keep his face impassive. He hoped they didn't suspect the last time he'd been this far from Cliffton was when he'd been fourteen—which was why he'd taken so long to find it.

The dwarves ducked inside the protected dome and slumped onto the benches. Drake joined them and dug into his pouch, popping his favorite snack into his mouth: slices of dried vrelk heart. The rich meat renewed his tired muscles. Bellor offered Drake a fresh biscuit from his pack and the young man accepted, offering the dwarf a leathery yet tender piece of dried meat.

"No, thank you." Bellor sipped from his water skin, then used a thin charcoal stick to write small angular letters into a leather-bound journal. Thor napped, laying his head on his shield while Bellor scribbled away.

A flight of thorn shrikes perched upon a nearby branch, staining it with their droppings. They spied on Drake with their beady eyes and chirruped until their high-pitched calls made him grind his teeth together. He wanted to shut them up, especially when they stretched their hideous wings, flaunting their demonic origins. He found himself wondering how many he could hit with a slender hunting quarrel and recalled his record: three with one shot. But he had no need to fletch new bolts with their feathers or take their meat to feed his dogs. Glancing between the birds and his two companions, he thought, *There's too many aevians—and dwarves—on the plateaus.*

The shrikes darted away, perhaps sensing his animosity. A dozen staerlings soon landed in the same place, adding their own white markings to the branch. Shaking his head, he understood perfectly why his ancestors called the plateaus *Ae'leron,* or "Winged Place" in the old tongue. Sighing, Drake recognized that the aevians—and the dwarves—were here to stay. *But I'll never like it.*

Bellor's weary eyes fixed upon their guide. "My friend, I have something important to tell you."

What now?

"Please forgive me for not sharing this news back in Cliffton." Bellor bowed his head. "Before we go any further, we have to talk about what I didn't want known by everyone in your village."

Drake gave him his full attention.

"We've heard your surname before. Bloodstone is a strong earth name, and is not common among Nexans." Bellor paused, appearing to ponder his next words. "Your father mentioned that Rigg Bloodstone is your cousin."

Drake rocked backwards. "Rigg?! He's like a brother."

Thor's eyes shot open.

"How do you know about Rigg?"

"We learned of him when we were in Nexus City." Bellor took a deep breath. "Before we began our journey into the forest. Rigg sold my people some Drobin artifacts he acquired near Armstead: a clan ring and some religious documents pertaining to our missing kin. We're certain he got them from the lost mine we call Quarzaak."

"Quar-zaak?" Drake squinted at Bellor. "That's the place we're searching for?"

Thor sat up. "Our kin chose that name."

Bellor asked, "So you know Rigg very well?"

"He's a little older, but we've hunted together a few times since we were young. My uncle Sandon brought his family and some other Armsteaders to Cliffton for the Moon Festivals. I haven't seen Rigg in over two years. You say you met him in Nexus City?"

Bellor tugged on his beard. "Actually, we never met him. Thor and I didn't conduct the temple business when the artifacts were purchased. Others handled the . . . negotiations."

"He shouldn't have haggled." Thor folded his arms. "He should have taken the original price."

"About Rigg. . . ." Bellor sighed. "I don't know how close you were. . . ."

Drake leaned forward. "He was like a brother. What do you know of him?"

"This may be a shock to you." Bellor's dire tone made Drake's jaw clench. "Rigg Bloodstone . . . is dead."

Drake felt as if a cloak drenched with freezing rainwater had spread over his entire body. "You tell me this now?!"

Bellor's eyes filled with remorse. "I apologize for not telling you earlier. We decided it was best to let you know after we'd left your village."

"Best?" Disbelief and anger contorted Drake's face.

"I'm very troubled to tell you of his passing." Bellor frowned. "I know his loss is a great blow."

"He can't be dead." Drake shook his head.

"Rigg was . . . murdered," Bellor said.

"Stabbed in the back," Thor blurted, "by hired killers."

Bellor shot a fiery glance at Thor.

Drake balled his fists.

"Rigg was on his way to the Temple of Lorak when he died," Bellor said. "He had already sold us artifacts belonging to our kin, and was going to provide information about where and how he recovered the items."

"How could religious papers and a clan ring get him killed?" *They're lying.* Drake touched the bloodstone on his belt.

"The ring and records were valuable." Bellor shifted on the shade-clover.

"Hired killers? Why? He was just a hunter from the Thorn-claw."

"He was in trouble with the smugglers' market." Thor almost smirked. "Criminals he cheated may have hired the men to kill him."

He couldn't have been a criminal. Impossible! Drake turned away.

"I'm sorry." Bellor moved his hand near the young man's

shoulder, hesitated, then didn't touch him. "I wanted to tell you earlier. Please forgive my hesitation at revealing this."

"Who killed him? Tell me."

"We don't know for certain," Bellor admitted. "Perhaps another buyer who wanted the items and information for themselves. A Drobin mine could be very profitable."

They're not telling me something. Drake kept his hand on his belt. "So you don't actually know who had him killed or why?"

"We don't." Bellor averted his eyes. "The smugglers who knew him denied hiring the assassins."

"They're criminals," Thor said. "They were lying."

"They blamed his murder on someone else," Bellor said. "Someone they didn't know—or wouldn't talk about—who they claimed was responsible."

Probably a gold-hungry Drobin merchant had Rigg killed. He's dead because of them and their greed. The slices of dried vrelk hearts Drake had eaten churned in his gut. He turned away from the dwarves and swallowed the bile that rose in his throat. Tears squeezed out of his eyes and his nose filled with mucus. The acrid taste in his mouth almost made him retch. His face reddened and he decided he couldn't be around the dwarves in such a state.

Shouldering his pack, he stepped out of the thorn-door and stared into the woods. A draught from his waterskin only dulled the bitter taste. He wanted to turn back, head for Cliffton, but his promise to guide the dwarves stopped him.

Bellor stood in the thorn-door, sad eyes aimed at the ground.

Drake imitated his father's hard trail-voice. "We should go, now. Armstead is still three days away." Hacking at the forest with vicious chops, he swung much harder than he needed to as vengeful thoughts sliced through his grief-stricken mind. *They're lying! Damn the Drobin. They probably killed Rigg themselves because he asked a high price for their treasures. Curse them! Maybe*

Laetham's right. Get rid of them at Blue Creek. Cliffton needs me. Jaena needs me and damn Laetham.

A sour burning filled Drake's mouth and he knew he tasted the need for revenge. *What else haven't they told me?* He remembered Thor's words, "He shouldn't have haggled." *Vrelk-shit! His life was worth ten times their worthless artifacts and I know why they told me. It was a warning. If I don't obey them, Thor will kill me too. I won't be the first human he's slain. No. I won't let it happen. They won't get me like they killed Rigg.* Laetham's words whispered in Drake's ears. "Get rid of them at Blue Creek, then come back home." A grim smile spread across Drake's face as tears stung his eyes.

XVIII

How much innocent blood stains my soul? How many young warriors have been slain while serving under my protection? Too many. I pray for the lives of Thor and Drake, but I fear something horrible may happen. Should I have told him about his murdered kinsman so soon?

—Bellor Fardelver, from the Thornclaw Journal

Bellor watched the Clifftoner's ferocious hacking as the Thornclaw was decimated by his onslaught. The War Priest directed Thor to follow at a safe distance while Drake savaged any plants that dared to get in his way. Green sap flowed from the wounded foliage as a rare daytime rain shower fell from the sky. Bellor imagined the forest was crying in pain. He sensed a darkness in the young man that had appeared in the gate tunnel, when Bellor had felt the presence of a hostile spirit.

"Bellor?" Thor whispered in Drobin. "He knows some of it now."

The War Priest nodded.

"You're not going to tell him any more, are you?"

"Of course not." Bellor shook his head. "It's better for him not to know. The Sacred Duty has fallen to us. He's just a young human with a different path. I'm not going to burden him with anything else, or recruit him to our cause. He's our guide, and with Lorak's blessings he'll help lead us to Quarzaak. Then his job is done, and we'll continue on our own."

"Good, I don't trust humans, especially ones who use the weapons of our enemies."

"Just pray we find Quarzaak and our kin alive. We can't do this alone." Bellor turned his gaze to Drake, who continued his merciless attack on the forest. *Did I tell him too soon? Great Lorak forgive me if I have made a terrible mistake.*

Hours later, Bellor heard the dull whoosh of running water in the distance as the late-afternoon sunlight filtered through the trees.

"Blue Creek." The young hunter glanced over his shoulder at Bellor, but avoided looking at Thor. "We'll soon be on a trail again. The shortcut is nearly over."

Bellor sensed Drake's anguish. His hard expression was a false front. *He blames us for Rigg's death.*

"A trail!" Thor gave a hearty laugh and distracted Bellor.

The three travelers dropped onto the dry edge of the riverbed. Dense brush and low arching trees broken by smooth, moss-covered boulders stretched east and west. Patches of sweet-smelling flowers and the buzz of insects added to the music of the water. Thor darted ahead and emerged onto a tunnel-like animal trail that ran parallel to the creek. He lifted his fists in the air and chortled with glee as he stood on the heavily overgrown path choked with thick vines and multitudes of ferns. Thor shrugged. "It doesn't look much like a trail, but thank Lorak."

"Follow me closely." Their guide stepped in front of Thor. "Walk where I walk. I'll lead."

Bellor observed how Drake marched east on the up-sloping ground while dodging the countless vines hanging over them.

"We'll follow it upstream to Armstead?" Bellor asked, moving past Thor.

Drake nodded as Bellor stayed a step behind the Clifftoner, who directed him to avoid a mass of low-hanging vines, even though he could almost walk under them.

Thor knelt at the water's edge, wetting his face and hands in the icy cold water. "Ahh! Invigorating." He splashed the water on his hairy cheeks several times and washed the twigs and dust from his beard. "Bellor, it's melt-water. Cold as the tip of a mountain's breast."

"Come on," Bellor called backwards, shaking his head at Thor's vulgar sense of humor while watching his companion wring the freezing water from his beard.

"I'm coming." Thor jogged to catch up and got tangled in a bunch of thorny vines.

"Thor, hurry up you hammer-dropper," Bellor taunted, "we haven't got time to—"

The heap of rope-like vines wrapped themselves around Thor's neck and body, squeezing him as if a dozen snakes had locked him in their green coils.

Drake darted past Bellor, his raised Kierka knife aimed at Thor's throat. Bellor gasped in horror as the blade arced toward Thor's neck while the vines held his friend tight, preventing him from lifting his shield to deflect the blow.

Bellor stood stunned by the human's hideous betrayal as Thor sucked in his last breath before meeting Lorak. The War Priest wanted to shout, throw himself in the path of the blade. All he could think was that Thor would be the eighth son in the Hargrim family slain by the weapon of the *Kierkaan*.

Raising his battleaxe in both hands, Bellor charged at Drake, readying a blow that would chop the treacherous human's spine in half.

Drake slashed over Thor's head, cutting a few vines away from the helpless dwarf. Bellor realized that the man had missed. The ropy vines pulled Thor off the ground lifting him by his neck and arms. The green stalks slithered over Thor, stifling his yelp as several of the tendrils curled around his neck, choking him.

"Don't struggle!" Drake shouted.

Bellor altered his axe-swing at the last possible moment, avoiding landing a maiming blow on Drake's back. The young human grabbed Thor's belt with one hand and slashed again at the constricting vines above the dwarf's head. The Kierka blade sliced through the plants until the vines released Thor from their deadly grasp.

The struggling dwarf fell hard to the ground with the severed, oozing vines still wrapped around his neck. Drake swung at more tendrils dropping to attack as Thor lay on his belly, gasping for air.

Bellor sprang forward, grabbed one of Thor's feet and dragged his friend away. Drake held off the writhing strands of the flesh-craving plant, backing away only when the dwarves were clear.

Bellor pulled Thor to his feet and they scurried away as fast as they could. They dashed up the trail and away from any low-hanging vines. Drake joined them, stopping a good distance from where the Thornclaw had attacked. Thor breathed hard as he unwound the vines from his throat, arms, and waist.

"What in the name of Lorak were those?" Bellor asked, sensing a change in Drake. It was as if the young human had cast off the darkness lingering within him.

"Constrictor vines." The Clifftoner surveyed the spot where they'd halted to catch their breath.

"They're not a myth." Bellor stared back.

"I wish they were." Drake scanned above them again. "It's good that I got to Thor before they pulled him into the trees. His struggling made them squeeze harder, and we would have never been able to free him." Drake glared at Thor and said in an angry tone, "I told you to follow closely. This is the Deep Thornclaw, not some orchard in Nexus City. I'm your guide and when I tell you to follow closely, do it."

"Praise Lorak for you." Bellor grinned and patted Drake on the back. Thor tried to catch his breath and examined his hands, which were spotted with blood. Bellor noticed Thor bleeding from a dozen puncture sites where the prickly vines had pierced his neck, face, and arms.

"I thought you were going to kill me"—Thor sucked in breath—"when I saw the *Kierkaan* coming toward my . . . head. Then you cut the vines . . . freed me. I can't believe a human saved my life with a Giergun weapon. How humiliating."

Bellor laughed and touched Thor's shoulder. "Ironic, my friend, not humiliating. Drake has honored you. You're alive. There's no shame in that."

Thor wrinkled his nose at Bellor. The bleeding dwarf turned to the young hunter with a serious expression. "I want you to know, Drake Bloodstone, that I, Thor Hargrim—" He slammed his fist to his mail-covered chest. "—pledge my hammer and friendship to you. We Drobin always repay our debts of honor . . . even to humans." The dwarf's toothy smile appeared behind his blood-speckled beard as he reached out and grasped Drake's forearm. "I've never had an honor debt to someone as tall as you before."

Grinning back, Drake matched him with a smile of his own.

"Do you hurt much?" Bellor asked.

"Of course not." Thor laughed. "I was a Champion in the Drobin army. It'll take more than a plant to kill me."

Drake asked, "Or do you feel—"

"I'm fine." Thor wiped his hands on his legs, then followed Bellor's lead and knelt to pray.

Bellor knelt and touched the ground with both hands praying silently. "Thank you, Great Lorak, for showing me the truth before I made a horrendous mistake. I would've lost them both, and so many have died while under my protection. I thank you for sparing Thor and Drake on this day.

"I also pray for the spirits of my dead . . . students . . . who have so recently entered your halls. I have shamed myself by failing them. Please give me the wisdom to keep this last one alive. Thor must carry on when I'm gone. I plead with you to give me the time, and Thor the desire, to finish his studies of Healing, Rune, and Earth magic so that he may become a War Priest in your service. It may fall on Thor to rebuild the *Dracken Viergur,* as I fear the vision I had of the battle between Bölak and Draglûne means that Bölak is dead, along with all his warriors. Please grant me the wisdom to follow the path before me and carry out my Sacred Duty." Bellor glanced up as Thor knelt beside him, looking more groggy than pious. "Thor, what's wrong?"

"I'm tired." Thor's eyes glazed over and he tilted forward, slack faced and eyes fluttering.

Drake sprang to Thor's side and supported his shoulders. "It's the constrictor vines. I didn't think—didn't know—if their poison would affect him since he was freed so quickly."

"Poison?" Bellor touched Thor's neck, examining the wounds from the thorny vines.

"Why didn't you say so before?" Thor almost slurred his words.

"I tried." Drake held Thor's shoulders. "It should pass."

"Are you certain?" Bellor scrutinized Drake's body language for any sign of doubt. The young man shook his head as uncertainty masked the Clifftoner's face. Bellor's heart sank.

Thor's eyes closed. Bellor slapped the lethargic dwarf across the face and shook him. "Thor! Wake up, you hammer-dropping oaf! Don't make me cut off your scraggly beard!"

Thor's eyelids fluttered open, "Not my beard, you old clump of. . . ." His eyes closed and he mumbled something incoherent.

"I can't lose him." Bellor's eyes pleaded.

"Over here, quick!" Drake dragged Thor toward the edge of Blue Creek.

"What're you doing?" Bellor tried to stop him and grabbed unsuccessfully at Thor's boots.

"The water will revive him. My Father said to never let someone sleep after constrictor vine venom has entered their blood or they may not. . . ."

Wake up, Bellor thought, as Drake reached the creek side and dunked Thor's upper body in the frigid water. Thor emerged gasping for breath, his eyes flew open and he flailed his arms.

"It's working," Bellor shouted. "Dunk him again!"

"We have to keep him awake." Drake dipped Thor's head in the water and roused him again.

They each took turns watching for griffins or plunging Thor into the water during the next hour. Each time Thor nearly fell asleep, they would dunk him into the creek.

"I'm awake! I'm awake!" Thor's teeth chattered together and he gasped for air. "I swear on my beard, the poison has worn off."

"Are you certain?" Bellor examined Thor's wide eyes.

"Yes." Thor pushed him away. "I wish you would have used the *zeitströmen*."

Bellor shook his head. "You'll be fine without it."

Drake winkled his face. *"Zeitströmen?"*

Bellor raised an eyebrow. "The *zeitströmen* is what we manipulate to use Healing magic. *Zeitströmen* means timestream."

"Timestream?" The young man's eyebrows came together.

"When either Thor or I use the Healing magic—"

"You both have it? Thor's a Priest?"

"No, no." Bellor shook his head smiling. "Thor's not a practicing War Priest. Not yet. He won't commit himself to the final ceremonies or training, though the last fifty years have taught him much."

"Too much." Thor rolled his eyes.

"We've delayed here long enough." Their guide stood up and motioned for them to follow. "If griffins are about, they would've heard us."

Bellor prodded Thor, and helped him stand. The weakened dwarf walked up the trail, then into the thick woods away from the creek where they searched for a campsite. As they picked their way through the trees, Drake said, "I still don't know what you mean by timestream."

Bellor smiled. "You see, Lorak has given Thor and I the gift of His most powerful blessing: Earth, Rune, and Healing magic."

"I've seen Healing magic before," the man said.

"Priestess Whitestar's Healing magic is similar." Bellor nodded, supporting Thor as he walked. "But Amaryllian magic is different. Thor and I channel the power from Lorak Himself."

Thor snorted. "Your Priestess must use *trees*."

Drake let a large frond snap into Thor's face. "You Drobin are strange folk to think so poorly of trees."

"Strange folk? Us?" Thor pushed away the plant, mouth hanging open in shock. "Your kin live in this terrible forest. Lorak didn't intend for civilized folk to live in places like this."

Bellor let go of Thor, who had to lean against a tree to keep himself upright. The War Priest shook his head. "There's a place for Earth and Tree magic. However, the magic Priestess Liana uses is not the same as the kind we use. Her abilities are limited by the tree she touches, whereas Lorak's magic has no such limitations. We touch the ground itself and draw from the entire plateau around us. We've no need to search for a tree. There is no place in Ae'leron devoid of earth or stone. Trees are another matter."

Resting his hand on an ironbark tree, Drake asked, "What does the timestream have to do with all this?"

Bellor rubbed his chin. "Only those who have touched the *zeitströmen* understand entirely. But know this: the timestream is all around us. It's like a great river carrying us all toward the future, always moving forward. However, when Thor or I use the Healing magic of Lorak, we change the flow of the timestream around the person we're healing. We move the person's physical body in the opposite direction of the timestream. We convince the person's spirit to return to the moment before they were injured.

"We guide them to the healthy state they were in during the moment before they were first hurt. As we touch the timestream we're caught up in its flow and risk getting swept away. Whenever we touch the timestream . . . we age quickly." Bellor touched his graying beard. "We sacrifice months or years of our own lives to use the magic. If we make a mistake, we can lose decades in a mere moment."

"Decades?" The young man leaned against the tree.

Bellor nodded, stared at Thor. "It can be very bad when the injured party was hurt more than a few moments in the past, but when a comrade lies dying at your feet you would do anything to save them, especially if you knew your own life depended on them surviving."

Drake asked, "Must you always touch the ground?"

"Yes, Thor and I must touch untainted earth or stone."

"Untainted?"

"The stone and earth of Ae'leron are blessed by Lorak, since He created the plateaus." Bellor grinned. "Lorak's essence can pass through the earth anywhere we go. We aren't limited by the availability of trees. Though there are rare places that have been corrupted, and Lorak's Healing magic cannot pass. That is, of course, until the place has been cleansed."

"What taints the earth?" Drake glanced back.

Bellor grabbed the Clifftoner's arm and looked him in the

face. "Wicked and murderous creatures—like dragons—can taint the ground with their dark essence. If they stay in a place long enough, they corrupt the land around them, making it impossible for us to contact Lorak or use His Healing magic. Dragons are the worst spawn of the Void. They must all be killed."

XIX

The land tries to kill us, but we will never turn back.

—Bölak Blackhammer, from the Lost Journal

Orange flames danced upon the small red stone in the center of their camp. Shadows cast by the flickering amber light played across the trunks of massive ironbark trees. Drake imagined the dark shapes were cloaked figures of men surrounding his cousin Rigg in an alley in Nexus City. The shadows grew taller, closed in, then stabbed him to death. The glow from the conjured flame hurt his eyes, making them water. *I should have been watching his back.* He rubbed away the accumulating moisture before the drops ran down his face. He tried not to let either of the dwarves see him wipe his cheeks.

Thor lay nearby, exhausted from the constrictor vine poison, while Bellor paced around the camp, inspecting the thorn bushes protecting them on three sides and gazing into the night. The older dwarf mumbled some kind of prayers as he passed behind the fire, causing hulking shadows to appear on the tree trunks, distorting his rounded features.

Drake chastised himself for even considering Laetham's vile idea of letting the dwarves die at Blue Creek. The venerable Priest had a good heart. There was no way he could have been involved in Rigg's murder. But what weren't they telling him?

"Something is down by the creek," Bellor whispered as he peered into the night.

"We shouldn't have had a fire." The young man looked away from the flame, thinking how stupid he was to allow one. His father never would have.

"Maybe it's just a vrelk?" Thor sat up. "Or a griffin."

There were vrelk migrating north. Big herds. Meaning that flights of griffins, manticores, and maybe even wyverns would be close by.

"*Löshun*," the War Priest whispered and the rune-flame sputtered out. "We could do worse than griffins." He and Thor shared a knowing look, making Drake suspicious once again.

"It's not that cold tonight, is it?" Thor got to his knees with an effort.

Bellor shook his head, told Thor to stop talking with a curt hand signal.

The whole exchange confused Drake. He glanced at the curdle-moss he had put all around the camp. It would mask their smell, though all the talking could draw in a flight of griffins.

Crunching sounds came from the direction of the creek. Drake made the hand sign for griffins—a fist with three fingers hooked like talons. Bellor reached for his axe as the Clifftoner spanned his crossbow as quietly as he could. As the lathe flexed back, it creaked like a bending branch. The latch clicked as the string locked in place.

Scratching and thrashing sounds carried from inside the creek bed. Something trampled through the bushes, slowly at first, then picked up speed.

Thor stood up gripping his shield. Drake aimed his crossbow forward.

"Will the warding hold?" Thor asked.

"I don't know." Bellor lifted his axe.

A large creature broke into a run and headed directly for their camp. Drake's finger touched the trigger when two huge, slobbering beasts crashed through the bushes. The pair entered the camp with jaws wide open.

The Drobin raised their weapons, ready to spill the blood of the monsters. The creatures avoided the dwarves, leaped straight at Drake. Stunned, he couldn't avoid their jump as they drove him to the ground and started licking his face and whining with glee. The two bullmastiffs yelped and pawed him, their foot-long tails wagging furiously.

Fighting back onto his knees, Drake hugged his dogs as they pressed their large heads and wrinkled faces into his. He wrestled with them, opening the saddle-packs strapped to their backs and fed them pieces of dried vrelk. They stopped whining and licking him as they chewed the food.

Picking burrs and thorns from their coats, Drake checked for injuries on their footpads. "Jep, Temus. Sit." They obeyed his command and stared at him with their tails pounding the ground, raising little clouds of dust. "Guard." The bullmastiffs looked around and sniffed the campsite inundated by pungent curdle-moss.

Jep smelled Thor, who fumed the entire time the big dog investigated him.

"*Stûnkenmutt.*" The dwarf glared at Jep and pushed away his wet nose. Jep backed off and sneezed in Thor's direction. The angry dwarf wiped the dog's moisture from his shield. "Stay away from me." Grumbling, he raised a fist. Jep didn't move and at one hundred thirty pounds, the massive bullmastiff would be a good match for Thor.

Jep canted his head to one side in apparent confusion and stared at Thor with his soft brown eyes. Temus didn't investigate the camp much and sat near Drake, while Jep sniffed around Bellor and Thor.

"Thor, Bellor, they can take over the watch."

"I suppose you trained them?" Thor eyed the young man.

"They're the best guard dogs in Cliffton. What's this, boy?" Drake asked Temus as he reached for the little wooden tube tucked into the dog's saddle-pack. He undid the leather string and freed the tube before opening it. He pulled out a tiny piece of tanned hide with a few black letters drawn on it in charcoal. A lump rose in Drake's throat as he read the note aloud, "It says: 'To guard the family.' It's signed, 'Father.' " Love for his father overcame him and his chest ached. Smiling, he remembered their last conversation at the gate and what his father had told him: *You are the family.*

Drake realized how much his father really did love him and hugged his dogs, burying his face in their short furry coats. After petting the dogs for several minutes, he pulled out a small wad of netting from his pack and strung it between two trees.

"What are you doing?" Thor asked.

"Putting up my hammock." The Clifftoner tied the strings around the notches he'd made in the trees so it wouldn't slide down during the night. "You two don't sleep on the ground, do you?"

"Of course we do." Bellor smoothed the patch of dirt he had cleared. "The ground is sacred."

Shaking his head, Drake climbed into the hammock and wondered how they had made it all the way to Cliffton without being eaten alive by fever ants. The dogs stalked around the camp, their frowning black faces scanning the forest with their ears pricked up at sounds of the night.

Thor leaned against a tree, still glowering at the dogs. Fascinated with Thor, Jep and Temus both stared at him. Jep kept ambling over and sniffing at Thor's boots or licking his shield. Drake watched the dwarf shoo the dog away repeatedly until sleep overcame him.

At sunrise, Drake awakened to see Jep curled up next to Thor.

The dwarf had his arm over the animal's chest and the two slept together like newborn puppies. Bellor woke up and the War Priest's muffled laugh woke Thor, who quickly roused himself and rolled away from the dog.

Drake grinned. "Thor, it looks like you made peace with Jep."

Thor pointed to Jep and then his own chest. "Your dog and me have an agreement, that's all. I won't slobber on him and he won't slobber on me."

Holding in his laughter, Drake wondered if dog slobber would rust Thor's shield.

After a quick breakfast, the company of five followed the Blue Creek trail toward Armstead. The young hunter taught the dwarves how to recognize the occasional masses of constrictor vines dangling across the path. Most of the vines were empty, but they saw the desiccated bodies of two thistle deer hanging in the flesh-craving plants, which had pulled the animals high into the canopy where only foolish scavengers would dare to look for a meal.

An hour into the march a swarm of bloodsucking flies began feasting on the companions. Drake slapped at the tiny aevians and told Bellor, "These flies are coming against the wind to get us. Strange."

"Maybe they like the smell of dog." Thor swiped at the bugs on Jep's head. Both dogs snapped at the air, trying to bite the insects landing all over them.

Pressing ahead to escape the cloud of hook flies, Drake noticed a dozen surikats heading downstream along the bank. He knew something had spooked them, and hoped it was nothing more than a rival mob of watchkats that had chased them away. He said nothing to the dwarves, but paid extra attention to the sounds of the forest as they marched into the rising foothills of the Wind Walker Mountains. Small waterfalls and a few pools filled with silvery fish drew their attention. Eventually the creek disappeared into a deep channel carved through the hills. Drake heard it flowing, and dared standing at the steep, crumbling edge for a look down.

Jep and Temus both paused and their ears pricked up. The dogs retreated back and nuzzled against Drake. "What is it, boys?" The dogs stared at him then looked forward and whined, their ears standing up.

"What's got them spooked?" Thor scanned the trees around them.

"I don't know, but Armstead is that way." Drake pointed ahead and went with the dogs on his heels. The dwarves followed them up the slope as a tremendous buzzing drifted from the next rise. The droning became louder with each passing step and Drake wanted to turn back, though his building curiosity compelled him to keep going. He crested the next hill and froze in horror.

Tens of thousands of flying red fever ants hovered in the air above the creek and darted under the canopy in buzzing clouds. Millions more wingless ants formed a thick carpet of finger-long segmented bodies as they swarmed on the south bank of the creek and across the connected branches that met over the water channel.

The reason for the colossal mustering was an uncounted multitude of big, black, hairy spiders clashing with them in the canopy and on the web bridges spanning the creek. Spider drones as big as a man's hand crossed the creek on web bridges or in the tree branches above. Paralyzed, Drake watched the endless struggle waged by Ae'leron's two most powerful bugs as their war for supremacy on the plateaus unfolded in front of him. Skin itching, he imagined bugs creeping down his back. "We better get out of here. One ant bite and we could get the red fever."

"It's the death-spiders I'm worried about." Thor scratched his arms.

Backing up, Drake said, "We'll have to cross the creek and circle south."

Bellor and Thor jogged after their guide as a swarm of flying ants buzzed toward them. Drake ducked and swatted an ant that landed on his neck. A death-spider drone dropped from above and landed on his pack.

"Hold." Thor grabbed Drake and with a quick blow crushed the arachnid with his hammer. The dead bug fell to the ground and Thor finished the job with his boot.

"Thank you." Drake smiled.

"You have enough pets already." Thor laughed. "Now find us another way."

Drake headed south, listening to the calls of the thorn shrikes as they entered the sparse trees at the edge of the grasslands. Their agitated, high-pitched trills made him pause, but he didn't hear the shrieking sounds they would make if griffins stalked the woods.

"Is it safe?" Bellor asked.

"No." Drake searched the canopy for holes. "This is griffin country."

"Bug country is worse." Thor rubbed the Kierka scar on his neck and scratched his arms.

"We'll travel along here"—Drake motioned forward—"and follow the edge for a while."

"How much will this detour slow us down?" the War Priest asked.

"Finding a way across Blue Creek put us back a couple of hours. We should still arrive in Armstead about two days from now, after sundown."

"Fine, as long as we arrive." Bellor followed Drake and Temus. Thor brought up the rear with Jep at his side. Temus pointed his short stubby nose into the grasslands and raised his ears. Jep darted to his brother's side and his ears pricked up. Both dogs gazed south.

Following the dogs' signal, Drake stared into the grassy plains. A dozen vrelk galloped into view as they sped across the open ground. The dogs looked at their pack leader, their faces begging for permission to race after the large six-legged beasts. "No. Stay."

Jep whined, pleading to chase the brown vrelk cows led by a bull with ten-point antlers. The massive specimens, taller at their muscled shoulders than the tops of the dwarves' heads, sprinted toward the forest, unaware of the companions. The vrelks' hooves pounded the ground, their thousand pounds of bulk flattening the grass as they thundered along.

The bull vrelk led the way, his six legs, three on each side equally spaced apart, powering him forward with his harem trailing behind. Drake thought about the short hunts near Cliff-ton and the scores of vrelk he had killed with his crossbow. He stared in awe as the small herd galloped in the open trying to quickly cross the favored hunting grounds of the griffins.

The vrelk pranced into the trees, their yellow-tan rumps disappearing into the shady forest. The crashing sounds of the herd continued for a few moments longer, but faded until only the excited bullmastiffs could hear them moving.

"Beautiful animals. Just seeing them makes me hungry for dinner." Thor ate a handful of slices of dried vrelk hearts and gave a few to each of the dogs.

Later that night, in a sheltered camp, Drake opened his pack to find something to eat.

"Here, I've made plenty of stew for us all. I'm afraid I don't have any salt for it." Bellor offered the young hunter a full bowl of the steaming liquid.

"Thank you. Oh, I think I put some salt in my pack." Drake

dug inside the big pocket and rooted around.

"All it needs are a few pinches." Bellor grinned. "Though I've already put some good Drobin spices into it already."

The Clifftoner pulled out a pouch of salt and closed his backpack. He ate the stew, which had an odd earthy flavor. He recalled one of Laetham's stories about Drobin putting fine sand or powdered minerals in their food and thought, *Bellor wouldn't put dirt into the stew, would he?* Drake shook his head and finished the hot meal without complaint, vowing silently to do the cooking the next night.

Thor picked a piece of meat out of his teeth and wiped his beard. "The meat your family gave us softens well."

"One more night in the woods and we'll be in Armstead. Then we can have some nice ribs or a juicy vrelk roast at . . . my uncle Sandon's house." The thought of having to tell his aunt and uncle about Rigg suddenly made him queasy.

"Is vrelk all you humans eat?" Thor slumped to the ground and patted his belly.

Lacing his fingers under his head and trying not to think about Rigg, Drake said, "It's good meat. What else are we going to eat out here, birds? Aevians are only fit for dogs." He rubbed Temus on the head. "And that's only when there's nothing else. Right boy?"

Temus snuffled and wagged his tail.

"I was wondering." Bellor looked up. "Do you think your family knows anything about our missing kin?"

"I don't know." Drake shrugged. He wondered about the kind of bond Bellor and Thor had with their long-absent family. His curiosity nagged at him and he decided to find out if he could pierce their wall of secrecy. "You two have come a long way to find your relatives."

After a moment Bellor said, "We have."

Thor sipped his tea as if he hadn't heard the question.

After another lengthy pause, Drake asked, "Were you both close to them?"

"A long time ago," Bellor said, "especially to the warrior who led them."

"Will you tell me about him?" Drake asked.

Thor's eyes asked Bellor permission to tell their inquisitive guide. The old dwarf nodded.

"They were led by my uncle," Thor said, "the great warrior, Master Bölak Blackhammer."

"Why have you risked so much for him?" Drake asked.

"We have taken no risks that he would not take for us if we were missing," Bellor said. "He would never stop searching for us. Bölak would give his life for either of us and we will gladly give ours for him."

The genuineness of Bellor's words made Drake reconsider the hateful words he'd heard about Drobin his entire life.

"Family is very important to us," Bellor said, "and Bölak Blackhammer is family to us both. He's my first cousin and Thor is his only living nephew. We're both close to the heart of the Blackhammer clan. Thor and I are second cousins. Master Bölak is our esteemed kin, and he traces his lineage from the ruling Blackhammer family. Thor and I are honor bound to find him and the others with him."

"My mother," Thor said, "the Honored Sister of Lorak, Daerna Blackhammer, was his only surviving sibling. I honor her by searching for my uncle, one of the bravest and most famous warriors our folk have ever known. She would've wanted me to find him."

"His trail has been difficult to follow," the War Priest said.

"He didn't leave word about where he was going?" Drake asked.

"My nephew," Bellor frowned, "liked to go his own way. When he left Nexus City forty years ago, he kept his destination a secret." Bellor yawned and lay back.

Drake considered asking them more, but he sensed they would disclose nothing else. He put his head down on his pack and pulled his cloak over himself to sleep. Temus rested beside Drake and the two of them stared at Jep and Thor, who snored in exactly the same rhythm.

As he drifted off to sleep, the young man wondered if Thor's missing uncle was still alive, hidden for over forty years in the Wind Walker Mountains. More likely Bölak was dead, his bones bleached white in a nest of griffins.

XX

How I long for the safe stone halls of home.
                    —Bölak Blackhammer, from the Lost Journal

"Where's Armstead from here?" Thor asked as he stood atop a hill looking at the Wind Walker Mountains before them. The steep slopes displayed the green of springtime.

Drake gestured to the snowcapped peaks in the distance. "Armstead lays at the mountain's foot, by a lake. We should be there before sundown tomorrow."

"Splendid," Bellor said as a cool breeze stirred his beard.

The companions hiked through the forest near the edge of the grasslands, always keeping under cover and watching for aevian predators.

"Bellor, do you know where the mine is?" Drake asked.

The dwarf stepped closer to his guide. "Quarzaak is south of Armstead. The records Rigg recovered described the mine as being five days south, in a canyon with a fast-flowing river. Do you know of such a place?"

"Why didn't you tell me before?" The young man turned away from Bellor.

"I didn't believe there was a need until we got closer to Armstead." The old dwarf shrugged.

"Do you know of a river?" Thor asked.

"The Boulder River is two days south of Armstead," Drake said, "and it comes out of a steep canyon. My father and grandfather hunted by it with my uncle Sandon and Rigg."

"Good, I wonder what your uncle can tell us about Rigg's discovery," Bellor said. "We learned so little about it before he was slain."

Drake tried not to think about his cousin and found himself wishing he could talk to Jaena. He ached for her, and wondered when he would see her again. He rested his hand on Jep's neck and the dog licked him. *At least the dogs are with me.*

"Drake?" Bellor asked, his tone grave.

"Yes."

"I want you to know that we won't tell your kin about the possibility of Rigg associating with criminals in Nexus City." Bellor touched the mountain-shaped Lorakian amulet around his neck. "Especially when we have no proof."

"Thank you, Bellor."

"Regardless of who Rigg associated with," the War Priest said, "he provided us with valuable artifacts, and we're most thankful for his efforts. If it wasn't for your cousin, we wouldn't be here."

Neither would I. Drake's stomach knotted up. *I'd be marrying Jaena.* He suddenly resented that Rigg had found the mine, starting the chain of events that took him away from Cliffton.

A distant rumbling echoed from the grassy plains. Thousands of vrelk emerged from the dusty horizon in brown waves of bobbing antlers and thumping hooves. They trotted toward the edge of the forest, keeping up a steady pace as they crossed the open grasslands. The sight of so many animals left Drake's mouth gaping open as he stared at the vast ranks.

Observing the speed of the herd, Drake reasoned that the vrelk would reach the forest after he and his companions had gotten clear of their migration route. "Come on." He led them forward at a brisk pace, making for a ridge that would become the far edge of the vrelks' path.

A pinpoint flash of fire, followed by a pillar of smoke, caught Drake's attention as it erupted at the rear of the herd where the rising dust cloud obscured the sky. Before he could think about the source of the flames the mass of vrelk reacted to the strange event behind them. The animals nearest the flames and smoke galloped at maximum speed. Fear spread to the rest of the herd and panic drove the animals forward in a mad dash.

The sound grew to a thunderous roar as the six-legged vrelk approached faster and faster. The terrified animals would reach the forest before the companions could get clear.

"There're so many of them." Thor stared in wide-eyed shock as he jogged along.

"We can't stay here." Drake scanned the forest for a place to take refuge. "We've got to get further ahead or the vrelk will trample us! Run!" He sprinted for the ridge, with the dwarves trailing behind, and looked back to realize that his short-legged friends were falling back and would never make it to the higher ground. He thought about climbing a tree, but couldn't think of a way to save the dogs too. Then Drake spotted a nearby mound of rock. "This way!" His voice barely carried over the din of the impending rampage closing in on them.

The animals leading the main herd penetrated the tree line as the stampeding mass of vrelk entered the forest and charged toward the companions. A deafening wave of thunder filled the forest and drowned out all other noise.

Sharp hooves splintered wood and crushed bushes as the vrelk surged forward. Drake reached the rocky hill and pushed his dogs up the steep face. The dwarves climbed up the rock with surprising ease. He scrambled after them as scores of vrelk stampeded around the base of the rock.

Dust and the musky smell of the herd filled the air as Drake knelt atop the rocky hill and beheld a sea of pointed antlers. Bellor coughed and rubbed his tired legs as the animals rumbled past on either side.

"Let's hope they don't block our way for too long." Thor crouched beside Drake.

The dogs whined and the young man feared they would leap off the rock as they nearly went mad with excitement. "No. Stay. Sit!" He grabbed Jep's collar as the dog bounced up and down, barking and yelping. "*Stay.*" Drake glared at the willful dog and watched as the thundering herd filed past in their uncounted thousands.

As the rear of the herd trundled by, pushing against the vrelk in front of them, he saw fear in their eyes. He smelled the rank odor of burned vrelk hair, but didn't see any marks on the animals. The Clifftoner turned to Bellor, preparing to study his reaction carefully. "There was a burst of fire on the plain that caused the stampede."

Bellor's face remained impassive. "It could have been a brush fire."

The dwarf's denial rang hollow, and Drake's intuition told him Bellor had seen it too. "It wasn't a brush fire." The young man pointed his finger at Bellor. "There wasn't any lightning to set one off, and the grass is still damp from the rains. It's as if someone caused the stampede to try and kill us. Or should I say, the two of you?"

Bellor shrugged and worry lines appeared on Thor's forehead. Neither of the Drobin said anything more. Drake gritted his teeth as he fumed over their denials.

The dust started to settle more than an hour later, leaving the companions covered in a layer of brown grit. They still perched upon their rocky refuge until all but a few of the stragglers had departed. "Time to go." Drake climbed down and the dogs followed, sniffing the fragrant ground that the passing herd had left in its wake. Jep and Temus wasted no time adding scent markings of their own.

"Ahh, *gak!*" Thor examined his boot smeared with fresh vrelk droppings.

Hiding a smirk, Drake led them forward and found the pummeled ground easy going, save for the piles of spoor. As they neared the ridge two dozen vrelk straggled across the grasslands toward the woods. Noticing how slow the animals ran, he realized all of them were injured. Most of them limped along without the use of all their legs.

The piercing scream of a vrelk a few dozen paces away made Drake whirl around. The afternoon sun partially blinded him as he spotted a lone, golden-winged griffin pouncing on a vrelk. White feathers covered the giant eagle head of the aevian demon, revealing its gender. *Females never hunt alone.*

The griffiness pressed her huge, lionlike haunches onto the vrelk and pinned it to the ground. A pair of giant eagle claws dug into the struggling vrelk's body as the creature severed the terrified animal's windpipe with her hooked beak, sending a splash of blood across her beak and white feathery head. Drake estimated the creature's wingspan to be at least nine paces from tip to tip, and her weight to be about seven hundred pounds.

Three more female griffins descended out of the sky and pounced on other straggling vrelk, crushing them with the momentum of boulders dropped from a cliff, shrieking with pleasure as they landed.

Jep let out one loud bark and Temus growled from the back of his throat as the predators savaged their prey. The largest griffiness looked up from her kill as blood dripped off her beak.

"*Quiet.*" Drake silenced the dogs and whispered to the dwarves, "We must leave now. She thinks we're after her kill, but above all, do not run while they can see us."

Folding her wings, the griffiness stepped into the forest, glaring at the five small creatures in the shady woods. Her long, lionlike tail came erect and her penetrating yellow eyes never left them.

Using his crossbow's front stirrup, Drake cocked his weapon before he and the dwarves backed away. He slipped in a bolt and aimed at the advancing beast. Drake froze in place when she let out a piercing shriek. *A direct challenge.* The other three female hunters abandoned their maimed and half-dead vrelk, two of which still struggled and tried to run, despite their broken bodies. The three others stalked into the woods, following their leader.

"Back up slowly," Drake whispered, as he began to retreat. The female griffins advanced one step at a time. "Watch the leader's tail. It'll twitch three times before she charges."

Bellor and Thor loaded their own crossbows as they backed up. The War Priest's lips moved offering a silent prayer.

Drake made eye contact with the lead griffiness as she lowered her head. He could faintly smell the coppery vrelk blood on the wind and the musky odor of the griffiness. The young hunter steadied his crossbow. He couldn't get the correct angle for a heart or lung shot. Her blood-spattered head blocked his aim. Stepping back carefully, Drake glanced around for any kind of refuge. *The ridge won't save us. Nowhere to hide and one shot is all I'll get. I've no chance with a Kierka knife.*

The tail of the griffiness twitched to the side. Once . . . twice.

Drake aimed at her left eye, his finger tensed on the trigger.

A dying bull vrelk launched itself forward as its six legs powered it off the ground one last time. Antlers pierced one of the trailing griffinesses' flanks and she roared in pain. The punctured aevian whirled around and slashed the dying vrelk with her talons.

The leader and the other griffins turned toward their sister, distracted by the commotion.

"Run." Drake fled into the forest with Thor, Bellor, and the dogs trailing behind. They all disappeared into the trees and Drake hoped that the griffins would not come after them.

The companions walked for another hour, then camped atop a green foothill. A lone cover tree planted by Gavin Bloodstone protected the old campsite from aevians or rain. The commanding view from the hillock gave them a clear look at the southern plains and the endless expanse of the Thornclaw Forest to the north. The white-topped mountains in the west reflected the light of the setting sun, which plunged into the Void on the eastern horizon.

The high vantage point allowed Drake to see a small, blackened area in the grasslands where he'd first spotted the fire. The great distance prevented him from gaining any clues as to its cause. He felt sure the dwarves knew something.

Woof, Temus barked, distracting Drake from his frustrating thoughts. The dog ate the second crow Drake had shot for him. Jep slept next to his brother with a full stomach, black feathers spread all around him.

"We'll reach Armstead tomorrow?" Thor's lips puckered as he drank Drobin tea from his tin cup.

"Before sundown, if all goes well." He scratched Temus' head as the dog chewed.

"If we stay out here too much longer," Thor gulped his rest of his tea, "our luck will run out."

"We could've been killed twice today." Bellor lay down, shaking his head. "Drake, we owe you and that vrelk a debt of honor."

The Clifftoner rolled his eyes, wanting to say, *If you owe me an honor debt, why don't you stop keeping secrets?* All he managed to say was, "If that wounded vrelk had known how many of its cousins I've shot, it probably would've let the griffiness kill me."

XXI

Signs and omens are the future whispering back to us.
—Priestess Liana Whitestar, passage from the Goddess
Scrolls

In the predawn darkness, Drake reached for Jaena's hand as they floated on a warm breeze high above the forest. The silvery moon rose behind her as it climbed above the mountains. Her skin and hair glowed with a golden radiance and her eyes sparkled like blue stars. Their hands came closer together, but something tugged at Drake's spirit, pulling him away from his beloved. Struggling to reach her, he stretched for Jaena's hand, suddenly realizing they both flew above the trees, gliding on the air with translucent wings that sprouted from each of their backs.

Face contorting in horror, Drake realized he was actually flying, a supreme violation of Amaryllian law. As if to punish him for the profane transgression, a tremor of force rattled through him, pushing him farther away from Jaena. Sorrow colored her smile as the distance between them grew. She faded to nothingness. Without her presence he plummeted downward, the forbidden wings abandoning him.

Drake startled awake under the cover tree as the land beneath him shook, making his hammock sway. *The tremor in my dream.* He peered through the branches at the massive, pockmarked, gray moon floating over the mountains and filling the sky. There was no sign of Jaena as another tremor shook the earth. The trembling cover tree released a smattering of leaves that drifted downward in a faint breeze. The dwarves sat up as the rolling tremor subsided.

Jaena's image filled his mind as Drake looked at Bellor and Thor, who both knelt in prayer with their palms pressed to the rocky soil in their camp atop the hill. When Bellor opened his eyes Drake said, "We have tremors here often, especially when the moon is rising."

Bellor smiled. "Lorak has reminded us that we walk across His earth. I've sensed the ground trembling since we entered these foothills."

"You have?" Drake rubbed the sleep from his eyes.

The War Priest wavered his hand slightly. "Not enough that you would detect, but as an Earth Priest I've been taught to be sensitive to Lorak's messages."

Lying back, Drake watched the moon dominate the mountains, making them look small as it rose ahead of the sun. "Jaena told me the moon calls to the plateaus. And that the land rises to meet the heavens."

"There's truth to that." Bellor took out his journal and a charcoal stick from the pouch on his belt. "The great stone moon is Lorak's creation. The plateaus rise at His call to meet the moon, as your Jaena has said." Bellor scribbled in his journal, then looked up. "The tremor was a good omen. The Mountain Lord resides in the land, and when His spirit arouses, the earth trembles. Lorak has arisen to watch over us."

Or he's sent us a warning. Drake remembered Jaena's glowing spirit being pulled away from him right before they touched.

Like the teeth of a gargantuan predator, the sharp, triangular peaks of the Wind Walker Mountains jutted toward the moon. White clouds blended into the snowcaps as they passed over the range of towering stone. Drake kept a watch on the gray moon as it traveled across the wavering blue sky during their march up the steep slopes of the forested hills.

Thor gazed into the distance as they reached the top of the highlands. "The peaks remind me of home."

Huffing and puffing, Bellor crawled to the top of the ridge. "Is this . . . the top?"

"Yes." The Clifftoner helped the old dwarf to his feet and tried not to acknowledge the burning pain in his own legs.

"Thank Lorak." Bellor let out an exhausted sigh as he surveyed the endless green expanse of the Thornclaw Forest below them.

Standing atop the limestone step-cliffs that guarded the approach to the Wind Walker Mountains, Drake thought, *Ethan and I should've seen this five years ago. At last I see it for us both.* His gaze followed the narrow ribbon canyon cut by Blue Creek that they had followed for most of the day. He tried to trace it all the way to the edge of the Void, but the treetops blocked his view after a few miles. He turned around to inspect the beginnings of Steam Valley, and saw the trail and the loose canopy formed by the branches of gnarlpine, needle-leaf, and brush-blossom trees.

"We shouldn't linger in the open." Drake scanned the sky and the dogs stopped sniffing the trail.

"I'm ready." Thor adjusted the straps on his pack, which bulged with his and most of Bellor's heaviest supplies.

Bellor stood up straight and slapped his legs as if trying to bring them to life. "Lead on then, Drake, before I roll off this edge."

The rocky path to Armstead snaked through the forest passing under the squat gnarlwood trees, their knotted branches twisted together as if wrestling for dominance. Drake guided the dwarves over the well-marked trail, hewn by axes in some places. They left the path when he sensed better protection along a different course. His short detours always led them back to the trail where they passed only two young cover trees, planted by the Armsteaders sometime after Drake's birth. He directed the dwarves to rest for short periods in both small refuges as he kept watch for mountain griffins.

Half an hour before sunset, Drake beheld the palisade walls of Armstead. Cleared ground separated the green-capped village from the alpine forest. Scores of cover trees grew in rings around a central tree near the shores of Cinder Lake. A log wall with sharpened points augmented the cover tree barrier that protected Armstead. An empty moat surrounded the village, giving additional protection from predators, fires, or flash floods. The narrow drawbridge beyond the earthen ditch was tight against the gatehouse.

"It's a bit like Cliffton," Thor said, "except for the mountains." The monolithic spires of stone loomed over the village. Rays of fading sunlight reflected off the tips of the peaks while the rest of the land lay cloaked in dusky shadows.

"My great uncle, Garrek Bloodstone, and a group of veterans from the Giergun War built Armstead a little after Cliffton was settled." *I wish I could've met Uncle Garrek.*

Next to the trail, Drake found a dusty wooden hailing horn dangling on a tree branch. He blew a bold greeting call and waited. A pack of guard dogs began barking immediately. "Show yourself!" A man challenged them from the gatehouse.

The Clifftoner picked up a dry tree limb to serve as a peace branch and scanned the sky before striding into the open and waving the branch above his head. With the dogs at his heels and the dwarves close behind he yelled, "Hail Armsteaders! I am Drake Bloodstone of Cliffton, and I bring two companions and greetings from my village."

Two crossbowmen appeared in the tower windows above the

gate. "Hurry! We'll watch the sky as you cross!" Spurred by the urgency in the man's voice, Drake dropped the peace branch and led the companions as they hustled across the open ground. The narrow wooden drawbridge lowered to meet them and Drake jogged across it and into the shadowy tunnel, which reeked of dogs. Eight female bullmastiffs growled from the back of the tunnel as a man with a short black beard held the pack at bay with the long handle of his axe and an outstretched arm rippling with corded muscle. Drake restrained Jep and Temus with a pointed finger. Both dogs tensed their bodies and raised their ears, smelling the scent of the females.

Stepping forward, the young man noticed the murder holes in the walls and ceiling. Bellor and Thor carefully examined the slits where defenders could shoot quarrels or thrust spears at anyone inside the tunnel.

"May the sky be clear." Drake raised his face, where he spotted two crossbows aimed at the dwarves. He wondered why three men guarded the gate. Something was very wrong.

"May the sky be clear." The black-bearded man's eyes didn't leave Drake. "It's been a while since I visited Cliffton, Drake Bloodstone. I almost thought you were Rigg."

A sharp pang of grief stung Drake's cheeks as he recalled his physical resemblance to his cousin.

"Elder Kovan." He strode forward and shook forearms with the man who reminded him of his father.

"Who are these two in your party?" Kovan glanced at Bellor and Thor.

"These Drobin are under Cliffton's protection. Priestess Whitestar and the Elder Council asked me to lead them here."

Kovan gave the dwarves a hard look. "Liana sent you with them?"

Drake nodded.

Kovan's shoulders relaxed a bit, though he didn't put down his axe.

Bellor opened his hands to the sky. "Greetings, Elder Kovan. I am Bellor Fardelver. Thank you for opening your gate to us humble servants of the Mountain God. My companion, Thor Hargrim, and I come in peace."

Thor tipped his head while holding his shield in front of his chest.

Kovan looked them up and down for a long moment. He shifted his axe to his other hand before resting it against the wall. Opening his palms to the dwarves, Kovan mirrored Bellor's peace gesture. "If the grandson of Gavin Bloodstone says you have the protection of Cliffton . . . I'm willing to offer you the protection of Armstead as well. You are all welcome here."

Unseen hands rapidly winched up the drawbridge and clamped it shut behind them. Kovan held his dogs in check as the companions exited the foul-smelling gate tunnel and walked into a small cover tree arbor. The peppery odor of the domed tree made Drake think of home, though the scent had a different quality than the trees of Cliffton.

Carrying his axe once again, Kovan flashed a subtle hand signal—stay alert—to the men in the gate tower. The Elder said, "I'm on watch until morning, but I'll take you to your uncle's house. Sandon and Tabitha will be pleased to see you—as well as a few others."

Drake barely heard what he said as he tried to figure out what had happened in their village.

"How are the skies over Cliffton? Have you seen any aevians?" Kovan asked.

"A few." Drake made certain the dwarves didn't see as he formed a hook with his index finger, flashing the wyvern-sign before poking his index finger against his heart to tell Elder Kovan it had been killed.

"Is your grandfather well?"

"The Priestess keeps him well taken care of," Drake said as he memorized the route away from the gate, noting that Armstead's entrance trails were far less complex than the mazelike ones in Cliffton. He also noticed the lack of shade-clover on the path and guessed that the elevation and winter snow prevented it from growing.

"All your folk are well?" Kovan's eyes lingered on the Clifftoner as he watched carefully for a reply.

"Yes." Drake heard the concern in Kovan's voice, the question within the question. Uncle Sandon would have to tell him what was wrong.

Sheltered cover tree homes appeared in the shadows. Kovan led them past the structures, which had arboreums constructed in the same manner as Cliffton's. Bullmastiffs barked from inside their yards and watchkats called out alarms.

A handful of Armsteaders stood in their thorn-doors to see who had entered the town so late in the day. An old woman gasped when she saw the dwarves. Most people stared harshly as they watched Bellor and Thor march through their village. The cold response in Cliffton seemed almost welcoming compared to Armstead.

"Here's your uncle's home." Kovan gestured ahead.

A pretty young woman with brownish-blond hair, light-blue eyes, and a beaming smile stood in the thorn-door of the cover tree across from Uncle Sandon's house. She ran out and hugged Drake tight. She whispered in his ear, her voice sultry, "Still handsome as ever, aren't you?"

Kovan cleared his throat. She pulled away from the hug, her alluring eyes never leaving Drake's.

The skinny and forward little girl he'd met during the Moon Festival in Cliffton two years ago had become a beautifully proportioned . . . *woman*. Drake couldn't stop himself from staring at her feminine features, which had bloomed since their last meeting. "Sherissa? Is that you?"

"Of course." She rubbed her lips together.

Three little girls who reminded Drake of what could have been Sherissa at various stages of her childhood scampered up behind her. "I've grown up since my father took me to Cliffton. I knew you'd remember me." She giggled with her little sisters, causing her lush, round breasts to draw his attention again. "You're not married yet, are you?" The little girls behind Sherissa held their breath with anticipation.

"Still as forward as I remember." Drake averted his gaze.

"*Sherissa.*" Embarrassment mixed with anger altered Kovan's expression.

"Well, are you?" Sherissa asked.

When he shook his head no, the little girls jumped up and down and chattered back and forth.

"Told you so!"

"See, he came for her!"

"Does he have a marriage branch?"

"Why can't I marry him?"

"Woodskull, he's for Sheri. You're too little."

"Be quiet, girls." Sherissa grabbed their shoulders and smiled at Drake. "I'm glad you came. I've waited for you for two years. It's so good to see you again."

With his eyes, Drake begged Kovan to help him escape.

"Leave him alone, Sheri. He's had a long journey. Get your sisters inside, it's getting dark and I have to get back to my watch."

"Yes, Father." Sherissa stepped closer, her eyes boring into Drake. "I'll see you in the morning?"

"No, we'll be leaving early." Drake shook his head, thought his grin must look ridiculous.

Sherissa pushed her hair away from her chest. "Don't leave

too early. You look like you need to *rest.*"

"Get in that house!" Kovan ordered Sherissa and her sisters, pointing with his axe. Drake obeyed as well, scurrying away from the young woman and toward his uncle's thorn-door.

Kovan caught up to the companions, a pained expression on his face.

"She's seventeen?" Drake asked.

"Turned this month." Kovan nodded.

"Not married or spoken for?"

"Not yet." Kovan sighed. "She still talks about you and Rigg. None of the young hunters here are good enough for her, though they all seem to want her for a wife. You being here with *them* won't help matters."

Drake remembered the festival in Cliffton when fifteen-year-old Sherissa had followed him and Rigg around everywhere like a lost puppy. He shook his head as a gang of hunters gathered outside the thorn-door, many touching their knives and scowling. Drake hoped that leaving Armstead by sunrise would be soon enough.

XXII

Truth. Why does it hurt so much when I find it? Innocence is its own truth.

—Bölak Blackhammer, from the Lost Journal

A sturdy new door of freshly cured wood from the heart of an ironbark tree opened before Drake and his companions. Firelight flickered through the doorway and the shuttered windows of the two-story house, which sat under the arches of a squat cover tree. The smell of roasted meat wafted into the pepper-scented yard. He expected a vigorous Uncle Sandon and his dogs to burst out of the house. Instead, a lean, weathered man with a noticeable limp hobbled onto the porch and peered through the twilight. The man's stubbled jaw and the dark circles under his eyes made the Clifftoner stop and stare.

The man rocked back when their eyes met. "Who's there?"

Drake wondered the same thing. He heard fear—or perhaps hope—in the man's voice. He knew it had to be his uncle Sandon, but what had happened? Who was this thin, pale, crippled man? "Uncle Sandon, hello, it's me, Drake."

"Drake?" His uncle squinted, locking onto the young man's face. "I thought you were. . . ."

He thought I was Rigg. He hoped I was Rigg. Drake smiled as best he could and stepped forward.

"What a surprise. Welcome to Armstead. I haven't seen you

in over two years. You've changed. I never thought you'd leave . . . I mean, I didn't think you could spare so much time away from Cliffton. Good to see you."

"Good to see you, Uncle." Drake shook forearms and felt soft flesh where there had once been solid muscle. "Our family in Cliffton send their greetings, and my father said he's sorry for not visiting."

"It's not an easy trip." Sandon smiled.

"These are my friends." Drake gestured to the dwarves. "I've guided them from Cliffton."

The muscles around Uncle Sandon's left eye trembled and his spine stiffened as he gaped at the dwarves. Drake wondered if his uncle suspected the dwarves brought tidings about Rigg and forgot to introduce them.

Sandon bowed his head to Bellor and Thor graciously. "I'm Sandon Bloodstone, pleased to meet you. This house has always been open to Drobin. Please, come in."

"Thank you, Master Bloodstone. Let me introduce myself, I'm Bellor Fardelver, humble servant of Lorak. I'm honored to meet you. This is Thor Hargrim."

Sandon ushered them into the hearth-room and waved to Kovan. "Have a good watch, Elder."

The guardian nodded as Sandon put a thick bar on the door and limped in after his guests. Drake noticed Jep and Temus sniffing at the floor by the doorway. "Uncle, what happened to your knee?"

"It's not bad." Sandon grinned with lips that were thin and colorless.

What's happening here? Dazed, Drake muddled through greetings and introductions between the dwarves; plump Aunt Tabitha who he met for the first time; cousin Janek, fifteen winters old with scraggly brown hair; and tiny cousin Ellie, twelve, though appearing much younger.

"We were just about to sit down to eat." Aunt Tabitha herded them toward the table and hugged Drake, a tense smile pasted onto her face. "I'm so glad you came. We've plenty for all and I've made a roast and seasoned it with some onion Ellie and I picked today. And I've got a spiceberry pie!"

Aunt Tabitha and Ellie served the flame-roasted meat with brown bread, boiled beans, and fresh goat milk. The dwarves accepted Tabitha's offer of salt for the juicy vrelk slices heaped upon their wooden plates.

The Bloodstones and the two Drobin consumed their food as they all followed the Nexan hospitality custom of not mentioning ill news until after the meal. Except for compliments about Aunt Tabitha's cooking, and praise for Uncle Sandon's fine home, few words passed across the table. Drake felt the dread hidden behind the faces of his aunt, uncle, and young cousins.

Janek ate only a few bites and took his food to Jep and Temus, who lay on the floor out of sight of the table. Wondering about Sandon's missing dogs, Drake ate a piece of spiceberry pie, which the dwarves declined, much to Aunt Tabitha's surprise. Ellie cleared the plates, Janek returned, and Drake shifted on the hard bench, wishing for a way to avoid the upcoming conversation.

"Tell me, nephew," Sandon spoke bravely, "what brings you"—his voice wavered—"all here?"

Drake glanced at Bellor, who had already volunteered to break the news of Rigg's death as they had trod the path to Armstead. The War Priest had said: "I have told families of their son's passing many times before. Too many times."

All eyes turned to Drake and blood rushed to his face. His cousins and Aunt Tabitha braced themselves for terrible news.

"How did you meet these two fine Drobin?" Sandon's question sounded like a retreat, as if the poor man already knew the truth.

"I was in Cliffton's watch tower when I saw a vortex of mist." He met his uncle's weary gaze.

"A bad omen," Aunt Tabitha mumbled. "Cliffton is too close to the Void."

The dwarves nodded in agreement, then Drake told of his search for little Neven and the aevian sighting at the garden. He didn't speak of his decision to ask Jaena to be his wife, instead skipping to the moment when he saw the dwarves and shot the wyvern. Unsure of what to say next, he looked at Bellor who took over the tale and described Drake volunteering to be their guide. He avoided mention of the reason why they wanted to come to Armstead and finally the War Priest withdrew his sacred symbol of Lorak, which had hung hidden around his neck, tucked behind his armor.

Bellor wrapped his stubby fingers around the pendant, a small sharp-peaked mountain crafted of bright silver. "Master Bloodstone"—Bellor touched the symbol to his heart—"I thank you for inviting us into your home so warmly, and you, Lady Bloodstone, for the fine meal. I know we Drobin are not welcome in these lands. Thank you very much for your hospitality. I must tell you that Thor and I are here because of your son, Rigg."

Janek and Ellie sat rigid, paralyzed by Bellor's words. Tabitha and Sandon grabbed each other's hands and both paled, faces tightening.

"Please forgive us," Bellor continued, "for not telling you the moment we arrived. We meant no disrespect and wanted to follow the hospitality customs of your people."

Sandon's lips trembled. "We haven't heard from Rigg since he left for Nexus City eighteen months ago."

"He's been gone so long." Tabitha's face wrinkled.

"Rigg did make it to Nexus City." Bellor pressed his lips together. "The Temple of Lorak was grateful to purchase some Drobin artifacts he recovered near here."

"Yes." Sandon leaned forward. "He found the Drobin mine, Quarzaak, south of here, in Red Canyon. He brought back a gold ring, some papers, and a small fortune in gold nuggets."

Bellor sighed. "I have some very bad news to tell you . . . about Rigg."

Sandon's shoulders sagged.

"He was a brave man," Bellor said, "and faced many dangers to bring us valuable and sacred relics to our temple. My people are eternally grateful for his courageous journey to return the Drobin artifacts. Sadly, he was ambushed on his way to a second meeting with my brethren. I'm very sorry, but he was slain."

The family gasped and tears flowed from Aunt Tabitha's eyes.

"We gave him a hero's burial in the cemetery behind the Temple of Lorak in Nexus City." Bellor touched Tabitha's hand. "I carved him a headstone in white marble myself. It reads, 'Honor to Rigg Bloodstone, finder of the lost relics of Quarzaak. May Lorak watch over his spirit.' "

The stricken look on Aunt Tabitha's face and the tears streaming down her cheeks made Drake turn away. Sandon rocked back in his chair, then stood up awkwardly, favoring his bad knee. He wrapped his arms around his sobbing wife. "I knew it," Sandon whispered as grief settled over the room like a cloud of choking smoke. Janek and Ellie turned to Drake for confirmation of their brother's death.

Nodding at them, the cold hand of grief squeezed his chest without mercy. Suppressing his own tears, Drake thought about Ethan and Rigg, knowing all too well how his cousins felt. *I've lost two who I would call brothers.*

Holding his wife, who buried her face in his gaunt chest, Sandon said, "I knew my son was in grave danger when he left. I've been preparing for this . . . moment. At least we finally know what happened to him." The gray-haired man choked back a sob. "How did he die?"

"He was struck from behind," Bellor said, "it was over quickly."

"I wish Rigg had never found that place." Sandon shook his head. "I blame myself. I'm the one who told him the stories of Quarzaak. Rigg brought a curse down on himself for taking those things. When he first returned home, he said there was something following him. I would have never let him leave if I'd known where he was going."

"What followed him?" Bellor asked.

Sandon stared at the old dwarf. "Manlike demons wanted the treasure returned. After Rigg had already left for Nexus, they came here looking for him. Two tall, winged creatures with the heads of bulls and cloven hooves smashed in the door."

"Wingataurs." Thor sat up straight.

"Wingataurs?" Sandon shrugged.

"They have the blood of dragons in them," Bellor said, "and are a cross between a minotaur-demon and a true dragon."

"Whatever they were, they wanted the treasure Rigg took," Sandon said. "They broke through our front door in the middle of the night and killed all three of our dogs."

That's why I didn't see his dogs. Drake leaned back to see Jep and Temus lying by the new door. He saw faint stains on the wooden floor and realized they were from dogs' blood.

Sandon's hands shook as he raised his arms like he held a crossbow. "I shot one of the demons. My bolt pierced its neck, but it didn't die. It bared its teeth at me and pulled out the shaft."

Sandon buried his head in his hands as the memory took hold of him. "It forced its mind into my own, prying into my very soul for the whereabouts of Rigg. It learned of the ring and the golden nuggets Rigg had taken from Quarzaak. But it didn't care about them. It just wanted to know what he had done with the book and papers."

Bellor clutched his pendant, his knuckles going white.

"It grabbed my leg, twisting it while pulling me down the stairs." His injured knee trembled and Sandon plopped down next to his wife as his knee buckled.

Drake's face burned with rage as he thought about his uncle being dragged through his own home. He imagined his mother or Jaena enduring the same fate in Cliffton because he wasn't there to protect them.

"It violated and tormented me as it searched my memories . . . and when the demon found out what it wanted—" Sandon clutched his knee, obviously in pain.

Ellie started to cry and Janek put his arm around his little sister.

"My mind was numb and my body paralyzed." Sandon rubbed his eyes. "The treasure it sought wasn't here. I thank Amaryllis the rest of my family wasn't hurt or tortured like I was."

Face trembling with rage, Drake inhaled slowly, his hand clenching around the handle of his Kierka knife. Sandon's face quivered and became even more pale. His wife reached out and held his hand as he said, "I'm afraid to sleep. The monster is still in my mind . . . reading my thoughts . . . and tormenting me." He collapsed against his wife.

Bellor stood up and strode to Sandon's side where he rested his hand on the man's shoulder. "I thank Lorak and Amaryllis that you're all alive. I will pray for all of you to be healed of your pain. Now I understand that Rigg's courage came from his father. All of you Bloodstones have gained the undying respect of my folk."

The War Priest handed Sandon a small white stone with a black symbol etched into it. "Carry this rune stone with you, and keep it next to your bed as you sleep. The demon will be kept from your dreams, and you'll have peace again. I promise in the name of Lorak that you'll be free of your nightmares."

Sandon nodded as he accepted the small stone. His hand stopped shaking when he held it in his fist. "I was worried about Rigg after he left." Strength and a measure of calm returned to Sandon's voice. "Ever since that day, I've had a bad feeling that's never gone away. He got himself into trouble in Red Canyon and brought it back here with him."

Bellor nodded, tugging on his beard.

"What's so important about those papers and ring anyway?" Sandon's fist pressed against the table.

Bellor sat back down across from Sandon. "The papers are religious writings, answering many questions. We seek knowledge of our kin who passed here years ago and the records from Quarzaak are great treasures our enemies wish to keep from us."

Still fuming, Drake asked, "Uncle Sandon, why has no word of these winged demons gone to Cliffton? We would have come to help hunt them down."

"Our Priestess said not to send word." Sandon shook his head. "We were afraid and didn't want to cause panic. Two aevians got past our defenses and broke into my home with ease. The only signs of their passing were hoofprints outside our door. Even the Priestess doesn't know how they bypassed the cover trees." He sighed. "Perhaps we should've told your folk, but what could you have done? They wanted Rigg, and we knew he was heading straight to Nexus City and wasn't going to stop at Cliffton."

"I'm sorry. It doesn't matter," Drake said, wishing he hadn't asked.

"We'll talk more tomorrow." Sandon breathed out a ragged breath. "My family and I would like some time alone." He barely held back tears. "There's much more to tell you. Terrible things have befallen us here in Armstead."

"I'm so very sorry for what you have lost." Bellor touched both Tabitha and Sandon's arms. "If there's anything I can do, I won't hesitate to help you. I understand how difficult it is to lose those you love."

"Thank you, Master Bellor." Sandon shook forearms with the old dwarf as Bellor's face crinkled, his eyes misting over with tears. The sorrow on Bellor's face made Drake remember the War Priest's words on their way to Armstead, *I have told families of their son's passing many times before. Too many times.*

XXIII

Why do I always seem to find myself in situations I never imagined would occur?

—Bölak Blackhammer, from the Lost Journal

Using the lantern Aunt Tabitha had given him, Drake guided the dwarves out the reinforced back door of Uncle Sandon's home. He ran his hand over the stout wood, wondered if it could stop a wingataur demon.

"Where is it, Drake?" Thor asked as they stood on the rear steps.

"What?" Drake held up the lantern to illuminate the yard shielded by the cover tree.

"The bathhouse?" Thor rolled his eyes.

"Sorry. I think it's this way." He led them around the side of the house to a small mud-brick structure built near the edge of the cover tree's ground-rooting branches. Small wisps of steam escaped from vents in the eaves of the square building.

Thor sniffed the air. "Minerals?"

"It's a hot spring." Bellor took a deep breath of air.

"How did you know?" Drake asked.

"I smelled the springs when we entered the village," Bellor said. "Your kin chose a good place to build a village and I know why the cover trees have grown quickly. The earth here is rich."

"My grandfather told me there are a dozen hot springs coming up in the village and a few cold ones." Warm, humid air turned to puffs of white vapor as Drake opened the bathhouse door. Entering the dark steamy room, he gazed at the sunken pool of clear hot water over a bed of smooth gravel. He noticed the water coming up from the ground and escaping out a hole in the far wall. Crude stone steps ran down into the shallow pool, which appeared to be as deep as Drake's waist. He lit several candles positioned near the doorway. "Now you can see better."

"The dark is no hindrance to us." Thor shrugged as he stripped off his armor and clothing.

"Sorry." Drake finished lighting the candles for his own benefit. "I'm not thinking tonight."

"You're tired, and it's been a difficult day for all of us." Bellor put his chain-mail hauberk with Thor's outside the humid bathhouse. Drake noticed both of them taking off necklaces, which had the sacred mountain symbol of Lorak hanging from them.

The dwarves waded into the pool and then submerged themselves completely, their beards floating in front of them before vanishing under the hot water. Drake followed, sighing as his sore legs relaxed. His skin tingled all over from the minerals and the three of them had ample room to move about and relax. They floated for a bit before taking turns sitting by the outlet drain and washing with harsh soap that cleansed the trail grime from their bodies.

Janek opened the door and carried in three robes, a washboard, and more soap. "Your beds are ready and you can wear these if you want to launder your clothes."

"Thank you, Janek." Drake took a washboard and scrubbed all his clothes trying to get out the dirt and sweat from the days on the trail. Thor and Bellor got out of the water and Drake's eyes widened when he saw the many battle scars on their stout, muscular bodies, which sprouted hair from everywhere except where the white lines crossed their skin. Both put on the child-sized robes, which weren't nearly broad enough in the shoulders or chest. The garments were still a little too long and dragged on the ground.

"I'll show you the loft where you'll sleep." Janek pointed to their armor. "I can carry that for you."

"If you wish," Bellor said, squeezing water from his under clothes.

Janek picked up the chain-mail shirts. "I thought they'd be much heavier."

"Drobin steel, light and strong." Thor hefted his and Bellor's weapons.

"Cousin, are you coming?" Janek asked.

"Soon." Drake floated in the water, luxuriating in the warmth for a moment longer.

"Don't tell my father I left the back door open," Janek said. "He hates that."

"I won't tell," Drake said, as Janek left with the clean and slightly water-wrinkled dwarves.

Still floating in the pool, the young man thought of home. He missed Jaena and memories of her soft lips made him wake up and imagine having her in his arms. The temperature seemed to be rising in the bath when he heard the door open again. Slipping deeper into the water he open his tired eyes. "Is that you, Janek?"

"Guess again," came a playful female voice.

Eyes popping open, Drake whirled around as Sherissa stood at the top of the stairs to the pool. She blew out the lantern and only a few flickering candles lit the steamy room. Her white linen nightgown outlined her body and the soft candlelight left little to his imagination. The cold mountain air outside had an interesting effect on her chest, and Sherissa smiled seductively when she noticed him staring. The young woman looked him over herself, apparently enjoying the view of his hard, athletic body. Too stunned to speak, Drake sank further into the water trying to cover his nakedness as Sherissa made eye contact.

"I'm so glad you're here and obviously thinking of me. I've never stopped dreaming about you. And now you arrive, less than a month after I've turned seventeen. I know you're here because of me, even if you don't. I'll be a perfect wife for you. You don't even have to ask. Once we're married you can take me back to Cliffton and we'll start our family there." She inched her linen chemise slowly off her shoulders to expose the ivory smooth skin beneath.

Drake knew it was wrong, but he yearned to see more as burning arousal took hold of him. Every part of his maleness wanted to give in to the lust building inside. Already stimulated by thoughts of Jaena, Sherissa offering of herself to him made him almost mad with excitement. She stepped forward and wet her full lips with her tongue. The filmy nightgown dipped lower, so that she was hugging it to herself by crossing her arms, leaving almost nothing to the imagination.

Seeing more of her body made his desire grow stronger. He thought of inviting her into the bath and exploring the passion he and Jaena had always resisted. A primal part of him begged to take her, while a persistent voice in the back of his mind pleaded to think of the consequences. It wasn't right. He knew it in his heart.

Drake thought of Jaena and his love for her. An act of lust might tie him to Sherissa for the rest of his life. Visions of children who looked like Sherissa's giggling little sisters flashed through his mind. He blocked out the possible future as Sherissa let her nightgown fall to the floor. He envisioned her curvaceous body pressed against his, kissing her neck—among other places—and the passion of sex with the obviously willing and beautiful girl. But it was wrong and he knew it. After a long breath his racing mind halted abruptly. He made a painfully right decision. "Sherissa . . . wait."

"Wait?" She scrunched up her pretty face. "What man would say wait when a beautiful woman comes to him like this?"

"Wait . . . I. . . ." He couldn't believe what he was saying as he fumbled for the right words. "I don't want to deceive you, Sherissa. You are beautiful, it's just. . . ."

"I know I am. I can have any man in Armstead, *or* Cliffton."

"I'll be leaving tomorrow and I didn't come here to ask—"

"Shhh. Don't say any more. I shouldn't have come to you here, now. I know the time is bad. I heard Tabitha crying a moment ago. Rigg's dead, isn't he?"

Not knowing what to say, Drake sunk deeper.

"I knew it." Sherissa wilted a little and held her head in her hands. "You're right, after our wedding is the proper time, but at least now you've seen what's waiting for you on our wedding night."

Sherissa slipped on her nightgown in a way that made Drake reconsider his refusal. That pure male part of him still wanted to invite her into the steamy water and quench the lust that was finally starting to subside. He turned away, thought of Jaena, and gathered his courage. When he turned back she sat on the bench, staring at him with a fake smile on her face that made him worry. He met her eyes and took a deep breath. "I'm sorry, Sherissa. I can't marry you."

Woodskull! A primal, angry voice inside his head screamed at him.

Surprise flashed across Sherissa's light-blue eyes, then immediately turned to anger. "It's that witch, Jaena, isn't it? She has some kind of hold on you, doesn't she?"

"Yes, I . . . no, I mean, uhhh. . . ." Drake wanted to be as kind as possible, but he had absolutely no experience to draw from. He would have preferred facing a charging griffin with his bare hands.

"What are you saying?" Sherissa's voice rippled with fury. "You must take me to Cliffton."

"I mean . . . I can't settle down. I'm not going back to Cliffton now. This is wrong, we can't . . . I've got—"

"I thought you were a man like Rigg, but you're just. . . ." A harsh guttural sound erupted from the back of Sherissa's throat. She stared at him with hatred pouring from her eyes. Tears of rage and disappointment ran down her flushed cheeks. "If you don't want me, there are plenty of *real men* who will marry me. You'll regret this."

She grabbed his clothing and the remaining robe off the wall and stormed out the door muttering, "I can't believe I was going to—"

The door slammed, bringing in a wave of cold air that blew out all the candles and chilled the room. Drake hoped the surreal encounter was over and for a moment he tried to pretend it was just a nightmare. A voice inside screamed, *It wouldn't have meant anything. You could still leave tomorrow.*

"No." Drake knew he had made the right decision. He remembered how he and Jaena had spent most of their teenage years not giving in to their primal urges. Jaena was usually the strong one who had said, "Wait."

Woodskull! The voice chastised him again as he tried to forget the whole thing. He knew he had hurt Sherissa terribly and wished he could've said things differently. Drake decided it was better to break the young girl's heart than to break Jaena's. There was only one woman he could ever really love, and Jaena would be worth the wait.

After waiting for a long time in the steamy bathhouse to be certain Sherissa had left and his family had gone to bed, Drake finally headed back into his uncle's house. Naked and embarrassed, he opened the door and shivered as the cold air slapped against his skin. Moonlight barely penetrated the thick branches of the cover tree, and at least the darkness would hide his lack of clothes.

Drake stepped into the night and something crashed into his back, slamming him to the ground. The air was crushed out of his lungs by the impact and rough hands held down his shoulders. Pinned and stunned, he heard a young man's voice filled with hatred. "If you ever touch her again I'll cut your damn throat. *Understand?*" The man pushed Drake's face into the ground and punched him in the ribs with a meaty fist. "Do you understand?"

Unable to speak because of the pain and lack of breath, Drake nodded.

"Good." The man punched him several more times on the left side, as if he was trying to break ribs. The pain came in sharp stabs that left him squirming as the knuckles dug in. He kept expecting the next blow to be from a knife. Helpless, he couldn't stop what was happening.

The attacker pressed Drake's face into the dirt. "You and your Drobin friends are not welcome here. You Bloodstones bring nothing but trouble." The man pushed off him. "Stay down." A hard kick to his crotch left Drake quivering and sucking in breath.

For a long time he lay in the cold, naked and shivering. The pain in his ribs and groin made it impossible to stand. It was as if his body had forgotten how to move. His feet and toes started to go numb. Drake managed to crawl to the back door and go inside. After a difficult climb up the steps to the loft, he laid his bruised body down and covered himself with two scratchy blankets. He couldn't stop shivering and the overwhelming sense of humiliation made him toss and turn, adding to his pain. He vowed to himself to never get caught off guard like that again. His hand closed on the handle of his Kierka knife. *Next time, I'll be ready.*

XXIV

I've almost forgotten what it feels like to fall asleep in a safe place.

—Bölak Blackhammer, from the Lost Journal

The small white rune stone lay on the table by Sandon and Tabitha's bed, its milky surface reflecting the moonlight that filtered in from a tiny window. Tears and nearly silent sobs kept them both awake as they held each other close. Eventually, Sandon and Tabitha drifted into a deep and restful sleep.

Rising from its lair in the Wind Walker Mountains, an evil spirit traversed distance and time searching for its chosen victim. Vrask approached in his ghost-body through the silver mist of the astral realm. Glowing white light surrounding the spirit of his target.

Roaring in anger, the dark soul of the wingataur demon repeatedly rammed into the shining radiance, which threw him backward every time. Repulsed and injured by the White Fire of Lorak, the evil entity fled back to his earthly form. He awoke from the astral sleep and Vrask's angry roar echoed through mocking stone halls. The lofty ceilings and lengthy tunnels absorbed his bellowing cry.

Even more enraged, the demon rose from the stone floor, his two cloven hoofs scraping against the rock as he stood. Vrask's massive fist slammed into a wall, sending chunks of stone flying in every direction. Hatred and violence consumed the bull-headed wingataur as he stomped off to find a new victim for his hate.

Vrask needed to kill.

XXV

I shall never forget the horrors of my past.
—Bellor Fardelver, from the Thornclaw Journal

Bellor jerked upright in the darkness, almost banging his head on the low ceiling of Sandon Bloodstone's loft. Lying back down, the Priest cringed as the images of crushed and blackened bodies flickered through his mind. He saw the broken limbs of the nine young dwarves, each with terror sculpted onto their dead faces. Their lips screamed silently and he couldn't bear the sight of their gaping mouths held open by the rictus of death. Curling into a tight ball, Bellor shuddered. *If only I'd prepared them better, they would have lived.*

Memories reared up in Bellor's mind. He heard the voice of the High Priest's chamberlain as they stood in Lorak's great temple in Drobin City.

"You're a fool, Bellor Fardelver. A great fool."

"But I've been summoned by the High Priest himself." Bellor pointed to the seal on the letter.

The chamberlain tossed it aside. "You can't trick me with this forgery. You've tried many ploys to gain an audience with the High Priest, but this is beneath even you. Where is your honor?"

"Do not question Master Fardelver's honor." Thor pointed at the white-bearded dwarf blocking their way. Two temple guards stepped forward, hands tightening on their axes.

"We're leaving." Bellor held his apprentice back as he retreated down the steps.

"Bellor the fool!" The chamberlain shouted, laughing with the temple guards.

Thor scowled. "I should challenge that thin-bearded coward and teach his champion a lesson for insulting your honor."

"If I wanted you to challenge anyone," Bellor kept his voice low, "I'd have left you behind where I know you'd brawl with all the other apprentices." Bellor sighed. "I do appreciate your confidence in me, Thor."

Bellor stared across Sandon's loft to where Thor slept. *Thank Lorak I didn't leave him behind or he'd be dead along with all the other Dracken Viergur.*

Lying awake and listening to Thor's breathing, Bellor wondered: *How long had it been after we left for Drobin City that my students were approached by the terrified miner?* His claim that a fledgling wyvern had taken up residence in the old coal mine on Slag Mountain could have duped even me. But why did they decide to help him on their own? *Because they followed my doctrine. Mine! They thought they could handle it because of what I taught them. Bellor the fool, indeed.*

Muffling a sob, Bellor prayed for understanding of what had happened next. All nine of the young fighters entered the abandoned mine, heavily armed and prepared to slay the wyrmkin. Not one had remained outside to guard the entrance.

Bellor thought of the evidence he found later showing that all of them were deep underground when something sparked and ignited the flammable gases within the tunnels. Fire engulfed the subterranean passageways and a great explosion blocked the entrance with tons of rock.

The plume of black dust that rose into the sky had alerted the sentries at Ridgehold, who later told Bellor about the black cloud and the miner who had spoken of the wyvern—although three days passed before he had heard the report.

The old War Priest wished he could forget the moment when he realized the tracks of his missing students led to the abandoned coal mine. Bellor coughed as if he was still choking on the black powder that had filled the air during the effort to clear away the rubble. Wringing his hands together, he could almost feel the coal grit chafing against his skin.

Six punishing days after the cave-in, Bellor, Thor and the miners had reached the remains of the nine dwarves. Five had died in the initial fire or been crushed by the collapsing tunnels. Four had been trapped under the rocks, surviving for several days before suffocating or succumbing to their grievous burns or shattered bones. Two had scraped the flesh from their fingers trying to claw their way out.

Searching for vengeance, Bellor hunted for the fledgling wyvern that had supposedly laired in the shaft and terrorized the trade road. He found nothing. The old miner who claimed he'd seen the wyvern had also disappeared and Bellor discovered that the mine had been abandoned for several years due to the dangerous gases seeping from the rock. The massive rune stones of warning had been removed. Bellor found them on a rise, over a hundred paces from the entrance, as if they had been flung uphill.

The ambush had been perfectly planned to kill Bellor's *Dracken Viergur* apprentices. The summons for him to see the High Priest had also been false, and made him seem even more of a fool to the Lorakian clergy who sneered at his final report of what had happened at the mine.

They mocked him when he told of the singular talon mark in a patch of dirt outside the entrance. Rock hid most of the track, but he knew what he saw right away. Dragon sign. He also realized the scorch marks on the rocks at the mine entrance were from a massive stream of flame entering the shaft from the outside. Not the inside as some suggested.

Dragon fire. Not an accident. It was a trap.

Tears welled up in Bellor's eyes and he wished he had trained them better. Twenty years of preparation had been nullified the instant the fiery breath of the dragon ignited the air inside the coal mine. Shadowy images of the nine burned bodies drifted in the darkness above Bellor. He prayed that his dead wife could somehow forgive him for letting all of their sons be killed, but Bellor knew he could never forgive himself.

My nine sons. I've failed you.

XXVI

Our Sacred Duty has become a force unto itself. It drives
us ever forward. Nothing will stand in our way.

—Bellor Fardelver, from the Thornclaw Journal

A wooden stair creaked in the silence as Drake descended from
the tiny loft where he had slept alone. Wrapped only in his
hunting cloak, he searched for something to wear and winced at
the pain in his ribs. Embarrassed by his lack of clothes, he
hoped to find something—anything—he could put on without
eliciting too many questions from his uncle's family. He reached
the ground floor and headed toward a closet near the entryway
when he noticed someone crouching in front of the hearth.

Aunt Tabitha stoked the embers with a poker. "Have a good
night?"

"Uhh . . . I . . . uhh. . . ."

"I found *those* scattered outside." She pointed to his missing
clothes, which hung over the back of a chair. "I think they're
dry."

"Oh, so that's where I, uhh. . . ."

"Left them?" She raised her eyebrows. "You can't fool me.
You remind me too much of Rigg, and I don't just mean your
pretty face. Rigg was always in trouble with Sherissa too. I
thought you were different."

Drake turned bright red. His ears burned and his ribs ached.

He had already decided not to tell anyone about what had happened.

Aunt Tabitha stabbed a log with the fire-poker. "Sometimes I wonder if Sherissa drove him away. I guess that girl can't resist a Bloodstone man. I hope she's married before Janek comes of age, or I fear she'll try to mount him too."

Drake had to get away. He couldn't take any more. "I'll get some more firewood." He was out the front door and into the darkness of early morning before he realized how stupid he was for not getting dressed. The mountain air was a cold slap on his bare skin. A troop of watchkats squealed at him and he thought they were laughing. He felt so foolish and wanted to bash himself over the head with the wood he picked up.

Jep and Temus bounded up to him and put their cold noses in places he didn't appreciate. "Stop it." He shooed them away and finished gathering small logs from the pile. He returned with an armful, barely able to hold the wood and keep himself covered. Drake entered the house and dropped the wood before facing Aunt Tabitha. *Please don't ask me any questions.*

"Maybe you should finish getting dressed before breakfast. I'll have food ready soon, so you can get an early start."

He tiptoed back up the stairs, almost forgetting his pile of clothes.

"*Men.*" Tabitha tossed a log on the fire and sighed.

Drake finished dressing upstairs and gathered his courage to face Aunt Tabitha. He arrived at the breakfast table with a sheepish grin and found Bellor and Thor sitting next to Uncle Sandon. The circles under Sandon's eyes seemed lighter, especially when he smiled.

"Thank you again for the rune stone, Master Bellor." Sandon took a big bite of vrelk sausage. "I haven't slept that well in a long time. No bad dreams. And I have them every night."

"It was my honor," Bellor bowed his head, "to help the father

225

of such a son."

"Thank you." Sandon smiled proudly, the sadness retreating.

"Good morning, Drake." Thor raised a cup of hot liquid to him.

Sniffing the drink, Drake detected a scent reminiscent of the hot spring out back and put it down.

Aunt Tabitha served them all large helpings of hot biscuits, vrelk sausage, and goat milk. "Eat a good breakfast, now. Before it gets cold."

Sandon took a bite of sausage, chewed once, and swallowed hard. He looked Bellor in the eyes. "I know you have a lot of questions, Master Bellor, and I still have a lot to tell you. Forgive me for speaking of such things during our meal."

"It's quite all right." Bellor bit into a biscuit.

Sandon gulped goat milk. "Disturbing things have been going on here ever since Rigg left. The Steam Valley isn't a safe place to travel, and it's gotten much worse over the last year and a half. After Rigg fled to Nexus, there was a great fire in the valley, which wouldn't be that unusual, but this one started in more than one place, almost at once."

"It wasn't lightning?" Drake asked, remembering the burst of fire on the plains. He glanced at the dwarves, who kept their expressions neutral.

"No. There wasn't a cloud in the sky. The blaze started near the entrance of Red Canyon, then the wind drove it north, following the Steam River. It burned the whole valley for three days. It was a nervous time for us Armsteaders. But thank the Goddess, the wind shifted five miles south of here. By the grace of Amaryllis the fire spared the village."

"What could've started it?" Drake asked.

Sandon sat back. "Kovan saw a dragon flying south over the Cinder Lake."

"Dragon?" Thor almost spat out his tea.

"How big?" Bellor asked, then took out his journal and prepared to take notes.

"Kovan couldn't tell exactly. Too far away."

"He's certain it was a true dragon?" Bellor asked.

"We've all seen wyverns and the like, and this wasn't a wyvern. As I was saying, the forest has been burned badly. There's very little cover left now in most of Steam Valley. Very dangerous to travel, just dead trees all over. Most of them haven't even fallen down yet, and the sky is so open. Aevians can easily see you."

Appetite gone, Drake shifted in his chair.

"It's worse, nephew. Three hunters have disappeared since the fire. Two of them, Taylon and Garent, were on the edge of Cinder Lake, fishing from the safety of the trees. We found their poles and gear, but nothing else. The whole village is in turmoil."

"Were there any signs of an attack?" Drake asked.

"We found hoof tracks like the ones the wingataur demons left outside the house. The tracks appeared right in front of them on the shore. It was as if they didn't see them coming, then landed, catching them by surprise. It was hard for me to understand how they wouldn't see them flying at them and we don't believe they came out of the lake."

"So you think they appeared and just carried them off?" Bellor looked up from writing in his journal.

"I know it sounds impossible. . . ." Sandon shrugged. "I don't understand how they didn't see them. They even had dogs with them. We found both of them dead and broken by the hunters' gear. Surely they would've seen the wingataurs coming."

"Maybe they couldn't be seen." Bellor pushed away his plate. A long silence followed as Bellor wrote more notes. Drake's meal threatened to come back up as the horrible notion of a giant wingataur demon appearing and attacking without warning sunk in.

Bellor looked up. "I've studied scrolls about wingataurs. They're ancient allies of true dragons, and have draconic blood in their veins. There are tales of sorcerer-wingataurs using magic to make themselves invisible or do worse things. From what you've said, it sounds like sorcerer-wingataurs are to blame for the disappearances, and perhaps the fires."

"What about the other missing hunter, was he ever found?" Drake asked.

"Dellen was hunting in the Steam Valley and disappeared about a week after the other two, leaving no trace. We still have no idea what happened to him."

"I fear for your village, Master Bloodstone. What your folk have gone through is terrible. Thor and I want to help, but we must know a few more things."

"Of course." Sandon nodded. "I'll tell you all I can."

"What do you know about Drobin being in this area?" Bellor asked.

"I know as much as any other man in Armstead about the Drobin who traveled through here forty years ago. I've heard all the tales and listened to all the villagers who met them. I've also spoken with those who traded with them in the years following."

"They did trade with your village, and didn't just travel through here?" Bellor asked.

"Yes, for about three years after they arrived. Some of them returned and traded mostly tin, and some silver goods in return for various supplies. My father traded with them in this very room for a silver cup. I'll show you." Sandon hobbled to a cupboard and brought out a finely wrought small cup that had tarnished black over the years and was in need of polishing. Triangular mountains like the ones looming over Armstead decorated the sides of it. "This will be used during Ellie's wedding feast, but with all that's happened, I sometimes wonder if

I'll ever see her wedding day."

"You'll see it, have faith, my friend." Bellor winked. "The rune stone will protect you. And so will we."

Drake saw hope in his uncle's grin. At that moment he knew he had to help Bellor and Thor, both for his uncle Sandon and all of Armstead.

The old dwarf carefully examined the craftsmanship of the silver cup. He passed it to Thor, who also studied it. "This was made quickly," Thor said. "The crafter didn't mark it with his clan symbol, family name, or hearth-name. It was obviously made for trading to humans."

Bellor shot his younger comrade a disapproving look. "I apologize for Thor. He meant no offense."

Thor set down the cup. "Bellor, everyone knows humans don't have the same expectations we do. It's no secret."

Bellor caressed the metal. "Master Bloodstone, do you know how to find Quarzaak?"

Sandon scratched his chin. "Your folk were very quiet about that. We always thought it was in Red Canyon because of the way they would talk about how beautiful the land where their home was. We always assumed the Drobin lived in Red Canyon."

"How many dwarves came through originally?" Bellor asked.

"Eleven or twelve when they first arrived. I don't think anyone remembers exactly how many."

Bellor wrote in his journal and both dwarves sat on the edges of their chairs.

Sandon leaned back. "They stayed a few days the first time we met them before they set off prospecting in the mountains. They found a rich mine, judging by all the metal they traded here in Armstead. Then after that first time, only a few would come at a time, heavily laden with all the goods they could carry. After two years, only one would come. It was always the dwarf called Dorlak."

"Dorlak?!" Thor sat forward, giving Sandon his full attention.

"Yes, he was a nice fellow, but could never stay long, and always said he had to get back." Sandon folded his arms.

"I see the handiwork of the great armorer and weaponsmith, Master Dorlak Silvershield, in that cup," Bellor said.

"You do?" Thor examined the cup again more carefully. "You think it's his work." The dwarf put the cup close to his eyes, scratched it with a nail, ran a finger around the edge, and even sniffed it. "It might be him. Maybe you're right."

"I'd bet my axe it was Master Dorlak," Bellor said.

"It's fine work. Quite nice, actually." Thor shrugged, still looking for some mark to identify the crafter for certain. "I'd know its maker if it were a weapon or piece of armor."

Sandon gazed at the cup. "Judging by the amount of goods Dorlak traded, the dwarves weren't making nearly as many items as when they first arrived. He would never tell us what happened to the others, though, and that mystery has been speculated about ever since Dorlak last visited Armstead. I was a little boy then.

"At first the town was overwhelmed with goods. Cups, bowls, knives, a few hatchets. They made excellent broadheads, and other things we would have had to travel for at least two weeks to trade for in the north. Metal goods were being bought right here, in the middle of nowhere. The dwarves couldn't keep up with the demand, and even though the items were rare, they always traded fairly and were honest. Then one summer, without any warning, they stopped coming.

"According to the tree marks that was approximately . . . thirty-seven years ago. We've never heard from them again and the legend of their lost mine has been with us ever since. I was only a child when they were here and don't remember them much. I'm still fascinated by the tales. I do have one memory of my father talking to a dwarf other than Dorlak. He was their leader, I think? I shook the fellow's hand. I remember his fist was very big, as big as my father's, and he had a golden ring on his finger."

Sandon looked at Thor's hand, studying the gold band on the dwarf's index finger. Drake inspected it too, noticing a shiny black warhammer embedded into the burnished gold.

Thor asked, "Do you remember if it looked like this?" He lifted his hand, displaying the ring in the morning sunlight.

Sandon looked closer, then rocked forward. "It looked exactly like yours. I'll never forget it."

"I am of the Hargrim family. My clan is Blackhammer. All members of my clan who have reached their hundredth year wear the same ring." Thor touched it to his chest, over his heart. "The inside is engraved with our hearth-names and titles. The outer side of each ring is nearly identical."

Bellor put his hand on the table and displayed his own golden ring. It appeared to be the same as Thor's, a lustrous black war-hammer embedded in a golden band.

"Show them." Bellor nodded to his apprentice, who took out another Blackhammer clan ring identical to the others.

"This band belonged to Master Dorlak Silvershield," Thor said. "I will always carry this ring. No matter his fate, he will always be remembered as one of the best crossbow-makers and weaponsmiths in the whole Blackhammer Clan. I shall never forget my time in his forge from my fiftieth to seventy-fifth years."

"Twenty-five years?" Drake's mouth hung open.

Thor nodded. "Master Dorlak is the one who taught me how to make my shield." Thor motioned at the round disc on the floor. "Long ago, after the Twelfth Giergun War."

Standing up, Bellor stared at Sandon. "Master Dorlak's ring arrived in Nexus City, carried by your son, Master Bloodstone. You met our clansmen who have disappeared two score years ago. That's little time for our folk. Over two hundred and fifty years have taught me the importance of family. There's little of mine left, and those that may be alive must be tracked down for the good of our folk. Thor and I have sworn an oath to find our kin and honor their commitments. Our Sacred Duty has become a force unto itself. It drives us ever forward. Nothing will stand in our way."

XXVII

Truth cannot be found in words, but in deeds.
—Priestess Liana Whitestar, Litany from the Goddess
Scrolls

Uncle Sandon led the way to Armstead's gate as the faint blue light of dawn filtered through the cover trees. Drake pulled his hunting cloak tight over his shoulders to fight off the lingering chill in the darkened pathways. He followed his uncle through many thorn-doors until they finally stepped into the arbor dome outside the gatehouse.

Two-dozen somber-faced hunters stood waiting for them on the ground while a few more watched from the enclosed gate tower. Most were young men. All held loaded crossbows. Jep and Temus stayed on either side of Drake, their bodies tense, sniffing the air. One of the tallest hunters, perhaps a year younger than Drake, glared at him hatefully. The Clifftoner knew it was the man who had attacked him the night before.

Sandon's smile faltered. "Good morning."

None of them responded with words, only black scowls. The oldest hunter among the group, a man with a half-ring of white hair around his bald scalp motioned to the closed gate tunnel. He pointed with a rusty and notched Kierka knife that marked him as a veteran of the Giergun War.

The message was clear: get out. Drake walked alongside his limping uncle toward the gateway, wishing Sandon could move

233

faster. The dogs and dwarves followed close behind. Sandon reached the inner door as Jep and Temus whined, sniffing the air. They were just as anxious to leave Armstead as he was.

Sandon pulled open the unbarred portal and a coppery odor overpowered the scent of dog urine inside the tunnel. Light streamed in over the lowered drawbridge, revealing the bodies of eight bullmastiffs, all dead and mangled. Three severed human heads lay beyond the slaughtered dogs in the middle of the bridge. Elder Kovan's blood-smeared face was among them. His glassy eyes stared right at Drake, his tongue lolling out from behind his purple lips. The gorge rose into Drake's throat and his head spun.

Sandon sagged against the gateway and let out a horrified groan. Drake couldn't believe it. There had been no alarm horn, no barking. Nothing. Eight dogs and three hunters massacred during the night and no one knew until the changing of the watch. Drake swallowed bitter vomit and a chill spread over his entire body.

Several breathless villagers—both men and women—burst through the thorn-doors. Many were half-dressed and all had panicked or confused expressions. Sherissa pushed her way through the crowd. Fear shone from her light-blue eyes.

"Where's my father?" The desperation in Sherissa's voice made Drake shudder. He still couldn't believe Kovan was dead. Guilt consumed him. *I never should have brought the Drobin here.*

The white-haired Armsteader had a stony expression as he glanced at Sherissa and the anxious villagers. "It's true. The night watchers are dead. All of them."

The arbor dome filled with gasps and murmurs.

"My husband?!" A young woman shrieked in horror and fell to her knees. Her cries stabbed into Drake's heart. His legs felt weak and unsteady. He could hardly draw breath and his chest ached to the fiber of the bone.

"See what you've done?" The tallest hunter pointed his crossbow at Drake. "They're dead because you came." Other villagers' faces twisted, becoming unrecognizable as madness took hold of them. They leveled their weapons at the companions.

Bellor and Thor put their backs to the gate tunnel and crouched defensively. Thor raised his shield and moved to protect Bellor.

Sandon addressed the bald veteran. "Elder Trevers, please tell your people that my nephew and his companions are not responsible for these . . . murders. It was the *demons* who attacked us." Sandon's voice trembled, his knotty hands pleaded for them to stop.

The Elder's grim expression was filled with judgment.

A stone hit Sandon in the shoulder and one struck Drake above the eye, forcing him backwards against the gatehouse. A gurgling sound made Drake glance back. A loop of rope had dropped from a window in the gate tower and landed around Bellor's neck. The noose tightened on the War Priest's throat.

"Stop!" Sandon shouted as Bellor's body lifted off the ground. Thor fended off the rope meant for him and uttering Drobin curses he tried to help Bellor. More Armsteaders took aim with their crossbows at Thor. "They came to *help* us. Don't do this. Please." Sandon shouted as the mob pressed closer.

"Kill the Drobin scum!" A hunter yelled.

Bellor's short legs kicked against nothing as he rose into the air, his face darkening as he began to suffocate. Thor held onto his legs as the War Priest tried to reach the rope over his head.

Drake drew his Kierka knife and in one lightning strike cut the rope strangling Bellor. The blade bit deeply into the wooden gate. He pulled his knife free as Bellor tumbled to the ground choking and gagging. The tallest hunter moved toward Drake. Jep and Temus immediately bared their teeth and gave low warning growls. The young Armsteader pointed his crossbow at Jep.

Drake lunged past Jep, swatting the crossbow aside with his heavy blade. The tall hunter released the missile and it streaked toward Thor. The Drobin warrior twitched his shield up at the last moment. The bolt slid along the metal and *thunked* into the gate. Another Armsteader shot a bolt as Thor threw himself on top of Bellor—who was trying to stand—and pushed the War Priest out of the way.

The tall hunter cocked a fist.

"Blayne, no!" Sandon shouted as Drake ducked a powerful blow which left the younger man vulnerable and off balance. Drake grabbed the Armsteader's big shoulder and drove his knee into Blayne's abdomen. The hunter doubled over and Drake kneed him in the face, then shoved him down. The young hunter fell to the dirt as blood coursed his broken nose.

Crossbowmen turned their weapons toward the Clifftoner. He felt the tension in their trigger fingers. All his muscles tightened, and he expected to be pierced in a dozen places.

"This is madness!" Sandon yelled.

Thor and Bellor backed into the gate tunnel pulling the dogs by their collars and eyeing the murder holes above them. "We have to go!" Bellor urged, his voice hoarse and weak.

A teenaged Armsteader targeted the dwarves. "Stop them! Kill them before they get away!"

Drake met the boy's hate-clouded eyes and understood the pain in his voice. He'd heard it in Ethan's years ago when he lost his father. Drake said, "The Drobin didn't do this! It's not their fault, don't you see?"

The boy squeezed the trigger. The bolt streaked toward the dwarves who dove out of the way. More Armsteaders aimed into the tunnel and Sandon pulled his nephew to the ground, trying to get him out of the way of the coming missiles.

"Run!" Drake shouted to the Drobin as he got free of his uncle's grasp. They had to escape, somehow get through the gatehouse and cross the open ground without getting riddled with bolts.

The dwarves picked themselves off the ground as Drake sprang toward the open gate.

Sandon stood up and waved his arms. "No, don't shoot them!"

A wooden portcullis slammed down in front of Drake, sealing off the tunnel. Clutching the crisscrossing wooden bars, he met Bellor's gaze.

"We're not leaving you." The War Priest grabbed the bars.

"No, I'll settle this," Drake said. "Take the dogs and go."

Resignation filled Bellor's eyes as the dwarves crouched under Thor's small shield. They hustled toward the drawbridge with the dogs, as hunters took up positions at the murder holes above them, ready to shoot.

Brandishing his Kierka knife, Drake turned to face over a dozen Armsteaders holding loaded crossbows. A great crash of wood rent the air. Another wooden portcullis had been dropped in front of the dwarves before they reached the drawbridge. The dwarves and the dogs were trapped.

"Kill them!" A hunter shouted.

"We will have our vengeance." Elder Trevers motioned to the men in the gate tower. "Kill the dwarves."

"This is not the way of Amaryllians!" Drake shouted. "This is not the justice of the Goddess!"

The Armsteaders hesitated and the dwarves stopped at the portcullis.

"The Drobin are *not* responsible," Drake said, knowing in his heart who had caused the terrible tragedy.

"Shut your mouth," Elder Trevers pointed his knife at him, then helped Blayne stand up. The young man shook off the daze from Drake's knee to his face. Trevers wiped the blood from Blayne's nose and had him stand by Sherissa.

"I say that I am responsible," Drake said. "I brought them here. This is my doing. Mine!" He thrust his Kierka high in the air. "I demand the blade truth. It is my right."

Sherissa slipped past Blayne and confronted Drake, who brought his knife back to his side. She slapped him hard across the face, her mouth contorting into a snarl. Sherissa hit him again, the loud slap stinging his other cheek. He didn't look away from her. After the third slap, Drake caught her wrist. "I'm sorry about your father. He was a good man."

Sherissa's lips trembled and her eyes misted over. "I hate you."

The air pushed out of Drake's lungs. "I know."

Blayne drew his Kierka knife. "Sherri, move away from him." The young woman froze, turned to Blayne who gave Drake a murderous look. "I warned you not to touch her again."

As Sandon took Sherissa by her shoulders and guided her away, Drake remembered Blayne's voice from the night before. The coward had jumped him outside the bathhouse.

"I didn't touch her last night," Drake said, while meeting Blayne's gaze squarely.

"He's lying," Sherissa's face twisted with shame and hatred. She turned to Blayne. "Kill him. Kill him for my father."

Drake couldn't hide his shock. He thought that even through all the pain of the last day, Sherissa wouldn't lie to see him dead.

"If it wasn't for you damn Bloodstones," Blayne spat, "none of this would have happened to us."

Nodding in acceptance, Drake turned to Elder Trevers. "If I'm killed, you must let the Drobin go." He looked at Bellor and Thor who now stood at the inner portcullis, surprised that his life had brought him to this point. "My life for theirs."

The mob and Elder Travers grumbled as Thor shook the wooden bars and cursed in Drobin.

"Don't do this," Uncle Sandon begged as Drake slipped off his pack. "It's not your fault."

It is, Uncle, Drake thought. *It is.*

Elder Trevers faced Drake. "Agreed. The blades will speak only truth. Your life for theirs." The veteran patted Blayne on the shoulder.

The hulking young man stalked forward. "I'm going to cut your throat for trying to have your way with her." Blayne stood with his feet apart and raised his Kierka over his right shoulder while stretching his left hand out to point at Drake's throat.

Mirroring Blayne's fighting stance, the Clifftoner stepped away from the gate so he could cock his right arm. His ribs ached as he raised his left hand. Jep and Temus growled and barked.

Blayne leaped forward immediately. The Armsteader brought down his Kierka with a mighty slash. Dodging aside, Drake avoided a blow that would have cut through his skull. He counter-slashed to drive Blayne back. The weight of the swing pulled him off balance and intense pain flared in his ribs. The Armsteader attacked again, forcing Drake against the gatehouse.

Heart racing, Drake couldn't remember any of the lessons his grandfather had taught him about fighting with Kierka knives. Blayne struck again. Drake parried the side-armed slash. Blayne's knife scratched across Drake's Kierka until their hand guards came together. Blayne pulled away first and made a quick slice. The knife cut the skin on Drake's arm. The surge of sharp pain made him angry and desperate.

A ghostly wyvern's head appeared in Drake's mind and an intense cold prickled in his gut, slowing his reflexes. *The blades will know the truth. You are guilty.* The whispering voice filled him with despair. Drake's guard faltered and Blayne slashed at his face, opening a cut across his cheek.

"This is not the way, Drake," Bellor said as a dark presence inside the young man tried to break down his resolve, sap his will to live. "You are not responsible. The wingataurs did this to sow discord. Don't sacrifice yourself for their crimes. Fight!"

Blayne thrust at Drake, who jumped back to avoid the hunter's long reach.

Thor and Bellor began chanting in deep tones, their voices mixing with the taunts and jeers from the villagers. Blayne circled, probing Drake's flagging defense, using his much longer arms to keep Drake at bay. The Armsteader kept trying to pin Drake against the gatehouse wall where Jep and Temus snarled and pawed at the gate, biting into the wood.

"Fierce dogs," Blayne smirked, "once you're dead I'll take them as my own."

"They'll tear out your throat."

"Then I better kill them before I go hunting for the Drobin."

A red-hot bolt of anger pierced Drake's guilt. Strength poured into his limbs again and the Drobin chanting invigorated him. He launched himself forward, slashing at Blayne's extended arm. Drake cut a line of crimson on the Armsteader's forearm.

The taller hunter gritted his teeth and lunged. The Clifftoner caught Blayne's elbow in his armpit and pinned it to his sore left side. Blayne grabbed Drake's knife hand in a vice grip as they locked together.

The pain in Drake's left side exploded into a furious, white-hot agony, but he kept a hold of Blayne's knife arm. The larger man forced Drake back and Blayne's breath choked him. "What's wrong? Sore ribs?" The Armsteader couldn't get his arm free, so he dug the handle of the Kierka into Drake's side. Grimacing in pain, Drake kicked Blayne in the groin.

The Armsteader sucked in his breath, then head butted Drake in the face.

Stunned, Drake smashed against the gate, banged his head on the wood and slid to the ground.

Standing over his fallen foe, Blayne raised his long blade in both hands.

"Move!" Bellor screamed before the curved blade descended.

Blayne's Kierka chopped into the wooden bars, burying itself in the gate right where Drake's head had been an instant before. Blayne tried to pull his weapon out of the wood and Drake raised his own heavy blade to cut off the Armsteader's hand.

Turning the knife before he swung, Drake slammed the dull side of the heavy blade into Blayne's wrist, shattering the bone. Yelping and clutching his broken limb, Blayne rolled onto his side. Drake stepped behind him and put the razor-sharp edge of the curved knife against the Armsteader's throat. Many of the villagers gasped and swore.

"Shoot him!" Sherissa yelled. "Make him pay for all he did!" She slumped to her knees sobbing. Several young men took aim at Drake, who used Blayne's body as a shield.

The Clifftoner stared at the villagers as blood streamed out of his nose, dripped from his forehead, cheek and arm. He felt his knife cutting into Blayne's skin. The rage missing from him during the battle erupted. "Is this truth?!" Drake glared at the Armsteaders in disgust, his body trembling. "How many more good men have to die today?" Few of the villagers would look at him. "I am not your enemy." He motioned his bloody chin at the dwarves. "They are not your enemy." He took in several deep breaths of air and tried to control his shaking. "Now let them go."

The Armsteaders whispered amongst themselves and turned to Elder Trevers. "Raise it." The outer portcullis groaned and clanked as the men in the tower winched it upward at the Elder's command. Many hunters kept their crossbows trained on Drake—he knew some aimed at his throat, others at his eyes. At this range, they couldn't miss.

Drake pressed the blade against Blayne's throat and glanced at his two Drobin friends.

"Get to the woods."

"You'll follow?" Bellor asked with concern.

The young man nodded, wondering if the old War Priest guessed his intentions.

Thor glared at the crossbowmen aiming at Drake, then put his thick fist against his chest and nodded at Drake before withdrawing. Bellor pulled on the dogs' collars. They whined and barked as Bellor dragged them across the drawbridge, then across the field into the forest. Drake glanced at the dead dogs in the tunnel and at the severed heads on the bridge. The men were killed because of him. There was no other truth. He could have let the Drobin die in the Thornclaw Forest. Instead he had brought them to Armstead, somehow triggering the attack.

The time had come. Drake stepped away from Blayne, giving the Armsteaders clear shots with their crossbows. He locked eyes with Elder Trevers and let his knife fall from his grasp. "My life for theirs."

The villagers took aim.

Drake's last regret was that he would never see Jaena again.

XXVIII

Perseverance must always be tempered with wisdom.
—Bellor Fardelver, from the Thornclaw Journal

At the edge of the woods Bellor hid behind a fallen gnarlpine tree. He prayed to Lorak that Drake would appear, but as the moments dragged on his hopes became a dying ember. Despair at losing the brave young man brought tears to his eyes. He vowed that Drake's sacrifice would not be forgotten.

"Those inbred humans have killed him." Thor's scowl masked his grief.

Bellor thought, *I should have found another way. Done something to stop what happened.* The wingataurs had sown so much fear in the village that the people had become the servants of demons, causing more terror and violence when they should have been banding together.

A man appeared on the drawbridge. Bellor's hopes sparked to life, then died out. The one called Trevers ambled out of the gate tunnel. The human's eyes searched the trees. Bellor sunk down, still keeping a line of sight to the Armsteader. Trevers got on his knees and carefully gathered the three heads into a sack.

More than a dozen crossbow-carrying hunters marched across the drawbridge with half as many bullmastiffs and assembled in front of Trevers. The Elder pointed into the woods indicating several directions—including the one where the Drobin were hiding.

"I knew it," Thor spat. "Vrelkshit-eating liars. They're coming after us."

Bellor led as they ran back to where they had tied the dogs. Jep and Temus strained at their tethers, whining and biting at the ropes. When the dogs were free they refused to go along with the dwarves and wanted to drag the dwarves back toward Armstead.

"We'll have to release them." Bellor struggled to keep Temus from running off. Thor kept Jep from escaping by hugging the dog tight, his face buried in Jep's neck. "Thor, you'll have to let him go."

Thor rubbed Jep's neck then released him. Jep bolted toward the village and Temus followed. Thor watched them go. "I always hated those dogs."

"Come on." Bellor darted into the trees. The War Priest hiked through the alpine forest as fast as he could. Violent barking erupted in the clearing near the village.

"Jep and Temus will slow them down." Thor's grin faded when the barking suddenly stopped.

Thor watched their backs as Bellor expected the hunters from Armstead to find them at any moment. The soft blanket of pine needles helped them obscure their tracks, though dogs would have little trouble catching their scent.

Bellor climbed over a fallen log. "We're going to have to find a stream, then travel in it to throw them off our trail."

"Why don't we just swim across the lake?" Thor rolled his eyes as both dwarves stared at the massive lake of dark water. Blown by the wind, small white-capped waves rolled south in the shadow of the Wind Walker Mountains.

Bellor sighed, "You're right. They know this country too well. They'll be ahead of us . . . waiting in ambush."

"And behind, driving us toward it." Thor slung his shield on his back. "Doesn't matter. I'd rather get shot in the front. Let's go."

For over almost two hours they hiked through the trees without any sign of pursuit until they reached the top of a low hill. Dead trees stretched for miles, filling the entire southern end of the alpine valley. Bellor stared at the open ground, gawking at the black and gray trunks, helpless victims of the fire that had consumed them eighteen months before. Most of the scorched trunks still stood, like sad sentinels watching over a graveyard. *This wasn't a natural fire,* he thought. *It was deliberate.*

"We have to cross this dead place with no cover?" Thor asked.

"Only if we want to find Quarzaak." Bellor inhaled the mountain air detecting no scent of the burned forest.

"Wingataurs will see us coming." Thor searched the horizon with a grim visage.

"There has to be a less dangerous way," Bellor said.

"There isn't." Drake stepped out from the fat trunk of a gnarlpine. Jep and Temus stood behind him, their tails wagging.

Bellor gaped in shock, wondering if he were a ghost. A bandage covered Drake's arm and the bruised knot on his forehead stood out like a knot on a log. His nose had swollen and Drake favored his left shoulder, carrying most of his backpack's weight on his right.

Thor let out a hearty laugh and Jep bounded over to Thor.

"What happened?" Bellor asked, closing the distance and examining Drake's injured arm.

"My uncle stitched it up." Drake gestured to his cloth bandage. "He had to boil the thread first."

"I mean, I thought they'd killed you." Bellor allowed himself a big smile, felt a burden lift from his spirit. "The Elder let you go."

Drake nodded. "My uncle stepped in front of me, or the young hunters would have shot me dead. Then Uncle Sandon told them we were going after the demons, that we would kill them all. Take vengeance for Rigg, Kovan, and the others."

"We will," Bellor promised.

"We thought they were hunting us," Thor said.

"No, they're searching the woods for the bodies of Kovan and the watchmen."

"Thank Lorak for showing them wisdom." Bellor laid his hands on the earth.

"Elder Trevers said the blade would have killed me if I were guilty."

"Truth should never be decided by knives," Bellor said, wondering where the abhorrent Nexan custom had started.

"And you beat that gangly goat-brained hunter, didn't you Drake?" Thor laughed, rubbing Jep's belly.

The young man looked away, shoulders sagging. Guilt weighed him down. Bellor remembered the dark presence of the wyvern-ghost inside Drake during the fight. Tiny venom ghosts must have injected themselves into Drake's spirit in Cliffton and had nearly caused him to give up—though Bellor's prayers while trapped in the gate tunnel had managed to burn them away.

Bellor had sensed the presence of the poisonous spirits in Drake when they'd left Cliffton, though he thought the young hunter had cast them out during the encounter with the constrictor vines. Obviously, they had hidden deep inside him. Bellor suspected that their guide was already susceptible to spirits of the dead, judging by his troubled aura. He would have to teach the Clifftoner how to release the negative energies that held him in the past and connected him to the Void.

Remorse sapped Drake's spirit and Bellor knew he needed to hear the truth. "It wasn't your fault those men were killed. The wingataurs have claimed this territory. More men would have been killed eventually no matter if we came. The blame is with the demons."

Drake turned away, pretending not to hear Bellor. He scanned the dead forest and open sky. "You asked if there was another way to go south. We're hemmed in by the lake on one side and Griffin Ridge on the other."

Bellor let the subject drop and gazed at the huge expanse of Cinder Lake to the east and the foreboding gray cliffs to the west.

"That way." Drake pointed to an area thick with burned trees. He loaded his crossbow and searched the sky, then walked down the hill into the burned forest. Bellor and Thor flanked him two steps behind as they all moved ahead with tentative strides. They marched past scores of burned trees and the miniature saplings growing around them.

The War Priest focused on the open sky and the sparse undergrowth where ground-walking griffins would have little trouble pursuing them. He realized this was an easy place to die, and Drake had just been given his life back. Now it was being risked again because Bellor wanted a guide. But they didn't really need the human any longer. They could get by on their own. It was needless to ask Drake to put his life in jeopardy repeatedly for them.

As they traveled further south, the forest became more spread out and open. Bellor's worried thoughts about Drake's life became amplified by the precarious nature of their situation, which had grown dire because of the massive desolation. Wingataur demons could be flying overhead, or worse, a dragon or wyvern. The dwarf decided they'd gone far enough. "We've got to stop."

"It's not even midday," Drake said, warily watching the sky. "We can keep going."

"No. We have to stop," Bellor said.

"Then I'll find us cover." Moments later the Clifftoner

ushered them under a dead gnarlpine tree that had fallen after the fire. They squeezed under its blackened branches, hiding within a small cavity formed by its burned husk. Jep and Temus guarded the entrance, their ears pricked up and their noses smelling the breeze scented with sulfur from nearby hot springs.

Hands on his crossbow, Drake clenched and relaxed his jaw as he peered out of their hiding place. "What's wrong, Bellor? Why did we stop?"

The War Priest finally let out a long sigh. "Drake, the time has come for us to part company. You've lived only twenty summers and I fear if you continue with us . . . you won't see another."

In disbelief, Drake and Thor stared at him as if he were a demon.

"Thor and I have to continue, it's part of our Sacred Duty. But you are so young. You couldn't even grow a full beard if you wanted to. You need to live, experience a life with your people. This is too dangerous now, especially after what's happened in Armstead. We're wide open for attack in this burned-out forest. If there's a dragon in this valley, and it attacks us, we probably won't survive. Go back to Cliffton. Bring a warning to your people about what happened in Armstead. We'll find our own way." Bellor frowned. "I don't want your death on my spirit. You've done so much already. Go home. Our arrangement is at an end."

Drake touched his chest with one rigid finger. "I'm making my own decisions. I'm not a Nexan servant you can just dismiss. I'm a hunter, and this is my land."

Bellor leaned forward. "You've been a skilled guide, and got us out of Armstead by risking your life. I'll not have that happen again. There's much you don't know about Thor and I, and our true purpose. It's better if you and your dogs go back. Record all you've learned about us, and the Drobin who came before." Bellor tried to hand Drake a sack. "You won't be able to read the Drobin words, but please take my journals. My Thornclaw Journal must not be lost . . . in case Thor and I don't return."

Drake pulled away, refusing to accept the bag.

"Please," Bellor begged, "this information must be preserved." He fixed his somber gaze on Drake. "Thor and I can find Quarzaak from here. Now go back and never come this way again until the trees are tall and green again. Please, keep the journals safe." Bellor again tried to hand him the small cloth sack. Drake pushed it away with his crossbow.

Thor scowled at Bellor. "What in the name of Lorak's Holy Blood are you doing? We need a guide. We need him."

"Quiet, Thor," Bellor warned through clenched teeth. "My mind is made up. It's not your place to question me."

"My place?!" Thor shouted.

Bellor sat up straight, "Thor, you—"

"Listen to me," Drake interrupted, "my cousin Rigg died because of what he found in Quarzaak, and my uncle Sandon and his family have been tormented for months. Who knows what's going to happen to them now? Three hunters are missing. Three are dead. They had families who depended on them. This isn't just about you and Thor looking for your relatives anymore. This is about my relatives too! Men are dead, probably because we came to Armstead. Don't you know what just happened? I was prepared to die to help you escape Armstead, and you still won't tell me what's going on? I deserve that much."

Bellor tore at his beard as guilt filled his entire being. Drake had risked everything for them, and hadn't received their trust in return because of his race. "I'm sorry. We didn't know if we could trust you before. Once a person knows something they cannot easily un-know it. Thor and I have already resigned ourselves to a bleak fate without much hope . . . but you have a choice. Go home. Marry your Jaena. Leave us to our destiny."

"Give me the choice." Drake pounded his chest. "What more can I do to earn your trust? I've already saved your lives. Let me decide if I return home or go on."

Bellor held his face in his hands before looking up. "You must understand me, Drake Bloodstone. I'm old and damaged. I've seen terrible things and fought too many wars. I don't want to see any more of the people that I care about killed." Closing his eyes, Bellor saw the turbulent aura surrounding Drake and the great strength of will inside him.

Bellor's eyes blinked open. "The old ways of the Drobin fade slowly. For us to trust humans is against everything we've ever learned."

"I am one man," Drake lowered his voice. "One. Judge me for who I am, not for all of the men who've come before."

"You are one man," Bellor said, "a good one I don't want to sentence to death. But I can see I must go beyond the old ways . . . or the Sacred Duty Thor and I have accepted will not be realized. I didn't see it before. Now I'm convinced." Bellor nodded at Thor. "Lorak brought the three of us together for a reason. I sense the cords of our destiny braiding together. I'm going to tell him everything, Thor, and let him decide his fate. He's right. We owe him that much."

Thor grinned. "I don't like needing a human."

"Enough of this." Drake was not amused. "What haven't you told me?"

Bellor leaned forward. "I haven't told you about the dragon who will enslave our world."

★ ★ ★ ★ ★

PART THREE
QUARZAAK

★ ★ ★ ★ ★

XXIX

We keep the truth from those we meet along our journey. We rationalize that it's for their protection. Sometimes I wonder if we're merely protecting Draglûne. Are we his unwitting pawns by keeping his secrets?

—Bölak Blackhammer, from the Lost Journal

Bits of scorched gnarlpine fell on the companions as they crouched under the fallen tree. Bent on its side the black trunk and brittle branches gave cover and some protection. The dogs continued their vigil prowling around and making Drake wonder what they smelled lurking in the burned forest.

The War Priest cleared his throat and smoothed his beard. "The attack outside Cliffton wasn't random. The wyvern had been following us."

"I thought so," Drake said.

"The lone aevian you slew outside your village may not be the only one sent to kill Thor and I."

Bellor looked into Drake's questioning eyes. "The one who sent the wyvern . . . is probably responsible for the Rigg's death."

"I knew you were lying when you said you didn't know who sent the assassins."

"We told you we weren't certain," Bellor said. "However, we have strong suspicions, despite our lack of proof. Assassins killed him. On whose orders is the most vital question. We suspect the one who gave the orders is the one who left the two

scars on the wyvern's neck."

"The marks were carved, weren't they?" Drake asked, remembering his grandfather's warning.

"Yes." Bellor nodded. "Wounds not deep enough to kill, but profound enough to always remind the beast who its true master was."

"Who?" Drake's fists tightened.

"A powerful creature whose claws are wrapped around every plateau of Ae'leron." Bellor raised his hand like a claw. "His followers worship him as a god, and ritually sacrifice their own children to appease his hunger. We call his servants the Cult of the Iron Death. Their master is diabolical and scheming, and has been building his power for hundreds of years. His servants lurk in almost every city of Ae'leron. They're loyal and ruthless and carry out his orders without question. He also controls many cunning aevian slaves, like the wyvern you shot.

"They are everywhere, always watching and waiting to do his bidding. He's their ultimate master, and they would do anything commanded of them or face a painful death. That wyvern traveled from the south, probably the Khoram Desert, judging by its scales. I'm sure our trip to Quarzaak was anticipated long before we left Nexus City. The wyvern had been sent to stop us.

"We're not merely searching for the lost mine of Quarzaak and our kin, we hunt for an ancient evil that has grown stronger during his long lifespan, which has lasted hundreds of years. He has many names: the Iron Death, the Betrayer, the Shapeshifter Wyrm, and the Dragon of Darkness. But to our folk, he is known as Draglûne, King of the Dragons."

The information sank into Drake as he realized their guarded secret was far worse than he had ever imagined.

"To face him is burning death." Bellor exhaled as if spewing fire. "If it is Draglûne who set the fires and was seen flying over Cinder Lake, we're in extreme danger. If he comes for us . . .

we're likely to be ashes on the wind. Only with preparation and divine providence can we survive. Lorak's magic can shield us from his fire breath, but unless I know he's coming and have time to invoke the magic, we're doomed. Even if we can ready all of our protections, we're greatly outmatched."

A dragon. Drake stared at Bellor.

"I don't know if you can understand the magnitude of my revelation," Bellor said. "Draglûne is not just a powerful aevian monster. He's the most vile—and perhaps the most devious—beast in all of Ae'leron. He hates all non-wyrm-kin and if he lives much longer, a reign of unimaginable destruction and terror will be inflicted upon the plateaus. There will be a great war that will affect us all."

Leaning against the tree, Drake thought about the powerful Drobin armies and the regiments of human soldiers. "If he's so powerful and will bring this 'great war,' why are you two lone dwarves after him all by yourselves?"

"We're not alone." Bellor sat up straighter. "Lorak is with us."

Drake raised his eyebrows.

"Don't insult our honor." Thor held up his fist, displaying his clan ring as if he was going to punch Drake in his already swollen face.

"Swallow your doubts, boy." Thor brandished his warhammer in two hands. "Master Bellor and I are both *Dracken Viergur.*" Thor used the Drobin pronunciation rolling the r-sound in **Drra**-ken, and emphasizing **Veer**-grr. "In your Nexan tongue we would be called dragon hunters. We're an order of Drobin warriors dedicated to hunting and slaying dragons and other wyrm-kin with our sacred weapons."

"*Dracken Viergur.*" Drake spoke without the Drobin pronunciation. "Strong name for hunters."

Thor nodded. "We follow in the footsteps of the *Dracken Vier-*

gur who have gone before us. We shall find Draglûne and kill him, or we'll die trying. We've sworn this in Lorak's name." Thor slammed his hammer into the earth, burying the head in the dirt.

"We two are left to carry out our Sacred Duty." The War Priest's shoulders sagged. "There were others. My *Dracken Viergur . . . students.*"

"What happened to them?"

"They were recently . . . murdered." Remorse wrinkled Bellor's face and Thor frowned. The old dwarf told the story about the coal mine. Tears formed in his eyes when he spoke of finding the bodies. "It had taken me over twenty years to train my nine sons, then in a few moments they were killed in Draglûne's trap."

Drake's mouth gaped open as he realized Bellor's own children had recently been killed.

"The journal arrived in Lorak's Temple in Nexus City a few months before my sons were slain. I think perhaps its appearance caused Draglûne to murder them. He knew we would soon be ready to hunt him down, and Draglûne wanted to eliminate as many *Dracken Viergur* as possible."

"You're hunting him now."

"We have no choice," Bellor said. "The *Dracken Viergur* stronghold was also attacked, while we cleared the rubble from the mine. The dragon lore contained there was destroyed by flame. More innocent dwarves died. Since those terrible days, only five months ago, wyverns have hunted us wherever we go. Thor and I have been marked for death by Draglûne and his servants. Our only chance is to find the other *Dracken Viergur* and band together to slay him."

"Your lost kin?" Drake asked.

Bellor nodded.

Thor pulled his hammer from the soil and brushed it off.

"My uncle Bölak led the *Dracken Viergur* who settled Quarzaak."

"Why'd they come to the Wind Walker Mountains?" Drake asked.

"Master Bölak and the other *Dracken Viergur* endeavored to find a place to live in peace," Bellor said, "and to prepare for the final battle with Draglûne. He thought the Iron Death wouldn't be able to find them here. My cousin Bölak thought it would be a secret place to prepare and avoid Draglûne's assassins."

"There's been no word in forty years," Drake said, "a long time."

Bellor smiled. "We've never given up hope that Bölak and the other *Viergur* are alive. We hope they've been preparing these four decades for the final battle with the wyrm. Though there's a chance Bölak and the others may have been slain. I wish I could know the truth about the visions troubling my sleep. I've seen terrible things in my dreams of what might have been. It's unclear to me if what I've seen is true."

He fears Bölak is dead, Drake thought.

"We'll find my uncle," Thor promised, "and join his eleven *Viergur.*"

"Will there be enough of you to face him?" Drake asked, imagining it would take whole armies to kill a dragon.

"Don't think Bölak and his *Viergur* were weak," Bellor said. "Draglûne feared them and wanted my cousin and the last of the *Viergur* slain. The wyrm saw our strength, and knew we threaten his power like no other on the plateaus. We know secret lore to slay dragons and wyrm-kin. Draglûne is afraid of the knowledge we *Dracken Viergur* possess."

"Some of that lore was taken to Quarzaak," Thor said.

"We thought it lost." Bellor reached into a sack and took out a pair of small leather-bound books, carefully wrapped in wool cloths. "This is my Thornclaw Journal," Bellor said. "I wanted you to take it and keep it safe."

"What's that other one?" Drake pointed as he saw only the front cover on the square journal. Dwarven rune letters were inscribed on it and the torn binding barely held it together. Some pages were in danger of falling out. Burn marks and dark stains, which could be dried blood, marred several of the pages.

Bellor held it reverently as Drake examined the obviously thinned book, thinking a significant number of pages were missing toward the end. "It's not whole. Where are the last pages?"

"We don't know," Bellor said. "This is the beginning of Bölak Blackhammer's private journal. We call this first section the Quarzaak Journal, because of where it was found. Your cousin, Rigg, found it in Quarzaak. He brought it to Nexus City, and the Temple of Lorak eventually acquired it.

"In these pages Bölak recorded the visions of the future that Lorak gave him. He saw the coming of the great war of destruction that Draglûne would try to bring to Ae'leron someday. Sadly, the last pages of his journal, along with Bölak and the rest of our kin . . . are still missing."

XXX

I saw Draglûne leading a vast army of winged demons.
They swept across the plateaus, killing every living thing in
their path. They burned the cities and villages, sparing
nothing from the flames of destruction. Lorak has shown
me the possible end of the folk of Ae'leron. I know that if
Draglûne isn't slain, my terrible vision will come to pass.
Our Sacred Duty must not fail.

—Bölak Blackhammer, from the Quarzaak Journal

A red fever ant as long as Drake's index finger crawled next to
him under the charred tree. He crushed it with his boot and
looked for more on the shadowy ground before scrutinizing the
battered pages of the Quarzaak Journal.

Bellor cleared his throat. "If it hadn't been for Rigg, we may
have never known about Quarzaak. The visions of Bölak
would've been lost entirely."

Wishing he could read the Drobin language, Drake scanned
the miniature, blocky rune letters covering the sheets of parchment. Bellor turned the pages, showing him the massive amount
of information contained within.

"It starts many years ago, when Bölak accepted his Sacred
Duty to slay Draglûne," Bellor said. "There are revelations and
visions sent directly from Lorak, but most of it is the story of
Bölak's journey to find Draglûne's lair. The Lorakian clergy has
dismissed it entirely, which is why they allowed us to take the

259

original. I suspect the copy in Nexus City won't survive long. They don't understand that this text is a priceless treasure, as it covers many years spent in the Drobin homeland. The section Rigg recovered ends when Bölak and his *Viergur* were mining Quarzaak and preparing to leave to hunt for Draglûne."

"Do you think the rest of the missing pages are in Quarzaak?" Drake asked.

"We hope so." Bellor closed the journal and wrapped it carefully before putting it in the small sack. "This journal is a weapon. There's dragon lore aplenty on these pages. Bölak's small book can kill Draglûne. It's more powerful than my axe or Thor's hammer."

Thor grunted in protest.

"The journal has told us much," Bellor said, "but the last pages must've fallen out, been removed, or were destroyed. We are greatly indebted to your cousin. He got the journal and Master Dorlak Silvershield's clan ring to us before he was killed. For that we're eternally thankful. It's fitting that you, Rigg's cousin, are helping to avenge him, and carry on in his place."

If I fall, who will take mine? Drake wondered. A throbbing pain pulsed through his temples, and he shielded his eyes from a ray of sun that filtered through the dead gnarlpine.

"Thor and I are alone in this," Bellor said. "It has fallen to us, and perhaps you."

"You should have help, from the Drobin king . . . someone," Drake said.

"The Drobin folk haven't cared about or heard of Draglûne for many years," Bellor said. "Bölak's stature as a great hero has faded, even though the Nexan and Drobin leaders know about him. They're wrong for underestimating the dragon king, and thinking his power has waned. He waits and builds his strength."

"Our leaders are fools," Thor said.

"That's what Lorak's High Priests call me, Bellor the Fool."

Disgusted, Drake shook his head.

"The High Priests have given me no support to rebuild the once great order of *Dracken Viergur* that defended our folk for many centuries." Bellor's tone revealed his anger. "I was the only *Viergur* Master left, but only my sons and Thor would follow me. Their resentment of Bölak and myself blinded them to the real threat. They didn't care that Bölak was gone, and most of them don't want him found now. Thor and I are probably the only ones who would ever look for him. The Priest Council even refused to believe Draglûne was to blame for my sons' deaths. They claimed it was a stray spark that caused the explosion. They didn't believe I'd seen a wyrm track or scorch marks from dragon fire."

Thor snorted. "They also said the fire that destroyed our *Dracken Viergur* Hall of Records and killed the dwarves there was a careless accident with a lantern. We don't even use lanterns. We can see in the dark! They call us fools?"

"They didn't want to admit it was Draglûne who struck so easily at the heart of our folk," Bellor said. "Their denials are perfect examples of how the Drobin have underestimated Draglûne. I fear we shall pay a heavy price for the complacence of our brethren, and all the while the Cult of the Iron Death is gathering vast wealth and information through illicit dealings and infiltrations. They're gathering strength for the coming war. Or perhaps they're feeding Draglûne's greed for power, gold, and blood sacrifice."

"I'm so sorry for all the kin you've lost, Master Bellor." Drake tried to imagine Bellor's pain from losing his sons.

Bellor sighed. "Yes. They're all missing . . . or dead. Most of them died seventy-five years ago when I first battled Draglûne."

"You fought him?" Drake sat up straight.

Bellor nodded slowly. "Seventy-five years ago, my axe had its first taste of wyrm's blood."

XXXI

There's no cover ahead. The aevian waits for us to move, but we can't turn back.
                    —Bellor Fardelver, from the Thornclaw Journal

High above the Steam Valley, rage consumed Vrask. The sorcerer-wingataur searched the ground with vengeful eyes, beating his leathery wings against the air as if attacking the wind itself. Powerful magic, strong wings and a belly full of fresh human meat propelled him forward, allowing him to rise high in the thin mountain air where he remained invisible to the eyes of his enemies. His large body made only a faint blur in the vast sky of blue. Vrask grinned, showing his fangs. He knew his prey would never see him coming.

Floating on the breeze with his Draconic magic, Vrask scanned the exposed valley floor. He searched for the Drobin Priest who had provided the rune stone that now thwarted him from entering the dreams of the human known as Sandon.

Vrask's grin turned to a snarl when he thought about being denied his nightly pleasure of torturing Sandon's spirit, even though there were many other humans he could visit while in his ghost-body. Sandon was his favorite though, and had impressed Vrask by surviving for so long after his visits had begun. None of the others lasted more than a year, but Sandon had lived almost eighteen months.

Vrask vowed to himself that he would find and kill the devious little earth creature that had given Sandon the rune stone. Then he would fly into the village, take the magic stone and crush it to dust. Maybe he would leave the dwarf's head in a bucket at the bottom of Armstead's well? He could hardly wait to cut the dwarf's body into long, slender pieces, just as he had the three night watchmen.

XXXII

Soon we shall face Draglûne and his Giergun army. I pray
for courage, both for myself and for the warriors under my
protection. Many of us will fall, but the wyrm must be
slain at any cost.

—Bellor Fardelver, Chronicle of the Eleventh Giergun
War

A sudden breeze sent dust and bits of the scorched wood swirling into the air. Rubbing the grit from his eyes, Bellor blinked
at Drake, considering how to tell the young human about Draglûne and all the brave warriors who had died trying to slay
him.

Thor nodded at him, encouraging Bellor to continue.

After taking a deep breath, Bellor met Drake's curious eyes.
"We call it the Last Battle of Drobin Pass. We knew that if we
lost . . . the war was lost." He paused, the wrinkles deep around
his eyes. "Thousands of Drobin and our Nexan allies had
already been killed in the days before the final fight. The Giergun army had attacked us . . . day after day, until we could fall
back no farther. We held our last defensive line for six days
against repeated assaults. We wanted their dragon commander,
Draglûne, to come . . . and we did our best to force him to try
and break our line, to smash his forces against our defensive
anvil." Bellor's voice crackled with emotion. "It was seventy-five

years ago, but I'll never forget what happened. . . ."

Bellor peered upwards at the sheer canyon walls of Drobin
Pass. The black-flecked granite mountains on either side of the
fifty-foot-wide gorge pressed together, forming a narrow chute
that snaked through the Dark Spire Mountains.

Draglûne cannot spread his wings in here, Bellor thought. *He
must come at us on the ground or not at all.* The War Priest ducked
under the low overhang of rock where thirty *Dracken Viergur*
and forty Kamarian Blood Warriors hid. *Dusk will bring the Giergun . . . and, perhaps today . . . the wyrm will come.*

"See anything?" Dorlak Silvershield asked as he checked the
braided cord on his powerful crossbow.

"Nothing yet." Bellor stroked his dark-brown beard and
prayed for patience. His was wearing thin after three days of
hiding in the cramped, rocky shelter watching the battle rage for
several hours each day. Though the fight lay only a few dozen
paces away, they had not been able to join it. He wondered if
Bölak was having the same frustrations in his position on the
opposite side of the gorge. He knew his old friend hated waiting. Bellor looked at the other side, trying to see into the dark
overhang where his cousin Bölak led a second group of
concealed *Dracken Viergur* and Blood Warriors.

The sunlight soon faded and drums made of dwarf-skin
rumbled from deep in the twisted canyon. As the booming
echoes reverberated off the granite, Bellor turned to his eager
troops. "The Giergun come."

The War Priest stared out of his hiding place, surveying the
battle lines formed by a heavily armored contingent of the
Drobin king's army. From his slightly elevated vantage point, he
saw the tall Nexan soldiers in the front ranks. The men stood
shoulder to shoulder in a tight phalanx, their line stretching
across the canyon in a slightly curved formation that curled

backward. Their fifteen-foot-long pikes pointed to the sky and Bellor thanked Lorak for the humans' presence once again.

Searching the canyon beyond, Bellor saw hundreds upon hundreds of dead bodies and broken weapons, the grisly evidence of the eight thousand Nexans, five thousand dwarves, and countless Giergun that had died in the three weeks of fighting. He whispered a prayer for the battle-tested group of five hundred humans that remained to help hold the line and counter the long spears of the approaching Giergun phalanx.

Bellor counted the ranks and estimated that less than a third of the Drobin king's army was arrayed near the front. He glanced back fifty paces and noticed many soldiers in reserve forming a second line in front of the massed catapults and ballistae.

"The Nexans will run today," Dorlak said solemnly. "They are broken men. My apprentices from the forge are more eager to fight than that poor lot of humans."

"The Nexans will do their duty," Bellor said, secretly wishing with Dorlak that the more reliable and fresher Drobin infantry could wield the pikes, but the six-foot-tall humans managed the long shafts much easier than the four-and-a-half-foot-tall dwarves ever could. Grimacing, Bellor knew the awful casualties of the war had washed away any trust the Nexans once had for Drobin generals. That problem would be important only if they held now. If they didn't hold here. . . .

Straining his golden-brown eyes, Bellor tried to see the heavily armored Drobin infantry standing beside their human counterparts in the first rank, but he caught only glimpses of their pointed steel helms and full body shields.

Forming up behind the pikemen, a troop of at least two hundred Drobin warriors in plate armor and carrying kite-shaped shields—a company Bellor recognized as the Steel

Guards—created a physical reminder that the men couldn't run.

The drums gained in volume and Bellor heard a horn bleating. Out of the shadows marched the Giergun, armored in full helms, iron breastplates, and bulky greaves that covered their feet and legs—the favorite targets of Drobin soldiers. Each had a rectangular shield with a thick spike jutting from the center. Their twelve-foot-long spears pointed out from the moving wall of metal. In the dusky light the Gierguns' greenish-gray skin looked black, but he couldn't see their yellow eyes—not yet anyway.

More Giergun horns sounded and Drobin catapults answered them, hurling round stones that *whooshed* through the canyon before rolling through the ranks of Giergun, crushing and maiming scores of the enemy. Huge ballistae released four-foot-long bolts that pierced shields and impaled Giergun soldiers. Scores of Nexan and Drobin sharpshooters rained down flights of quarrels from the heights, and more crossbowmen on the canyon floor sent their missiles arching into the coming Giergun.

Crossbow bolts shot by the Giergun filled the air over the defending army. Men and dwarves fell dead or wounded as quarrels needled through gaps in their shield wall, punching through armor or slits in helms. Soldiers died screaming, and Bellor wondered how many more times he would have to bear witness to the savage slaughter.

An earsplitting roar filled the canyon, and Bellor's heart thumped hard as he heard the sound he had been waiting for. A gigantic iron-gray dragon burst out of the darkness, its huge head looming over the marching Giergun. At first Bellor thought it was Draglûne, the draconic lieutenant general of the dragon king, but he saw the long gray bullish horns jutting from the monster's forehead.

It can't be! Gasping, Bellor knew that only a five-hundred-year-old dragon could have horns so large. He realized the draconic monarch himself, the great Mograwn, had come to punch through their last line of defense. *He wasn't supposed to come!* Bellor tried not to panic, but his inner voice screamed, *Where's Draglûne?! We prepared for Draglûne!*

Ranks of Giergun marched in front and on both flanks of the ancient dragon. Flames smoldered in Mograwn's mouth, and the War Priest immediately began invoking the fire-protection magic for himself and his warriors.

Screams of terror erupted from the Nexan pikemen as the dragon appeared. Human captains barked commands and most of the soldiers leveled their weapons at the Giergun, but others dropped their pikes and tried to flee. The troop of Steel Guards kept the men from falling back. Drobin War Priests touched the frightened soldiers, using Lorak's power to give them courage and return to stand beside their brothers.

For a moment, Bellor wished he stood with the War Priests on the line, as he had so many times in the past. *But I have a different duty. Please, Lorak, let me honor you this day.*

Mograwn roared again and the Giergun marched faster toward the prickly hedge of Nexan pikes. Just before the Giergun reached the pikemen, a wave of orange fire surged from Mograwn's mouth engulfing the center of the men and dwarves. Few were shielded from the flames, and scores were melted or cooked in their armor where they stood. Men and dwarves became puddles on the ground. Warriors burned as if tufts of dry grass had been stuffed inside their armor.

Shrieks of dying dwarves and men filled the canyon, the thin gorge amplifying their death cries. But the Drobin line had not totally collapsed. It held firm on the flanks, though the middle had been annihilated.

The advancing Giergun clashed with the remaining pikemen, while some of the green-skinned soldiers dashed through the open center to be met by the hammers and axes of the Steel Guards.

The surviving Nexans began to retreat, holding the Giergun at bay with their longer weapons as Drobin axemen in front hacked at the Giergun's spears, sundering the shafts. The progress of the charging Giergun suddenly halted when the Steel Guards closed ranks, slaying the first waves of their foes with ruthless efficiency.

Bellor lost sight of Mograwn for a moment in the smoke. He dared hope the dragon had retreated, then saw the shadow and realized the dragon king had leaped into the air. The gigantic wyrm crashed down upon the center of the pitched battle crushing Giergun and Drobin alike under his massive bulk. His spiked tail—longer than a sentinel ironbark tree—swept left and right, knocking aside Nexan pikemen and Giergun on the flanks as if they were toys. Flames spouted from Mograwn's mouth, immolating most of the remaining Steel Guards and Nexans, who began to flee for their lives. The wyrm finished off the survivors, raking them with his claws like scythes through stalks of wheat.

Lines of Giergun sprinted forward to guard Mograwn's flanks and Bellor watched a scant number of his brothers trying to escape as the dragon king and his Giergun soldiers advanced.

Bellor prayed that his *Dracken Viergur* and Blood Warriors would remain unseen as his enemies advanced toward the second line. The ground trembled as Mograwn stomped forward, his four thick legs crushing bodies flat. The old wyrm tucked his wings tighter to his back and kept his head low as catapulted stones and ballista bolts as large as javelins streaked toward him. He batted some away with his foreclaws, others deflected off his bony forehead, while a few bounced off his iron scales. Bellor knew that only missiles enchanted with great Earth magic could pierce his thick scales, but the stones bludgeoned him and slowed his advance.

In answer to the missiles that the Drobin hurled at him, Mograwn spat balls of fire that sailed over the second Drobin line. The fiery spheres ignited several of the catapults and ballistae, killing and scattering their crews.

Bellor watched the dragon's right flank, where at least sixty Giergun marched in loose formation. Packed ranks of thousands of Giergun came behind Mograwn. The *Dracken Viergur* would have little time to strike before enemy reinforcements arrived to defend their leader.

The dragon monarch passed Bellor's position, and the War Priest raised his axe as he crawled out of the overhang. He charged and forty Kamarian Blood Warriors leaped out, quickly passing him and attacking the surprised Giergun vanguard. The unarmored and lightning-fast Drobin warriors caught their foes by surprise, slicing and hacking down their much-taller opponents. The Kamarians threw themselves into battle, slaying over half of Mograwn's flankers before the enemy knew they had been ambushed.

Bellor led the second wave, directing his thirty *Dracken Viergur* to dart past the surviving Giergun and toward their assigned attack points on the exposed wyrm. The Kamarians opened the way to the dragon's flanks, and few of the *Dracken Viergur* were forced to stop their charge.

Ducking a blow from a Giergun's mace, Bellor sprinted for Mograwn's right rear leg. The Giergun tried to swing again, but the fearless Blood Warrior, Wulf Ironfinder, slashed the brute's legs apart. Before the enemy could sink to the ground, Wulf pierced its throat and followed Bellor.

Barely acknowledging Wulf's presence, Bellor brought his battleaxe down hard, cutting through the iron scales with his enchanted weapon and partially severing the largest tendon of Mograwn's lower leg. Wulf chopped in the same place and Bellor struck again, causing the wyrm's leg to buckle. More *Viergur* hacked at the dragon's other leg muscles, aiming for the most vulnerable spots with their enchanted blades.

Mograwn's entire rear half slumped to the ground. The other *Viergur* had won through and done their part as well. The dragon's forelegs fell out from under him, and Bellor knew all the wyrm's legs had been hamstrung—*right according to plan*. Roaring in pain, the dragon whirled its head around and tried to beat its wings, but the tight canyon and overhanging rock prevented Mograwn from flying out of the trap.

Dorlak and his sharpshooters released four bolts that flared with silver light and pierced the dragon's neck. Jolts of energy coursed through Mograwn's head as three more steel-tipped quarrels hit the wyrm's other side after Bölak's warriors released their own missiles.

Mouth opening wide, Mograwn sprayed rivers of fire over his flanks and burned the spaces between himself and the canyon walls. Flames washed over Bellor and his brothers, but Lorak's sacred magic kept them impervious to fire. Praising Lorak, Bellor watched the remainder of the dragon's bodyguards being roasted alive.

Mograwn's tail lashed forward, sweeping burning bodies of Giergun and Drobin along with it. The spiked appendage impaled or crushed many *Dracken Viergur* and killed most of the Kamarians as it swung from side to side.

Narrowly avoiding the dragon's counterattack, Bellor hugged against Mograwn's side and charged toward the wyrm's neck and head. He didn't have time to mourn for his dead companions, many of whom he had served with for decades. Raising his axe, Bellor's eyes locked onto the spot on Mograwn's neck where a major artery lay beneath the scales.

One step away from chopping into the dragon king's flesh Bellor felt a titanic gust of wind caused by the dragon's partially flapping wings. He flew forward through the smoky air, rolling head-over-heels across the canyon floor.

Bellor's head bumped against the ground, but he clung onto his axe and arrested his tumble by digging his blade into the ground. Blood ran down the side of his scalp as he stood up to face the wounded dragon. To his right he saw a scant few of his brother *Dracken Viergur:* Bölak, Nalak, Wulf, Gillur, and Tharak, who had also been buffeted forward by the dragon's wings.

Mograwn's hateful gaze bored into Bellor and his fellows as the wyrm lay on his scaled belly. All four of the dragon's legs hung limp, hamstrung and almost useless. But the wyrm didn't quit. The king used his long tail and massive wings to grab onto the canyon walls and pull himself backward. Bellor realized the draconic aevian would pass through the wall of flames he had created when scouring his flanks, or his Giergun soldiers would come through and protect him before he could be finished off.

"Dracken Viergur!" Bölak Blackhammer screamed as he charged forward with his blacksteel hammer, *Throrkrush,* in one hand and round shield in the other.

"Lorak!" Bellor shouted, following as fast as he could, and knowing they had precious little time to complete their sworn duty before the Giergun arrived to rescue their wounded leader.

Fifteen paces never seemed so far to Bellor as he chased after Bölak. Six strides before they could attack, Mograwn's mighty wings flapped again, sending a wave of ash-filled air blasting into their faces. Bellor fought with all his strength, but he flew backwards along with all his five brothers.

Pushing himself off the ground—now twenty paces from Mograwn—Bellor glanced backward to the Drobin second line. Dorlak Silvershield's dragon-killing weapon rolling forward to the front rank. A wagon with a huge ballista mounted upon it emerged with a long, slender bolt loaded into the cocked weapon. A team of dwarves—trained by Dorlak—aimed the giant crossbow directly at Mograwn.

Bellor prayed their aim would be true and saw the dragon king's red eyes go wide when he saw the ballista. The draconic monarch opened his mouth to breathe out a ball of fire, but as he took in a breath, Dorlak and the *Dracken Viergur* sharpshooters released their second volley of bolts. The shafts hit Mograwn in the side of his throat and he flinched in pain, but he spat the ball of flame, which missed the crossbow-wagon, instead consuming the Drobin soldiers beside it.

Bölak charged again and Bellor followed with the others. As they neared their enemy a massive shape descended from above and behind Mograwn. Bellor stared at half-spread-out wings that slowed the falling wyrm. Face twisting in horror, he recognized the thickly muscled draconic body and realized Draglûne, the lieutenant of Mograwn, had arrived to rob them of their victory.

Boom! The second dragon's landing shook the earth. *The battle is lost!* Bellor despaired, but he charged toward certain death hoping to take one of the wyrms with him. "For Lorak!"

Mograwn beat his wings again causing a third gust of wind that knocked Bellor and the *Dracken Viergur* back down. But once the wind had stopped the giant ballista released its long bolt and the missile flared with a radiant silvery light as it flew straight at Mograwn. Bellor realized it would take the wyrm king in the mouth, penetrate into his brain and kill him dead.

Draglûne lurched over the wounded dragon and snatched the magical bolt from the air, catching it in his claw the instant before it could hit his wounded king.

"No!" Bellor shouted as he struggled up and charged with his five companions. Roaring in triumph, Draglûne raised the Drobin bolt then plunged it into the side of Mograwn's chest, burying the shaft deep into one of the wyrm king's lungs.

Mograwn swiveled his head, staring in disbelief as Draglûne locked his giant claws onto the helpless king's wing joints. Bellor heard a loud snap as the wings were wrenched from their sockets.

Draglûne tossed the limp wings aside, then crushed the mortally wounded Mograwn even closer to the ground. The king's spiky tail whipped forward like a scorpion's and bludgeoned Draglûne on the back of the head. Then the spiky appendage wrapped around the younger dragon's neck.

Bellor heard the shouts for Dorlak's giant ballista to be winched back for another shot as Draglûne struggled to pry the king's tail from his neck. The traitorous dragon used his great foreclaws to unwrap the now-limp appendage, then slid backwards off Mograwn's bleeding body.

Dorlak and the others shot their crossbows and half a dozen glowing silver missiles streaked toward Draglûne puncturing the scales near his shoulders, but none scored a fatal blow. Bleeding from his neck, where the sharp tail had cut him, Draglûne stared at the small band of six Drobin who pressed their attack.

Bellor thought the wyrm made eye contact with Bölak, who ran faster and screamed, "Blackhammer!"

The powerful winch of Dorlak's ballista latched the cord into place and Bellor knew they would soon release a second bolt. But the betraying wyrm bounded up, digging his claws into the granite cliff and ascending the sheer canyon like a colossal spider.

The ballista released its missile. The shaft clattered against the canyon wall, narrowly missing Draglûne, who soon crested the top of the gorge and disappeared.

Bölak led Bellor and the other four *Viergur* forward. They stopped their charge and approached the dying wyrm with measured caution. Red blood leaked from Mograwn's many wounds, and one of the dragon's scaly eyelids closed. Undaunted, Bölak cocked his arm and circled to the right of Mograwn's head, while Bellor angled to the left. Wulf and

Tharak followed Bellor, while Nalak and Gillur moved with Bölak.

The fire behind Mograwn faded. Bellor stepped forward as countless ranks of Giergun prepared to attack. *Mograwn must die before I do.*

Striking like a snake, the dragon king's head darted toward Bellor with jaws opened wide. Bölak threw his hammer and *Throrkrush* struck Mograwn on his temple, stunning the once-mighty dragon. The wyrm's fiery mouth snapped shut before it could close around Bellor's small body. The dragon's huge head fell hard to the ground at Bellor's feet and the king of the dragons lay helpless in front of him as scores of Giergun charged toward them, howling curses.

In an instant, the War Priest summoned the most potent wyrm-killing magic of Lorak and raised his already sanctified axe. The weapon—enchanted by the Master Forge Fathers to slay wyrms and their kin—chopped down on the dragon king's neck. The glowing blade sliced through the iron scales, severing an artery beneath and burying itself deep into Mograwn.

Bellor felt the holy power of Lorak coursing through the axe and mingling with the dissipating energy of Mograwn, who had invoked Draconic magic as he lay dying. Bellor sensed the opposing magic mixing together, infusing the axe with the last emotions of Mograwn. Pure hatred charged the battleaxe and surged into Bellor's soul, making him want to kill Draglûne more than anything.

Giergun soldiers swarmed around Bellor, but he didn't see them, or Wulf, Bölak, and the others desperately fighting to protect him. Lost in the psychic death throes of Mograwn, Bellor heard the dragon's voice thundering in his head, *MY SON HAS BETRAYED ME!*

Hundreds of charging Drobin warriors from the reserve joined the battle, rallying around Bellor and the surviving *Vier-*

gur. The War Priest's eyes shut tighter, but he saw Mograwn rise up in his mind's eye and scream, *I will have my revenge!*

Fragments of Mograwn's hate-filled essence entered Bellor's axe and imprinted themselves into the enchanted metal. The blade glowed crimson as it took on the rage of the dying king. Bellor heard the axe speak inside his head with Mograwn's voice: *You will call me, Wyrmslayer.* . . .

XXXIII

Why do I risk my life and hunt Draglûne? Is it love for what I've left behind, or hate for what lies ahead? The answer is both. I must do all I can to save my homeland from the destruction Draglûne will bring.

—Bellor Fardelver, from the Thornclaw Journal

Sitting alone on the hard bench in the watch tower, Jaena Whitestar stared into the Void. After five days, the pain from saying good-bye to Drake still squeezed her heart. Turning away from the white abyss, she studied every crack and knot in the wooden tower, hoping to see some sign that Drake had been there. Jaena saw nothing and turned back to the Void, imagining his face in the clouds and wondered if there was anything she could do to keep him alive. He had gone into great danger and she blamed herself for helping him leave the village.

The magic of the Goddess tingled in her palms, reminding her of the awakening that had taken place since Drake had left. A door had been opened in her soul that day, and the magic had poured out, bringing her closer to becoming a full Priestess of Amaryllis. The process of channeling the mystical energies of the Goddess were becoming clearer to her every day since.

A wisp of ephemeral cloud rose from the Void, floating above the layer of mist before dissipating to nothing. She watched other bits of vapor rise and disappear, or form odd shapes that she didn't expect: a wyvern's barbed tail, a dragon's claw, each one different than the last.

A sudden epiphany made Jaena sit up straight. She realized that many of her recent dreams weren't dreams at all. They were visions of the past and possible futures. She thought about the dream that had come to her over and over: Drake entering the valley surrounded by snowy mountains and two eagles watching him from above before screeching a warning. Jaena knew if he kept going into the valley he would put the village, and himself, into great danger. But last night's dream was different than the others. She realized that if she kept her mind's eye open she could see the choice he would make—if she let herself. But she couldn't bear to look.

Hanging her head, Jaena held in her sobs and rocked back and forth as the pain in her heart gnawed at her spirit. Cloaked in despair and worry, Jaena opened her eyes and saw a few tiny wood shavings on the tower floor. Picking them up gently, she held them in her palm and studied every little curl in the wood. Jaena looked at the star charm on her wrist that her beloved had carved for her and realized the dried-out shavings had come from it. They must have been in the tower for months. Jaena remembered the day Drake had given her the bracelet. She could see his face as he handed it to her as clearly as if he was standing in front of her now. Love for him made her ache even more and she couldn't hold in her sobs.

Wind whipped into the tower and blew the wooden shavings out of her hand and into the Void. She lurched forward trying to grab them. Helpless, she watched them drifting down toward the misty Underworld. The clouds seemed to twist below her, turning into the grinning face of a wyvern that promised to take away her beloved forever.

You can't have him! Jaena wanted to scream. She held in the words and sat on the bench again, praying that Drake would come back and not step into the valley. Her palms tingled once again with magic, and she knew there were things she must also do if he was to survive and return to her. Jaena vowed that when she next had the dream, she would find a way to see if Drake would go into the valley or come home. A startling realization jolted through her. *If I can learn to see the future more clearly, I can see what dangers Drake will face. I could save his life if I could warn him of what is to come. Can I alter the future and save him, or will I cause his death in a different way?*

The clouds below swirled into the head of a dragon, then dissipated into nothing. An overwhelming sense of doom caused tears of despair to roll down her cheeks.

XXXIV

The danger grows with each passing day. I won't show my
fear to the *Viergur*. They must not see my concern. I must
be as strong as the hardest rock in all the mountains.

—Bölak Blackhammer, from the Lost Journal

The wrinkles around Bellor's face deepened under the shade of
the fallen tree as the old dwarf leaned toward Drake. "We are
going into the mouth of the dragon. One mistake, and only a
path of cinders will mark our passing. Thor and I go to our
deaths willingly. You don't have to. I still encourage you to go
back. Think carefully before making your decision."

Drake pondered what he had just heard, and what could
happen if he continued with Bellor and Thor. While he
considered, Jep and Temus paced nervously, scenting the breeze
and glancing about with anxious eyes. He stared at the white-
tipped mountains and Cinder Lake in the distance.

Freezing lake water seemed to splash into his face when he
remembered Jaena's vision. She had said he would be in a valley ringed with snowy mountains and gnarlpine trees would be
all around him. His heart skipped a beat, and he remembered
that Jaena said if he stepped into the valley he would put all of
Cliffton in great danger and may never return home. She had
told him that eagles would screech a warning. But he was
already in the valley—and why would aevians warn him? The
only birds he'd seen or heard were mountain jays fluttering

through the branches. *Maybe it was nothing? Just some strange dream she had.* Drake turned away from Cinder Lake and realized he had already put his village in danger. Anyone helping the enemies of the dragon king would be punished brutally.

The image of Kovan's severed head and the mangled dogs in the gate tunnel flashed through his mind. When would the demons come to Cliffton? Would he be on watch and suffer the same fate as Kovan? Would his people turn into a vengeful mob like the Armsteaders had, shouting and blaming each other? He knew he couldn't let it come to that. Drake turned to the dwarves, his mind clear. "Rigg was murdered by Wingataurs, and they broke into my uncle's house. Both Armstead and Cliffton are threatened, especially if it was Draglûne who was seen over the lake. I know that only when these valleys are safe . . . only then can I return home."

Bellor's smile had a touch of sadness. He grasped Drake's forearm. "I am honored to have you with us, for as long as you choose. I will do everything in my power to keep you and your dogs alive."

Thor smiled. "As will I." The stout dwarf reached for his pack. "We better get moving."

"Wait." Drake stayed Thor's hand.

"What is it?" Thor scanned for danger.

"The dogs." Drake motioned to where they paced. "They sense something."

Bellor gazed upward through the branches of the tree and studied the sky. "We should stay here for now."

"I agree." The Clifftoner picked up his crossbow as Bellor kept looking through the burned branches.

"We'll wait until nightfall," Bellor said. "The vision of both dragons and wingataurs is worse at night . . . and we're going to have to get past the watchers of this valley without being seen."

"Then we can't follow the banks of the Steam River. Too

much open ground." Drake knew his father would scream at him for what he was about to propose. "There is another way."

Bellor raised an eyebrow.

Drake pointed west. "Griffin Ridge."

"There's no other way?" Bellor asked.

"We could backtrack to the Thornclaw," Drake said, "then take a couple of days and cross miles of open plains where the vrelk are migrating. At least on the ridge the griffins might not see us coming."

After the sun had set and darkness cloaked the valley, Drake led the way north, backtracking into the unburned woods. Late that night he changed course and marched due west until they found the forest ridge bordering the valley. The companions made camp at the base of the cliffs and didn't light a fire.

After their cold supper, Drake inspected the braided string on his crossbow, checking for weakness or slack. "Once we get to the top of the cliffs, we can follow the ridge south until we reach the Boulder River."

"At least up there we'll know what to expect," Bellor said.

Thor grimaced. "I'd rather fight Draglûne."

Thoughts about the fire he'd seen on the plains compelled Drake to ask, "Was it Draglûne who caused the vrelk to stampede? Did he try to kill us?"

"I caught only a glimpse of the flames," Bellor said. "Besides, there was too much dust. I didn't see a dragon. If it were him, why wouldn't he just kill us himself?" The dwarf shook his head. "Perhaps he was just hunting vrelk as they crossed the grasslands? If it was him, maybe he didn't know we were there."

"It *was* Draglûne," Thor said. "I've seen the color of his fire before."

"You have?" Drake asked.

Thor let out a deep sigh. "Only moments after Mograwn fell

dead from blows from *Wyrmslayer* and *Throrkrush,* I had my own meeting with Draglûne. . . .

Hundreds of wounded Drobin warriors sprawled on the floor of the massive cavern. Thor breathed through his mouth, trying to avoid gagging on the scent of punctured bowels and fresh blood. He shivered, imagining how brutal the battle must be in Drobin Pass. Despite the risk, the young dwarf wished he could be there with the adults. He would fight on the front line with his uncle Bölak's core of *Dracken Viergur.* Someday, when he was old enough, he would join his famous uncle. For now, he would get as close to the front as he could by helping with the wounded who had been carried down from the pass and into the capital, Drobin City.

"Thor, please help me with this." Daerna Hargrim, a Sister of Lorak and Thor's mother, motioned for him with a bloody hand. She had finished stitching the flesh together and now reinforced the dressing on the dwarf's stump with a thick bandage. "Hold up his leg."

Thor followed her orders as she expertly wrapped the stump where the warrior's foot had been severed, all the while re-assuring him with her calm voice and gentle touch. Thor marveled at her composure. For days, his mother had barely slept as endless streams of wounded had come through the cavern. He was certain that there were no warriors on the battle line with as much stamina as Daerna Hargrim.

Thor's gaze wandered. The small coal fires scattered around the cavern to keep the injured warm revealed that more bleed-ing soldiers were being brought in by exhausted bearers. A dozen Sisters of Lorak and their assistants rushed to help.

"Where will we put them?" Thor asked, wondering how any more could fit in the overcrowded cavern.

"We'll make room here," Daerna said, indicating they would

move the soldiers even closer together. She always found a way.

Thor and his mother prepared to move an injured warrior when Daerna stopped and rigidly faced the entrance to the cavern. Fear intruded into her soft brown eyes.

"What is it?" Thor whirled around as frightened Sisters fled the entrance dragging wounded soldiers with them. A wave of panic—that felt like a hot wind—swept across the chamber. Those who had not regained consciousness suddenly woke up and cried out in terror. Others who could still move, crawled toward the small exit tunnels.

Unable to comprehend what was happening, Thor focused on a lone dwarven warrior who stood blocking the cavern entrance. His eyes glowed red with an otherworldly fire. Leathery wings sprouted from his back and he grew into a giant. His body expanded and his neck lengthened. His hands became claws and his head elongated and grew black horns. Iron-gray scales became the size of shields as they sprouted from his flesh. The dwarf grew into a massive true dragon. His bulk crushed those lying on the floor near the entrance and shattered the stone steps leading down into the room.

The exits were clogged with terrified dwarves. Daerna turned to Thor as the wyrm opened his mouth. She dove onto her son, pushing him down as the dragon spewed torrents of fire. His mother used her body as a shield, hugging Thor and pulling his arms and face into her body. Her long braid caught fire and Daerna's scalp blazed like a torch. Thor felt the heat, smelled the burning hair and tried to roll his mother away from the flames. She pinned him under her, all the while praying to Lorak for protection—not for herself—but for her son.

The dragon stomped about the cavern, burning and crushing whomever he could. A few wounded warriors stood to face him. He batted them aside and sent his fire into the tightly packed exits where the Sisters were trying to help the wounded escape.

Screams of terror were choked off as the dragon immolated scores of Drobin.

Thor finally slipped out from under his mother's burning body and smothered the flames with his bare hands. He rolled her on her side as she blinked back tears of agony.

"*Mother.*" Thor held her blackened hand, praying to Lorak to save her life, to take his instead, for she was a worthy servant of the Mountain God, unlike him.

Daerna's lips trembled. She whispered, "My son, you must live." Her soft brown eyes closed for the last time.

Thor kissed her hand and stood to face the dragon who once again crouched near the entrance. The cavern was filled with flames and choking smoke. The young dwarf drew his dagger and prepared to charge the beast. Heat from burning corpses kept him back and he choked on the noxious smoke, then fell to his knees.

A voice boomed like thunder in Thor's mind, knocking him down beside the body of his mother.

"*I am Draglûne, the new king of the dragons! This is a warning to all who oppose my reign. I can strike anywhere I choose. Tremble in your halls of stone, for someday I will return and slay all of your folk!*"

Thor wiped his eyes. "My mother gave her life so I would live to hunt Draglûne." The dwarven warrior fixed his hard gaze on Drake. "Know this: Draglûne will die before my eyes, and I'll avenge my fallen kin."

Drake considered the two dwarves in the light of this new knowledge. "So many terrible things have happened to both of you. No one should have to endure what you have."

"We all pay our own price," Bellor said. "The survivors of such things are maimed, body and soul, but worst off are the restless spirits of the dead who cannot find their way to Lorak's Halls."

The hair on Drake's arms stood tall after the mention of restless ghosts.

"The spirits of the dead are often dwarves with unfulfilled vows," Bellor said. "They won't leave this world or go to the next. I've helped guide many of them, though it's very difficult to make them go against their will. So they stay in eternal agony, never able to complete their sworn duty, or pass on. It nearly broke me to walk through the battlefields and find so many spirits who wouldn't leave."

A chill lingered in Drake, and he had to suppress the unease in his heart. Something needled at him, and he saw the Void in his mind's eye, but he couldn't face it. Not yet.

Early the next morning, Drake led the way after finding a place to ascend the four-hundred-foot stone cliff. A water-cut chute led all the way to the top. He guided the dwarves and dogs up the narrow defile past boulders and spiny plants. The end of the climb proved to be more difficult than he'd expected, and it took more than an hour to finally reach the top.

Cresting the rocky ridge, Drake looked west. The expansive grasslands and the Void beckoned in the distance. The ocean of white clouds appeared as if it was going to rise up and overwhelm the plateau with its sheer immensity.

Once the dwarves and the dogs joined him, the young man got them off the exposed promontory and took refuge under the thorny trees and spindly thickets of devil's club. They fought through the tightly packed stalks of spiky plants and around the jumbled granite formations.

After another hour of hard travel, the companions and the anxious dogs stumbled out of a thicket and into a clearing beside an overhang of rock. The wind shifted and the musky smell of griffins and the sharp scent of rotting flesh filled the air. The bones of vrelk, thistle deer, and mountain sheep littered the ground, also peppered with large, tawny feathers and griffin tracks.

Crossbow ready and eyes searching, Drake stepped away from the empty nest site, ushering the dwarves to go back the way they had come. The rumbling growls of Jep and Temus alerted him to the presence of something hiding in the brush. Hackles rising, the dogs bared their teeth. Pointing his crossbow at the bushes, the Clifftoner sidestepped away from the clearing. He waved the dwarves to go while he guarded the rear with the snarling dogs.

A griffin as large as Jep exploded out of the brush, springing toward Drake with its talons and a hooked beak aimed at his throat. Drake's bolt impaled the young monster in the chest, but its momentum carried it forward. The wounded beast knocked him onto his back, pinning him against the bushes.

Jep and Temus tore at the griffin's haunches, nearly dragging it off their master. Thor and Bellor struck the juvenile aevian in the back, their blows ending its twitching. Drake pulled himself out of the bushes and felt blood trickling from lacerations on both arms.

"How badly are you hurt?" Bellor asked.

"Only scratches," Drake said, though his sore ribs throbbed and his arms burned with pain as he tried to reload his crossbow.

A griffin's piercing shriek made Drake jerk backwards and drop the bolt he was loading. "Go!" Leaving the shaft on the ground, he pushed the dwarves away from the nest. They ran as fast as they could, Jep and Temus loping behind.

The aevian's call echoed down the ridge. *A second youngling or an adult?* He wondered how many griffins could hear the high-pitched, screeching call. Trying to control his fear, Drake followed Bellor, then lost sight of Thor as he crashed through the dense brush further ahead. Another griffin shrieked nearby. A dull crunch silenced the aevian's battle cry. Five steps later, Drake hopped over the body of an immature griffin. Blood leaked from its cracked skull, matching the fresh stains on Thor's warhammer.

Another ear-piercing shriek echoed across the ridge.

"How many more," Bellor gasped for air, "are there?"

"At least one," Drake said, "probably more."

Bellor ran out of breath four thickets later. "Stop . . . for . . . now." He sprawled on the ground, trying to catch his wind.

Jep and Temus licked Drake's bleeding arms, hindering his attempts to reload.

"We've got to keep . . . moving," Drake said, finally succeeding at cocking his crossbow. "When the adult griffins return . . . and find the young ones dead—"

"They'll come after us." Bellor pulled himself to his feet. "Let's hope they're on the plains hunting, but we better get going."

Taking over for Thor, Drake guided them as fast as he could. The companions kept snaking southward, fighting their way through the clinging thickets. When the sun set, they paused for a quick meal and some much-needed rest, then continued on with Thor leading the way. Unhindered by the darkness, Thor and Bellor found ways through the brambles, while Drake kept his ears open for sounds of pursuit.

The pattern of almost nightly rain showers continued and soaked them utterly. Despite being chilled and exhausted, they didn't pause until an hour before sunrise. Once the sun's light filled the horizon, Drake urged them on again. For the rest of the day and most of the second rainy night on the ridge, they hiked as rapidly as they could, stopping only twice, and never for more than an hour.

On the morning of the third day, the half-roar, half-shriek of an adult griffiness reverberated through the trees, waking the exhausted companions after only a few minutes of sleep.

"They've come." Bellor struggled to sit up and raise his axe.

"Only one." Drake shook off his fatigue, a burst of nervous energy coursing through him. "She's calling for her sisters."

Thor glared at Bellor. "Let's stand against them, before you and Drake are too tired to fight."

The dogs stopped licking their sore paws and whimpered.

"No." Bellor forced his exhausted muscles to help him sit up. "We go before more arrive."

Drake rose and began cutting through the thicket with his Kierka blade. The calls of at least five griffins thundered behind them a half hour later.

Thor growled through clenched teeth. "Now we'll have them!"

"Keep moving under the trees." Bellor pushed the younger dwarf ahead.

The dogs snarled, glancing behind them as the sounds of pursuit intensified.

"This way!" Drake tried to surge forward. The fatigue in his legs held him back.

The pack of griffins crashed through the brush, gaining on the companions. Drake ducked branches, wending his way forward. Bushes slapped his face and cut his hands. Suddenly, the thicket disappeared, recently incinerated by a massive fire. The ground was almost totally clear—except for the darkened trees.

For an instant Drake's heart leaped with joy. He could run at full speed, but he realized the griffins could run much faster in the burned-out terrain. Mind reeling, his shoulder smashed into a charred tree. The impact sent him sprawling to the ground. Acrid ashes stirred up by the collision filled his mouth. He coughed as the dogs followed fast on his heels. Jep and Temus stopped to guard his prone form. The dwarves exploded out of the thick brush, stumbling onto the razed ground.

The feathery heads of seven griffins appeared behind them. Hungry eyes met Drake's as he sprang to his feet. The dwarves reached him and the three of them, plus the dogs, faced the griffins.

A large female with a bristling head of feathers emerged from the brush. Drake aimed at the lead griffiness. He knew her yellow eyes, having seen them after the vrelk stampede. She cocked her head to the side and he thought she remembered him too. An eighth griffin, a gigantic male with a thick mane of golden feathers, appeared beside the lead female.

"I'm waiting!" Thor shouted, banging his hammer on his shield.

The griffins hesitated, sniffing the air and burned ground.

"What're they waiting for?" Thor asked.

"Back up . . . slowly." Drake grabbed Jep's collar and pulled the growling dog with him. Temus followed and the pack of griffins made low, wet, rumbling sounds that vibrated through Drake's chest—but the aevians didn't move forward.

After a few paces, Bellor said, "They won't come after us."

"Why not?" Thor asked in a tone that made Drake wonder if he was disappointed.

"They won't leave their territory?" Drake kept stepping backwards.

"They're afraid of us." Thor bared his teeth.

"No," Bellor whispered, "they're afraid of the dragon."

XXXV

We're close to Draglûne. One misstep and we could be
dead, or worse, slaves of the wyrm.
                    —Bölak Blackhammer, from the Lost Journal

The companions descended from the burned section of Griffin
Ridge in a narrow defile filled with scorched shrubs and fallen
trees. Drake led the way, kicking up gray ash with each step.
The fine grit coated his clothes, irritated his eyes, and left a bitter taste in his mouth that he couldn't spit out. Blurred vision
threw off his steps and his footfalls slapped against the rock
much too loudly. Looking at the ribbon of sky he thought, *If the
griffins overcome their fear . . . or if Draglûne comes. . . .*

A hawk's piercing cry caused Drake to point his cocked
crossbow at the sky. The raptor flew parallel to their course,
then disappeared. Quickening his pace, he herded Jep and Temus in front of him. Bellor and Thor followed behind, navigating the rocks much better than he did.

"Steady on, lad." Bellor touched Drake's shoulder. "We're
almost to the bottom."

Momentum dragged the young man down the sloping rock
and his exhausted leg muscles fought against gravity. The slope
finally ended and he sagged to his knees, weariness overcoming
him.

"We can't stop now." Thor helped Drake stand. The Clifftoner wobbled, then matched Thor stride for stride. He kept

thinking about why eight griffins had let them go. The very idea of the vicious predators being afraid of anything made his stomach twist into knots. *What if the dragon heard the griffins and is waiting for us?* He glanced upwards.

Something touched Drake's shoulder and he shied away.

Bellor froze, his hand in mid air. "It's me."

"Sorry, Bellor. I'm . . . I guess I'm. . . ."

"You're just overly tired. Me too." Bellor's face looked pale. "I want you to have these." The War Priest handed Drake a half-dozen crossbow bolts with rune symbols on the shafts and narrow, steel points designed for deep penetration. "They're enchanted with Earth magic and will be very potent against wingataurs."

"Thank you." Drake loaded one, putting the rest in his leg quiver along with his and Ethan's thorn bolts.

"We must remain vigilant," The War Priest said. "The dragon may be close."

The roar of the two rivers filled the burned woods, foiling the companions' ability to hear much beyond their immediate surroundings. The dead trees had once been vibrant stands of old growth brush-blossom. Even in death, the trees partially hid the companions when they arrived at the tumultuous intersection of the Boulder and Steam Rivers.

Hiding in the shadows, Drake looked upstream, where the Boulder River disappeared inside the rocky walls of Red Canyon. Under his direction, Jep and Temus crept forward beside a fallen log and stood in the shallows, lapping at the fast-moving water. Next, Thor stood watch while Drake joined the dogs and filled his belly with refreshing liquid. He splashed water on his face, scrubbed off the ash, and wished he could lie down on the cool stones for a moment. Instead, he searched for a way across while the dwarves both drank their fill.

Huge rocks churned the water to a white froth and spring

runoff created rapids and deep whirlpools. Downstream, the rounded ends of several giant boulders poked out of the river, forming a path nearly all the way across. The rocks sat close together in the middle of the channel, reminding Drake of miniature versions of the Lily Pad Rocks. Instead of falling into the Void, the penalty for failure would be a battering on the rocks and then death in a churning whirlpool.

"Are you sure Quarzaak is on the south side?" Drake asked.

Thor and Bellor nodded.

"We'll have to cross there." Drake pointed downstream.

Bellor eyed the proposed route. "Even I can hop those distances, although Thor and I will sink like stones if we fall in." Bellor picked at his chain-mail hauberk.

"The jumps aren't big," Thor said, "and we can reach Red Canyon by nightfall once we cross."

Drake hiked downstream to the rocks. He kept to the shadows as he waded into the frigid, thigh-deep water carrying his boots. He climbed onto the first stone, then helped Temus climb up with him. Shaking as much water off his legs as he could, he glanced at the rapids below and pulled on his boots. The Clifftoner sprang gracefully from the first rock to the second, to the third, the fourth, and all the way across. Temus didn't want to be left behind and followed eagerly after getting over his fear before the first jump. Thor followed first, powering through his jumps all the way. Jep sprang after him, wagging his tail excitedly between leaps.

Standing on the first rock, Bellor stared at the next stone.

Come on, Bellor, Drake thought, *you can make it.*

Bellor jumped. Crossed the first gap. He leaped across the second, landed awkwardly. The old dwarf wobbled, teetered, was unable to get his balance and flailed his arms.

"No!" Thor screamed over the roar of the river.

The old Priest fell headfirst into the rapids and disappeared

293

beneath the swirling water.

Jep leaped into the river and disappeared below the surface. Thor struggled to pull off his chain-mail hauberk in preparation to dive in, while Drake sprinted downstream where he could pull Bellor or Jep out. He leaped onto some rocks and positioned himself near the main channel of the river, straining to see Bellor or Jep below the turbulent flow.

Thor splashed feet-first into the water, then vanished from sight.

Drake lay on his chest reaching into the freezing river. Heart pounding, he waited as Temus whimpered on the bank and ran back and forth. A moment passed with no sign of Bellor, Jep, or Thor. *They've been down there too long!* Drake jumped to his feet, preparing to dive in.

A hand thrust from the river. Drake dropped, grabbed the wrist and pulled with all his might. A dwarf clambered up on the rocks, coughing out water.

"Thor!" Drake turned from him and put his arm back into the freezing current. Thor coughed and retched as Drake's hand started to go numb. A thousand needles stabbed into his arm. "Bellor! Jep!" He kept his hand in the water. "Bellor! Jep!"

Thor's coughs became sobs as the moments passed.

Numb with shock more than cold, Drake pulled his empty hand from the water.

XXXVI

How would I carry on without Thor? And if I fall, will he
have the strength to go on without me?
　　　　　—Bellor Fardelver, from the Thornclaw Journal

Sheltered under living brush-blossom trees on the south side of
the Boulder River, Drake and Thor stood in stunned silence.
Temus watched the river and whimpered.

Guilty thoughts stabbed Drake in the back like white-hot
bolts. *Why didn't I take Bellor's pack? I should have carried it for
him. I should have found a better route across. I should have held
Jep's collar.* He imagined Bellor and Jep's bodies being carried
downriver until they fell into the Underworld where blood-
spattered griffins and other demons would tear their corpses
apart.

Temus' ears pricked up. He barked and then ran downstream
at full speed.

"Come on!" Drake yelled, sprinting after his dog. Thor chased
behind and Drake thought Temus barked again, but he realized
the sound originated from further down the river. *Jep!*

Around the bend, Temus stood in the shallows barking. Jep
stood on a half-submerged rock six paces from the shore, cut
off by frothing rapids. Clinging to the same rock, Bellor hung
on as whitewater pulled at his lower body.

"Hang on!" Drake screamed, trying to figure out a way to
reach them.

Thor arrived a few moments later as Drake labored to drag a fallen tree as big around as his thigh into the river. With Thor's help they moved the log into position and both stood in the shallows where they floated it to Bellor's rock. The power of the river pressed the log against the stone, holding it in place. Jep jumped onto the dead trunk and ran ashore.

"Grab it!" Drake yelled as he tried to keep his footing on the slippery bottom.

Bellor's trembling hands locked onto the log.

"Hold on!" Thor shouted, as he and Drake pulled Bellor to the bank. They dragged the shivering dwarf out of the river and amid joyful laughter took cover far under the trees.

Jep pranced over and stuck his wet nose into Drake's face before doing the same to Bellor.

"Jep found me." Bellor rubbed the dog's neck. "I grabbed him and he swam to that rock. I'd been under for a while when I felt him beside me. I grabbed his tail and he pulled me to the surface. I owe Jep my life. I won't forget that."

"*Good dog.*" Drake hugged Jep and pet Temus.

Jep pulled away and pranced over to Thor, where he shook himself dry. The scowling dwarf bore the brunt of the dog fur-scented water. "*Stunkenmutt!*" Thor growled and wiped away the water, trying to hide his smile. "At least you had a bath."

A low rumbling growl from Temus made the companions whirl around. The dog stared at the riverbed. The winged shadow cast by the flying creature stretched from bank to bank and quickly disappeared as it flew toward Red Canyon.

The companions stood speechless and shocked. The dogs huddled against Drake and he felt bitterly cold as he realized how big the dragon's wingspan had been. It was much larger than he imagined.

"Was it Draglûne?" Thor asked, not even trying to hide his concern.

The War Priest sagged into the ground. "We'll find out soon enough."

The shrill chirping of birds and the roaring river blocked out the sounds of the companions as they passed beneath the brush-blossom, aspen and gnarlpine trees. Drake marched first, his crossbow loaded with a bolt enchanted with Earth magic. The dogs followed close behind, their subdued demeanor mirroring his. Bellor followed the bullmastiffs and Thor watched their backs with his hammer ready in one hand, shield in the other.

Picking his way through the shadowy trees, the Clifftoner paid close attention to his dogs, hoping they would perceive a threat long before his lesser senses ever could. The dragon sighting spurred him to focus, though thoughts about home kept intruding into his thoughts. Just a week ago he had held Jaena in his arms and finally decided to marry her. A surge of homesickness and a longing for her overwhelmed him. He wished he could be there by her side and not here, marching into constant danger. But this was something he had to do, both for Jaena and all the people he loved. After what had happened in Armstead, there was no turning back. Too many men had died already because of the dragon and its minions. If there was anything he could do to stop it from causing more harm, Drake would do it.

Through a break in the abundant trees, the half-mile-wide mouth of Red Canyon rose in the distance. Monolithic cliffs towered on either side of the river, blocking the view of the snowcapped mountains. Judging by the roar of the rapids, the Boulder River moved even faster as it exited the canyon.

The dwarves stared at the lofty red walls, almost entirely vertical and several hundred feet tall. A ledge of white stone ran along the rim, with hardy needle-leaf trees perched on inaccessible ledges high above the canyon floor, where only the wind or aevians could reach them.

Bellor stared in awe. "Drake, please tell me again what you know of this place."

For the second time he explained what his father and uncle had said about the colossal ravine snaking backwards for miles. The cliffs were actually made up of several individual plateaus, each with a flat top covered with trees. The walls were nearly continuous, forming natural barriers on either side of the river. Red Canyon curved and followed the meandering waterway, congested with gigantic reddish boulders.

"I can see why Uncle Bölak would want to live in such a place," Thor said.

"Magnificent," Bellor agreed. "We'll camp inside tonight."

Thor whispered in Drobin as they got closer to the red walls.

"I apologize," Bellor said, "Nexan doesn't have the right words to describe the beauty of the stone here. Ever since we read Bölak's description in his journal, we have wanted to see it. He wrote it was 'blessed by Lorak' and had 'the most magnificent red sandstone I've ever seen.' He was right. This place is sacred."

"Did they know about this place before they came here?" Drake asked.

"The Kamarian Blood Warrior, Wulf Ironfinder, an old friend of mine, was their scout. He discovered it while exploring this area many decades ago. He trekked through the Thornclaw before either of your villages were built."

Bellor slipped back into Drobin as he and Thor studied a waterfall cascading down hundreds of feet to splash into an oval pool before joining the river. Drake paid extra attention to the sky while the dwarves stood ogling the canyon. He traversed around an area full of the sandy mounds of large fever-ant colonies. The finger-long black ants marched on the ground, forming long lines that crisscrossed the canyon floor.

"Ouch!" Thor slapped his legs. Several ants climbed the dwarf's body.

"Get away from the mound!" Drake shouted, grabbing a leafy branch to use for an ant-brush. Thor scurried away from the huge anthill while Drake caught up to him and brushed off the bugs as fast as he could.

Moments later, far away from the mounds, the young man inspected the two coin-sized welts forming on Thor's legs.

Thor grimaced, squeezing his eyes shut. "They burn like fire."

"Woodskull." Drake shook his head. "You're lucky you didn't break one open. You could've gotten stung hundreds of times. And if you'd somehow survived that, you'd end up dead from the fever. Hopefully you won't get sick with it now."

During the rest of the day they avoided several fields dotted with dozens of anthills. The gorge wasn't as wooded as Drake had hoped. He guided them from shadow to shadow, using stands of trees or the huge boulders strewn across the canyon as cover. Several times he stopped to study the canyon far ahead, making certain the rock formations hidden in shadow weren't actually a perched dragon.

When the light faded in the late afternoon and the canyon rim became too dark, the worn-out companions made camp in an overhang beneath the cliffs. Despite their screen of trees, they didn't dare make a fire.

Drake cleaned the trail dust off his crossbow. He carefully inspected the lathe, finding no cracks on either arm of the bow. The latch and trigger mechanism appeared in perfect working order. He put a new string on for good measure. He touched his thorn bolt for luck before placing it back in his leg quiver, then inspected the sikatha thorn he had been crafting into Ethan's thorn bolt. He worked on it with his boot knife, preparing it for a point and fletchings.

"We're close to Quarzaak. I can feel it." Thor scratched behind Jep's ears as the hungry dog lay panting at his feet.

"I wish we knew exactly where it was," Bellor said. "Bölak wrote something like the entrance was 'on the cliff, above the foot of the throne.' "

"We'll find it." Thor scratched the ant bites on his leg.

Drake's eyes kept drooping shut. After he had almost cut himself twice, he put the thorn bolt and boot knife away, then lay down with his back against the wall of the canyon. Fatigue from the last four days of no sleep and constant trekking made it impossible for his eyelids to stay open. As he settled in he noticed Jep and Temus begin to pace back and forth. Their ears pricked up as they stared into the night. He knew he should open his eyes. . . .

Both dogs growled, then barked in alarm. Drake's eyes popped open as he reached for his crossbow. He sat up and peered into the night. When he saw what approached, Drake knew his weapon would be useless.

XXXVII

They come for us. We're outnumbered. We must find a
way to hold them back.

— Bölak Blackhammer, from the Lost Journal

"Wake up, wake up!" Drake shouted and pointed into the darkness. "We've got to go!"

Thor and Bellor sprang up. The forest floor was coming
toward them. A writhing carpet of black fever-ants approached
them in a flowing swarm as wide as the Boulder River. The
dogs snarled and whined. Drake grabbed his pack. "Come on!"

The dwarves dashed away as thousands of the finger-long
insects streamed over the companions' abandoned camp, then
turned. "They're following us. What's happening?" His flesh
crawled at the sight of the rampaging insects and he remembered
how painful Thor's bites had looked.

"Keep going!" Thor urged.

Bellor struggled to keep running without dropping his armor
and other gear. They hurried through the forest and entered a
large grove of aspen trees. The pale moonlight reflected off the
white trunks of the young trees and green leaves rattled a warning in the breeze.

Deep throaty growls from the dogs sent chills down Drake's
spine. The companions stopped as Jep and Temus stared into
the trees. Ears and tails raised, the dogs glanced left and right,
as if tracking two different threats, in front and behind. The

darkness coupled with the white and black striated bark of the aspens ruined Drake's efforts to see through the web of shadows.

"What is it, boys?" Drake paid close attention to the dogs.

Thor raised his shield. "The dragon?"

"I don't know." Bellor slipped on his chain-mail shirt and put on his pack.

A teeming swarm of millions of fever-ants poured through the trees ahead of them. The insects flooded forward in an undulating dark tide. Drake gasped and stumbled back as the companions turned to run. An equally large swarm of ants came from behind.

More deadly insects flooded out of the trees. "To the river!" Drake yelled.

"We're trapped!" Thor shouted as the ants encircled them.

Drake's heart beat like a drum as the vast sea of fever-ants closed the distance around them. He imagined them crawling over his body, biting him thousands of times as they ate through his cheeks, crawled up his nose and inside his mouth until they filled his lungs before eating through his insides. "Climb the trees!"

"No!" Bellor shouted. "Stand your ground, the trees won't save us." Bellor took out a bag of white powder. With Thor's help, the dwarves sprinkled it on the ground in the shape of a circle seven paces in diameter while intoning Drobin words of power.

"Stay in the circle," Bellor commanded as they finished.

The noose tightened as the first bugs arrived at the scant bits of powder making up the ring. Seeing the insects' segmented bodies and hooked mandibles made the ant-bite scars on Drake's hands sting painfully.

The swarm halted at the white powder as if they'd run into an invisible wall. Drake fell back to the center of the circle, clenching his teeth in horror as they were entirely surrounded by the living sea.

"Will it hold them?" Drake asked.

"As long as we don't break the circle or attack them in any way, they won't get in. It will even hold demons at bay," Bellor said, "but not dragons."

Drake expected the ants to cross the flecks of white powder and skitter into the circle. They crawled along the edge trying to find a way in.

The sound of two heavy feet crunching the ground outside the ring echoed in the trees.

"The dragon comes!" Thor raised his hammer.

"That's no dragon," *Dracken Viergur* Master Bellor said, "but we must take precautions. We may need the *schützenfeör* before this night is over."

"What?" Drake glanced at the old dwarf.

"Fire-protection magic, *schützenfeör.*" The War Priest's hands glowed red as a dim aura of fire enshrouded his body. He touched Drake, Thor, Jep and Temus. The fiery aura disappeared from Bellor when he had touched them all.

After Bellor touched him, Drake's skin felt cool while fear scraped his insides.

Something moved in the forest in front and then behind.

"I can hear two of them," Thor said, "one there, one back there." He pointed into the woods. "Wingataurs?"

Bellor shrugged and Drake aimed his loaded crossbow into the trees, wanting to run out of the canyon as fast as he could. He heard two distinct sets of loud footsteps on either side. The creatures broke their way through the tough undergrowth snapping small trees and trampling bushes. The sounds grew louder on both sides as the creatures crashed through the forest.

The fast-moving monsters sped directly toward the circle. Drake heard the ominous sounds and could see bushes and trees being crushed—but nothing was there except a faint blur in the darkness.

"Draconic magic!" Bellor shouted. "They're invisible."

The unseen creatures charged them from two sides at full speed, plowing through the ants and leaving distinct hooflike footprints as they crushed the swarming bugs. Thor faced one and Drake the other as they prepared for the demonic onslaught.

Fighting the urge to flee with all his willpower, Drake's hands trembled on his crossbow. Less than twelve paces away the monsters charged hard and fast.

"Don't shoot!" Bellor pulled Drake's crossbow to the ground as he shot the missile into the dirt at their feet. "If you attack, they'll be able to come into the circle."

The invisible foes stopped dead in their tracks right outside the ring. Fever-ants parted in the wake of the demons giving Drake knowledge of their precise location. He drew his Kierka knife and cocked his arm, smelling their foul breath. He wondered what Kovan had seen before he died.

The creatures snorted and the ants surged forward like a black wave. The protection spell held them back. The invisible demons roared, then retreated into the trees beyond the thick ring of fever-ants. Drake watched the impression of their cloven hooves crush the insects as they stepped away.

The slicing sound of sharp metal cut the air, then through wood. An aspen tree fell creaking towards them as it crashed through the forest. Drake and Bellor dodged its trunk. They couldn't avoid its thin branches, which scratched and battered them before it slammed to the ground.

Another slicing sound and a second tree fell towards them, threatening to smash Drake into the earth. The third one fell and a fourth tree was soon on the way. He couldn't avoid the tree branches, and along with the dwarves and dogs kept narrowly avoiding the falling trunks.

"Can they break the magic with the tree trunks?" Drake asked.

"No, only if we attack them." Bellor dodged the falling trees and the ones on the ground.

"Do something, Bellor!" Thor yelled. "Use the Earth magic."

"I'll break the circle if I do." Bellor yelped as a branch struck him in the arm.

The dogs nearly ran into the swarm. Drake's hold on their collars weakened. He sidestepped the plummeting trees and pulled the yelping dogs with him. More aspens fell, crisscrossing their ring with tree trunks and branches that pummeled Drake to the ground.

A branch glanced off Bellor's head and he fell stunned. Thor barely managed to pull the War Priest's limp body out of the way of another falling log. The sound of chopping echoed close by.

Another tree fell and Drake couldn't see anything except the writhing blanket of deadly fever-ants. He lay on his side and rolled left to avoid another tumbling log. Jep eluded Drake's grip and dodged right. The dog skipped out of the circle into the morass of fever-ants.

"Jep!" A hewn tree blocked his way as Drake lunged forward.

Bounding over the fever-ants, Jep stood on a log as he tried to get away from the biting insects. Ants swarmed over the bullmastiff. He shook some of them off and snarled at an unseen foe that stomped forward. Jep confronted the demon as the bugs tried to bite through the dog's fur. Drake held Temus back as the dog tried to rush to his brother.

Thor dashed to where Jep had broken the circle and spread more white powder as ants poured in. The dwarf crushed many of the bugs with his foot as he sealed the circle tight again. He turned and stomped on the others as they sped toward Bellor's unconscious body.

305

Jep leaped into the air, jaws opening wide. He was caught in mid-jump and lifted up by the invisible monster. Jep's jaws snapped and he barked ferociously.

Using all his strength, Drake restrained Temus to prevent him from rushing out to save his brother. Long wounds appeared on Jep's side. Blood spurted out, as if he was being torn open by sharp claws. Drake gasped as Jep was raised higher then brought down savagely. Two sharp horns pierced through Jep's abdomen in midair. The dog howled in agony, impaled by the once invisible horns now covered in Jep's blood.

"No!" Drake screamed, keeping a firm hold of Temus.

"A sorcerer-wingataur!" Thor yelled as he smashed the last of the ants that had broken the circle.

Jep's spasming body was lifted off the horns and the dog's blood spurted onto the beast exposing its location. A loud roar erupted from the monster as it hurled Jep's body away. Drake stood paralyzed as his bloody dog flew toward him. An instant later, the bullmastiff smashed into him, knocking Drake onto the pile of trees crisscrossing the circle.

Crouching behind fallen trees that provided him with cover, Drake held Jep's body in his arms as the dog jerked and yelped. Thor shielded Bellor's body with his own as the dazed dwarf recovered from the blow to his head.

Jep's coppery-smelling blood soaked into Drake's clothes as he made a futile attempt to hold pressure on the terrible wounds. Choking back tears and horror, Drake knew his mangled dog was going to die.

Thor pushed Bellor under the cover of branches and set his shield over the War Priest's face. He crawled closer to Drake and laid his hands on Jep. "Lorak, I ask you for strength."

Drobin words rumbled from Thor's lips. A green radiance flowed out of the center of Thor's palms. The wounds on Jep's back began to close and Drake remembered Bellor's words about the Drobin Healing magic. Drake imagined the dog's physical body being pushed back along the timestream to the moment before he was injured.

"Great Lorak," Thor whispered, "please help me fight the flow of the *zeitströmen.*"

A thunderous roar from a demon blasted over them. Thor flinched and lost focus. Thor's arms trembled then he fell forward onto Jep as if the dwarf's body was being pulled into a raging river.

Thor's muscles bulged as he tried to pull away from Jep, then fell backwards. Thor's beard had grown slightly and the dwarf seemed to have aged right before his eyes—but the healing wasn't finished and Jep's wounds remained.

The dog whimpered, then stopped breathing and lay motionless. His life's blood oozed onto the ground from gaping abdominal wounds.

"I've failed." Defeat spread across Thor's face.

Bellor tossed aside Thor's shield and crawled toward Jep. Determination burned in the War Priest's eyes.

"Can you save him?" Drake asked as Jep's warm blood leaked through his hands.

Touching the dog's body, Bellor closed his eyes. "Jep clings to this world because of you. There's still a chance if I can pull him backwards through the *zeitströmen.*"

Bellor prayed and touched Jep's limp body. Drake imagined months slipping away from the old dwarf's life. A bright green light emanated from Bellor's chest and the radiance flowed down his arms, out his palms and into the dog. In only a few moments the massive wounds slowly closed. Bellor pulled away, shoulders sagging, his beard slightly more gray and looking utterly exhausted.

Jep opened his eyes and tried to get up. Drake hugged him tight, feeling the mended flesh and drying blood where there had just been fatal wounds.

"Thank Lorak, the time-distance wasn't too long." Bellor collapsed onto the bloody ground.

Thor hung his head. "I shouldn't have failed."

Temus licked his brother and then barked at the monsters lurking in the woods.

A deep roar of frustrated rage erupted from one of the invisible beasts hiding in the trees. The fever-ants mustered around the protective circle at a more frenetic pace.

"Thank you, Bellor, thank you, Thor." Drake helped Jep stand. "I thought he was gone."

Bellor grinned. "Not while he's under my care, and I always pay debts of honor."

"We should get under the branches." The Clifftoner motioned for his friends to take cover under the fallen tree trunks. He looked for signs of the unseen demons, heard only the chittering sounds of the ants cutting the shrubs and grass to shreds.

"How's your head?" Drake asked Bellor.

"Just a nasty bump. It's nothing, really." Bellor shrugged off the injury. Using the powerful Healing magic had affected him much more adversely.

"Dwarf skulls are an inch thick." Thor knocked on his forehead and grinned at Bellor.

Waiting for something to happen, Drake tried not to look at the ankle-deep blanket of fever-ants. He could hear the skin-crawling, scraping sounds of millions of ant bodies rubbing against each other and tearing up the plants around them. As the moments dragged on he thought the sound grew louder and louder.

"Look." Thor pointed to the trees at the edge of the clearing. "The stumps have clean cuts. One axe blow must've cloven through them."

Drake tried not to think about the force and sharpness

required to cut through the hard aspen trees. He really didn't want to consider what the wingataurs' axes would do to his soft flesh.

"We must get rid of these insects," Bellor said.

"How?" Drake asked.

"We'll pray for the rain to come," Bellor said.

"It would take a lot of rain," Drake said.

Bellor smiled, placed his hands on the earth and began to pray. A short time later Drake smelled moisture in the wind. Small drops began to fall, then larger ones as the ever-faithful rains poured from the sky. The ants' tightly packed formations gradually began to flatten and disperse. Moments later, the water falling from the canyon walls collected into small streams. It ran through the woods and toward the river, sweeping away more bugs. The white powder turned into a thick paste that clung to the ground.

When the wind and rain finally stopped, only a few hundred ants milled around the circle. A whizzing sound heralded the appearance of a small boulder flying through the air. Drake ducked as the rock passed within inches of his head. Another stone struck the tree trunk that Thor crouched behind. The companions took cover behind the fallen logs and crawled under them as much as they could. Stones as large as human heads dropped from above and others were hurled from the woods. Drake cowered with his friends among the fallen trees, trying to avoid the deadly hail.

The cascade of rocks halted as fire fell from the sky. A burning bush crashed into the pile of wood surrounding them.

"They won't have me in a bonfire." Thor leaped up and grabbed the flaming shrub with his bare hands. Drake expected Thor's beard and clothing to erupt in flames, but he seemed impervious to the fire. Pulling the bush out of the deadfall, Thor fell on top of it, smothering the flames with his chest, while Bellor extinguished several small fires with his bare hands and pushed mud onto them.

Drake thought the wetness from the rain protected them, then remembered the Drobin fire-protection spell as a second burning bush landed beside his leg. He couldn't feel the heat at all and stomped out the fire, gaining confidence when his clothing didn't burst into flames. Six more flaming bushes landed in the circle. The companions extinguished them and kept the fires from spreading.

A shadow passed high overhead, and the low scratching sound drifted from the trees.

"Are they gone?" Thor asked.

Bellor shook his head and Drake's heart raced while he waited for the next attack.

Moments later Drake heard someone running very fast along the stony bank by the river beyond the trees. Thor squinted toward the sound. "I see a human fleeing for his life."

The dogs barked and the running man yelled, "Drake!"

Though unable to see through the darkness, Drake immediately recognized the voice. "Uncle Sandon! Over here! Run!"

The man sprinted toward the circle and crashed through the undergrowth and trees. Struggling to catch his breath, the sweat-soaked man raced toward them hopping over logs and dodging spiny shrubs. Ten paces from the circle, he tripped and collapsed on the ground.

"Get up!" Drake shouted.

Sandon tried to stand, then groaned in pain as he fell back down. Something pulled him backwards by one leg. His uncle screamed in terror as an unseen foe dragged him away.

"Help me! Please!" Sandon begged, stretching his arms and grasping in vain at the undergrowth.

Drake lunged forward. Bellor grabbed him by the belt and

pulled him backwards. Thor tackled the young man to the ground and they crashed onto the logs.

"Let me go! It's my uncle, we've got to save him." Drake fought Thor who tried to pin him down.

"That's not Sandon!" Bellor shouted.

Resisting with all his might, Drake tried to pull away from Thor, who crushed him like a boulder with steel arms.

"That's not Sandon!" Bellor shouted. "Your uncle couldn't run like that. It's a trick of the Draconic magic. Don't believe it. That's a demon, not your uncle."

The man screamed again for help as he was lifted by his legs into the air. He grabbed onto a tree and begged, "Please, Drake, *help me!*"

Sandon lost his grip and was dragged into the woods. His screams of terror and pain continued. Drake heard cracking and thumping, followed by agonized wailing.

The sounds of torment stopped several moments later. Drake took his trembling hands slowly off his ears, and prayed to Amaryllis that Bellor had been right.

XXXVIII

The demons have us trapped in the circle. We must break
the siege.

—Bellor Fardelver, from the Thornclaw Journal

A loud snort came from the woods. Huddled under the fallen
aspen trees, Drake heard the sharp cracking of a tree limb.

"They're watching us," Bellor said, glancing into the darkness. "We must be ready, especially if the dragon attacks."

"I'll keep watch." Thor's eyes barely stayed open.

"The dogs and I will stand guard." Drake tried to shift away
from the aspen branches poking him in the back. He knew he
couldn't sleep—even if he wanted to.

"Using the Healing magic has exhausted Thor and I. We must
rest."

Drake and the dogs started their vigil as wind began blowing
through the trees again. Rain fell in great torrents until the early
morning. The drops pattered endlessly on his hooded cloak,
soothing him to sleep.

The sun rose over the canyon walls in the morning. Frozen
to his very soul, Drake felt like he hadn't slept at all, but knew
he'd drifted off a few times before sunrise. He noticed Bellor
and Thor were awake and the War Priest looked somewhat older
in the morning light.

Bones creaking, Bellor stood up and scanned the trees. Thor
brushed the mud off his bloodstained clothes.

"I want to take a look by the river," Bellor said.

Bleary-eyed, crossbow ready, Drake and the dogs led the way through the woods. His boots crunched on dead fever-ants with every step. He paid close attention to the dogs, in case the demons waited in ambush.

At the riverside, Jep and Temus lapped at the water. Thor refilled their waterskins while Drake and Bellor inspected the tracks in the mud. Cloven hoofprints stood out in the muddy spots, then changed to human boot prints where they had heard the running during the night.

"I see the tracks. It's just hard to believe." Drake ran his fingers over the outline of a boot heel, then touched the hoof-prints preceding it.

"Believe it," Bellor said. "There'll be much worse to come. Surviving last night was a gift from Lorak. We learned about our opponents and they studied us as well. When we meet them next, blood will flow." Bellor lifted his weapon in two hands. "My axe will taste the wyrm-kin's blood. *Wyrmslayer* has great power against any creature with dragon blood and the winga-taurs will feel its bite."

"We better get moving." The Clifftoner glanced at the rising sun, and wondered if the dragon had also watched them during the night. He ushered them back under the trees.

Bellor put down his axe and took out Bölak's Quarzaak Journal. He translated some of it aloud: "We followed the river, until we were almost within crossbow range of the great falls. Wulf climbed the cliff on a narrow path that started near the foot of the throne before calling down to us, saying he reached the caves he had discovered so many years before. The entrance was high up on the southern cliffs, with a great view of the falls. I see the approaches can be easily defended, and could be held by few determined warriors." Bellor scrutinized the words on the page. "I'm not sure what he means by the 'throne.' "

"We'll know it when we see it." Thor marched forward without pausing. Bellor nodded as they all walked west toward Red Falls and the head of the canyon.

Drake and the dogs took the lead, keeping under the trees and watching for any hint of danger. A crow on the ground drew his attention. "Are the wingataurs able to change into small creatures?" Drake motioned subtly to the black-feathered aevian that watched them.

Bellor shook his head. "Sorcerer-wingataurs can assume the shapes of human or dwarf-sized creatures. Draconic magic is very powerful, but it has its limitations."

"The enchanted bolts you gave me will kill them?" Drake touched his leg-quiver.

"Yes," Bellor said, "but only if they penetrate deep."

Whirling to his left, Drake shot the crow. Bellor and Thor jumped with surprise as he released the bolt. The bird fell from its perch, wings askew.

"Temus, fetch." The dog retrieved the dead bird, laying it at his master's feet and wagging his tail as saliva dripped from his mouth. "Good boy." Drake patted Temus, removed his bolt, and cut the bird in half, giving a portion to each dog. After cleaning the shaft, he put it back in his quiver. "They fly true, Bellor."

"They fly true with you shooting them. Thor and I have practiced with crossbows for many years, but I doubt we can match your skill."

Thor wrinkled his nose.

They followed the narrowing canyon walls that stretched high above their heads. Drake noted every possible ambush point or break in the thin canopy of aspen and brush-blossom trees. He suspected that if the wingataurs were watching them, they were invisible and downwind—or the dogs would have smelled them. "What are the wingataurs and the dragon waiting for?"

Bellor looked into Drake's eyes. "You mean, why don't they attack?"

"They're cowards," Thor said.

"They'll come when we're most vulnerable," Bellor said. "As far as the dragon . . . I don't know what has kept it away. I fear we'll find out soon enough."

Eyes burning from lack of sleep, Drake refused to let fatigue claim him. The tension from being constantly alert was a heavy burden. He started to see movement in the shadows, hear noises in the woods, though nothing was there. He felt slower than normal, not as sure of himself. "Should we rest?"

"We can't stop now," Thor said.

Bellor considered the request.

A howling call in the distance startled Drake and the dogs' ears pricked up.

"A wingataur." Bellor lifted his axe.

"See, we can't stop now," Thor said, "or we'll give them more time to set a trap for us."

Sighing heavily, Drake trudged along. A short time later another howl seemed closer. His finger lay poised on his crossbow's trigger as the dogs' tails perked up.

The quietness of the next couple of hours frazzled Drake's nerves even more. "Where are they?"

"Still watching us," Bellor said, "probably up ahead."

Through a gap in the trees, Drake caught his first glimpse of Red Falls. The roar of the cascading water filled the canyon. As they approached, it increased to the volume of a continuous thunderstorm. The rushing water plunged five hundred feet as it squeezed through a narrow defile of rock high above the canyon floor where the walls pressed together. Vertical cliffs hemmed in the river. There was no way to go further.

The companions had to yell to be heard above the falls. They wouldn't be able to hear their enemies sneaking up on them. With a grim expression, Drake searched for a sign of the 'throne' Bölak wrote about.

Thor shouted, "That big ledge halfway up the cliff," he pointed, "has trees on it and looks like it has the armrests of a chair on either side. And a high back like a king's throne."

Bellor stared at the rock formation. "We'll find a way up. That has to be the giant throne Bölak wrote about."

Watching for danger, Drake kept an eye skyward. As they approached the "throne," the dogs' tails stood up. Cautiously, the companions moved closer to the base of the throne rock. Several dry water runoff chutes snaked down from a gigantic fan-shaped hill that turned into the throne. The red stone hill looked like a fractured ramp up to the seat of the chair, but it was unclear if the chutes extended all the way to the seat or ended at a cliff.

"Water made these trails long ago." Bellor pointed at the dry chutes, then spoke just loud enough to be heard above the roar of the falls, "I'm certain one of these is the 'narrow path' Bölak wrote about. But which one to take?"

A half-dozen water-cut trails angled up steeply from the foot of the throne. Each one twisted and turned, hiding where it originated. The trails disappeared in the upper reaches of the promontory as they rose higher. All of the paths could be walked up easily, but none stood out as the right way to go.

Jep and Temus turned away from the rock and growled. They sniffed the light breeze coming out of the woods behind them.

Bellor glanced at the trees, apparently trying not to draw attention to his actions. Drake stepped to one of the trailheads and urged the dogs to follow him.

"Be wary," Bellor said, "the wingataurs are close."

Thor scanned the woods and raised his shield to cover his chest. "I'll watch our backs."

"Choose a path," Bellor ordered the Clifftoner.

Taking the lead, he picked one in the middle and crept up the narrow, uncovered trail. His back tingled because of the lack of protection from aevians. He expected the wingataurs to attack at any moment. He struggled against the urge to crouch among the rocks and scan the sky.

"Steady on, lad," Bellor said.

Even with Bellor's reassuring presence behind him, Drake couldn't relax. The way became much steeper after the first turn, and the incline made his legs burn. The walls closed in as they ascended higher. Drake couldn't see very far ahead as he followed the dark-red sandstone, stained black where the water had run over it for centuries. The path forked and Drake led them to the right. The chute ended at a short cliff which appeared to be a waterfall during the wet times.

"We'll try another way," Bellor said, as Thor led them while backtracking downward. Drake thought the left fork looked promising and for the hundredth time he made certain a Drobin bolt enchanted with Earth magic was loaded into his crossbow.

The second path Drake chose led them to higher ground overlooking the canyon. He crouched below the steep cliff in front of the seat of the throne with his back to the rock face. The seat loomed over a hundred feet above them and Thor found a path ascending the cliff that circled around the side.

"Perfect place for an ambush," Bellor whispered.

Thor bared his teeth for an instant, then waved the other two ahead.

Drake started up, traversing the narrow ledge-trail, only one pace wide. Jep and Temus hesitated before following, then Bellor came, with Thor bringing up the rear. The width of the trail didn't worry Drake, but when it curved around the side of the throne-rock, he stared down at a four-hundred-foot drop-off. He saw the path angling toward the east arm of the throne, and they had to keep going.

Cool wind tousled Drake's hair. The spray from Red Falls, thundering to his left, misted the air and muffled the sound of his footsteps. The height gave him a spectacular view, but also made his heart beat faster as he stepped forward, trying not to look down.

After a few steps, the ledge narrowed to only a half-stride wide. He approached the precipice. A natural staircase had been carved by water erosion through the armrest of the throne. "Looks like this slot leads into the seat," he yelled to the dwarves. Drake inspected the way forward and realized it couldn't be seen from the base of the canyon. The red staircase-like path was enclosed on both sides by high, smooth walls.

Inside the hidden stairway the rock shielded Drake from the wind. Bellor followed and Thor lingered behind on the ledge with the dogs inspecting the cliff.

A boulder hurtled toward him from the top of the chute. "Ambush!" Drake's reflexive step back made him bump into Bellor and they nearly fell over.

"Look out!" Bellor shouted, pointing skyward. Another rock plummeted toward Drake from above. Pushing Bellor backwards, he dodged the skull-sized rock.

The smaller stone exploded upon impact, spraying fragments and fine red dust everywhere. Bellor pulled Drake with him. They made it back to the ledge as the rolling boulder burst out of the chute, narrowly missing Drake's leg. The stone fell hundreds of feet and crashed into the trees below.

"Follow me!" Thor yelled, edging onto a thin ledge that disappeared further around the cliff toward the main wall of the canyon.

A second boulder tumbled down the chute. "Go!" Bellor yelled, prodding Drake and the dogs to follow his kinsman.

Chasing after Thor, Drake kept glancing at the sky as Bellor dashed right behind him. They rounded the corner of the narrow ledge, Drake hugged the cliff face as Thor led the way to a low cave mouth. "Come on," he yelled, ducking and crawling inside.

Drake scurried in after Thor and the dogs, but Bellor lagged behind by a few steps as he navigated the narrow trail.

The sound of a rock whizzing through the air made Drake cringe even though he was inside the cave. He reached for Bellor as the War Priest dove forward. The stone smashed into Bellor's backpack, the rock knocking the old dwarf to the ground. Drake grabbed Bellor's outstretched arms and pulled the old dwarf's limp body into the recess of stone.

"Bellor!" Thor clambered toward his mentor's side and took over pulling him in.

Drake aimed at the tunnel opening as wind whistled into the cave. He refused to blink from the dust stinging his eyes.

Groaning in agony, Bellor gnashed his teeth together.

"Bellor?" Thor reached to help, but hesitated to touch him.

"My pack . . . took . . . most . . . of the blow. I'm all right."

"You're a miserable liar." Thor helped Bellor turn on his side, eliciting gasps from the injured dwarf.

"Help me sit up." Bellor struggled to a sitting position against the cave wall.

Jep and Temus growled menacingly at something outside. Drake's anger boiled and he scooted forward, kneeling inside the entrance and searching for a target.

Reveal a demon to me, Amaryllis, and I'll send it back to the Underworld. Drake heard the *whoosh* of wings and dust rose from the ledge in front of him. He saw a faint blur and pulled the trigger.

The enchanted bolt *thunked* into solid flesh. A demonic wail echoed in the canyon and the monster's bony hooves clattered against the ledge-path.

Drake considered springing forward and trying to finish off

319

the monster with his Kierka knife. Closing with a wounded demon would be dangerous, but he might not get another chance. Blood dripped from the Drobin bolt that protruded from the wingataur's unseen body only a few paces away and he decided to strike. The Clifftoner unsheathed his knife and stepped closer to the entrance.

"Don't!" Bellor shouted.

Drake held himself back and watched as the Drobin bolt—and the wingataur he had shot it into—sailed off the ledge and disappeared around the bend in the cliff.

A boulder smashed into the ground outside the cave and exploded. Shards of rock pelted Drake's face before he could turn his head. He fell backwards in excruciating pain. "My eyes!" Drake rolled on the ground, felt the blood on his face and realized he was blind.

XXXIX

It may be a trap, but we must go on.

—Bölak Blackhammer, from the Lost Journal

Jep and Temus guarded the cave entrance as Drake writhed on the ground, blind and gritting his teeth in agony.

"Hold still!" Thor pulled Drake's hands away from his face, and squeezed his entire waterskin into the young man's eyes, washing out the fine red dust. The water eased the pain and when Thor finished his vision started to return.

"Can you see?" Thor asked.

Drake blinked rapidly. "Almost." He rubbed the last of the dust from his face gently, feeling the shallow cuts on his skin.

"Good." Thor patted his shoulder. "Now keep watch."

"Keep watch?" Straining to see any sign of the wingataurs, Drake wiped his face and peered out from the small cavern. The dogs sat beside him on the stone floor; their noses, ears, and eyes searching for the demons.

Water from the falls scented the breeze and Drake let it cool his face while trying to ignore the stinging in his eyes. He blinked away the pain and looked up and down the steep cliff. He noticed a large pile of red and tan stones scattered on the valley floor directly beneath the cave mouth. He guessed the rock had been dumped there.

Glancing back, Drake saw Thor hovering over Bellor, who seemed to be recovering from getting hit by the rock.

"Broken bones?" Thor asked.

"No. I just lost my breath, and my shoulder is bruised."

"Your backpack probably saved your life, lessening the blow." Thor looked at Bellor's pack, which didn't show any obvious signs of damage.

The War Priest moved his left arm and gasped in pain.

"I should use the Healing magic on you before any more time passes," Thor said.

"No, too risky." Bellor grimaced and waved Thor away with his good arm. "I don't want you touching the *zeitströmen* again. You need more training. Remember last night? It's too dangerous."

Shame flashed in Thor's eyes. Drake assumed that failing to heal Jep at the circle the night before had caused Bellor's stern response.

"I'll be all right in a moment," Bellor said.

"Bellor." Thor cast his gaze downward. "I have to tell you—"

"I'll be all right," Bellor said through clenched teeth.

Thor bit his lower lip, then crawled away to investigate the rear of the low cavern that would keep even the dwarves bent at the waist.

Once Thor had gone, Drake asked, "Is the Healing magic really so dangerous?"

Bellor's expression hardened. "It could kill him. Last night Thor lost control and was fortunate to have pulled out of the timestream before he lost decades of his life." Bellor's expression softened. "I've seen novice Priests like Thor slumped over their fallen brothers after a battle—dead of old age. Their hair turned white, bodies wasted by the passage of hundreds of years in only a moment's lapse of concentration. They couldn't control the *zeitströmen*, nor could they pull away from it. It can kill as easily as it can heal."

"I didn't know. . . ." Drake wondering how much time Thor

had lost. "You both risked much for Jep."

Bellor grinned. "Thor will do practically anything to save a comrade who has gone with him into battle. So will I." The War Priest looked at Jep, then back to where Thor was exploring alone. "Thor, how did you know this cave was here? There's no mention of it in Bölak's journal."

Thor came back slowly and kept silent.

"What is it?" Bellor asked after a long moment while testing his arm, which moved a little easier.

Thor stared at the cave entrance. "I saw a dwarf on the ledge out there when we were attacked."

"What? A dwarf?" Bellor blinked as Drake inspected the path again for some clue.

"Yes," Thor said, "and he gave a secret hand sign of the *Dracken Viergur.* He motioned for me to follow him and then took the ledge-path that led here."

"Who was it?" Bellor asked. "One of Bölak's warriors?"

"He looked familiar," Thor said, "but I didn't recognize him. He was younger than me, and had a blond beard."

"Younger than you?" Bellor shook his head. "It couldn't have been one of Bölak's *Viergur.*"

"Where is he now?" Drake asked, suspecting it had been a shapechanged wingataur.

"I don't know." Thor frowned.

Bellor sneered. "Draconic magic. Has to be."

Drake slapped the rock. "We're trapped in here. The demons will kill us if we try to escape using the ledge."

Thor crawled to the back of the tunnel. "No, it couldn't have been a trick. There's a way out." He inspected the sides of the cavern. "There's a fissure here. It goes into the cliff. We can climb it. There're even a few pieces of copper and silver ore here too. It's high quality and has been crushed by a rock-press or a hammer. Our kin must have dumped waste ore down the

323

fissure from above. The dwarf I saw probably went up this way. Come on, look."

Jep and Temus guarded the entrance while Bellor and Drake crawled back to see Thor's discovery. They inspected the four-foot-high crack. Drake could barely see in the dim light. The fissure ran between two massive mountains of rock that had split apart in an earthquake long ago, leaving a gap that ran the full width of the cave, almost five paces.

Dropping a stone into the crevasse, Drake listened to it bounce off the walls below. He realized the wide crack extended far below the cave. A faint breeze blew out of it and he guessed it probably exited the cliff and landed on the pile of tailings on the valley floor.

"Wait," Drake said, "if we climb up there and fall, we'll probably slide right out of the cliff."

"Bellor and I are too surefooted," Thor said. "It's not that steep. Even the dogs can make it."

"We could go back outside," Bellor said, "and take our chances on the ledge. Or we can crawl up this fissure. Either way is risky, especially if it was a wingataur masquerading as a—"

"It wasn't," Thor said. "I know what I saw. He was a *Dracken Viergur.*"

"Then why didn't he wait for us?" Drake asked.

"It doesn't matter . . . for now," Bellor said. "If we meet him again, I'm certain we'll find out the truth."

"What if it's a trap in there?" Drake asked, hating the idea of climbing up into the crack, especially with the dogs at risk. "I'd rather face them outside than in that dark hole where I can't see anything."

Thor pointed up. "I'd rather have a strong stone roof over me than open blue sky where the wyrm-kin could be anywhere or drop more rocks on us."

"Thor's right. Going back out there doesn't seem promising." Bellor rubbed his hurt shoulder. "Besides, I think there were two of them hurling rocks at us out there, probably the same two from last night. Unless there's a third one who could have shapechanged. The ambush outside would've been fatal if we hadn't found cover in here. I think the demons would've preferred we hadn't discovered this cave."

Thor stuck his head into the gap. "This has to be a tailings chute and maybe an escape tunnel. There's got to be a way into Quarzaak."

As much as he didn't want to mention it, Drake said, "There are rock leavings at the bottom of the cliff—right below this crack. There's a good-sized pile down there."

"Our kin must've used this to dump rock from the tunnels above," Bellor said, "and I believe this fissure angles toward the seat of the throne and down like you said. This has to lead right into Quarzaak. Only one way to find out." Bellor motioned for Thor to start climbing up.

"I'm not taking the dogs in there without light," Drake said, "and I'm not waiting here."

"We'll fix that." Bellor took a milky quartz stone suspended from a leather necklace out of his pouch of rune stones. *"Laampfeör."* A soft gray-white light emanated from the rock and lit the cavern with a pale radiance.

"What's that?" Drake asked.

"A glowstone." Bellor handed it to Drake. A tiny rune had been painted onto the glowing crystal. He expected it to feel warm, but the stone was cool. As he put the necklace on, he realized he wouldn't be able to hold his crossbow and crawl up at the same time. Drake stowed the bolt, released the tension on his weapon and reluctantly slung it over his shoulder.

Thor climbed first, Drake followed, shepherding the dogs in front of him. Bellor came last, favoring his hurt shoulder. Crawling on his hands and knees in the slanting tunnel Drake kept thinking about one of the dogs sliding downward into the blackness and not being able to stop—or worse—getting wedged between the rocks down in the crevasse and dying there after many days of agony because he couldn't get them out.

However, the dogs made their way up confidently, as if they enjoyed being encased in the fissure with no bottom. Small pieces of rock skittered down past Drake as Thor ascended the angled stone in front of him. The Clifftoner assumed most of the loose pebbles had been dumped down because they didn't look like the red and white stone they climbed. He found greenish-flecked rocks scattered in niches along the way.

Without Bellor's light he would have been terrified. Even with the reassuring glowstone his hands shook as he climbed up what would have been an easy challenge above ground. Locked inside the mountain, Drake's nerves pulsed with constant danger messages.

After several minutes of climbing, Drake bumped his head on the ceiling. He muffled a curse as the walls seemed to press tighter around him and he hunched over even more. He stared up as the fissure became vertical. The only way to progress would be to wedge themselves into the crack and pull themselves up, which would be impossible for the dogs.

"Shhh, I found something," Thor whispered from the right as he investigated at the fringes of the light.

Head aching, Drake crawled next to Thor who had found a flat, level recess with enough room for all of them to stand up straight. The glowstone revealed the dark slide they had ascended. He couldn't see any sign of the cave where they had entered the fissure. "What now?"

"Humans," Thor muttered under his breath while caressing the wall. "There's obviously a door here." He examined the stone very carefully, as if smoothing out a wrinkle in a blanket.

Bellor slipped past Drake and the dogs. Both dwarves examined the rock until Thor announced, "Here, I found the hinges. It swings inward."

Drake had no idea what they were talking about and thought he could feel the weight of the stone pushing down on him. He wanted out before an earthquake compressed the walls together and turned them all into a thin, red paste.

"I think this is the keyhole." Bellor pointed to a tiny opening in the rock. "But where's the key?"

"It's got to be close by." Thor searched and began examining the walls near the door, then stepped to the edge of the light. Moments later Thor's probing hands found a loose rock and he pulled it out to uncover a secret cavity. "Bless Lorak." Smiling, Thor removed a short bronze rod with metal teeth protruding from three sides.

"How did the dwarf get in if the key is still there?" Drake raised one eyebrow.

"He probably had an extra one, or he opened the door, replaced the key, and went inside," Thor said as he slid it into the keyhole and wiggled it around before rotating it one full turn. Metal groaned defiantly inside. The lock released with a click and the stone portal slid inward a hand-width. Dust settled out from the tiny cracks as if the door had not been opened in a long time, revealing a natural cavern more than fifteen paces across and oval in shape. The reddish ceiling appeared to be twice as tall as a man, and piles of crushed gravel covered the floor. The dogs whined and nuzzled Drake, who patted their necks.

Thor whispered, "Looks like a rock-press room. I see a Drobin-built stone-crusher. Mineshafts go into the wall at the back of the cavern. And one natural tunnel out of there. This must be Quarzaak."

"Silver ore?" Bellor asked.

"Yes, and copper," Thor whispered then ducked outside the room. "Just like we saw back down there."

Bellor clicked the stone door closed in case their voices carried into the tunnels beyond. "I hope there are no wingataurs in there."

"You think the wingataurs are inside Quarzaak?" Drake asked. "What about the dwarf?"

"I don't know, but they could be, unless it's under siege. I don't believe the door has been opened in a long while, so the dwarf didn't come in through here."

"There could be another way," Thor said.

"Unlikely," Bellor said, "but what worries me more is not knowing where the dragon is."

"Dragon?" Drake's mouth became very dry and he could barely swallow.

"The dragon seen over the lake must be with the wingataurs." Bellor touched his beard and worry carved deep lines into the War Priest's face. "If they're in here, the chance of the dragon being present is high. Especially if there's a chamber big enough for it to make a lair. We'll hope to meet him there."

Hope? Drake thought. *These dwarves are insane.*

"Before we go any further, I want to protect us like I did last night in the trees. The *schützenfeör* will shield us from the dragon's fiery breath. The magic won't last more than a few hours though."

Drake's brow furrowed. "You mean we were only protected from fire for part of last night?"

"Yes, but I can reinvoke it if I have to." Bellor chanted softly under his breath and his hands glowed red as they had the night before. Hypnotized by the amazing magic, Drake watched as a faint aura of crimson fire surrounded Bellor's body. He touched them all, then the aura disappeared. "We won't be burned to ashes, but beware the smoke from what the flames burn. Smoke kills as easily as fire."

His mouth becoming more parched, Drake asked, "Bellor, do you really think Draglûne is here?"

"It's possible. We should pray that we have found him in one of his lairs away from his army of wingataurs. He has at least two guarding him though. Hopefully not any more. But we must be prepared for him or his minions, especially in case the dwarf Thor saw actually was a wingataur."

"A wingataur wouldn't know the *Dracken Viergur* hand signal," Thor said.

"We hope. . . ." Bellor locked his eyes on Drake. "But if we face The Iron Death, aim for his neck or chest—like you did at Cliffton against the wyvern. Wyrms are vulnerable there . . . if you know where to shoot. I wish we had more time. I'd teach you many things about killing dragons."

"Where do I aim exactly?" Drake asked.

"If you can pierce its windpipe or heart, you can severely injure or even kill a wyrm. But Draglûne is terribly powerful, well armored; and if he is here, we have almost no chance with our few numbers and limited weaponry. The usual tactics won't work for us."

What are we doing here? Drake thought, *This is a suicide mission.* He wondered if sliding down the fissure would be preferable to going through the door to Quarzaak. His memory of Bellor's story of the Last Battle of Drobin Pass made him shudder. Dozens of *Dracken Viergur* had attacked the dragon, and only a handful had survived.

"Surprise would've been our greatest weapon, but that's gone now. We'll have to go for the kill quickly if we face any wyrmkin," Bellor told Drake. "Once the fight begins, we'll have little time. If the battle goes on very long we'll surely be killed. The *schützenfeör* will protect us from fire, but the claws and teeth of wyrms are deadly in close combat. Stay away from the head . . .

and watch out for the tail. None of that really matters, though."

"Why?" Drake asked, trying to remember everything Bellor said.

"We're not going to fight him that way." The War Priest gave Thor a knowing glance. "There's another way to deal with dragons in their lairs. It only takes two Earth Priests with the power of the Mountain God. You don't need to come any further, Drake. I shouldn't have brought you this far."

"But you need me. I have bolts enchanted with Earth magic. I can fight."

"I know you can, but it's better if you take the journals and get out of these caverns. Thor and I will stay and finish this."

"What are you going to do?"

Bellor touched the rock and whispered, "This sandstone has many fractures. It's vulnerable and so is the dragon. We're going to bring the entire cavern down on him. Not even Draglûne can stand against a mountain. He'll be crushed."

"But how will you escape?"

"There won't be time," Bellor said. "We'll get as close to the wyrm as we can and start the Stone Chant. He'll breathe his fire upon us, but we'll be protected. When he closes to finish us with his claws, we'll bring down the cavern with Lorak's power."

Drake couldn't believe what they were going to do. "What if wingataurs interrupt your chant? You said it yourself, the dragon will be protected."

The War Priest shifted uncomfortably. "It will be difficult, especially without surprise, but we'll find a way. You don't have to come, Drake," Bellor said, "you can stay here with the dogs and keep the wingataurs off our backs. Thor and I will go in. We've been preparing for this for decades. We've already resigned ourselves to our fate—but you don't need to die."

For an instant, Drake thought about leaving them. "No, I'm going with you. When you start your chant, I'll keep you safe long enough for you to bring this whole damn canyon down on him."

Remorse tainted Bellor's smile as the old dwarf grasped the young man's forearm. "I am honored to go with you into battle, Drake Bloodstone. Your family would be proud of your courage. Pray with me now." Bellor reverently touched the stone. "Great Lorak, give us courage to face our enemies. Honor us with your strength as we go together into battle as brothers in arms."

"Together." Thor raised his blacksteel hammer and patted Drake on the back. "Lorak will protect us. He favors those who avenge their kin."

Drake thought about his dead cousin Rigg, poor tormented Uncle Sandon, the three missing hunters, Kovan and the mutilated villagers in Armstead. What would happen if Draglûne and his wingataurs attacked Armstead again, or Cliffton? Would they burn down both villages and kill his family and friends? Jaena, Tallia, all the Bloodstones, little Neven, Mae, Edeline and all of Ethan's family—everyone—would be slain by the dragon and its minions.

Drake loaded his crossbow with an enchanted Drobin bolt and prayed, *Amaryllis, please let my aim be true. Let me give the dragon a mortal wound before I die.*

Checking and rechecking his crossbow, Drake expected to get only one shot before the dragon or the falling rock killed him and the dwarves. He knelt beside Jep and Temus and fed them dried meat from their packs. He rubbed their bellies and hugged them as they ate. "Good boys. I'm sorry, but I'm not coming back. You'll have to find your own way home."

XL

Revenge, or justice? I can't decide which is more important, but revenge keeps me going.

—Bölak Blackhammer, from the Lost Journal

Entering the cavern, Drake expected a massive storm of flames to fill the chamber. He stared into the darkness and heard a click behind him. Bellor locked the door and the War Priest pocketed the bronze key. Drake imagined them all fleeing for their lives and not being able to open the nearly invisible stone portal.

Jep and Temus whined from the other side and pawed at the stone, their nails scraping against the rock. "Shhh, good dogs." Drake touched the door. They kept whining and the sad sound knifed into his heart. He thought, *It's for the best. At least they'll have a chance to escape out there.*

The dogs whined louder, and Bellor looked back at the wall. "We can't have them making all that noise." He glanced at Drake. "Perhaps we should bring them along?"

"Maybe they'll be safer in here with us," Thor said.

"Open it." Drake tried to find the keyhole as relief tinged with sadness spread over his entire body. He told himself they would find a way to escape when the end came. The excited dogs burst in and he quieted them as they entered Quarzaak. When they were calm, he had them fall into place beside him— Jep on the right, Temus on the left.

Following behind Bellor and Thor, Drake's glowstone lit the cavern with a soft light. The dogs stayed on his heels as they all moved tentatively across the chamber, filled to the ceiling with piles of crushed rock. The glowstone shone against the reddish walls and the vermilion gravel on the floor.

Thor crept across the cavern filled with the piles of ore-flecked rocks, his feet crunching with every step. Five tunnels lay at the far end and they all listened for anything coming toward them. Thor paused for a moment to inspect the rock crusher in the center of the chamber. It was made with two large stone wheels, one set atop the other, that could be rotated using wooden handles to pulverize the rocks placed between them. Rune symbols had been painted upon the stones, and Drake wondered if the machine was magic.

"*Dracken Viergur* built this crusher," Bellor whispered.

Thor grinned. "Uncle Bölak must have been here."

Hoping Thor was right, Drake peered into the largest natural passage over five paces high that exited the cavern. He stared down the tunnel, but it turned abruptly and blocked his view ahead.

Thor led them toward the tunnel. They passed in front of the excavated mine shafts. Drake couldn't turn away from the dark holes cut into the rock. Scattered rodent droppings on the ground intrigued Jep and Temus, who sniffed the floor eagerly. The dogs looked into the central mineshaft and their ears pricked up. Following their gaze, Drake pointed his light directly into the tunnel, then gestured to the shaft where the bullmastiffs focused their attention. A low scraping sound grew louder.

Aiming into the darkness, Drake stepped back. The dogs and dwarves stood at the Clifftoner's sides with weapons ready. A scurrying sound preempted the arrival of two brown mice. The rodents scampered out in a hurry and disappeared into the rock piles. Something else bounded down the tunnel. Drake's eyes locked onto the demon. A small, iron-gray dragon creature one and a half strides long from snout to tail froze in front of them on its four slender legs. The surprised little monster gawked at Drake with beady, onyx eyes. The dragon pressed its tan belly against the stone.

Targeting the wyrm-kin's head, Drake noted the immature wing buds protruding from its back. A tiny stinger grew on the end of its tail. He thought it was the spawn of some type of four-legged breed of wyvern. Sharp claws, long fangs, and a pair of horns gave the aevian a fierce look, despite its lizardlike body being smaller than the bullmastiffs. The baby dragon creature observed the companions with what Drake thought was interest instead of fear.

"Don't kill the dragonling. Steady the dogs before they bark," Bellor said with his calmest voice. "If we're wise, we'll win this battle before it begins."

Doing as he was told, Drake held the dogs back as Bellor carefully took out some dry vrelk meat and tossed it at the feet of the little dragon. It sniffed and then ate the jerky, swallowing the strips whole and then looked for more.

"What are you doing?" Drake asked as Bellor fed the demon.

"You feed Draglûne's offspring?" Thor's whisper became a snarl.

Bellor fed the little monster some more meat. "We'll capture it and then we'll have a hostage."

"Why not kill it and move on?" Thor readied his hammer for a throw as the sharp tail twitched while it gulped down the food.

Drake didn't like the look of the barbed stinger and pressed the dogs further back.

"I have no love for wyrm-kin either." Bellor tossed another piece of jerky. "But we can use it to our advantage."

"You want to *capture* it?" Thor's outrage hissed from his lips.

"Since it's running around here alone," Bellor said, "they may have no idea we've gotten into Quarzaak. The wingataurs may not have found the tailings-chute entrance. Maybe this little one's mother and father think we're still trapped out there." He tossed another bit of meat.

"What do you mean, mother and father?" Drake asked. "Two dragons?" He didn't want to think about two. He focused on keeping the dogs calm and making sure they didn't startle the little dragon. Jep and Temus stood tall. He could feel their muscles tensing. Jep strained against Drake's hand, itching to go forward.

"I don't think there're two dragons." Bellor fed the dragonling some more, and prepared to lasso it with a short rope he had pulled from his pack. "This one seems to be half-wyvern. Look at its tail. It has a stinger, like a wyvern, but four legs like a dragon. It's a crossbreed. It must have a wyvern parent. We'll have to watch out for the stinger once I rope it. I'll have to cover the tail with a sack."

Thor glared at the dragonling. "True dragons mating with wyverns? Disgusting."

"Maybe I shot its mother at Cliffton?" Drake shrugged.

"That one was male." Bellor threw another piece of meat to the creature, which ate it ravenously. With each throw, Drake noticed that Bellor inched the wyrm-kin closer to him.

Thor scowled. "Let's just kill this wyrm-kin and move on."

"I'll shoot it." Drake's free hand slipped away from the dogs as he took aim.

"This is leverage." Bellor shook his head. "Opportunities like these can't be overlooked, especially when we're so out-matched—assuming there is at least one dragon here."

Unable to contain himself, Jep lunged forward, growling. The little dragon darted down the largest tunnel as Bellor threw the lasso much too late. The wyrm-kin moved so fast that neither

Thor nor Drake could attack.

Bellor angrily twisted his beard.

"We should've killed it." Thor glared at Bellor. "We'll regret this."

Maybe we should have left the dogs outside? Drake thought, ashamed at their actions and his inability to control them.

Thor walked cautiously after the dragonling and Drake aimed his crossbow ahead as the companions traveled out of the tailings room. The crunch of their footsteps on the stone made Drake cringe. He thought every step echoed like a drumbeat as they crept down the wide tunnel, which allowed them to travel three abreast.

The glowstone revealed the craggy red walls with dark clefts and shadows all along the passage. Wingataurs could hide in ambush in many places. After a short walk, the tunnel ended at the beginning of another cavern. Drake scanned a large chamber at least five times the size as the first one they had entered. His light barely reached the far side. Piles of crushed ore and a mortared stone furnace with a chimney reached to the ceiling.

"What's that?" Drake noticed black runes covering the stone structure.

"A crude smelter," Bellor said, "though this one didn't use charcoal or wood."

"Earth magic once fueled it," Thor said.

"Daylight." Drake pointed to a dim speck of light at the ceiling where the chimney reached the apex of the cavern.

"It must be the vent hole for the smoke." Bellor gazed up at the faint glow.

The young dragonling hissed from atop a mound of rock before scurrying down the only tunnel out of the chamber.

"Follow it," Bellor said, "but be watchful for a trap."

They trailed the skittering wyrm out of the smelter room and down a circular tunnel of red stone four times as tall as Drake, and wide enough for the three of them to walk abreast with the dogs behind. The little monster's stinger-tipped, iron-gray tail rounded a corner and disappeared.

The glowstone winked out. Blinded in the pitch-blackness, Drake felt as if his lower body had been dipped in icy water. The thundering of hoofed demons charging toward him in darkness sent bolts of fear shooting into him. He stumbled back and tripped, his crossbow flying from his hands as he hit the ground.

"Blackhammer!" Thor screamed.

Jep and Temus barked ferociously at the approaching creatures. Drake recognized the sound of the wingataurs' blades slicing through the air and remembered the aspens being cut down outside the circle.

A loud clang on what had to be Thor's shield resounded in the tunnel. Drake smelled the demons' repulsive, musky scent and foul breath. The battle raged as Drake lay blind and helpless in the darkness, tensing as he waited for a chop from a wingataur's weapon to sever one of his limbs.

Crimson light emanated from Bellor's axe blade as it slashed through the gloom. Drake's eyes began to adjust to the faint glow, but he still couldn't see the demons. Thor sidestepped and spun forward, his hammer swinging low at what had to be the wingataur's leg. Thor's weapon smashed into something and Drake heard a deep, pained groan.

Bellor's axe halted in mid-swing as metal clanged on metal. An invisible opponent knocked the old dwarf backwards. Bellor kept his footing as the dwarves faced two opponents.

Thor swung again and his hammer glanced off something. Before the dwarf could attack again, he rolled backwards as if struck by a powerful blow and crashed into Drake. Both of them sprawled on the cavern floor. The sharp hooves of a wingataur clomped right in front of them.

Barking viciously, Jep and Temus lunged forward. Drake

heard the clatter of retreating hooves and dove for his crossbow, which lay against the cavern wall. Bellor whirled forward and swung his axe in a wide arc to create a space in front of the dogs. A demon yelped in pain as *Wyrmslayer* tasted demon flesh. The crimson axe glowed brighter, bathing the tunnel in blood-hued light.

Leaping to his feet, Thor raised his shield and cocked his arm while Drake aimed at the space in front of the dogs where he guessed a demon stood. He squeezed the trigger with a vice-grip, launching a dwarven war bolt. The shaft sank deep into its target, piercing what had to be the monster's gut. He wished he could see through the cloaking draconic magic as he spanned his crossbow. Before he could finish reloading, retreating hoof beats signaled the wounded monsters' withdrawal.

Bellor held his flaring bloody axe over his head and yelled a cry of victory down the tunnel, *"Wyrmslayer!"*

"Run faster, demons!" Thor shouted and banged on his shield.

The hoof beats stopped and a deep and coarse voice with a thick accent yelled back in Nexan, "We'll roast your flesh, stunted ones. Come into our fire-maker."

The wingataur's words echoed in the tunnel and wedged themselves into Drake's eardrums, which suddenly ached sending pain through his whole head.

Bellor's face contorted with murderous rage. The War Priest spoke with a bloodthirsty tone. "We must pursue them. *Now.* While we have them on the run. They won't break my magic again. *Feörscheinen!"*

The glowstone on Drake's neck shone even brighter than before and hurt his eyes when he glanced down. He gawked at Bellor's maniacal expression and wondered if the trapped essence of the dead dragon king, Mograwn, had possessed him. Vengeful power radiated from *Wyrmslayer* and the axe glowed red as Bellor squeezed the handle, his injured shoulder apparently healed. He appeared to want to charge after the demons and cut them to pieces.

Thor held him back and the War Priest took several deep breaths while praying silently. He used all the willpower he could muster to overcome the axe's need for draconic blood. After a few moments, an uneasy calm returned to Bellor. "We must be very careful now. If we walk into a dragon's trap here, we could meet a quick end."

"Are they trying to lure us ahead?" Thor asked.

Bellor's expression became much more placid and the glow in the axe subsided. "Perhaps, but we must go forward regardless."

Swallowing hard despite his parched mouth, Drake's hands trembled. He gulped several quick breaths, trying to steady himself. Fear coursed through him as he silently repeated the mantra of the Bloodstone Way. *Forget yourself, focus on the moment, permit no distractions.* He said it over and over again, but his hands would not stop shaking.

XLI

An evil shadow hangs over us, ready to take the lives of my warriors.

—Bölak Blackhammer, from the Lost Journal

Blackish-red drops of blood marked their trail as the jagged tunnel wormed and twisted onward. Drake saw no sign of the dragonling, but noticed scuff marks left by the cloven hooves of the fleeing wingataurs.

Aiming his crossbow at the edge of the darkness, he whispered the Bloodstone mantra to himself like a calming wind. His hands barely shook as Bellor marched a step in front of him on the left, with Thor to the right. Jep and Temus followed as the companions moved forward.

The glowstone's light revealed a spherical cavern with a smoke-blackened ceiling. The grotto lay at the intersection of four separate tunnels, with faint rays of daylight streaming in from one of the exits. The light filtered past a stout wooden door with rusty bronze hinges and a heavy wooden bar. The wingataurs' blood trail led into the largest passage that sloped upward and lay opposite the barred door. Blood had trickled down from the angled tunnel, leaving long streaks that ran into the room.

Bellor motioned for Thor to scout ahead as Drake's finger brushed against his crossbow's smooth trigger. Thor crept forward along the wall and peeked out the tiny window in the wooden door. "Main entrance," he whispered.

"That's one way out, but let's see where the wingataurs and the dragonling have gone." Bellor pointed to the blood trail as they all walked slowly toward the widest tunnel. Thor and Bellor carefully inspected the way ahead and Drake lent his tired eyes to search for signs of ambush or traps.

"Water carved most of this tunnel originally," Bellor whispered, "but a lot of stonework has been done to make it wider. See the pick and chisel marks?" White scratch marks gouged the irregular surface of the wall.

Thor pointed to the rock. "The wingataurs must've done this. Drobin would never have cut stone so crudely."

"Why would they make it wider?" Drake asked. "This tunnel is high and wide enough for them."

Bellor's grave look made Drake think of one good reason to make it bigger. *A dragon.* A reeking odor drifted down the tunnel, reminding him of rotten foot-sweat mixed with dog vomit. Jep and Temus sneezed and hung back behind him, afraid to continue.

"What's that stench?" Drake asked.

"Dragon." Bellor wrinkled his nose. "We're close to its lair."

Thor marched a bit ahead and Bellor followed a step behind. Drake watched them and had to exert all his resolve to keep his own feet moving. Jep and Temus brought up the rear on his heels. Drake wanted to ask Bellor why they kept going, but all he could do was press his lips together and hope that the fire-protection magic would indeed shield them.

The glow of sunlight appeared ahead and a faint breeze brought an even stronger scent of death. The stench intensified as they passed over the remains of a wooden gate that had been burned to ashes many years in the past. The pivoting gate had been ripped out of the stone, no longer guarding the tunnel and blocking water from flowing into Quarzaak. Drake noticed a gutter in the stone that must have been carved by the dwarves to drain water away from the entrance.

Beyond the sundered gate Drake expected to see a titanic dragon waiting to kill them. Instead he beheld a natural overhang in the side of the cliff. It lay open to the canyon, with a domed ceiling and sunlight streaming in from the massive opening in the cliff face. Over thirty paces wide, the portal overlooked the falls and much of Red Canyon.

"A dragon's lair-cave." Bellor nodded as he surveyed the area.

"But no dragon." Thor scowled.

"It may yet return," Bellor said, "while we stand here like fools. Let's be quick with our search and get back down to the smaller tunnels. We must see what we can learn of our foe. Be on guard, it could return at any moment."

Drake nodded, then looked out from the shelf and watched the falls plunging down the canyon walls. The constant roar of the water made it hard to hear as the dwarves moved into the cavern. He covered them, scanning the sky and keeping two fingers on his crossbow's trigger.

"I didn't see this shelf from below," Bellor said. "I must look more closely when we're on the canyon floor again."

Wrinkling his nose at the foul-smelling half-cavern, Drake glanced back at the lair-cave. Black streaks from running water scarred the red stone. Water dripped into a small pool in the back. He imagined water continually seeping through the rock, filling the place with little streams.

Standing in the demon's den, Drake sensed something else besides the smell lingering in the air. A vague chill radiated from the rock, the cold brushing against his skin like the prickly leaves of a stinging nettle plant. Considering the strange sensation, he surveyed the bones of vrelk, thistle deer, mountain goats, and the parts of at least three griffins. The remains lay strewn everywhere, but no insects buzzed around, sparing a fresh vrelk carcass. "Even the flies avoid this place." Drake tried to spit out the foul taste in his mouth. "Shouldn't we get back inside?"

"We won't stay much longer," Bellor said.

The dogs sniffed at the rotting meat and whined their disapproval. Neither Jep nor Temus touched the hundreds of bones scattered on the floor. Surprising Drake, Jep stayed close for once and didn't explore.

"Over here," Thor called out. "This must be where it sleeps."

The impression of a huge creature was imprinted in the fine red sand.

"Big." Drake realized it had to be much larger than the wyvern at Cliffton.

"More than forty-five feet long, including the tail," Bellor said. "It's not a very large dragon, thank Lorak. I wish there were tracks. This stone is hard to read."

"Where has it gone?" Thor asked, standing alert and watching over Bellor while Drake and the dogs kept their own vigil. "It's been here recently."

Kneeling, Drake used all his hunter's skill to follow the blood trail of the wingataurs. The drops ended at the sheer cliff. "Bellor, the wingataurs flew away, right there."

"What about the dragonling?" Thor asked.

Drake shrugged, unable to see any sign of it.

"The dragon must have taken its offspring away," Bellor said. "I would have done the same. But it might come back to evict us from its lair."

Thor glanced at the sky. "Maybe the dragon was hunting? The wingataurs might have gone to find it and took the dragonling with them."

The numerous carcasses made Drake wonder about how the dragon killed its prey. He imagined the wyrm diving on them from above and crushing them or burning them with fire. He wondered if the spirits of the animals the dragon had eaten still remained, now restless ghosts trapped within the cave.

"A dragon would hate living here," Bellor said, "there's cold water seeping in, and it's exposed to the wind. This place would be torture for it. The small tunnels below would prevent it from getting around anywhere but up here, though it could poke its front half into the entry-room, but that's all."

Thor grunted in agreement.

"I wonder," Bellor said, "why was the tunnel widened? A dragon could use its Draconic magic to shapechange if it wanted to enter Quarzaak."

"Maybe it couldn't shapechange," Thor said. "Doesn't that prove that the dragon wasn't the dwarf I saw outside?"

"It still could've been one of the wingataurs," Drake suggested.

"It wasn't." Thor crossed his arms. "Come on. The dwarf has got to be down there somewhere and I don't like this place."

"We're exposed here," Drake said, "we need better cover."

"Let's check the lower tunnels," Thor said.

Bellor nodded. "There might be more wingataurs or worse things hiding down there. Still, we must explore it."

Jep and Temus loped out of the lair-cave, which Drake thought should've been the dream of any dog, with meaty bones all over to be chewed and savored. They hadn't touched anything. He glanced back and shivered.

"You felt the taint of the wyrm—its evil—didn't you?" Bellor asked.

"Is that what that was?" Drake blinked at the old dwarf.

"You sensed the demon spirit of the wyrm. It has tainted that place with its vile aura," Bellor said. "I remember the first time I felt the residue of a dragon-spirit. It was long ago, when we found an abandoned den of Draglûne, back when he led the

Giergun armies. Wyrm-kin of great power have a presence surrounding their being. It leaches into all things . . . rocks, trees, even stagnant water. The wyrm's spirit has seeped into the stone here, and it draws power from its lair, making its magic stronger. If that place is ever to be cleansed, it will take very powerful magic."

"What about the taint of the wingataurs?" Thor asked.

"The aura of sorcerer-wingataurs should be easier to remove," Bellor said. "I assume their stain will still be potent, and if we are to weaken them, we must eradicate their lingering aura." The War Priest met the young hunter's questioning gaze. "None of us want to die, but we certainly don't want to be slain in that lair-cave or any other places tainted in such a way."

"What do you mean?" Drake asked.

"If we fall dead in there," Bellor said, "our spirits would not be able to find Lorak's Halls."

"Because of the taint of evil?" Drake asked.

Bellor nodded. "Our spirits would stay here, trapped between worlds."

A cold restlessness shifted inside Drake's chest. Ethan's face flashed through his mind as he considered Bellor's words: *Trapped between worlds.*

XLII

How many Drobin bodies will we discover in Quarzaak?
Will we find Bölak's remains, or does he still live after all
these years?

—Bellor Fardelver, from the Thornclaw Journal

A musty smell filled Drake's nostrils as his glowstone revealed
the tall passage carved by water and time. Thor led Drake, Bellor, and the dogs deeper into Quarzaak. Jep and Temus walked
slowly, their nails clicking on the stone floor of the snaking passage.

The tunnel widened and Drake stepped into a rectangular
chamber with five archways, each outlined with mortared stones
cut into blocks. One of the entryways was large enough to ac-
commodate a wingataur's height. The others were five feet tall,
high enough for a dwarf. A pair of smashed doors lay on the
ground under the largest arch, which had a rune-inscribed
keystone set above the opening. A solitary door made of
ironwood blocked one of the smaller archways, with a thick
branch barring the portal. The dogs' ears perked up as they
sniffed at the roughly constructed door.

"What is it, boys?" Drake asked.

Thor raised his shield and Bellor motioned for him to open
the way. Thor slowly lifted the bar. The dogs moved closer and
Drake winced as the branch scraped across the ironwood. Temus growled and Jep's head jutted forward. Thor used the little

spike on top of his hammer to push open the unbarred door. It squeaked as it swung inward and a rancid smell wafted out of the dark room. Drake shone his glowstone past the threshold.

"Please, don't hurt us," a weak voice pleaded from within.

Thor lowered his shield and weapon. The dogs stepped forward, tails wagging. Drake couldn't believe his eyes. Two emaciated men cowered in the corner of the tiny stone chamber. They shielded their eyes from the light and squinted at the companions.

"Thank the Goddess," Drake said, wishing he recognized the two scraggly-haired men. He guessed they were two of the missing hunters from Armstead. "Don't worry. We're here to help." Drake lowered his crossbow. "You're free."

"Free?" The black-haired man asked, his nearly toothless mouth hanging open in disbelief. He looked older than Drake's father, and his skin hung loosely over his bones.

"The demons are in false shapes again," the brown-haired younger man whispered.

"No." Drake shook his head. "You're free. This is no trick."

"We are?" the younger man, no more than twenty-five, asked. The mottled purple and yellow bruises covering his face and body made him look like a battered piece of living, breathing meat.

Drake tried to sound hopeful, "You're free. Come out of there. We won't hurt you."

"Rigg, is that you?" The younger man asked.

"No." Drake took a step back. "I'm Drake Bloodstone, Rigg's cousin."

After the two men crawled out of the room, Drake helped them stand while pretending not to notice the rank smell wafting from their pale, gaunt bodies. Their bloodstained clothing needed to be burned. He glanced into their prison chamber at human waste, pieces of a blanket, and a few well-cleaned animal bones. A tiny trickle of water ran down the back wall and he imagined them having to lick the stone for a drink. The nightmare the men had been living hit Drake harder than Blayne's head butt.

The older man touched his sunken chest. "I'm Taylon. This is Garent. We're from Armstead. We thought we were going to die here."

Garent mumbled something, his sunken eyes staring at the putrid cell.

"Don't worry, lads," Bellor said, "you're safe with us."

"We'll—I'll take you home." Drake didn't know what else to say.

"Are there others alive in here somewhere?" Bellor asked. "Perhaps there are dwarves here, or another man from Armstead?"

"Alive?" Sadness washed across Taylon's face. "There was another, Dellen. He was killed a few days ago. Vrask came and dragged him out of our cell and beat him to death in front of us."

"We don't know why he was so angry. We'd done nothing. But he killed him. Right there." Garent gestured to the floor where Thor was standing. A stain on the ground appeared to be from blood. Thor moved off the smear and shook his head.

"Which demon was Vrask?" Bellor asked.

"The wingataur with the longer horns." Garent bit his lip. "He's far more cruel than Grallk."

The two men suddenly turned away from the companions.

"What's wrong?" Drake asked.

"You asked if there was anyone else in here," Taylon whispered. "There's your answer." Taylon pointed toward the tall archway behind them. Drake turned and for a fleeting moment saw a young-looking, blond-bearded dwarf staring at them with sad gray eyes. For an instant Drake smiled, hoping there were more dwarves in Quarzaak. But as he looked closer, he noticed that the light from his glowstone passed through the spectral outline of the dwarf.

Gasping involuntarily, Drake realized the dwarf's bare feet didn't touch the floor. The apparition levitated higher, turning away from them in utter silence. A hideous wound ran down the length of the dwarf's spine, exposing his backbone and vertebra underneath.

Hearing the crash of metal on stone, Drake whirled around to see Thor on his knees, his shield dropped beside him. Thor's face wrinkled and his lips trembled as he stared at the ghostly figure that disappeared down the tunnel.

Drake stood paralyzed, shocked at what he had just seen.

"His body is in there." Garent motioned beyond the tall arch. "The wingataurs killed him long ago."

"You've seen his remains?" Bellor asked.

Garent nodded. "The wingataurs nailed it to the wall in that room above the forge. Not much left, just a skeleton and withered flesh. He roams the halls and taunts the wingataurs and Verkahna. They can't destroy him, though they tried many times."

"Nailed—above the forge?" Bellor's body tensed. *"Sacrilege."*

Thor stood up, ready to follow the ghost. "It was him that I saw outside. We must help him. Please Bellor, we must lay him to rest."

"We shall." Bellor put a hand on Thor's shoulder and turned to the two men. "Who is Verkahna?"

"She's a dragon," Taylon said.

"You didn't see her?" Garent asked.

"She's gone," Thor said, "fled with her dragonling."

Drake offered Taylon and Garent food and water. The grateful men ate ravenously. Sensing their pain, the dogs nuzzled against the men, lending them their furry warmth. Drake suspected the strain of their imprisonment would take much longer to heal than their physical wounds. A firm resolve took hold of him, and he didn't care about anything except getting them home safely to Armstead and their families. He wrapped his cloak around Taylon. "Don't worry. I'll look after you both."

"We must attend to the ghost," Bellor said.

Turning to the hunters, the Clifftoner promised, "I'll get you out. Don't worry."

"Thank you, thank you very much, Rigg—I mean, Drake. Sorry, you look so much like him."

"I always have."

Taylon shivered despite the cloak. "When I saw you, I thought Vrask had finally recaptured him. Vrask always promised to find Rigg and bring him back here."

"Rigg was a slave here before we were captured." Garent touched Temus and rested his hand on the dog. "He wasn't here long. He escaped. I wish we knew how. We've been trying to figure that out a while."

"He escaped?" Thor asked.

Of course he did, Drake thought. *Rigg would never have stopped trying.*

"We tried several times to get away," Garent said, "but they always caught us. The Drobin ghost tried to help us, though all he ever did was lead us to his body or a blank stonewall by the rock crusher. There's no way out in either place."

Drake, Bellor, and Thor exchanged knowing glances and the Clifftoner thought about the hidden door at the tailings chute.

"He led you to his body?" Bellor asked.

"Many times," Garent said. "The wingataurs slept in that room with his bones." He pointed to the tall archway.

"The ghost scared us at first," Taylon said, "but he never did anything to hurt us. He tried to distract the wingataurs when they were beating us."

"Did he speak?" Thor asked.

Taylon shook his head.

"What else do you know about Rigg?" Drake asked, as he put the dogs on guard at the entrance to the cavern, worried the wingataurs might return.

"We learned a few things," Taylon said, "when the wingataurs beat us. They told us what they were going to do to Rigg when they caught him. We know they tried to find him in Armstead. They wanted to get back some papers he took from here."

"They looked in Rigg's house in Armstead," Garent said. "We were in town when they attacked, though Rigg had already gone away. Part of the reason the wingataurs captured us was to see if we knew anything about him. I guess whatever he stole was very important to them and their master."

"Their master?" Bellor asked.

"Another dragon," Taylon said. "Draglûne, the dragon king. He sent the wingataurs and Verkahna here to find something important."

"They couldn't find it," Garent said. "It was some valuable treasure Draglûne wanted."

Opening his mouth to speak, Drake stopped because of a glance from Bellor. He wanted to tell the poor men about Bölak's journal and guessed that it was most likely the treasure sought by the wingataurs and the dragon.

"Vrask wanted to use us as slaves." Garent touched his bruised lips.

"The demons didn't like being slaves of this she-dragon, Verkahna, did they?" Thor smirked.

"Slaves?" Taylon raised one eyebrow. "They weren't Verkahna's slaves. They were her watchers. She hated them. They spied on her and made certain she didn't leave Quarzaak except to hunt. It was punishment for her to be here. They enjoyed taunting her as much as they liked hurting us. They gave all the orders, not Verkahna."

"Ahhh, I understand." Bellor stroked his beard. "The winga-taurs were her wardens. Draglûne banished her."

XLIII

Lorak's Fire purifies the body and soul. It burns away evil and leaves only the pure essence of life.

—Bölak Blackhammer, from the Quarzaak Journal

Standing guard with his dogs, Drake listened for cloven hooves on the stone floors of Quarzaak. The Armsteaders sat beside him, praying that the wingataurs and the dragon would not return. Drake tried to look confident and give them strength, but with only a few hours of sleep in past days his nerves were frayed. Every shadow held a lurking threat and his imagination summoned little demons that seemed to hide in the darkness, waiting for him to turn his back.

Thor and Bellor made final preparations to follow the dwarven ghost and enter the heart of Quarzaak. The old War Priest drew a rune onto Thor's forehead with charcoal paint as he chanted in Drobin. Drake could hardly believe the deep bass sounds—which no human could make—came out of Bellor's mouth.

"Ho-**lig**-feörr-um-**Lorr**-ak. Ho-**lig**-feörr-um-**Lorr**-ak." Bellor chanted softly as Thor drew a similar rune onto Bellor's forehead.

The chanting suddenly stopped and the dwarves stood up with serious looks on their faces. Bellor's body glowed with a red aura and he touched Thor saying, *"Schützenfeör."* Bellor approached Drake and touched him as well.

"The fire-protection magic? I'll need this?" Drake asked as the fiery aura disappeared.

"Only if you wish to release the great burden clinging to your soul," Bellor said.

The hair on Drake's arms stood up and the urge to flee overwhelmed him. He started to step away. Bellor grabbed his arm and the fear inside him instantly retreated. The War Priest also protected Garent and Taylon with the magic. "All of you must come with us. The danger has not passed, but you have the favor of Lorak and His protection. You will not be harmed as Thor and I cleanse away the taint of evil from Quarzaak and re-sanctify the forge room. While we work, you must watch for our enemies. The wingataurs will sense this assault on their power."

"I'll keep watch," Drake said.

"We'll help," Taylon said, as he and Garent nodded. The Armsteaders and the dogs stood with Drake as the dwarves chanted in unison using their deeper-than-bass voices. "Ho-**lig**-feörr-um-**Lorr**-ak. Ho-**lig**-feörr-um-**Lorr**-ak." The two Drobin stepped forward shoulder-to-shoulder, singing their sacred hymn. They clutched their silver pendants, holding up the holy mountain symbol of Lorak as they marched forward.

The low-pitched words reverberated in Drake's ears as the dwarves stepped over the shattered doors beneath the archway. They led the way down a short curving tunnel, which opened into a large rectangular cavern with rounded corners.

The glowstone around Drake's neck barely illuminated the grotto at first, then became much brighter as the volume of the chanting increased. He took the crystal off his neck and held the blinding light away from his face.

"Ho-**lig**-feörr-um-**Lorr**-ak! Ho-**lig**-feörr-um-**Lorr**-ak!"

The natural cavern sparkled as Drake stared at the slender stalactites hanging from the high ceiling and the few broken stalagmites on the floor. He wondered why the stone sparkled so much, then saw thousands of small quartz crystals embedded in the rocks.

The diamond-like gems glittered like stars, captivating Drake with their twinkling display. Shifting his gaze away, he looked at the broad stone hearth and smithy area built in the center of the far wall. A black anvil stood in front of the forging area. The remains of an animal carcass rested on the anvil. He guessed the wingataurs had used it for chopping meat. Bloodstains and animal parts littered the area. The sharp smell of rotting flesh made his stomach churn.

A human head with flesh still clinging to the bone and the skull of a dwarf hung prominently from the wall. Drake wished he had never looked away from the ceiling—especially when he realized the carcass on the anvil was part of a human torso.

Nailed to the blackened trunk of the old tree beside the hearth was the desiccated husk of a long-dead dwarf. His skull and bones were visible through shrunken skin and scorched clothing. The dwarf's remains had been tied to the log to prevent them from falling off. It appeared the poor Drobin had been lashed to the tree and then nails had been driven through his body. Soot from the fireplace below had further darkened the remains.

A natural hole in the ceiling through which smoke could pass loomed over the dwarf's skull. A stone chimney had been built up to the hole, but there was a large gap where smoke had shaded the ceiling. Mortared stone walls enclosed the forge area on three sides, with a large hole punched in one. Drake imagined a wingataur's fist smashing through it.

Bellor and Thor focused their attention on the forge and the body of the dwarf, while Drake looked at the sleeping-furs on the floor at the end of the room and the animal carcasses hanging on wooden hooks.

The dwarves stopped chanting as they trod carefully, examining every corner of the cavern. Bellor sprinkled white powder over much of the room while he and Thor searched. Besides a few forging tools, they found one large wooden chest. Drake left the dogs and the Armsteaders watching the entrance and stepped over to see the discovery.

Thor opened the lid cautiously, discovering two small sacks of golden nuggets and silver aer'bor coins minted more than fifty years ago. They also found crossbow bolts, hammers, knives, nails, hinges, cups, bowls, pots, plates, and a silver-plated comb—almost all of which were made in Quarzaak. Thor also found a pouch of rough, uncut gems and a Blackhammer clan ring with the name of Gimur Stonebuilder engraved on the inside.

Thor claimed a small steel throwing-axe and tucked it into his belt. Bellor found one page from the Quarzaak Journal. Dried reddish mud on it reminded Drake of the dirt beside parts of the Boulder River.

"Perhaps the demons found this when Rigg escaped?" Bellor held up the paper.

"That would've told them he had the journal," Thor said, "but where are the rest of the missing pages?"

"Perhaps they're still hidden, or lost in the forest when Rigg escaped?" Bellor shrugged. "This page is damaged. I can read: 'We have forged many weapons to defeat the wyrm-kin, though more will be needed. Steel is difficult to craft in this place, but with Lorak's magic and Dorlak's skill we have forged scores of fine tips for our bolts. The Wyrm will soon feel the bite of our crossbows.' There's more, and it's all in Bölak's handwriting."

Thor lifted a large leather bag out of the bottom of the chest and took out a Drobin-crafted double crossbow. Its wooden stock—reinforced with blacksteel—stretched over two feet in length. Two powerful crossbows had been joined together, one on top of the other. He couldn't believe that instead of wooden lathes, each of the bows was made of flexible steel.

Unable to take his eyes off the unique and powerful weapon, Drake marveled at the ingenious cocking mechanism sitting between the two-level stock. He saw that by turning a handle, a metal winding device would pull back both cords. He inspected the fascinating steel ratchet bar with teeth that could be pinioned back by rotating the handle, thereby rotating a metal wheel inside the stock. "A crank wheel attached to a toothed bar? Amazing."

"The winder is called a krannekin," Thor said, "a Drobin invention."

Drake realized the cocking mechanism could be attached to one or both of the crossbow's thick cords. He also saw that two bolts could be loosed together or independently, depending on how the pair of triggers were pulled. The thick cords seemed to be in perfect condition and Drake desperately wanted to hold the weapon. "May I?" he asked Thor, who grudgingly handed him the double crossbow. Drake pulled the butt against his shoulder and couldn't believe how light the weapon was despite its metal. "Flexible steel bows? How is it possible?"

"A Forge Father with hundreds of years of experience and secret knowledge of Forge magic crafted it," Thor said. "Bellor and I knew the inventor of this weapon's unique krannekin."

"You knew him?" Drake asked.

"That crossbow and the axe I claimed were made by my old teacher," Thor said, "the Master Weaponsmith, Forge Father, and *Dracken Viergur,* Dorlak Silvershield." Thor gestured at the charred corpse on the wall. "I served as his apprentice for fifty years, and we worked to create the flexible steel and perfect the double krannekin. That crossbow is Master Dorlak's greatest achievement and he made it for one purpose. To kill Draglûne."

"The time has come," Bellor said, as he and Thor marched

away from Drake toward the forge. They stared up at the dwarf's corpse while Drake and the Armsteaders carried the chest of Drobin artifacts to the entrance of the forge room.

"Ho-**lig**-feörr-um-**Lorr**-ak! Ho-**lig**-feörr-um-**Lorr**-ak!" The chant erupted from the dwarves again. They repeated it over and over, the volume increasing until their incredibly deep-bass voices echoed throughout Quarzaak. Drake's ears hurt and he felt the sound vibrating through his body.

Taylon and Garent pressed their hands over their ears for several moments before they tugged at Drake, urging him to leave. Enthralled by the thundering noise, he shrugged the men off as Bellor raised his right hand and a small burst of fire erupted from his palm. The Armsteaders pressed themselves against the wall and slid to the floor as the War Priest threw the red-orange flame at the forge where it exploded before leaping to the hearth beside it creating a second fire. Visible waves of heat poured from the blazing fires and filled the entire cavern. A crimson radiance eclipsed the glowstone on Drake's necklace and bathed the grotto with a scarlet light.

Go now, before it's too late! A familiar voice in Drake's head begged him.

Bellor's golden-brown eyes locked onto Drake and the Priest's gaze froze him in place. The young man stared at the fires then gasped as the corpse on the tree began to change as a ghostly image appeared in front of it. The spirit writhed in agony, slowly becoming the image of an elder dwarf with gaping wounds that bled freely. Drops of spectral blood fell into the fireplace causing sparks to shoot upward like tiny phantoms. The apparition of the blond-bearded dwarf thrashed as if in excruciating pain, trying to break free of his bonds. He stared down at Thor and Bellor, pleading with sad gray eyes for release from the torment.

"Master Dorlak!" Thor cried out.

"We have come to set you free from your misery," Bellor shouted at the tortured ghost. "In the name of Lorak, I release you from this existence."

The ghost pulled its transparent arms and legs from the tree at last and floated forward over the anvil. It changed from a young dwarf with smooth skin and a blond beard to an old dwarf with weathered skin and a white beard.

"Master." Thor fell to his knees.

Bellor motioned with his hands and a faint golden light appeared in the ceiling and shone down on the spirit; but a dark cord of malevolent energy tied Dorlak to the scorched body nailed to the wall.

"Dorlak Silvershield, go to Lorak's Halls. Your time here is finished." Bellor pointed to the light, then glanced back at Drake, closed his eyes. Even with his eyes closed, the War Priest looked through him—inside him. Bellor's voice echoed in the cavern. "Cut the dark cord that binds you and pass into the beyond."

Fear washed over Drake as he heard Liana's voice in his mind. *He has bound you for too long. Cut the dark cord, and let him go.*

Run away! A young man's voice urged as Drake stumbled backwards.

"Release yourself from this world." Bellor looked away from Drake and back at the Drobin ghost. The spirit slowly shook its head.

He doesn't want to go. He's afraid. Don't make him leave. The inner voice pleaded with Drake.

"We will continue your Sacred Duty," Bellor said, "you've done your part and suffered enough."

The spirit hung in the air, a look of defiance on his translucent face. Thor reached inside his belt pouch and brought out a Blackhammer clan ring. He held it aloft and the ghost moved over to him, staring at the golden band. It was the ring Drake had seen in Armstead, the one Rigg carried to Nexus City.

"Master Dorlak, this was yours." Thor held the ring higher. The spirit nodded.

"Master." Thor bowed. "I'll carry your ring and your legacy to honor you. Rest now. Please."

The ghost touched an open hand to his chest, then motioned to Thor.

"Master Dorlak wishes to help us," Thor said.

"I know." Bellor nodded. "We must let him help. Then perhaps he'll depart." Bellor gazed into the eyes of the spirit. "You know we search for Bölak and hunt for Draglûne. Can you help us find Bölak and the other *Viergur?*"

The ghost nodded its head and mimicked slipping a ring on its transparent finger, then Dorlak motioned to Thor.

"Thor, if you put on his ring," Bellor said, "he'll have power over you and can enter you, possess your physical body. He may not leave, and I may not be able to cast him out. You know once a ghost has been invited in they are difficult to remove."

The spirit glanced at Drake with an expression filled with sorrow. The Clifftoner's knees trembled and he turned away as dead eyes looked at him.

"He was once my master," Thor said, "and your friend. He was noble and good."

"But we don't know what this existence has done to him," Bellor said, "he may have been twisted by the transformation and the evil of this place."

"I'm not afraid. We must know what he knows. This might be the only way to find out what happened to Uncle Bölak and the others, and to give him peace. If I don't do this, we may never know what happened to our kin."

Bellor sighed. "I will help all I can."

Thor slipped on the ring and raised his arms with open

palms. The ghost descended toward him and hovered above the ground, looking into Thor's brown eyes.

Amaryllian superstition, and a deep-seated fear, made Drake want to shout at Thor, tell him to reconsider. The Clifftoner said nothing as Dorlak pressed his ghostly palm against Thor's open hand and touched the ring. A light flashed from all around them. Dorlak's essence poured into the band of gold and disappeared. Thor collapsed. Before he hit the floor, Bellor caught him and eased him down.

Thor's eyes shot open and instead of the brown eyes Drake had come to know, he saw the gray eyes from Dorlak's ghost staring with an otherworldly depth.

"Thor, are you all right?" Bellor cradled his head.

"It has been so long since I've seen you, Bellor Fardelver." A voice slightly different than Thor's came out of his mouth, speaking accented Nexan. Dorlak Silvershield's eyes fixed on the War Priest.

Bellor wiped away his own tears. "I'm so sorry for what you've gone through, old friend. It's nearly over now. Tell us what happened here."

"Master Bölak. . . ." Thor choked and shut his eyes. "He left with everyone . . . except Gimur and I. He said, 'Guard Quarzaak and finish the weapons.' "

Bellor smiled. "It was always your calling."

"We were too old, too slow . . . for the hunt," Dorlak said.

"Where did Bölak go?" Bellor asked.

"To see a human who could find Draglûne. A wizard called Oberon."

"But there are no wizards left alive," Bellor said.

"Our ancestors failed to kill this one," Dorlak said, "and we couldn't find the dragon. Bölak left something behind before he departed." The dwarf's gray eyes opened wide and he grabbed Bellor's arm. *The Quarzaak Journal.*

"Where is it?" Bellor asked.

"Hidden away." Dorlak's eyes searched the room. "The wyrm-kin must never know where it is."

"They're gone," Bellor said.

Thor shuddered. "Three winters after Bölak left, they took Gimur by the river. A demon assumed his shape, but I wouldn't open the door. He didn't know the secret sign. Verkahna burned the upper doors and three wingataurs came in. I fought them for as long as I could. I slew one with a wyrm-slayer bolt. I couldn't stand them off alone. I fell in front of the forge." Dorlak wept and Drake glanced back down the tunnel. The dogs seemed restless and he wondered if they heard something behind them.

"What about the journal?" Bellor asked.

"Verkahna and the demons asked me where it was. Gimur had already refused to say anything. They broke into his mind and killed him trying to find where it was hidden. I suffered many days of pain, but Lorak sustained me . . . until I became a shade of my former self, cursed to roam these halls because I failed to defend them."

"You did your duty," Bellor soothed.

"Draglûne sent them here to find the missing journal," Dorlak whispered. "They must have the new journal he carried with him. Draglûne wants all traces of Bölak destroyed. He told Verkahna not to return until she had found Bölak's records."

"She was exiled," Bellor said, "forever searching for what she cannot find."

"Verkahna couldn't go home," Dorlak said. "Then the Bloodstone man arrived. I showed him where I hid my clan ring . . . and where the Quarzaak Journal was hidden. He escaped with most of it, but they went after him." Thor's muscles bulged and he grabbed for his hammer. "Then *he* came here."

"Who?" Bellor restrained Thor's arm.

"A true dragon." The struggling dwarf tried to break from Bellor's grasp. "In the shape of a wingataur. It was Draglûne himself. The Iron Death had learned that the Quarzaak Journal and my ring had been taken to Nexus City. He came here to find out what was happening. Draglûne commanded Verkahna and his servants to get back the journal, and she was to remain here as further punishment, for letting it slip through her claws for so many years."

Bellor rocked his friend gently. "Please, tell us where we can find the rest of the journal."

Dorlak whispered softly, "The sacred smoke shows the way."

"Thank you, Dorlak. You can finally rest now."

"I've waited for you to come for many years." The ghostly gray eyes burned into Drake. "Kill Draglûne with my crossbow."

Dorlak's eyes closed for a moment, then the gray eyes stared out one last time. A slight smile formed on his lips as he reached his hand toward the ceiling where the quartz crystals glittered in the firelight.

"You'll be with Lorak soon," Bellor whispered. "Sleep, old friend." Bellor recited a Drobin incantation as the gray eyes closed. The War Priest traced symbols in the air above Thor's body and whispered as Dorlak's clan ring glowed with iridescent light, then nothing.

Thor coughed and a faint globe of white light shot out of his mouth and floated in the air.

"Pass on, Master Dorlak, we will show you the way to the Halls of Lorak," Bellor said. "He awaits all his devoted servants."

The orb of swirling energy hovered and then slowly rose to the ceiling of the cave before passing into a patch of light near the rock chimney.

Thor's brown eyes glazed over. "Is he gone?"

"Not yet." Bellor helped Thor sit up. "We must finish re-sanctifying the forge room before he can pass to the next world.

The stone must be cleansed and doing so will alert the wingataurs, perhaps summoning them to attack us." Bellor turned to Drake. "Be ready for them."

Thor stood up and the two dwarves raised their hands and sang together.

"Ho-**lig**-feörr-um-**Lorr**-ak! Ho-**lig**-feörr-um-**Lorr**-ak!"

Red fire appeared in Thor's right hand. Both of Bellor's palms filled with the dancing flames. They took aim at the sleeping-furs of the wingataurs and threw the fire, which streaked through the air, engulfing the animal furs in a crimson blaze that consumed them without leaving ashes.

"Grott feör!" Thor and Bellor shouted in unison as the whole forge area blazed, encircling them in a shroud of fire. Feeling no heat and smelling no smoke, Drake wondered if he was hallucinating, but he knew it was real.

Bellor and Thor threw the cleansing fireballs all over the room, scouring the walls and floors, erasing all signs of the wingataurs from the cavern. Drake couldn't feel the heat on his skin, but he feared the power of the flames and fought the urge to flee.

The demonic wail of wingataurs echoed in the forge room. "Hurry!" Drake shouted. "They're coming." The monsters were somewhere near the entrance of Quarzaak.

Bellor and Thor turned to face the remains of Dorlak Silvershield. They threw their magic fire and ignited the tree in a fierce explosion. The wood and Dorlak's desiccated remains turned to ashes. The inferno also destroyed the skull of Gimur Stonebuilder, and the head of the hunter from Armstead.

Bellor turned and met Drake's frightened eyes as a large flame grew in the Priest's hand.

"What are you doing?" Drake asked. "The wingataurs are coming."

"The fire will not burn your flesh, Drake Bloodstone, but it will cleanse your spirit." Bellor raised the flame.

Drake instantly forgot about the approaching demons as a thought flashed through his mind. *Part of my soul will be destroyed if the fire touches me.* He felt a terrified presence clinging to his body, like ghostly fingers clutching at his shoulders. He stepped away from Bellor, closing his spirit to the purifying flames. In Drake's mind's eye, Ethan reached up at the moment when he fell from Thorn Bolt Rock.

Take my hand, or the Void will claim me forever! Ethan's voice echoed in his mind. He reached for his friend, his physical hand missed him. Drake's spirit crossed the distance and their spiritual hands met. Suddenly, a massive weight tried to pull Drake into the Void.

I won't let you fall! Drake resisted with all his strength and hung on, dragging Ethan toward him, pulling him up from the Underworld and into a protective embrace.

A demon roared right outside the forge room and Drake opened his eyes. He wanted to fight the wingataurs and guard the dwarves while they finished the ceremony. The spiritual act of saving Ethan had drained all his strength. Drake stumbled and fell to the ground.

The stone floor pressed against his cheek. *Ethan didn't fall. I saved him, pulled him to my side. Why can't I move?*

Like an icy mist rising from the Void, a deep sense of failure clung to Drake as he lay there, unable to lift his head. Then he knew, faced the truth at last. Grabbing his friend's spirit hadn't saved Ethan. *I've doomed him. And myself.*

Jep and Temus snarled and barked. Cloven hooves clattered on the stone right in front of Drake.

XLIV

We shall have our moment against Draglûne soon enough.
  —Bölak Blackhammer, from the Quarzaak Journal

The foul, musky scent of the wingataurs filled Drake's nostrils, but he couldn't find the strength to lift his head from the cold stone of the forge room. He waited for the blow that would soon kill him and trap his soul in the physical world like Ethan's and Dorlak's had been.

"Grott feör!" Bellor and Thor shouted and red light shone through Drake's eyelids. He imagined the spirit-fire exploding from the chamber and felt the weakness instantly vanish.

The wingataurs roared in pain. Their hooves pounded the stone as they retreated away from Drake's prone body. Strong arms pulled him up. He realized Thor and Bellor were lifting him. The aura of spirit-fire shrouding the dwarves had faded, but Drake felt the power radiating from them both.

"What happened to me?" Drake asked. "I couldn't move."

"I don't know," Bellor said, "perhaps the vile taint of this place affected you, though we've weakened the demons by cleansing the heart of their power."

"Now is the time to face them," Thor said.

The sharp hoof beats of the wingataurs echoed from the tunnel. They were still close. Garent and Taylon regained consciousness and huddled behind Drake, terror masking their faces.

"The wingataurs should have never come back." Thor raised

his hammer.

"Time to pay our debts of honor." Bellor hefted his axe in two hands and the dwarves marched forward.

As the Drobin strode away, Drake swallowed his fear, trying to put aside the responsibility he felt for dooming Ethan to an existence trapped between worlds. He cocked his crossbow. The demons would pay for what they had done to his family. "Wait here," he told the Armsteaders as he loaded an enchanted Drobin bolt. "Jep, Temus. Come."

With the dogs on his heels, Drake marched behind the dwarves down the twisting tunnel. Thor gave him a grim smile when he fell in with them.

"Wyrm-kin!" Bellor shouted. "We shall send you back to the Void!"

The sounds of the wingataurs' hooves stopped, perhaps beyond the entrance room. Each step brought Drake closer to the demons. He tried to slow his breathing and listened to strong words of power that Bellor chanted under his breath.

Bellor slowed his stride as Drake's glowstone shone into the sphere-shaped cavern. The sunlight that had come in through the main entryway had faded to almost nothing. Drake's eyes darted between the two open tunnels where the wingataurs could be hiding.

The dogs growled toward the larger tunnel that led up to the lair-cave and Drake wished his glowstone's light would reach farther as he aimed into the darkness.

Clattering hoofs pounded on the stone as two unseen wingataurs charged them from the direction of the dragon's lair-cave. Drake saw a blur and noticed the ground being scuffed where the hooves must be striking the rock.

"*Un-thoo-lan!*" Bellor shouted the words he had been chanting for several moments as the monsters entered the cavern. A flash of white light outlined the pair of eight-foot-tall monsters.

They became visible, allowing Drake to see them clearly for the first time. Brown fur and dozens of blackish scales covered the grotesquely large humanoid bodies of the demons. Each had leathery, batlike wings folded behind them as they ran forward with their massive bullheads lowered. Long horns pointed like spears and red eyes glared at Drake and the dwarves. The wingataurs charged, with wicked battleaxes clutched in their heavily muscled arms.

Deafening roars from the demons made Drake flinch as he shot a bolt at the shorter-horned beast that sped toward him and Bellor. The off-course missile struck its left thigh and the creature stumbled, breaking its charge, then stood upright and shambled forward.

The long-horned wingataur charging Thor limped as well, and Drake knew Thor had previously injured it.

"I'll finish you this time!" Thor shouted, baring his teeth as Drake reloaded.

The wingataur roared its own challenge as it lunged at Thor. The monster swung its axe toward the dwarf's head, but Thor expertly dodged and struck the tall monster in the same leg, making it howl in pain. But it didn't fall down and cornered Thor against the cavern wall.

Backing up, Thor darted aside as an axe chop dug into the stone wall. Thor struck the shaft of his enemy's weapon with his blacksteel hammer and broke off the large blade from its wooden handle.

Thor yelled in triumph. The wingataur didn't care and swung its meaty fist at Thor's head. The blow glanced off his shield. The impact flung Thor against the rock. The side of his face smashed into the wall.

"Thor!" Drake shouted as two clawed hands reached for the dwarf's throat. An instant before the demon could grab him, Thor whirled around and hit the beast on the snout with his hammer. Stunned by the shot, the wingataur stumbled and fell onto its back.

Jep rushed the wingataur Thor had struck down. Drake knew it was the same demon that had almost killed Jep the night before at the circle. Snarling, Jep attacked the fallen demon locking his powerful jaws onto the beast's throat as Temus lunged forward and tore at its left arm.

The second wingataur stumbled forward and attacked Bellor, who swung *Wyrmslayer,* cutting a gash in the creature's side. It tried to strike back with its own axe, missed as the bolt protruding from its leg slowed its slicing counterattack.

Fumbling with his crank-lever, Drake tried to reset his crossbow. His hand slipped and he failed to lock the string in place. Bellor drew the wingataur away from Drake by hacking at the demon's leg.

As Bellor and his opponent circled each other, Thor stepped on his fallen wingataur's right arm, pinning it while the dogs tore into the monster's flesh. Thor stared at the wounded creature and spit blood on its head—right between its eyes. Grabbing one of its longhorns, Thor slammed his hammer down in a mighty blow, cracking the skull right where his bloody spittle had marked it.

Bellor spun right and swung *Wyrmslayer* with all his strength. His blow missed and his shoulder, injured by the boulder when they entered Quarzaak, suddenly fell limp. He lost his grip on his axe during the backswing, unbalancing himself and leaving himself exposed.

The latch on Drake's crossbow caught the cord as the demon towered over Bellor. The creature smashed the butt of its axe into the old dwarf's chest, crumpling him to the ground. The wingataur raised its weapon above its head with two hands for a killing blow.

Drake's arms jerked up, his crossbow aimed by instinct and

reflexes. He felt the weapon bounce as his bolt shot forward. He watched the thick shaft slide off his crossbow and close the distance. The perfect point of Drobin steel found the wingataur's heart, burying itself deep. Gasping in pain, the demon stared with surprise at its fatal wound. With one final effort, the bull-headed monster brought its axe down into Bellor's left shoulder, cleaving through the dwarf's muscles and crushing bone. The War Priest screamed in pain, rolling on the ground in agony.

Rushing forward with his Kierka blade in hand, Drake slashed at the wingataur, cutting open its throat with one great slash. The dying beast tumbled to the ground, choking as it reached for its gushing neck wound.

Bright blood poured from Bellor's mangled shoulder as Drake picked up *Wyrmslayer*. With one blow he hacked off the wingataur's head. The blade glowed red and Drake felt the hate inside the weapon. The axe wanted to kill more wyrm-kin—especially Draglûne. Drake understood that the blood of the wingataur had ignited a fire inside the weapon. A surge of power emanated from the steel, filling Drake's muscles with furious strength.

"Bellor!" Thor knelt beside his fallen comrade cradling his head while Jep and Temus licked Bellor's hands and nuzzled him with their noses.

Loathing thoughts against wyrm-kin consumed Drake as blood leaked from the deep wound on Bellor's left shoulder. Drake screamed unintelligible curses at the dead wingataurs and felt the urge to mutilate the demons' bodies. *Wyrmslayer* glowed bright crimson. Drake stood paralyzed. Burning hatred filled his soul as he watched his friend dying.

"Bellor?" Thor shook him gently and old Priest opened his eyes.

"My time . . . has come. Let me go. Don't risk yourself for me," Bellor choked out the words.

Thor grabbed Bellor's arm. "Let me try."

"No," Bellor said through clenched teeth. "Thor . . . you are the *Dracken Viergur* Master now. Keep your vows. Do your Sacred Duty. Find Bölak and . . . slay Draglûne." Bellor put his sacred mountain symbol in Thor's hand. "Cover me with good stones." The elder dwarf's golden-brown eyes fluttered shut. Thor sobbed as Bellor breathed out a ragged breath.

Watching Bellor die pushed Drake into a frenzy. He hacked the head off the other wingataur and then chopped into its chest. The force of his repeated blows knocked the axe from his hands and he fell backwards beside the prone dwarves.

The rage left him and sadness suddenly replaced his anger when he saw the blood pulsing out of Bellor's wound. "His heart beats. He's not dead yet. Can't you save him?" Drake asked.

Tears streamed down Thor's face. "He doesn't want me to try." Anguish poured out of Thor's eyes. "I've never been able to heal a wound like this one."

"You have to try!" Drake shouted.

Thor sat up and a look of determination spread across his face. He clenched Bellor's sacred symbol tightly. Thor began to invoke Lorak's most potent Healing magic. He touched the stone floor and Drake knew he was connecting with the earth and delving into the *zeitströmen* so he could pull Bellor's spirit to the moment before his terrible wound. The words of power flowed off Thor's tongue as he touched the timestream, dipping his hands into the turbulent flow around Bellor. Drake prayed to Lorak and Amaryllis to save Bellor as he watched as Thor work.

Magic poured out of Thor and into his friend as the healing energy surrounded the old dwarf. The apprentice Priest's body trembled as he struggled to harness the power. He gritted his teeth and strained as if he was trying to keep a massive boulder from sinking into a lake. The blood vessels in Thor's forehead bulged and he let out a loud scream. Bellor glowed with an aura of emerald light. The wound began to heal, starting from the inside and moving out to the surface of his skin. A few strands of Thor's earthy brown hair faded to gray and Drake guessed he aged several years as raw time ravaged his body. "Bellor!" Thor screamed, his body spasming before he slumped over his mentor.

The aura of soft green light flowed around the two dwarves and Drake remembered Bellor's story about novice Priests healing their brothers after battles. He knew Thor would die unless he somehow pulled him out of the timestream.

Grabbing Thor, Drake dragged him off Bellor and hoped it was enough.

Both dwarves lay unmoving and Drake thought both of them were dead. Guilt and horror overwhelmed him. *I've killed them both. Why did I ask Thor to try to heal Bellor?* Drake lay down and prayed. *Please Amaryllis.*

Thor's eyes popped open and looked at the unmoving War Priest. "Bellor? Wake up."

Bellor's eyelids fluttered open and he reached for Thor.

"Are you both . . . all right?" Drake asked.

Thor crawled forward and Bellor pulled Thor's head to his chest and hugged him. A warm breeze blew from the large tunnel behind them. Growls from the back of the dogs' throats sent shivers prickling across Drake's back. Bellor stared into the big passage and mouthed a word, "Dragon."

Shocked into paralysis, Drake saw the three weapons he had discarded: his crossbow, his Kierka knife, and Bellor's axe. The dwarves appeared too weak for the Stone Chant that would collapse the cavern, and Drake felt totally defenseless. He thought, *I didn't even manage one shot at the dragon. It's all for nothing. Bellor will die anyway and we'll die with him.*

Resounding inside Drake's mind, an oddly feminine voice spoke to him. He heard strangely accented Nexan words, *"You've killed my slaves, but spared my child. This . . . pleases me. However, move toward your weapons and you shall all die."*

Expecting a torrent of flame to engulf them at any moment, Drake thought of Jaena and what they could have had together.

"Name yourself, wyrm," Bellor challenged out loud, while lying on his back, making Drake realize the dwarves heard the voice too.

"I suspect the slave-humans have already told you who I am. I have taken the name Verkahna, and am known by it among the desert people."

"Curse you then, Verkahna," Bellor said. "Show yourself."

"You're so eager to die, aren't you? I must say that I've enjoyed your display of fighting and magic. You are worthy opponents—for a pair of worthless wingaturs—but one such as me would kill you quickly, especially now."

"Verkahna," Bellor's lips curled with disdain. "We have come to reclaim our stronghold. You are not welcome here. Depart now."

"Bold even now when you can't even stand up to be slain?" The voice in Drake's head hissed with disapproval. *"No matter, you should understand that I was never welcome here, dwarf. This has always been an undesirable place for me. Now, I've told you my name, but who are you? I know two of you are War Priests of Lorak— who should both be dead many times—and that your Earth magic thwarted my slaves' attempts to kill you last night in the canyon."*

Bellor glanced at his axe buried in the wingataur's chest. "Pity you didn't come to us last night, but soon you shall feel our wrath."

"Your wrath, dwarf? I don't wish to feel it, and you don't want to feel mine."

"You planned all of this, wyrm." Bellor snorted. "But your

tricks will fail."

Verkahna let out a low rumbling sound from the back of her throat. *"As for tricks, I play none."*

"Hah!" Bellor spat, "Lies come easy to dragons."

"That's true, dwarf. Your shrewdness and courage have already gained my respect. By your mere presence here, I know you are either accomplished warriors, or very stupid ones."

"We are accomplished enough to slay you," Bellor challenged and Drake thought about leaping for his crossbow—but the time it would take to load it made him consider going for *Wyrmslayer* instead.

"No need for more threats," the she-wyrm laughed. *"I am reasonable, and I know if we engage in battle, there will be one of two outcomes. Either I will kill all of you—the more likely outcome at the moment—or you will slay me and then hunt for my spawn. Neither is worth the risk. Don't you agree?"*

"We never agree with wyrms," Bellor said. *"We'll take back what is ours and slay you, dragon. There will be no negotiations."*

"You can have this terrible place. I don't want it, and never have." Verkahna made a loud hissing sound that filled the cavern. *"You don't think I'd choose this tiny hole as my lair?"*

"Then who did, Verkahna?" Bellor asked.

"I suspect you know."

"Who is your master?" Bellor asked.

"I tire of questions, dwarf, and you won't answer mine, so it's time for me to give you my thanks."

Thor shielded Bellor's body with his own and Drake pushed the dogs, trying to get them to run out of the cavern. No attack came as the dogs pranced away, and still the wyrm stayed down the tunnel out of sight. Jep and Temus stood at the edge of the cavern, alternately watching Drake and glancing toward the dragon's voice.

"My slaves are dead and I finally have a good reason to be gone

from this place. However, I feel indebted to you—my liberators. You could've killed my dragonling, and yet you didn't. More importantly, you've given me cause to depart this cold place. I owe you your lives twofold for what you've given me."

"You owe us nothing, wyrm," Bellor said, "it is we who owe you."

"Revenge? Perhaps you do owe me that. However, it isn't I who threatens you."

"Your kind threatens us all." Bellor glared into the tunnel.

"Perhaps. Shall we make a bargain?" The wyrm let out another hiss. "You've given me two gifts: freedom from this mountain and the life of my child. I shall give you two gifts in return. For now I can give you this frigid tomb of stone. You can have this awful cave and all the lost souls that go with it. My spawn and I will depart. I vow to never come back and will gain much pleasure from that promise."

"We don't trust dragons," Bellor said.

"I don't either, dwarf. We agree on that at least," Verkahna said. "The second gift will have to wait for some future time, as I will still owe you for sparing my dragonling."

"You owe us nothing," Bellor said, "and I don't believe anything a dragon says."

The wyrm's laughter made the inside of Drake's mind itch and burn.

"Then go, or we shall drive you out." Bellor managed to rise up a bit.

"I've already left," the voice in Drake's mind seemed distant.

"We must stop her from escaping." Bellor reached weakly for his axe as Drake grabbed his crossbow and moved toward the large tunnel where Verkahna had been hiding.

"No!" Bellor shouted, "Drake, open the door. We'll go out the other way."

The Clifftoner threw open the barred door and ran outside with the dogs. As he finished loading a bolt, Thor and Bellor limped behind him, the two dwarves supporting each other.

Sunlight partially blinded Drake as he searched the sky. A massive serpentine creature with giant wings passing far above him as if she had just taken flight from the lair-cave. Squinting in the bright glare, he couldn't see well enough to shoot and blinked to clear his vision.

As he took aim, he saw the scaly blackish orange aevian appeared to be a cross between a wyvern and a true dragon with a long slender body and four limbs in addition to its giant wings. Verkahna's front legs and torso were also much wider than a wyvern's snakelike body. Drake caught a glimpse of the small dragonling clutching its mother's back as she flew over Red Falls.

"She's out of range. Too far." Drake's face flushed with anger.

Bellor stared into the distance shielding his eyes from the light. "Another time, wyvern-dragon. We'll meet again."

XLV

No matter what has befallen us during our journey, the power of Lorak has never deserted us.

—Bölak Blackhammer, from the Lost Journal

Drake watched Verkahna as she soared with her dragonling over the peaks of the Wind Walker Mountains. He turned away only when no sign of her remained, praying she would keep her vow and never return.

He followed Bellor, Thor and the dogs back to the entrance of Quarzaak. The dwarves paused outside the short tunnel that led to the main doorway. Grimacing in pain, Bellor sagged against the stone, holding his recently healed shoulder, still covered in blood. His clothes and armor bore the marks of the wingataur's axe and Drake held up his friend.

"Bellor?" Thor said with concern while helping to keep his mentor upright.

"The day is wearing upon me." Bellor managed a weak smile. "Don't worry, Thor. You've mended my body, but my spirit is hard to convince that such a painful wound never happened."

"It was a hard wound to heal." Thor smoothed a lone streak of gray in his once-all-brown beard.

Bellor stared at the younger dwarf. "I don't wish to guess how many years you sacrificed to heal me today."

Thor smiled. "Not as many as you've lost for me."

"Bellor, how old are you really, with all the healing you've done?" Drake asked.

"I've lived through two hundred forty-three winters, but the magic I wield has made my physical age over three hundred and fifty."

Wide eyed, Drake stared at the gray-bearded dwarf.

Thor laughed and tapped the Clifftoner on the arm. "Don't worry. *Dracken Viergur* don't die of old age. We're destined for heroic deaths battling wyrms." He stared up at the sky. "Perhaps soon."

Bellor looked at Drake very seriously. "That's what I told him five decades ago when I convinced him to become a *Dracken Viergur*. Much has happened since I took him on as my apprentice." Staring at Thor with proud eyes, Bellor put both his hands on Thor's shoulders. "Today you've earned special distinction among our folk, Thor Hargrim. You expressed your true gifts and passed the final test of a *Dracken Viergur* Priest, the test of great sacrifice. From this day forward, you're my former apprentice. If you wish, you shall be known as Thor Hargrim of clan Blackhammer, Champion of the Drobin army, Servant of Lorak, and full *Dracken Viergur* Priest."

Moisture formed in Thor's eyes and he said, "I'd heal you again in an instant, Master Bellor, for it was no sacrifice, it was my honor."

"It would be my honor if you were . . . my son." Bellor's lips trembled.

After locking forearms, Bellor and Thor embraced each other and Drake thought of his own father. For a moment, he wished he were more like Bellor.

Drake also thought about going home. Task done, he would return to Cliffton and marry Jaena. The wingataurs were slain and Verkahna had been driven from the lands of his people. He reasoned that Verkahna must have been the 'dragon' seen over Cinder Lake. With Quarzaak retaken, he could return to Cliffton with honor and see Jaena again.

"There's much to do inside." Bellor wiped his eyes, then marched into Quarzaak and inspected the dead bodies of the wingataurs. He stared at the body Drake had chopped apart with *Wyrmslayer* and glanced at the young Clifftoner with a knowing expression.

"We'll burn the corpses later." Thor kicked the one he had slain.

Leading the way, Drake escorted the dwarves back toward the forge room. Along the way they found Garent and Taylon and told them the news. Together, they entered the forge. No sign of magical or mundane fires remained in the extremely clean room. Dorlak's corpse and the head of the hunter, Dellen, were both gone. All evidence of the wingataurs and their filth had disappeared. Even the broken stalagmites on the ground were whole again. The quartz crystals shone even brighter now, as the grime coating the rock had been washed away. The scent of clean, wet stone filled the room and Drake sensed a beneficent aura radiating from the rock.

Near collapse, Bellor and Thor sat down to rest while the dogs guarded the entrance. "Drake." Bellor motioned for him to come closer. "There is something you can do for me."

"Anything." Determination etched itself onto Drake's face despite his fatigue.

"We must find the rest of the Quarzaak Journal."

"Where is it?" Drake asked.

"The sacred smoke will show the way." Bellor pointed to the natural chimney above the forge. "It must be up there. Forges and hearths are sacred to us. Please, climb up and find the secret place where Dorlak must have hidden the journal. Thor and I must rest now. Please, do this for me."

"I will."

Bellor smiled, closed his eyes, and fell asleep. Drake climbed the wall beside the hearth where the remains of the dwarf had been nailed to the black tree moments earlier. After reaching into the soot-covered chimney, Drake used his glowstone to light the way into the dark hole. Barely wide enough for him to squeeze into, he managed to pull himself inside the vertical shaft.

Fear made him stop. He didn't know if he could climb up. Gathering his strength, Drake pushed his body into the tight space. He wedged himself between the walls, straining his muscles to keep from falling.

Lifting himself with his arms, Drake inched upwards for what seemed like forever. Stopping to rest, he found himself dangling far above the hearth. His muscles trembled with fatigue as he tried to stabilize himself. If he fell, he would break bones and his skin would be peeled off his hands as he tried to slow his descent.

Don't think about falling. Keep going. Drake climbed again, wedging himself in the shaft until he found an impassable spot where the chimney wouldn't allow his shoulders to pass. He pulled himself toward the narrowing. A horizontal tunnel branched to the side where he could barely fit. Drake worried about getting stuck and was terrified of losing the glowstone that dangled from his neck.

The fearful thought of being trapped in absolute darkness as the rock pressed in around him made him pause. His heart pounded and he couldn't move.

"Focus on the moment." The sound of his own voice calmed him. He took a deep breath and slipped into the tunnel, his shoulders scraping the sides of the passage as he crawled.

After slithering a short distance he found himself in a small cavern where he could stand up. Fresh air greeted him and he stretched out his cramped body, enjoying the scent. He sneezed out the soot and dust from the chimney.

Moonlight found its way into a tunnel at the other end of the tiny cavern. The sounds of birds flapping their wings told him there was indeed another way out. He found a small wooden chest covered in spider webs and inscribed with Drobin runes. He brushed aside the cobwebs and opened the ancient wooden box. Inside he found a few dozen loose pieces of paper that looked very familiar.

The missing pages of Bölak's Quarzaak Journal!

Rigg hadn't taken the loose pages, which had fallen off the back section with the rear cover. Carefully, Drake put them inside his shirt. He found nothing else in the box and after closing it decided to explore the tunnel nearby and look at the other way out.

The surprised mountain jays flew away as Drake approached, leaving nests full of speckled eggs. He gazed out the window in the rock at the bright moon and the sky filled with stars. He thought the ghost of Dorlak had been right, climbing the vertical cliff would be harrowing. His courageous cousin Rigg had made the treacherous climb, and Drake knew he could not have done the same.

The thought of falling made him shudder for a moment and remember Ethan. Drake didn't want to fall to his death, and decided to climb back down the chimney rather than climb down the cliff. Even if he slipped, the chimney would be a much shorter fall.

Debris clung to Drake's skin and clothing, painting him black and gray as he landed on the ground beside the forge. He left behind a trail of ashes as he walked out of the smithy. He glanced back at the cinders on the floor and remembered when Bellor had said Draglûne's fiery breath would burn them to ashes.

Bellor and Thor were fast asleep when Drake returned. He put the journal pages on Thor's shield and placed a small stone on them to assure they wouldn't accidentally blow away.

Garent, Taylon, and the dogs were sitting just outside Quarzaak. They sheltered inside the entrance tunnel and stared at the night sky beside a small fire. He told them of his discovery and slumped by the fire.

"We should've known the ghost was trying to show us the way out all along," Taylon said.

"The climb down the cliff would have killed anyone but Rigg," Drake said. He thought about his dead cousin, wanting to be more like him and truly understanding how brave Rigg really was. Drake leaned against a rock. "Rigg escaped from here, alone. I could never have done what he did."

Taylon smiled. "Rigg was a great man. But Drake, you've done what he could not. The wingataurs are slain, the dragon driven away, and we are free again. I know he thought of you as a brother and today he would be so proud."

Tears filled Drake's eyes. Silently, he vowed to return to Cliff-ton and record Rigg's feats of courage in the *Bloodstone Chronicles*. Someday, perhaps, he would record his own.

XLVI

I asked the *Viergur* to look inside themselves for the answer. I know Lorak gives us everything we need to make the right decisions. We must only listen to His voice, which speaks through our hearts.

—Bölak Blackhammer, from the Lost Journal

The dawn light warmed Red Canyon as the sun rose over the sharp white peaks of the Wind Walker Mountains. Drake sat up on the hard ground where he had slept inside the entrance tunnel of Quarzaak. Spray from the roaring falls scented the air and tickled his skin when the breeze blew southwest.

Jep and Temus stared at him with their big brown eyes and wagged their tails. The two Armsteaders slept nearby, rousing when their rescuer got up. After picking up the glowstone, Drake made his way into the chilly junction room and past the slain wingataurs. He found Bellor and Thor reading the missing pages of Bölak's journal inside the forge room.

Thor hopped up. "You found them."

Smiling and wiping the sleep from his eyes, Drake marveled again at the glittering cavern and blazing fire in the hearth.

"You look awful." Thor grinned.

The Clifftoner realized his skin was still covered in black ash from his agonizing climb up and down the chimney.

Bellor put down the page he was reading. "These entries detail the last few months before Bölak and the *Viergur* left

Quarzaak. They're very important. Thank you very much for finding them."

"You're welcome," Drake said, as he leaned against the forge. His whole body ached and muscles he didn't know he had were knotted from the climb. Examining himself, he realized he had scrapes on his bruises and bruises on his scrapes.

"You better sit down." Bellor offered him a bench near the hearth. "Now we know more about what spurred Bölak to leave Quarzaak and search for this wizard called Oberon."

Drake cleared his mind and focused on what Bellor said.

"I'll translate what Bölak wrote: 'The scouts from Khierson City have returned after a six-month trek in the south. Nalak and Wulf learned the spies of The Wyrm are very active. The Cult of the Iron Death is strong in Khierson City among the humans, but not among the Khierson dwarves, thank Lorak. The slaves of Draglûne are also influential in the Mephitian enclave in Arayden and in the Khoram Desert.

" 'Draglûne has instructed his cultists to prepare for major attacks in the southern cities, which are far from the eye of our king. The Wyrm has plans in motion to seize power. If he does, he'll establish a hold that may lead to our downfall. I'm also very troubled about what I've seen during my prayer vigils. The terrible visions of the future have been coming more frequently now. There's little time to stop Draglûne. If we don't act now, we may be too late to defeat him.

" 'We'll seek out the wizard, Oberon, whom I believe we can trust. If his powers are truly as great as I've been told, he'll be able to find Draglûne's exact location. Then we'll hunt The Wyrm and slay him. We must act soon. Draglûne's teeth have sunk too deep already. If his hold becomes more established, we may never be able to thwart him or his Cult of the Iron Death.

" 'We've also learned Draglûne will use the Amaryllians and Mephitians against us. He'll infiltrate the ranks of their Priestesses and bend their followers to his will without the humans ever knowing it. Very soon I shall take Wulf, Nalak, Dalor, Killian, Karek, Gillur, Tharak, Mordrek, and Doran on a trek to Snow Valley. We will begin our hunt and may not return to Quarzaak for many years.' " Bellor looked up at the young man. "Drake, do you understand?"

Nodding, Drake thought about what Bellor had read. The journal mentioned infiltrating the ranks of the Priestesses. He worried for Jaena and Liana. Were they Draglûne's targets?

"Bölak wrote this almost forty years ago." Bellor put down the page. "Many of the things my nephew wrote about could've already happened. There's no way for us to know what's transpired."

"What're you going to do?" Drake asked.

The War Priest pondered the question as Drake thought, *I need to warn my people after Taylon and Garent are safely back in Armstead.*

"Thor and I will leave as soon as possible and find the wizard, Oberon," Bellor said, "or his descendants. Perhaps they still live in Snow Valley. They may know where Bölak traveled, or even where Draglûne is hiding. We have a detailed map to find Oberon's tower. The map is on the last page of the Quarzaak Journal with a short entry. Listen to what Bölak wrote: 'I leave this record for those who may come after me. I'll start a new journal tomorrow, and pray that none of these records will ever be lost.' "

The sun warmed Drake as he scanned the cliffs of Red Canyon with his dogs and his crossbow at his side. Garent and Taylon munched on his trail rations and enjoyed the light on their pale skin as the dwarves explored the tunnels inside Quarzaak.

Bellor and Thor are good on their own, Drake thought, confident the dwarves would have no trouble finding the pass to Snow

Valley, especially since they had a map. They didn't need a guide. His duty was done. He would go home to Cliffton, warn his people, marry Jaena, record Rigg's deeds, and become a guardian and path warden again. *They don't need me to join their hunt for Draglûne. Bellor won't ask me to go with him. Garent and Taylon need me to get them home, then I'll go to Cliffton.*

Sighing, Drake worried that Verkahna would return and attack someday. If she did, his place was close to home. The great camaraderie he felt with Bellor and Thor had to be put aside. He remembered his grandfather describing the ties his fellow soldiers had for each other after facing battle in the Giergun War. Strong bonds formed between them and they became brothers in arms. Grandfather's friends would die for each other—and often did. Now he knew how his grandfather felt.

Leaving Bellor and Thor would be painful, but it was time to get the Armsteaders home and then protect Cliffton until his dying day. He was a guardian. It was his Sacred Duty.

Drake and the dogs stood outside Quarzaak in the rocky seat of the throne. Gnarlpine trees shaded them from the midday sun. Garent and Taylon said farewell and started hiking down the rocky trail. Drake heard their packs rattling with a few fine metal goods crafted decades before by the dwarves of Quarzaak. Some of the treasure would be taken to Armstead and a little to Cliffton. Drake accustomed himself to the weight of the golden aer'bors Bellor had given him.

Sadness and guilt filled Drake's heart as he prepared to leave the two dwarves. He had a different path, while they would stay in Quarzaak a few days before they headed south for the wizard's tower.

Standing dumbfounded, Drake couldn't find the words to express his feelings of friendship and solidarity toward Bellor and Thor. They had accepted him, regardless of his human blood, and he had come to respect and trust them as well. The five of them—including the dogs—had become as Bellor had said that morning, like the strands of a braided rope. Now he was greatly weakening it.

Drake held Bellor's forearm with two hands. "I'll never forget you, Master Bellor."

"Nor will I forget you, Drake Bloodstone. Have faith, Lorak has a plan for us all." Bellor hugged Drake tightly. "Our paths have crossed for a while . . . and for that, I'm grateful. You'll always be an Earth Brother to me. May the sky always be clear for you."

Thor hugged the dogs and whispered Drobin words into Jep's floppy ear. Despite his sniffles, Thor kept a stern expression when he let go of the bullmastiffs and faced Drake. "It's a pity you won't be with me to practice shooting the double crossbow we found," Thor said. "I need someone with a bit of skill to test my aim against. Bellor's getting old, you know, and I don't want to embarrass him with my sharpshooting."

Smiling and gazing at the powerful crossbow covered with Drobin runes of power, Drake wished he could have loosed a few bolts from it. Shooting it would only make him want it more. He embraced Thor and patted him on the back. "My friend, watch out for Bellor."

"I'll keep him safe." Thor smiled. "It's what I'm good for."

Pulling away, Drake waved. He couldn't bear to linger any longer and fought back his sadness as he hurried to catch up to the Armsteaders. He watched out for aevians as he marched down the trail, trying to blink the blurriness away from his eyes.

Five days after leaving Quarzaak, Drake, the dogs, Garent and Taylon marched through the trees outside Armstead. The two men's voices buzzed with excitement at the prospect of seeing their families again. The joy beaming from their faces made Drake smile and the newly freed hunters pushed the pace despite their debilitated bodies.

Pride swelled from Drake's chest when he thought about his role in rescuing Garent and Taylon, and avenging his cousin. Still, he couldn't stop thinking about the repercussions of Verkahna escaping with her dragonling. Would she or her spawn return and threaten Armstead or Cliffton? He hoped not, and told himself the villages were safe.

Drake prayed to both Lorak and Amaryllis that Bellor and Thor would find Bölak and the other *Dracken Viergur*. Together the Drobin would slay Draglûne and all his wyrm-kin. His friends knew the truth about Quarzaak and had a fresh clue about Bölak and his missing warriors. Their Sacred Duty was far from over, and Drake had helped get them on the right trail again.

"Armstead!" Taylon shouted as they looked across the clearing. Garent grabbed for the hailing horn and blew it as loud as he could.

"I can't wait to see my family." Taylon's voice squeaked. "They've been alone for so long. I wish I would've never left home."

Do I wish the same thing? Drake wondered. A horn call greeted them from the gate tower of Armstead. Garent and Taylon strode forward waving at their folk, but Drake lingered at the forest edge, watching over them with his cocked crossbow.

"Come on, Drake!" Garent shouted. "We're home!"

"You'll go to Cliffton tomorrow." Taylon motioned for him to come. "They'll treat you well this time."

"I'm sorry." Drake shook his head. "I better not go in. I've got to get back to my own family."

The two men paused, then both dashed back and hugged the Clifftoner.

"Thank you. Thank you for everything." Taylon squeezed Drake's shoulders.

"Here." Drake handed Garent a pouch of gold nuggets, a silver hair comb and several other items they had found in Quarzaak. "Please, give my share to Uncle Sandon and Aunt Tabitha. And tell them about Rigg."

"You won't come in?" Taylon asked. "Your uncle's family will be so sad."

"Tell them I'm very sorry. I just have to go now."

They spoke their final words and the men promised to relay all of Drake's messages to his kin. When Taylon and Garent disappeared inside Armstead, Drake ran into the forest. The dogs loped after him, tails wagging. A sense of urgency invigorated Drake's tired legs. He felt a powerful connection to the people he loved. He had to get to them. *I have to protect my family.*

XLVII

We don't choose our destiny. It chooses us.
                    —Bellor Fardelver, from the Thornclaw Journal

Peace filled Drake's heart after five days in the wild forest. Gliding between the gnarly trees and thick shrubs, he and the bullmastiffs followed the tracks of their quarry. A cool breeze caressed his face and he smelled a sign on the wind. The dogs scented it too. "We're close, boys."

Cresting a low rise, Drake saw a plume of smoke rising from a campfire. He inhaled the odor of burning gnarlpine and smiled at the tiny camp below him.

Bellor and Thor sat around the fire at the edge of a meadow in Snow Valley.

"Brothers!" Drake shouted, raising his crossbow over his head. The dwarves saw him standing on the rise and leaped to their feet. Jep and Temus bounded down the hill toward the dwarves and Thor's hearty laughter boomed across Snow Valley.

The piercing cries of two eagles shattered the moment. The aevians flew over Drake.

Jaena's vision.

He remembered her words. "I saw you looking into a beautiful valley surrounded by tall, snowcapped mountains. Gnarlpine trees were all around and you were looking for something in the valley. Two eagles flew over your head and screeched a warning. "Drake, if you go into the valley . . . your life, and the lives of everyone in Cliffton will be put in danger. If you go into that valley, you'll be gone for a very long time. You may never return."

Jaena's presence was with him as he watched the two eagles fly in different directions. They were a mated pair, bound together for life. *They're saying farewell to each other, not warning me.*

Jaena's dream said he would endanger Cliffton if he went into the valley of the eagles. With Verkahna and Draglûne still out there, he couldn't sit and wait for them to arrive at Cliffton. If they came to his home, it would already be too late. To guard the village he had to hunt down the wyrms and kill them.

Because he was a hunter.

Drake sat in camp with the two grinning dwarves. Bellor said, "You've chosen the hard road and I praise Lorak for your decision."

Glancing at the trees above him, Drake said aloud for the first time what he'd been thinking during the days he'd tracked them. "As long as Verkahna and Draglûne are alive, my family isn't safe. I can't hide and pretend there's no danger. Years from now my home might be attacked. I'd have to live with the knowledge that I chose to do nothing. I won't let another tragedy happen when I could've prevented it." He sat up tall. "I can do something if I go with you." He thought about his uncle Sandon being tormented by the demons, his cousin Rigg being killed because of what he'd found in Quarzaak, and Kovan and the others who were murdered while on watch.

Staring into Bellor's eyes, Drake said, "I can't turn my back on what has to be done. I've always done the jobs no one else wanted to do. I'll sacrifice anything for my people, and you two are my brothers now. My grandfather would agree. He taught me to do what's right and I'll hunt the wyrms until the end. I've found my way, and like both of you . . . I'll become a hunter of dragons."

Thor handed Drake the rune-inscribed double crossbow. "Then you're going to need this."

XLVIII

The spirit world is a place where love can be touched.

—Priestess Liana Whitestar, litany from the Goddess
Scrolls

Jaena sat on the platform nestled among the high branches of the giant cover tree above the Shrine of Amaryllis. Her back rested against the massive trunk that sprouted from the most sacred place in Cliffton. She stared past the thorny branches of the tree as the full moon rose over the Thornclaw Forest.

Jaena breathed deeply, infusing her lungs with the peppery scent of the leaves around her as she focused on the glowing moon. Her mother sat beside her and also gazed into the gray face of the sky.

The two women performed the Moon Ritual as they had almost every night. This time Jaena knew the meditative ceremony would end differently than it had before. Liana had taught her daughter many new secrets in the two and a half weeks since Drake had been gone, and Jaena had experienced a further spiritual awakening.

Tonight will be my biggest step into the spirit world. I'll become a full Priestess under the face of the moon. Jaena concentrated on balancing her mind and body. Years of practice had given her a mastery over the flow of her spirit-energy. The trancelike state of soul healing opened the final door as her seven wheels of light came into balance. Her skin tingled and she was surrounded by the swirling magic of Amaryllis. *I'm ready.*

Jaena opened her third eye of prophecy. She could see the moon above her, though her sapphire eyes were hidden behind closed lids.

"Mother, I've balanced my spirit-energy." Jaena spoke with her mind.

Her mother's voice resonated within Jaena's being. *"Build up your spirit-energy and prepare yourself for the transformation into your astral form."*

Jaena focused on her aura, feeling it grow around her during the next hour of intense meditation. She felt the invisible particles of her spirit vibrating faster and faster. The moon rose over the forest in the distance and became a globe of silver light. Jaena's spirit reached for the sky and she floated above her body. She felt so free and wonderful having shed the confines of her flesh and the limitations of the physical world.

A sense of foreboding suddenly crept into Jaena's thoughts. *It's happened. I can feel it.* Once again Jaena saw her vision of Drake. She watched him walk into the mountainous valley. A pair of eagles flew over his head. One flew south, the other north. They separated to hunt. The birds would return to each other and their nest only when the hunt was over. *He's gone into the valley.*

Tears moistened her eyes, and she knew it would be a long time before she would ever hold him in her arms again. Jaena saw danger ahead for Drake and for Cliffton. *I can still help him—if I can learn to see his future—and warn him of the dangers he will face.*

"Jaena." Her mother's voice was a whisper of wind. The spirit-form of Liana Whitestar floated next to Jaena. *"The spirit world is open to your conscious mind at last. You're a full Priestess now."*

"He's gone from me, Mother. I miss him so much."

"You may go wherever your spirit wishes to travel."

"I want to see Drake and tell him I love him."

"Then go to him, daughter. Distance means nothing in the spirit world."

"How can I find him?"

"Look carefully and you'll see golden cords of energy connecting your spirit to all the people you've ever met."

Jaena was stunned when she saw over a hundred golden cords, some smaller than others. She recognized most of them and knew whom they extended to. One large one went directly to her mother's spirit-form. *"The cords connect everyone I've ever met?"*

"They link you with everyone living, and those who've passed to the Afterlife."

The most radiant cord led to Drake. It was much thicker than the rest and pulsed with the energy of love.

"Mother, can my cord to Drake ever be broken?"

"Only great evil can sever a link as strong as yours and Drake's. Manifest only good things with your mind and they'll become reality. Now go to him, daughter."

Jaena's astral body followed the glowing cord leading to her beloved. She passed through a world she had seen many times in her dreams. Jaena barely looked at the strange images and colorful clouds of light streaking by her fast-moving spirit. She found Drake almost instantly. He lay on the ground under a tree in a high mountain valley. He slept soundly beside four other beings—his companions—his brothers. Strong golden cords connected each of the figures to Drake. She saw powerful links between him and the two dogs. Jep and Temus loved him unconditionally. He was their world. They would never abandon him or leave his side. They loved him with every fiber of their souls and would follow him anywhere.

Shining cords extended from Drake to Bellor and Thor. The

Drobin were kindred spirits—hunters like him. They had the same strength and fire as he did. Jaena's third eye of prophecy hinted at the indestructible bonds that would join them in the future.

The dwarves didn't detect her invisible spirit-form, though Jep and Temus sensed her presence. The guard dogs watched the air above Drake as he slept. Jaena assured them she meant no harm and the dogs understood her telepathic message of love for them and Drake.

Focusing on his physical body, Jaena saw the vibrant multicolored cloud of light surrounding him. For the first time in her life she saw his aura clearly. It defined the essence of his spirit and she could see the love and the guilt he carried with him.

A dark cord connected Drake to Ethan's spirit, which hid beyond the reach of Jaena's senses. She knew Drake couldn't cut the link between them—not yet. Neither Ethan nor Drake were ready. She knew they both had much to learn before either of their spirits could move forward and accept their destiny.

Jaena hesitated before approaching Drake, then willed her astral body to glide closer. She softly touched his spirit with her own and felt him awaken. Jaena read his troubled thoughts. He stirred in his sleep as she caressed his face with an invisible hand formed entirely of energy. She spoke to his mind. *"I have come to you. This is no dream."* Jaena wrapped her spirit-self around him and they joined together body and soul. *"Drake, my beloved, you're my soul-mate and always have been. Our connection will never fade away and I will always love you."*

"Jaena," Drake responded with a thought.

"I'm here with you, my love." She touched his spirit. *"I know you will be gone from me for a long time. I've read your thoughts and know of the duty you've accepted. We must not be afraid, because our spirits are joined for all time and shall never be apart."*

"*I wish I could go home.*" Drake held her. "*And be with you now, get married, start our family. But I have to go on. I have to do this for you and for Cliffton.*"

"*I know. Evil threatens us. You must carry out your duty for more than just our village and me. You do it for our entire world. I can see your spirit needs to go on this journey. It's your life path, and you must follow it.*"

The golden cord between Jaena and Drake pulsed, as if it sensed something threatening their link.

"*I'll see the journey to the end.*" Drake's spirit glowed with power. "*If the dragon is not destroyed our children will never be safe.*"

Jaena almost cried when he mentioned children and their spirit-bodies melded into a soul-touching embrace. Their life essences flowed together becoming a cloud of swirling golden energy. Jaena experienced the sheer joy of the moment as pure bliss. They loved deeper and more fully than they ever had before, sharing every bit of themselves with each other. Spiritual love went beyond anything either of them had ever shared. The effects of it resonated into both of their physical bodies.

Back in Cliffton, Jaena's breath came quick and shallow as the feeling of ecstasy coursed through her physical form. Drake's own body trembled as the rapturous energy flowed through him. The electric bliss both of them felt grew many-fold. The stimulating charge became the most intense pleasure each of them had ever felt as it built higher and higher.

Jaena sensed Drake's spirit closely tied to his physical form and she felt him being drawn back into his body by the ecstasy sweeping over them both. The waves of pleasure reached a crescendo of sensation and Jaena felt Drake being pulled away from her. As both of them peaked their spirits returned to their physical bodies. Jaena opened her blue eyes and stared up at the moon as a sad smile formed on her lips.

★ ★ ★ ★ ★

Drake awoke, breathing hard. He stared up through the branches of the tree and focused on the massive bright moon dominating the clear sky. His body tingled from an incredibly intense dream and he thought he smelled the sweet scent of Jaena's hair. *Was it a dream? It was so real.*

He stared at the luminous moon and the glittering stars and wondered if Jaena was also looking into the night sky far away in Cliffton. Drake picked out the brightest white star and thought of his true love. He knew in his heart she was doing the same thing at that moment. He could feel the psychic bond between them grow stronger.

She was here.

After falling back asleep, Drake dreamed of Jaena. He knew that no matter how far away his journey would take him they would always be connected with a golden cord of love.

The End of Book One

ABOUT THE AUTHOR

Paul Genesse was born in 1973 and four years later decided that he wanted to be a writer. He loved his English classes in college, but pursued his other passion by earning a bachelor's degree in nursing science in 1996. He is a registered nurse on a cardiac unit in Salt Lake City, Utah, where he works the night shift keeping the forces of darkness away from his patients. Paul lives with his incredibly supportive wife Tammy and their collection of frogs. He spends endless hours in his basement writing fantasy novels and adding to his list of published short stories. Learn secrets of the world and view maps of Ae'leron by visiting www.paulgenesse.com.